HELCYON
THE ASHEN KNIGHT

HELCYON
THE ASHEN KNIGHT

KEVEN ALBERS

Cinnamomo Publishing

ISBN: 979-8-9996497-0-6 paperback
ISBN: 979-8-9996497-1-3 ebook

Helcyon: The Ashen Knight
Book One of the Helcyon Trilogy

Cinnamomo Publishing
cinnamomopublishing@gmail.com

For more information, visit:
www.kevenalbers.com

For Marion.

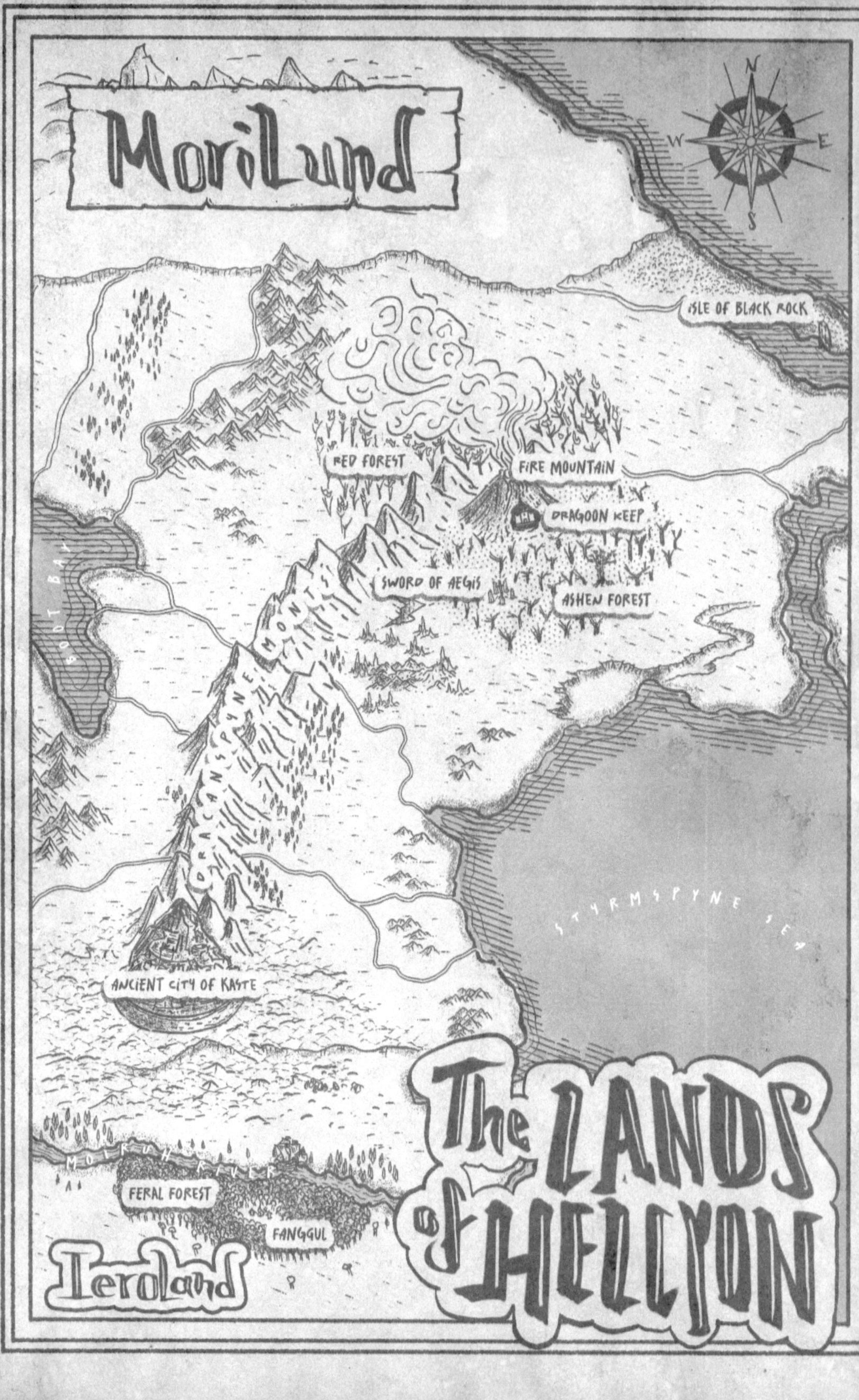

MoriLund

N
W · E
S

ISLE OF BLACK ROCK

RED FOREST

FIRE MOUNTAIN

DRAGOON KEEP

SWORD OF AEGIS

ASHEN FOREST

BOOT BAY

DRACANSPYNE MONTS

STYRMSPYNE SEA

ANCIENT CITY OF KASTE

FERAL FOREST

FANGGUL

Ierdland

The LANDS of HELLYON

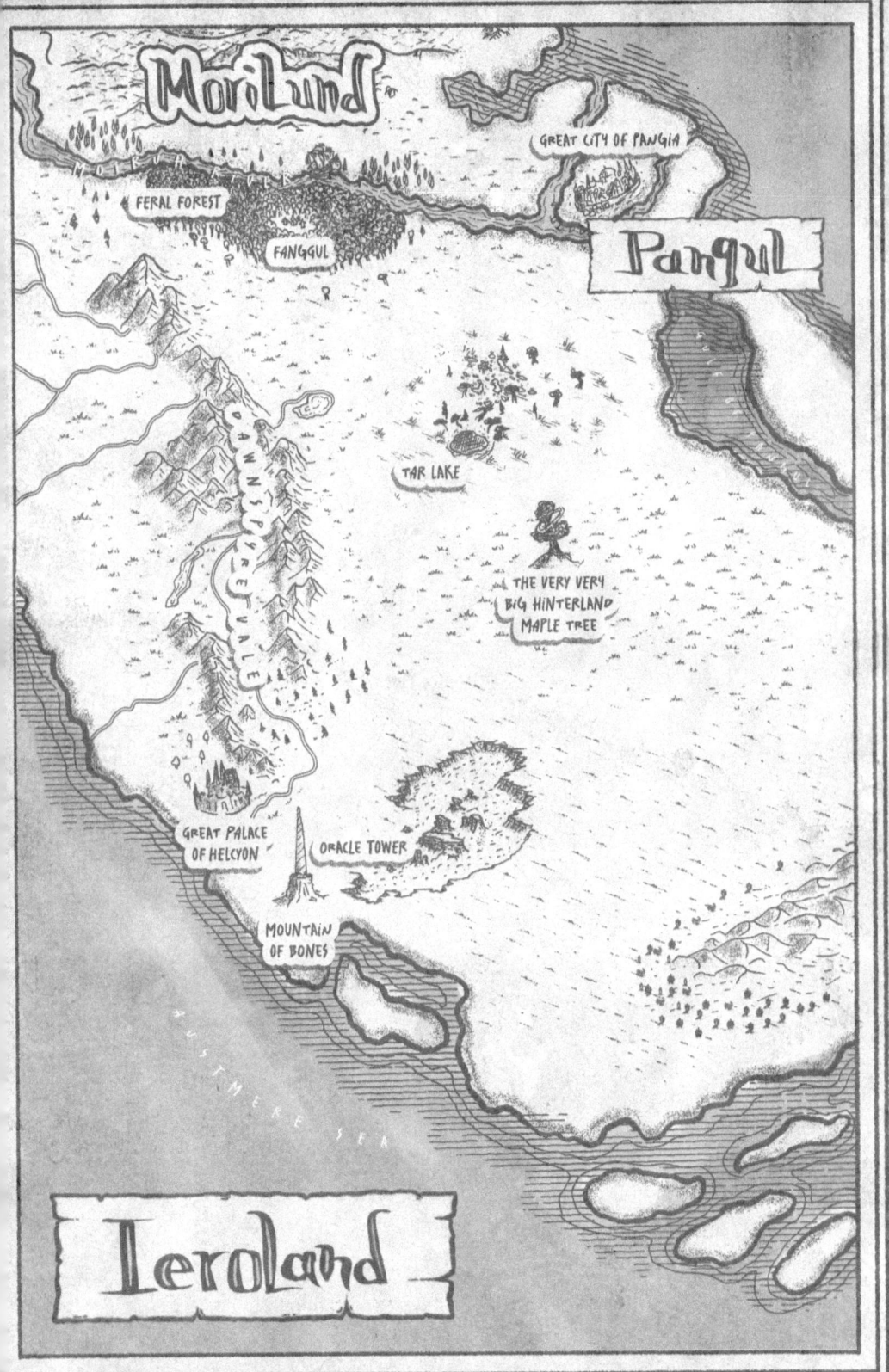

Light shines brightest in the dark; colors bloom richest in the gloomiest days of despair; hope drills deepest into the cruelest clay of calamities, and whispers ring loudest from the lips of the silenced.

—Everett Porter

ZERO

THE SCORCHED lands of Helcyon are cast in perpetual gloom by never-ending clouds of billowing coal dust. Vomited into the sky from a hollowed-out volcano seated in the northern country of Morilund, at the northern tip of the Dracanspyne mountains, where the mighty spewer of pewter's moniker is marked on all Helcyon maps as Fire Mountain. Within the flaming bowels of Fire Mountain, at the crux of a massive molten-lava lake is the stronghold known as Dragoon Keep. It is in this bastion, and from his throne of fire and brimstone, the Ashen Knight mercilessly reigns over all.

It is believed the malevolent clouds embody the ashes of all the lives he had taken in his conquest for absolute power. And now the dusty dead choke the air and blot out the sun, moons, and sky, skillfully stifling nearly every living thing to the brink of desolation and death for nearly a thousand years. And as some dark prize for his gruesome victory, the Ashen Knight was rewarded with immortality. To this day, he sits upon his cauterized throne with a charred iron grip tightly coiled around his kingdom of ruin.

Be not afraid, dear reader, Helcyon is not your world.

Not yet.

Helcyon and the melancholy comprised therein was fabricated by a father while shipped off a great distance to war as a way to bond with his thirteen-year-old son, Bobby Porter. The father prompted his hand to pen and pen to plot an imaginative escape of whimsical delight within the ethereal plains of a story's pages, enriched with characters and adventures privately scribed for just the two of them.

Tragically, this story—his story, was woefully cut short, before it was finished. And we know what happens to things left unfinished, don't we? Especially those items borne out of misery. They manage to continue on, festering, fomenting, and growing beyond even their creator's control or intention; mutating and adapting until it develops a life of its own. Born incomplete, the thing will pine, yearn, and consume to fill its gaping hole. It will latch itself like a lamprey onto the closest kin to its creator, and present itself in the guise of a legacy, but instead of imbuing and ameliorating the world it was abandoned into, it will burn it down to ash.

Please, let me stop here and apologize. I do not mean to get so dark so soon; I don't want to scare you away. I suppose I should introduce myself. It is the polite thing to do, after all, since I've already taken up so much of your time. My name is Bobble Gentles, and I am the Librarian in Chief of the greatest library in all Helcyon, in the province of Pangul within the Great City of Pangia. And though we house the largest collection of living knowledge, my favorite section of the library to frequent is the *Unfinished Works In Progress* section. Here, the innumerable shelves are brimming with books upon books of writings that have not been completed and still wait for their conclusions, finales, and endings. And let me assure you, there are many more unfinished books than finished ones, vastly more unheard stories than heard ones. This lends credence to the notorious Helcyon adage, "We inherit the stories of our fathers." Or if you prefer, mothers... let's just say it's an old adage, and if you permit me, I may emend the proverb to bend to a more modern ear and perhaps say, "We inherit the stories of our progenitors," there, more progressive, yes? Albeit not as catchy...

Anyway, it is here that I, from my world, found my way to you in your world. You may be wondering, how is this possible? Well, let me first state that I, being only a custodian for the writings of all living knowledge, it is important to note that I don't fully understand the mysterious workings of everything in our world, for I am not its author, nor its narrator of incessant exposition, but rather just a mere bibliothecary and amateur logophile, with a propensity for meddling with unfinished or underdeveloped oeuvres to the human experience. However, what I do know of this particular section's enchantments, I will gladly share with you. You see, when a book or piece of writing is unfinished, it so happens to be open to the influence of any inky hand. And I, with some compunction, have inked quite a few with my own, this one included, clearly.

So here we are, and should you indulge me a little further, I will answer the question you clearly forgot to ask: why am I speaking to you so directly? Please, my mute, yet vigilant inquisitor, accept this as my reply: I've worked here in The Great Library of Pangia for most of my life, and over the many years of my vocation as Librarian In Chief, I've learned how to listen attentively to all the books under my charge. Because libraries, I'm sure you well know, are places of profound silence, and the ideal space to hone one's ear to the distant calls of stories. Held within the numerous quiet reading rooms are books that speak in a variety of tones and themes; Some happy, some sad, some angry, some comedic, and many a mixture thereof. But it is only the unfinished books that are never read and cannot speak, but instead, wail and whine in fear of being completely forgotten. The oldest and first book ever to grace the halls of this great library is the unfinished piece of perfect writing that weeps the loudest and is the history of our lands, the blueprint to our sorrow and suffering, and the very same book you are holding right now. In your world, it may go by another title, but here in Helcyon, it goes by the working title of *The Traveler's Guide To Helcyon: Sights, History, Tips On How To Defeat the Ashen Knight*.

I must admit, it is very likely that to you, this book does not hold the same importance as it does for me. For this might be one you happened upon at random. One that you plucked haphazardly out of a pile of hundreds, thousands, or millions even, and may just as haphazardly toss back. But for me, what you hold in your hands literally is my world. It accounts my past, voices my present, and very much determines my future, as with all Helcyonites. Its story is not finished until you finish its story.

Now, if you are intoning at this very moment: hold on, hold up, hold it, every story or book is unfinished until read from front to back, then it seems, you, my dear reader, are not only inquisitive but part of the Inquisition. And are very clever to catch on to my little ruse of getting you this far, in the hopes that you will continue further.

Fine, if you are to gleefully hold my feet to the burning coals, I admit, you are right. Nonetheless, my plea to you is very much in alignment with this book; I, too, do not want to be forgotten. I, too, want to see a resolution to our current melancholy. I, too, want to see evil defeated and good triumph. I, too, want to find closure to all our open wounds, so we can heal again. And because this story is unfinished, its ending not yet written in stone, I have hope.

Of course, I make no illusions that there won't be some hardships along the way, but one must immerse themselves in the dark to see the light.

Well, my hand has become so blackened and slick with ink I can barely hold my quill pen. And the northern winds are blowing a nasty chill into my chamber. I feel as if they are harbingers harking harrowing news by which only the darkest minds of deviled masters can imbue.

I best take my leave, and I do so with my spirits, to some small degree improved, knowing I've helped you become slightly less unfamiliar with my home of Helcyon.

Be good, and be well, dear reader.

—Bobble Gentles
Librarian in Chief of The Great Library of Pangia

ONE

HULMICK **M**ULHICK stretched, shaking sleep from his lengthy limbs. The crow of dawn had barely begun, and he was already awake. One glance at this lanky figure, and you might suspect he was the descendant of a giant twig.

He sat up, teetering on the edge of his bed, quietly observing the dawn mature from dark gray to a lighter gray wash of light through his small bedroom window. His pale, gaunt face, marked by forty rough revolutions around the unseen sun, bore the burden of the previous night's raging winds in the form of purple crescents under his eyes. Yet, his eyes, glassy as they were, still shimmered with candid optimism.

Outside, northern gusts persisted, hissing and howling in contempt, rustling the cobalt-blue leaves of the towering maple tree that brought Hulmick immense solace. It stood as a wooden sentinel over their modest dirt farm.

Despite the windstorm's violent thrashing, its sinister whips and icy bites proved futile against the majestic timber. The tree rose four hundred feet, its trunk measuring thirty-six feet in diameter, and supported a blue crown that stretched one hundred and fifty feet outward. Locals revered it as the original tree of life, while scholars and botanists named it the Very Very Big Hinterland Maple Tree.

On their maps, this unique feature was the only notable landmark amidst the monotonous dirt plains of the hinterlands. Although specks and swathes of wild blue grass peppered the fields and rolling hills with color, the maple tree was the only entity in these parts teeming with such vigor and strength.

This was with the exception of Hulmick's thirteen-year-old daughter, of course. Though she may have been as tiny as a splinter in comparison to the majestic tree, her heart and muscle matched its might. A miraculous birth had granted her divine super strength and agility.

After several minutes of tranquil contemplation, Hulmick's gaze shifted from the gentle sway of the tree to his slumbering wife, Hyln. Her endearing imperfections were displayed in their raw beauty in sleep's serene stillness. She snorted and turned over on her side. What more could he desire than this compassionate, gentle wife and their daughter—a blessing straight from the Plebeian heavens? A loving smile tugged at his lips.

If clocks existed in Helcyon, one would sound an insistent 6 a.m. alarm. Hyln would inevitably curse the din and silence the device with a decisive punch. However, as such bothersome mechanisms were absent, Hulmick's boorish yawns, stretching, and dressing was enough to stir his wife. In protest, she buried herself deeper under the heavy patchwork blankets, bemoaning the morning's arrival and her husband's departure.

Hulmick's morning priority was always his morning cup of brewhaha, or as others might call it, plain black coffee. Once the hot, dark liquid met his lips and trudged down his throat, he would declare of his brew, "Ha-ha! I'm awake now!" Preparing for a second sip, he eyed his tar-like beverage with skepticism, then defended his poor brewing skills aloud: "Function over taste, I say," before enduring another wincing gulp.

Now dressed and energized, he crossed the main room of their ancestral farmhouse in three elongated strides. Upon reaching the front door, he swung it wide open, instantly meeting the wrath of the winds. Nonetheless, he welcomed the burgeoning day with a deep, invigorating inhalation of the cool, dewy air.

"It's a remarkably brisk morning for spring, I must say," he did say.

He tightened his coat around his neck with one hand, clutching his steaming brewhaha mug in the other. Ignoring the wind's bluster, he stepped out into the swirling outdoors, leaving the front door wide open.

Hyln rolled over repeatedly in bed, grunting irritably with each rotation. Before long, she was as snug as a frosted ham, swaddled tightly in her blanket. Despite her best efforts to remain ensconced in bed, the invasive wind created havoc in the tiny house, its whistles sharp and its chill biting. Unable to endure it any longer, Hyln, more of a bedraggled moth than a butterfly, emerged from her blanket cocoon, her hair in disarray. She tumbled and grumbled her way to the front door and slammed it shut with a resounding crash.

"Every morning," she muttered to the thin air, "by Porter, I swear, one of these days that man…" Her words trailed off, half-asleep and too weary to continue verbalizing her maledictions. With a slump, she returned to bed.

Hulmick had wittingly left the door open, so as he lumbered toward the barn and heard the slam come from behind him, his thin lips grew wide in an upward swirl, for he knew this wasn't necessarily the most effective way to wake his entire family, but it was an amusing one.

———————

ZENOBIA PULLED HER face out from deep within the crater of her pillow; pale red impressions were drawn and pressed all about her dopey expression, warrior markings from her nocturnal battles, battles she gleefully fought. Some children might complain that the melee of combat within their snoozing heads would be a terrible nightmare, but for Zenobia, they were welcomed dreams of delight.

The sound of her mother slamming the front door woke her, and it was evident straight away by her loutish yawn that she was indeed her father's daughter. She rubbed the red creases from her freckled face. Sprang from her bed and padded her way through a maze of old hard-covered books that littered her floor in tall stacks between her bed and the bedroom door.

She played as if she were a giant towering hundreds of feet over a helpless city; the Great City of Pangia came to mind, but she was delicate enough not to knock over any of the buildings as she crept through.

Argh, tiptoe, Roarrrr, tiptoe, Arr, tiptoe.

To her mother's reluctant joy, her daughter's face peered at her doorway.

"Time to git up and at-em, mama," Zenobia beamed, sharing a similar delight in rude awakenings as her father. "I dreamt a-mighty fine dream last night."

"Lord, is there no rest for the tired?" came an exasperated muffle from under the lumpy patchwork.

Zenobia hopped on the bed with a thunk.

"Nope."

Hyln, after a moment of stillness, finally unveiled her head from under the covers, fluttering her eyes until they adjusted to the light; she regarded her daughter imploringly.

"Can you please go tell your father all about it? He loves hearing your silly dreams. I need a little more sleep."

Zenobia crimped her brow. "Silly?" she pouted. "Ain't nothin silly 'bout battles, mama."

Hyln squeezed Zenobia's round face between her palms. "Honey, when it's all in your head, it is."

Zenobia stuck her tongue out at her mother, leaped off the bed, and stomped out of the room.

"You are a wonderful gift of annoyance, Sweet Bee," Hyln called out, "and tell your father..." Hyln proceeded to give Zenobia a message to relay, one not-so-friendly sounding.

As Zenobia swung back by her room to snatch up one of her books, a thought struck her, a comeback to her mother's dismissal of dreams. So she shouted back at her mother, "Wha begins in the head, mama, bound to end up in the real world. Dreams ain't nothin' but a way to help folks prepare for 'em."

With no reply from her mother, Zenobia grunted and then flew out the front door, doing a little slamming herself.

Hyln, in her newly acquired silence, expelled a great sigh of relief and burrowed back under the blankets.

———————

EVERY MORNING, HULMICK swung open the barn doors with enthusiasm and a broad grin and chuckled, "Good morn, Golly!"

But Golly, their beloved pet cow and the sole animal on their small dirt farm, never made a solitary sound of salutation in return. Not even a moo. Golly was more interested in eating than socializing, hence her complete lack of manners. However, Hulmick happily took the sounds of chewing as her tacit acknowledgment.

Golly ate anything and everything plant-based, even the bland bungleroots that looked as odd as they sounded and tasted even odder. This knotted root vegetable was the only food-like thing their dirt farm yielded in abundance. Bungleroot soup was a staple on the Mulhick's dinner table. It was nothing to write home about, but it wasn't anything to snub your nose at either.

"*Function over taste,*" was the family motto.

Hulmick petted Golly and took delight in the serenity of her hypnotic mastication and care of little else.

'If she wasn't a-movin', she was a-chewin,' the merchant (who had sold Golly to Hulmick five years prior) had declared as he leaned on the cart, panting heavily from loading a barrel of sweet maple syrup.

The syrup was Hulmick's payment for a few tattered books for Zenobia and the short, dumpy cow that had been eating nonstop throughout their transaction.

The merchant's tongue had a nasty habit of peeking out, poking the corners of his mouth, seemingly with a will of its own. Hulmick couldn't help but stare at the merchant's crooked mouth in anticipation of the peek-a-boo tongue. So when the merchant finally turned his back to open the barrel, Hulmick exhaled, relieved to have a momentary reprieve from the man's lack of control over the slimy pink muscle.

Then, with a greedy grunt, the merchant plunged his finger into the barrel, scooping up an unwholesome amount of the golden molasses. He smacked his lips around his syrup-coated digit, savoring the taste in a display of moist mouthy enthusiasm.

"Buff whin sheesh a-movin', sheesh wheelly movin'," the merchant continued, despite his finger firmly wedged in the hole below his bulbous nose.

Hulmick watched for an intolerable amount of time, both fascinated and repulsed, as the man suckled his finger clean, finally withdrawing it with a pop, only to be followed by a glistening strand of saliva.

The merchant's eyes grew wide, sparked by some realization that Hulmick wasn't privy to. The merchant's tongue slipped out—prodded the air—then slipped back.

"Now, this here is the sweetest dang syrup I've ever tasted," he confessed with a gluttonous grin. Then, without another word, jammed his finger back in his mouth, and departed hastily.

Hulmick stood there with his new acquisitions, watching the merchant ride off, vanishing over the hill long before the sound of his lips smacking finally faded.

He turned to observe the creature next to him, Golly, still chewing, oblivious to the exchange that had just taken place.

"You've got quite the appetite, huh?"

Gnawing was Golly's only reply.

At first, Golly's small stature was a disappointment. And when Hulmick discovered months later that she was infertile and incapable of producing milk, he felt swindled out of an entire season's worth of maple syrup.

But the way Zenobia took to her that first night he had brought her home changed everything. Zenobia, who'd never seen such an animal in her life, excitedly plucked the runtish bovine straight off the ground in a big sweeping hug, causing Golly to momentarily stop chewing in shock at the strange sensation of having all four hooves suspended in the air.

Hulmick knew then that the animal was more than just livestock.

"Got to be gentle, my love," he cautioned, worried for the poor creature. His daughter's Herculean strength never ceased to amaze him.

Zenobia set Golly down, gently petting her and cooing in her ear.

In that moment, Golly was now part of the family.

At present, Hulmick took another sip from his mug, his tongue recoiling from the bitter taste.

"You know, a little cream would help take the edge off this," Hulmick joked, winking at the bovine. The jest was a regular utterance of his, as it seemed to be a universal power of all fathers never to grow tired of their own repetitive fatherly jokes, deriving greater pleasure with each iteration.

"Welp," sighed Hulmick, "time for us to get to work, old girl." He fastened a harness around her neck and pulled her towards the doors. After one last grab at a mouthful of grass, Golly reluctantly followed.

Zenobia raced toward them, hugging a large book.

"Mornin', daddy! Mornin, Golly!" she hollered over the discordant whistle of the wind. Once she reached them, she skidded to a stop.

"Daddy, I gone had the most wonderful dream. I gone fought the Dragon King in an epic battle of brawns, and wit too, of course. And for a spell, we was head to head, an even match, it mite could gone eitherwhichway—but I rolled up under 'em, than leapt above 'em and with the most mightiest swipes of my sword, plumb chopped off its evil serpent head. An' all the folks cheered me good for savin' 'em!"

Hulmick lovingly took in the sight of his thirteen-year-old daughter.

"Sounds like an adventurous night you had. Someday they'll tell your tales in a book and sing paeans a-galore of 'Zenobia the Head Roller,'" he said with a chuckle, eyeing her small frame swallowed by oversized work clothes.

Her trousers, too long for her short legs, spilled over the tops of her loose boots. A leather belt, looped three times around her waist and fastened at its innermost hole, held up her father's old linen shirt, which hung from her slender shoulders like a burlap sack, the sleeves rolled up to her knobby elbows. A moth-eaten wool vest completed her disheveled look.

"And as your reward for a victorious battle: work. You ready?" Hulmick mused.

"You bet Imma ready for some sweet maple syrup," Zenobia beamed.

Hulmick laughed. "Well, last night was cold, so we can expect much sap today." He tousled her untidy hair, haphazardly tied in a ponytail. "Your mother up?"

"Yupp," chirped Zenobia, "but she said yer not permitted back 'til midday at the earliest." She cocked her head, trying to remember the words correctly. "She said the winds oughta flog thatyer smirk off yo face by then."

Zenobia looked at her father, waiting for him to explain, but Hulmick just scratched the back of his neck and snickered. He then gestured to the large book Zenobia held. "What's today's book?"

"A Hero's Call: Legends of the Knights of Ieroland."

"Sounds like a good one," Hulmick said, smiling, a grin resilient against the raging air.

He took six large wooden buckets from Golly's wagon and handed them to Zenobia. She looped her arm through all six handles and sprinted up the hill towards the giant maple tree.

AFTER TAPPING THE sixth and final spigot into the tree trunk with her bare hands, the bulk of her work was done; all that remained was waiting for the sap to fill the buckets, a task as slow as watching a snail build a cathedral. That's where her book came in handy.

She climbed forty feet up the tree in a single breath, settling on her favorite branch. Leaning against the bark, she balanced her hefty book on her knees.

The winds were such a pestilence that she doubted she could read in peace. Glancing across the horizon, she sought to gauge the weather. She loved the view from her perch. From there, she could survey the entire landscape, and if she squinted just so, she could transform the blue grass into a vast ocean. The rolling hills became turbulent sea waves. She imagined herself a daring captain seeking adventures of fortune and fame.

Captain Zenobia of the Magnificent Maple.

Though she had never seen the ocean, she was confident it mirrored her imagination. She scanned the expanse for land ahoy from her high lookout until her gaze fell to the ground. Her lofty height made her father and Golly resemble tiny figurines. She observed as they maneuvered the wooden wagon, her father pausing every few steps to unearth bungleroot from the field and toss it into the cart.

"Oy, first mate!" she called out behind her at the tree, her voice gravelly.

"Yesem, Capn'," she responded in another tone.

"What says the galley? What's on the menu for supper?"

"Bungleroot soup, Capn'."

"Again!"

"Yupp."

"As capn' of thisyer vessel, I pledge war on all bungleroots!" she exclaimed, thrusting her hand into the air to emphasize her decree.

"But than what would we eat, Capn'?" her other personality questioned. "We'd starve."

She lowered her arm. "Good point, first mate. That's why I need you at my side. You make fair'n true statements. We best not wage war on the underground vegetable after all..."

Zenobia slumped back against the tree, resting her chin on her book cover.

"...but swallow our pride instead, as we mus' with 'em bungleroots."

A shiver ran up her spine.

Were the winds finally getting to her?

No. The winds had ceased, the air eerily vacant, as if something scared the squalls away. She peered toward the North to see where they might have skedaddled to, but she was startled to see a dark fog creeping towards their farm on all sides. The gloomy clouds glowered and darkened further, turning an ominous shade. The tranquil air turned icy, and gray flakes appeared, drifting down like... snow?

But it was spring; it couldn't be snow.

Extending her arm, she opened her palm to the sky. A dark speck landed in her hand. She scrutinized the fleck closely, smearing it across her palm with her index finger.

Ash?

A shiver of dread ran through her.

"Zenobia! Zenobia!" her father's voice rang out from below. His high-pitched call set the neighboring dogs barking. She couldn't locate her father or Golly, only the toppled and abandoned wooden cart.

"Zenobia!" her father called again. This time, she caught sight of him as he sprinted toward her.

Arriving at the base of the mighty maple, he yelled in a panic, "Get down, and get inside now!" His command was more brittle than firm, undermined by a nervous quiver in his throat.

"What is it?" Zenobia shouted from up high. "Whats a-matter?"

"Please just do as I ask. We must go inside!" pleaded Hulmick.

Zenobia, puzzled by the sudden fuss, was not easily frightened. Yet, the terror in her father's tenor was unlike anything she had ever heard before, stirring a sense of alarm. She leaped from the branch and landed solidly beside her father. Hulmick snatched her wrist and bolted back to the house. His long strides made it challenging for Zenobia to keep up without stumbling over the swiftly accumulating ash.

The fire in the hearth of the main room snapped and twisted violently in objection to the sudden gust bursting through the open front door with Hulmick's hasty entrance, dragging Zenobia in behind him. Hyln, seated near the fireplace mending a boot, stood up startled.

"Hulmick! What has gotten into you?"

"The Devil," Hulmick responded curtly as he slammed the door shut and bolted it with a plank across iron brackets.

"What's wrong? Where's Golly at?" Zenobia probed her father.

Only after verifying the security of the barricade on the door did Hulmick face Hyln and Zenobia.

"We are in grave danger," he said with lips pale as a corpse. Then whirred past Zenobia to the center of the room, bent to one knee, and flung aside a threadbare rug to reveal a hidden door within the floorboards.

Zenobia had assumed this concealed entrance led to a food storage area, a six-by-six hole in the ground. However, it now occurred to her that it might serve a different purpose. She moved towards the window, scanning for Golly through the thickening haze and heavy soot-fall, her visibility outside reduced to a mere few feet. The grounds now covered in inches of ash, it appeared to her like winter for the dead. Squinting, she could just make out the outline of the massive maple tree. And near it, within the gray fog, something stirred. As she focused her eyes, the mist swirled around a dark, fluctuating mass that grew larger and darker, eventually assuming a more distinct, ominous form. Two words instantly chilled her to the bone—

Ashen Knight.

"Get over here!" Hulmick yelled, lowering Hyln into the hole.

"That's the Ashen Knight, ain't it?" Zenobia asked, wide-eyed, the corners of her mouth rising. She'd never seen a living legend before; all the stories in her books were just that, stories. But seeing a monster in the flesh held a particular morbid fascination for her, a sentiment her father clearly did not share.

When Zenobia failed to move away from the window, Hulmick rushed over, urging her toward the hole.

"Get in, now," Hulmick begged. "He's nearly here!"

In the eerie silence of the fog, the hollow sounds of a horse's hooves hammering against the earth thundered louder and louder as it loomed nearer, like the drumming of impending doom.

The moment Zenobia's feet hit the bottom of the hole, Hulmick closed the hatch above them. Zenobia and Hyln moaned for him to join them, but Hulmick quieted them, replacing the rug over the hidden entrance as a disguise. Hyln trembled, gripping her daughter close to her. The demon didn't scare Zenobia, but the thought of losing her parents did. This fear alone paralyzed her limbs into stillness and tongue mute. She had to trust her father's judgment. Hyln and Zenobia clung to each other as tightly as they held their breath; their ears attuned to the intensifying clomps of the unseen demonic steed and its rhythmic steel-shod hooves—

CLOMP, CLOMP—

which had carried its master a great distance to their little hovel—

CLOMP, CLOMP—

from its dank stables in the Dragoon Keep—

CLOMP, CLOMP—

for what possible reason—

CLOMP, CLOMP—

she could not—

CLOMP, CLOMP—

fathom...

The animal snorted to a halt just outside their front door.

Zenobia felt the atmospheric charge like a swarm of pins prickling her brain. The clomping had ceased, but her mother's heart continued clomping within her cagey chest, a frantic rhythm thumping loudly and fast against Zenobia's temple. The air hissed and shuddered with their shallow gasps.

Silence...

Waiting...

FLOOSH!

The front entrance burst into an unnatural, violet flame, a sign of dark sorcery. The inferno rapidly reduced the barricade to char, licking the seared edges a moment more before evaporating back into the ether as quickly as it had appeared.

Hulmick cowered near the fireplace, eyes tightly shut, his gangly arms a trembling shield before his face. He remained in this clenched position until he dared to open one eye, then the other. He sighed with relief, finding himself unscathed. He relaxed his protective stance and leaned forward slightly to examine his fortification; the door was still intact but now brittle as burnt leaves. His top molars grated against his lower ones. His heart skipped a beat, then doubled up. The fire beside him crackled—

An iron fist punched a hole through the charred door. Hulmick nearly swallowed his tongue as he reeled back in fright as the wood disintegrated around the gantlet. A second fist joined the first, ripping apart the remainder of the burnt lumber, reducing it to a pile of soot at the foot of a colossal figure encased in black armor. A deep purple cape fluttered behind, kicking up a blizzard of embers and ash. Hulmick coughed and choked in the noxious cloud of debris, waving his hands to clear the smoky air. His eyes stung and watered, and he wiped furiously to clear his vision. As his sight refocused, he found himself face-to-face with the towering figure of twisted metal.

From below the floorboards, Zenobia struggled to discern what was happening. It was bad enough that her view was limited by the slats of wood and the weave of the rug above, but with the added obstruction of the thick smoky haze, it was driving her a little more than batty. Hyln tightened her hold on her daughter to still her squirming. Finally, Zenobia stilled herself, turning her ear to the knight's haggard breathing as he wheezed from behind his full-faced helmet.

If Hulmick had the courage to stand tall, he would have been close to eye-level with the menacing knight, but instead, he bent over, caught in a half-bow of fear, staring at the scorched emblem of a flame emblazoned on the Ashen Knight's breastplate—a symbol of the Order of Fire.

"Wha—what can I d-do for you, m-my lord?" Hulmick shuddered.

The Ashen Knight remained silent, surveying the modest dwelling. His eyes, two glowing orbs of hot coal buried deep within the slits of his helmet, drifted across the room until they finally settled on Hulmick.

"Is this he?" the Ashen Knight's voice crackled through the air, a seared, tortured resonance of an eternal firestorm.

Hulmick crimped his brow. "I-I beg your p-pardon my lor—"

A bursting inferno erupted from the fireplace, nearly igniting Hulmick's trousers. He flitted to one side, exclaiming, *Holy gosh!*

The blaze vanished the next instant, leaving a great chill frosting the air, as if all the oxygen and warmth were sucked from the room. The Ashen Knight's smoldering eyes steamed in the cold. Hulmick's shallow breath emerged as a frail white cloud before his numbing nose, whisked upward into a swirl as something ghostly passed through it. And then, from nowhere and everywhere at once, came an otherworldly whisper:

"Yesss. It is he."

Hulmick ferreted his eyes about, searching for who—or what—had just answered. But there was no visible source for the ghastly voice. Eventually, his gaze returned to the burning orbs of his unbidden guest. With an exhale so profound his slender body nearly collapsed in on itself, he slumped forward, glancing at the floor where he believed his wife and child to be. He kept his eyes there for a moment, saying a silent goodbye. Feeling the heat of that terrible gaze still fixed on him, he straightened his posture.

Drawing in a deep breath of icy air, he addressed the burnt knight. "I will not r-resist, my l-lord," he stammered.

The Ashen Knight regarded the condemned man a moment before extending his hand. A spray of coarse black particles buzzed from his steel fingertips, coalescing around Hulmick's narrow wrists, solidifying into granite shackles.

From below the floor, Hyln suppressed her whimpers. Zenobia strained to make sense of the scene through the tiny gaps between the floorboards. When the dust finally cleared, she saw her father in chains. She nearly burst through the boards, held back only by her mother.

"Please don't," Hyln softly wept. "Please," she begged again.

Zenobia settled, but kept her focus locked on her father. Powdered ash dusted over them, stinging her eyes, as the heavy boots of the Ashen Knight turned on their heels and clopped back outside. An invisible tether yanked her father in tow. She caught a glimpse of his mournful eyes just before being dragged from view.

Hyln didn't need to see to know they were gone. Her cries—finally freed—filled the small space, her sobs deafening. Zenobia rocked back and forth, clenching her jaw, grinding her teeth. The feeling of helplessness was overwhelming... but worse still was the certainty that she could have done something, but didn't. Her father needed her. Her heart pounded the war drums in her chest—a call to arms. A surge of determined energy welled up inside her. She could no longer sit idle.

So she acted.

In a flash, Zenobia threw open the hatch, leaped from the hole, and sprinted after her father, a roar resounding in her wake. Hyln emerged in a flurry of panic and tears, calling for her to stop. But Zenobia didn't hear her—couldn't—over the pounding of her own blood in her ears. She tore across the ash-choked field, her legs driving harder than ever. Each stride sent the world teetering as she dove headlong into the whirlwind. Her lungs flared with pain, but she pushed on. The freezing air stiffened her limbs, but she forced hot blood through her veins. Ash stung her eyes, but she charged forward, blindly sprinting into the unknown.

She caught up with the Ashen Knight astride his monstrous black mare by the great maple tree. He was yanking her father forward with an invisible chain, each jerk threatening to pull him off his feet.

In the moment's chaos, Zenobia saw her father's mouth open in a shout, though she couldn't make out his words. She imagined he was pleading—*Go back! Go back!*

But it was too late.

Zenobia tugged at her father's arm with every ounce of her strength, nearly wrenching it from its socket in her desperation. But the enchantment binding Hulmick to the Ashen Knight was unbreakable, shrugging off even her supernatural might.

"Get away. Go back!" Hulmick begged his daughter.

She refused.

The Ashen Knight drew his long sword, *Black Star*, forged and tempered by the lives it had taken, equal to the population of ten cities.

Suddenly, Zenobia felt something clasp around her chest.

"Let go, my love." Her mother's voice rang clear.

Whether out of respect for her mother's plea, or a daughter's inherent obedience, Zenobia released her hold on her father. Now unmoored, Hyln swiftly scooped up her daughter's petite frame and swung away from Hulmick. In the whirl of the spinning world, Zenobia glimpsed the gleaming blade of *Black Star* slicing toward them...

And then she was airborne, caught in a seemingly endless free-fall, until a jarring impact sent her tumbling, skidding across the ground. Shaking off the daze, Zenobia peered up to find her mother on her knees, her face stricken with terror. A mere scratch marred Hyln's right cheek, but even the slightest wound from the Ashen Knight's cursed blade was enough to bring certain, agonizing death. The cut blistered almost instantly, searing her cheekbone, splitting the skin as it cracked and blackened. In a flash, it spread—like a flameless wildfire—from her cheek to the rest of her head, and then consumed her body entirely. It was over before Hyln could scream from the agony of being broiled alive. She was wholly scorched into a smoldering sculpture of cinders, incinerated in place, petrified into a black silhouette, arms outstretched toward Zenobia, as if clawing for her daughter's embrace one last time.

Hulmick plunged his face into his shackled hands and wept.

The Ashen Knight cantered his midnight mare toward Zenobia, where she lay motionless.

"P-please m-my lord. Spare m-my daughter. Pleeease!" Hulmick's voice shook uncontrollably.

But the Ashen Knight, unmoved by his sobs, continued forward. His mare stamped closer until he was nearly on top of her.

For Zenobia, reality unraveled into a gray wash of blurred shapes, lines, and shadows. Her hearing was clotted by the hum of a low, droning buzz. She felt neither the ground beneath her nor the pump of her heart. *Was she dead?* For a fleeting moment, she considered the possibility. But the taste of ash on her lips and the sharp stink of sulfur and charred steel told her she was still very much alive. Piercing through the blur and buzz came the Ashen Knight's voice: arid, rasping, and hollow. And his gaze, burning, inescapable. For a split second, she thought she saw her mother's face reflected in his fiery eyes. But then it vanished, swallowed by the flames. The secret of the Ashen Knight's immortality revealed itself in that terrible glare: each soul taken by his sword granted him another year of life. But Zenobia was too lost to make the connection.

"This is your doing," the knight scorned, each word a lash. "This is your fault."

The words resonated painfully in her ears as a million stabbing daggers in her heart. Her numb stare traced along the razor edge of the knight's sword... until it landed on what lay beyond its tip. It pointed to the remains of her mother.

With a kick, the Ashen Knight reared his horse onto its hind legs, the beast exhaling fire from its snout. Another kick brought its hooves crashing down, mere inches from Zenobia's immobile form. Defiant, she didn't flinch. Her body seemed no longer to take orders from its reckless captain.

In one swift motion, the Ashen Knight wheeled the horse around, galloped toward Hulmick, and hoisted him onto the stallion's back. Then, like thunder hammering the ground, they tore off northbound, vanishing into the thick veil of the fog.

Some time passed.

Then the northern winds returned, whirling with the same careless cruelty as before. Their turbulent touch dispersed the fog... and then turned on what remained. They carved through the charcoal figure of Zenobia's mother, wearing her down bit by bit, until she broke apart in a swirling storm of black specks, scattered across the ugly sky. Until she was nothing more than a ghost in Zenobia's tormented mind.

Her mother was gone.

Zenobia burst into tears, her eyes burning as she wept. She raged against the nasty northern winds, her anguished cries harmonizing with their mournful howl.

TWO

I **DON'T KNOW** why I can't cry.

When I was younger, I had a cat. He was all white with a pink nose that had one small dark spot on it. He was practically an albino, except for that little black spot. His name was Hunter. He was named that because he liked to hunt mice and bring them into the house, but he would never kill them. Otherwise, we'd probably have called him Killer. Anyways, he just wanted to show us that he could catch them, then he would bring them back outside and let them go. He was practically outside all the time, but he always came home at night for dinner and to sleep in my bed. One night he never came back. I mean, he always came back, except that one night. I didn't sleep at all that night. I stayed up waiting for him. I guess I did fall asleep because I woke up to my dad putting me back in bed, and as he tucked me in under my covers, I asked him if I could wait up for Hunter, but he shook his head and said he would be fine and that he would find his way back home eventually and for me not to worry. He didn't ever come home. I cried for two days straight. They tried to make me stop by taking me to the pet store. They told me I could have anything I wanted, but I didn't want another cat or pet of any kind after that. Even when my dad went away, on tour—a tour of what I was never told. But even then, and it was my ninth birthday, my mom asked if I wanted a dog, or turtle, or a snake even. My mom is petrified of snakes, so she really must have wanted me to have a pet, but I said no, not even a snake.

I don't like crying anyways; it's gross, it's messy, it's exhausting. I mean, no one likes crying. They're always trying to get you to stop if you do cry. But now everyone keeps looking at me like I'm some weirdo for not crying. I figured my mom was doing enough crying for both of us. She's crying now. I can hear her through her door, through both of our doors, and they're both closed. It's been two weeks since the funeral. I mean, I do feel sad, I do. I just can't make myself cry just because the adults want me to. Maybe if my mom let me see my dad, maybe then I would cry, but it was a closed casket, and she kept telling me that it would be too much for me to see him like that. Like what? I didn't know what she was going on about. I didn't even want to go in the first place. I didn't pay much attention to anything that was going on. I just worked on my map. I like drawing my map. I'm almost finished. I guess the only time I did pay attention was when my dad's bosses said some nice things about my dad. He was a hero. My dad was in the army—sorry, I mean, in the Marines, there's a difference. His bosses looked very proper in their army suits—sorry—marine suits. The kind they would wear to a funeral. They didn't cry, but they were sad like me.

I think my mom stopped crying. It must mean it's almost time to go to school. Yeah, she just knocked on my door, telling me to be ready in fifteen minutes. I'm glad she stopped just opening my door without knocking. That was annoying. But now she doesn't even open my door at all; she just talks through it from the other side. Sometimes I feel like she has a hard time looking at me, especially after she's been crying.

I've almost finished my map. I'm adding something new to it. Something my dad didn't include in the stories he wrote for me. I'm not big on fantasy-type stuff, like Dungeons and Dragons, but my dad was. That's why he wrote fantasy stories for me. He created a whole world for me, and he's a good writer too. I like being creative, too; that's why I'm drawing a map of my dad's world. But I'm adding some stuff to it, new stuff, he wouldn't mind, he liked my ideas. Sometimes he would even put them into his stories, like the time I suggested he put in a talking bird named Lymrik that always talked in rhymes, like lyrics in a song, except my dad made him speak fancier than a song. Now I'm adding a special weapon called the Sword of Aegis; sounds pretty powerful, huh? I don't know what it does yet. But it's powerful.

He wrote the stories when he was away. Sometimes he would record a video of him reading a new chapter to me. Sometimes I still watch them, but he preferred that I read. He said it was good for me to read. Reading was important. I like to read, except when I come across some hard word and have to go look up what it means, it takes me out of the story.

My mom just knocked again. Ten minutes, she says, and she'll be waiting in the car. I put all my papers in my backpack. I'm reading from my dad's book today at school for a book report presentation, and I'll be showing my map too. I'm a little nervous about going to school. I've missed the last couple of weeks, and I'm super behind on everything. Plus, I don't feel like telling people why I've missed so much school.

I can hear the car running outside. My mom left the front door open. But I'm just kinda standing at the top of the stairs; my stomach isn't feeling all that well. I use the upstairs bathroom, but I don't really have to go. I just fill the sink with cold water and put my entire face in it, and hold my breath for as long as I can. I feel a little better.

My mom is waiting. As I head back downstairs, I stop at my mom's bedroom. Her door is open. I look inside and see a box and some of my dad's medals spread out on one side of her big bed. The side of her bed that's neat and tidy; the other side is a real mess: dirty dishes, crumpled Kleenexes, dirty laundry covering empty medication bottles. I don't know how my mom does it. Keep one side so clean and tidy while the other side is in such shambles. "Shambles" was how Doctor Misty described my mom's handwriting when she was writing the checks. Doctor Misty is currently expanding her expertise by studying graphology, which is the study of handwriting, I think. "Shambles" wasn't a technical term, Doctor Misty said, but it was an accurate one, she told my mom. My mom had already written the checks, but that didn't stop her from ripping them up. Then my mom tells me Misty is not a real doctor.

Standing in the hall, I look at a door opposite my mom's bedroom door. It leads up to the attic. That's where my dad's things are. I guess my mom was up there earlier to get his medals. I wonder why. Looking at the attic door makes my guts rumble. So I look back into my mom's room at the tidy side of the bed where the box and medals are. I go in. I haven't been in here in a long time. It looks different. Her closets are half empty, and her dressers bare. Only a few family photos are left standing. There are four packing boxes on the floor that has a bunch of my dad's things in it. Next to the boxes are my mom's potted plants and potted flowers on small tables by the window. My mom likes gardening. She's got a real green thumb, that's what Mrs. Palmer, our next-door neighbor tells me about my mom. She would describe me as being green behind the ears. She even likes to call me Greenbean as a little nickname. I think she likes the color green. My mom likes spending a lot of her time in the garden out in the backyard, she's really fond of her plants and flowers, but these flowers and plants kinda look sickly now. Ignored, I guess.

It's cold and dim in here, and the light from the windows is almost completely cut off, except for one part of it. Feels like the coldest room in the house. It doesn't take long for my eyes to adjust. I'm staring at the box on her bed. It makes my stomach queasy. I don't know why; it looks like a box that a cake would come in, except that it's plain brown with nothing on it but my dad's name. I look at my dad's medals. There's like five of them; some are round, one is a hexagon, and most of them have a bald eagle on it, but one is in the shape of a cross with a ship on it. I pick the cross one up. It's heavy. I pin it to my shirt. My stomach feels a little better. I look in my mom's mirror. It's tall and shows the whole body, but I take up about half its height. I ignore how my hair is a mess and hangs in front of my eyes; I have to constantly shake my head to see. I ignore how I've got dark circles under my eyes, and how my double chin has a giant pimple on it, how my shoulders collapse inwards and down into my chest, creating a small hump at the lower back of my neck between my shoulder blades; how my clothes are too big for me in some places and too small for me in others. I ignore all that and just concentrate on the medal and how it looks pinned on me. It's shiny and beautiful, but it looks dull and awkward on me.

I put it back on the tidy side of the bed with the others. I put my hand on the box. It's made of rough cardboard, but I keep it there for a moment. I try to guess what's inside. I don't think it's a cake. I can't bother to guess, so I just open it and see a plastic bag filled with gray powder. I close the lid. My stomach aches again.

I jump. Not because I'm scared, but because a bird surprises me. It found the little clearing in the window and plopped right down, blocking what little light was left coming in.

I have a neurological aversion to surprises. That's what Doctor Lambert told me. Anyway, the bird just came out of nowhere. I don't know if I have an avian aversion, but this bird is weirding me out. It seems to be staring right at me with its glossy black eyes. It's a strange-looking bird, bigger than most birds I've ever seen. It has a long tail that is very colorful, like a peacock, but it's not a peacock. Its head is a shiny blue that simmers a bit of green as it jerks its neck about. Its body is brown, but aside from that, it looks like your standard bird.

It's pecking at the window with its stubby beak. I think it's knocking, asking me to let it in. So I do. Boy, that was a mistake—it rushes right in very clumsily and is not very good at flying at all. I drop to the floor, out of the way. Its claws swiping at thin air, nearly taking my eye with it. It flies sideways right into one of my mom's plants, tipping it over and spilling out dirt. It then zigzags right into the bed, wildly beating its wings about, each one on its own timing and rotation, opposite its pair. Its hooks shred my mom's side of the sheets, and its legs wobble at the edge of the mattress as it tries to jump up.

I run to the bed to protect my dad's medals and the box from the bird's clumsiness. It finally thrashes back into mid-air again, lifts itself up, dips, and then rises again, and manages to flop itself on top of my mom's bureau. Its clawed feet scrape along the top of her cherry wood dresser, leaving scratches all over it. It shakes its entire body like a wet dog would, starting from its head and following through to its tail, shaking out its shameful performance as a bird, no doubt. It then tucks its wings to its sides and gains some composure. It raises its head high and looks down at me, head constantly twitching and bobbing from side to side, up and down, not knowing how to stay in one place, I guess. It makes me nauseous just trying to keep track of it.

"Well..." I say to it, "What do you want?" I ask out of politeness, not expecting it to answer.

But it does.

"A tad more tubby than once I knew,
The distant boy I still pursue.
A prize lies near,
Its gleaming sincere,
Laid at your feet meant just for you."

It says in a very human voice. Who knew birds could talk? I mean, I've heard parrots talk, but not like this. This bird talked with such urbanity— I had to look that word up one time—it means being sophisticated and refined. At first, I thought it meant urban insanity. *Urban insanity* is how Mrs. Palmer described the city. It was getting crazier and crazier every year, she said. Anyways, the bird sounded kinda British. Was it just mimicking like a parrot, or did it actually understand what it was saying? I didn't know, but as impressive as its talking was, I couldn't just ignore how it called me fat. That was kinda mean for a bird to say.

"Hey," I say, "I'm only thirteen. I'll grow out of it." I hope that's true. I didn't like being chubby. You're always the target for the mean kids when you're big. "What do you mean by a prize anyhow?" I ask the bird.

"Heroes harken when great needs grow,
Answering cries, their courage on show.
Not a hero's might,
I find insight—
Though what does my small birdbrain know?"

Says the bird, a little annoyingly.

"That's the prize?" I ask, not thrilled at all about it. "I don't even understand what you're going on about, but I think you just insulted me again."

I look around for something to shoo the darn bird back outside. I spot an umbrella in one of the boxes. I grab it and hold it like a baseball bat, ready to swing, but I don't because the bird distracts me by gnawing on something chained around its feathered neck. I didn't notice it before but I can't help but stare at it now. It's a very shiny gold and silver cylinder the size of my thumb. The bird snaps the chain off; it falls onto the dresser near its sharp feet. The bird clicks and clacks backward, scratching more as it leans forward and nudges the cylinder towards me with its beak. Once it rolls the container to the edge of the dresser, it looks back up at me, all twitchy with its big, glossy eyes. It gives me goosebumps on my little back hump. I just look at the bird, the best I can, keep track of him and say, "What? What is it?"

It puffs out its feathered chest and raises its head high again to look down on me the best it can, and says:

"'Tis time to leave, my task complete,
The prize to bury 'neath your feet.
To heed the call,
Stand firm, don't fall,
Let hero's steps know no defeat.
"When hearts do break, it leaves a mark,
And lost souls roam through shadows dark.
Seek life anew,
Let truth ring true,
And light your way with hero's spark.
"Farewell, my friend, for paths must bend,
Beyond awaits your fairy tale end.
A tale unsaid,
By voice now dead,
Still calls to you—adventure to attend."

The bird spreads its short wings and batters them obnoxiously about, sweeping up air that blows my hair right into my eyes. After a few more awkward moments, the bird eventually takes to the air like a bowling ball, as if it had never learned what a straight line was, it jerks itself from one side of the room to the other. Managing to knock over a family picture on my mom's night stand before bouncing off another potted flower and right into the closet, knocking my mom's clothes off the rack, snagging one of my mom's blouses, getting it caught around its head, but it manages to shake it off. Finally, the stupid fowl finds its way back outside. I slam the window shut just behind its feathered rump. I let out a great big sigh, glad it's finally gone. I look around my mom's room—it's in shambles!

I involuntarily drop the umbrella onto the floor, not because I'm frightened of my mom honking the car horn. I've just developed a high sensitivity to sudden and abrupt noises. According to Doctor Peters, anyways. I liked Doctor Peters. He let me play with his acoustic guitar while he spoke to my mom. But my mom said he was too expensive because he was a real doctor.

It must be getting really late 'cause she's really going at it with the horn. I rush out the door but skid to a stop at the doorway. I eye the shiny cylinder. I snatch it up in my hand and continue on running downstairs and out to the car.

I'm in the car, and my mom just stares at me. I thought we were in a rush. So why are we just sitting in the driveway?

"Are you going to be okay?" she asks. "If you're not up for it—"

"I have to go back to school sometime," I say, wanting her to drive instead of just looking at me in that way like I was about to get upset.

My mom finally looks away, almost as if she did read my thoughts. She stares out the front windshield, all quiet-like. She seems nervous around me. I hope she doesn't cry. Mom, if you can read my thoughts, don't cry, okay? She doesn't. But I don't think she can read my thoughts because I kinda really actually don't want to go to school.

"I have something important for us to do after school." My mom then says as she puts the car in reverse. "It'll be good for us," she continues while backing out of the driveway, and we're on our way.

I keep looking at the cylinder for the rest of the ride to school. It's warm and feels like it's getting warmer as I roll it in my hands, studying the detailed carvings on it. It looks like little gold tree branches and leaves wrap around the silver part of it. I'm trying to figure out how to open it, but I can't.

"What's that?" my mom asks.

I stuff it into my pocket. "Something I found." I shrug.

"Oh," she says.

It's quiet for a bit.

My mom turns on the radio. We listen to a morning show with three grown people going on about silly, stupid things. They're laughing and talking over each other and making silly, stupid sound effects noises. I don't understand what they're going on about, *urban insanity*, I think. I ask if we can turn it off, but my mom says it's better than silence. I don't mind the silence. I can think better in silence. My mom says she overthinks already, so anything that makes her think less is better. My mom says she thinks I think too much and should be feeling more. That's what Doctor Tillman told her. I overheard them. My mom likes Doctor Tillman; I'll probably be seeing her again. She's a real doctor who is cheap. But in the meantime, I ask, *Feel what?* She doesn't know. I think she needs to think more, and then she would know.

We arrive at Thorncliff Middle School. My mom kisses my forehead and hugs me. She always does this when dropping me off, but she really takes her time this time. She reminds me not to be late after school when she comes to pick me up. "I won't," I say, and get out. She waves at me and waits for me to wave back, but I don't and just stand there looking at her, then she drives off.

I don't go in right away. I kinda just hang out front for a few minutes, watching all the other kids hurry inside with their groups of friends. My stomach feels queasy again.

The first bell goes off. I'm still on the front steps, except now alone. Well, I was alone until I see Brock and his goons. Teddy and Lucas strut towards me from the bike racks. Boy, my stomach is really having a go at it now, like it was suddenly switched onto the spin cycle of a washing machine.

"Hey, Porker!" Brock shouts as he comes up to me with his goons behind him. "Long time no see. Thought maybe they sent you to fat camp or something. Except you look fatter now. Eating your feelings again?" He shoves me. I fall hard. The cement steps jab into my back pretty good. "Stop blocking the way, fatty." Brock and his goons laugh. He really hates me. I don't know why or what I did that made him hate me so much, but I'm the only kid he picks on in the whole school. He's like my nemesis. I just stay lying there, looking up at them as they step over me. There's lots of room next to me on the steps, but they're having a really good time stepping over me. Thankfully, they don't hang around long. They hurry inside, still snickering and chuckling. I don't think they want to be late for class, 'cause they're always late and always getting in trouble for it. I just sit there thinking, even evil kids have friends. My stomach goes from spin cycle to tumble dry. I don't know if it's because I'm hungry or about to be sick. I decide to just sit as still as I can and hope it passes.

I stare up at the clouds. I try to make shapes out of them, but I can't. They're just white blobs to me. I'm currently suffering from imagination deficiency disorder, IDD for short. This is according to Doctor Tulip, whose own IDD had led to her having a cat named Max Therapy. He's an emotional support cat, but I don't know who for. He was so quiet and sneaky, I kept forgetting he was even there until he suddenly appeared behind me and stared at me as if I was some mouse he was hunting. He kept doing this, and I wouldn't say I jumped every time, but he didn't not put my nerves on high alert.

I don't know how long it's been, but long enough that my butt falls asleep. It tingles when I finally stand up. Pins and needles, I hate that feeling. I rub my butt; I feel the cylinder in my pocket, so I take it out of my pocket. It's cracked open. Probably when I hit the steps. I snap one eye shut and peek inside with the other. There's something in there. The rim of the cylinder cuts against where my fingernails attach to my finger, and the skin is dried and chapped, and it bleeds a little as I dig out whatever's in there. I finally manage to pull it free. Rolled up inside is a leaf. I unroll it. That's odd, it's a blue maple leaf that feels warm and has small blue leaf veins that glow. I bring my eye as close as I can to it, just before it goes all blurry; the little veins appear to have a glowing fluid flowing through them. If I turn the leaf upside-down, it kinda looks like a blue heart with veins pumping blood. From where to where I don't know, but it makes the leaf seem like it's alive.

The second bell screams. I jump, not because I'm a scaredy-cat, but because... well, I think you know by now. Anyways, I should go to second period. I'm supposed to read my dad's story and show off my map.

THREE

The Traveler's Guide To Helcyon: Sights, History, Tips
On How To Defeat the Ashen Knight

CHAPTER II: WAR ENDS

Three things can harden a man's heart into a lump of coal.
An abhorrent betrayal of the utmost perfidy, a profound
loss of the utmost tragedy, and trudging the bottom of the Lake
of Enlightened Fire. Amduat Lanmarc suffered all three, and in
that order. And it not only annealed his heart into solid black
rock, it created a monster the likes of the devil himself.

ON THE HARSH ISLE OF Black Rock, the Northern Winds are a death
sentence for many. And tonight, the bitter squalls—sharp as knives
and quick as silver—were out for blood. Like invisible assassins,
they cut through Amduat's tent, akin to his own blade slicing through
hundreds of enemy soldiers just hours earlier, coloring the cursed
grounds with splashes of vivid red. The landscape was strewn with
ubiquitous smooth fist-sized black stones, the very feature that gave
this region its name, stretching as far as the eye could see, to the
storm-ridden coastline. The treacherous terrain made stable footing
nearly impossible for his soldiers and cavalry during the height of
battle. But they were determined. Merciless. And in the end, they
emerged as the victor.

Huddled as close as possible to the blazing brazier at the center of his capacious tent, a fitting accommodation for his rank of general, Amduat grappled to steady his trembling hands, laboring over a basin to scrub blood from his stained flesh. His large hands were not just coated in the ruddy fluid of that evening's bloodshed but also bore indelible calluses and scars from a life spent in warfare. Yet among these rough markings was a contrasting emblem of elegance, a gold ring wrapped around his fourth finger, the hue of the eternal sun. Twirling the band, he lost himself momentarily in its radiant glow as if it conjured warming memories that subdued his chills.

But his respite ended abruptly, severed by the biting and icy gust that stormed into his tent, ushering in the arrival of three of his commanders, who planted themselves across him after tossing aside the canvas entrance. Instead of acknowledging these grim and tattered-looking men, Amduat bathed his face in the pinkish water. He winced as the glacial liquid bit into his flesh, a cold kiss of reality. Rising to his full height, he greeted his marshals.

"At first light, we press towards Dragoon Keep. We may be the last of our armies standing, the last bastion of hope, but we shall seize victory. This day will be one of pride, brothers."

Likho—the most imposing of the three men, though still lacking Amduat's height and broad shoulders—stepped forward, a patch covering his right eye. His voice was low.

"It is already over, my Lord."

Small red rivulets streamed down Amduat's face, narrowly missing his steely sapphire eyes, their gaze now anchored on Likho.

"What is over, brother?"

"The war, my Lord. It has ended."

Amduat let his gaze fall away. His hand swept down his face, casting excess droplets of crimson wash into the fire. The flames hissed. He took a seat, bringing his eyes to his ringed finger, deep in contemplation.

"Lord...?" Likho said.

"By what authority?" Amduat asked, without lifting his gaze.

"Meaning, Lord?"

"By what hand has this mercurial war, raging barbarously for three centuries, fought by our father, and his father before him, and his father before that—

"A war in which all our forefathers soaked their steel in the blood of our enemies... only to have their blood shade the blades of that same nemesis—

"By what hand of fate, or divine providence, on this very night, under the glare of the seven blood moons that bore witness to the slaughter of a thousand men, has suddenly swooped in and killed this war?"

Amduat finally lifted his eyes to meet Likho's, scrutinizing him through the flickering flames between them.

There was nothing but silence.

Likho glanced at his companions with his lonely eye. Saxon and Englo were as reticent as they were puzzled.

Amduat stood abruptly and rounded the fire, bridging the distance between him and his quiet lieutenants.

"To what mysterious plot have I been kept blind?" he challenged. "No man, save the king, outranks me, so this swift and unexpected conclusion baffles me.

"Enlighten me, brother: what god, clinging to his apparatus, has imposed this sudden end to the war?"

"No god, my Lord," Likho finally replied, "and the apparatus was no more divine than a quill. It was King Armis, alongside Prince Horee. An armistice was signed no more than two hours ago. There is a truce between Ieroland and Morilund. And though we were hilt-deep in bloodshed as the ink dried, the news arrived only moments ago."

Turning to another of his marshals, Saxon, Amduat inquired, disbelief lining his voice. "Is this true?"

"As true as dawn breaks in the south, milord," Saxon confirmed.

"I understand the hesitation in accepting this as truth, my Lord," Likho continued. "There has been nothing more intimate to our being, nothing more profound to our knowledge, and nothing more taxing to our souls than this war. But I speak with absolute veracity when I say, it is finally over."

A pause followed, where only the whistling wind dared comment. Amduat jerked some life into his limbs and clapped Likho on the shoulder. "Well then," Amduat chuckled. "We set for home at the break of the eastern light. Until then, the men shall heartily drink themselves senseless, basking in the good news."

He circled back around the iron brazier and poised himself over a wooden crate beside his bed. "This has accompanied me into every campaign," he reflected, "into every battle... every dark corner of Helcyon." He stooped down and extracted an ornate, silver-framed, gold-trimmed portrait of a young woman in modest attire, her beauty so profound it inspired painters, singers, and poets to conceive their most brilliant works. Yet, for Amduat, a mere knight and general, this delicate muse roused him to the heights of his own acumen, though his gifts did not manifest itself in paintings of flowers, jubilant songs, or romantic poetry... but in a tableau of death, leaving behind swaths of bloody corpses that rivaled Nex, the Conquer of Conquers.

The firelight danced in his wet eyes as he gazed upon the painting. "It has served me as a reminder," he said softly, "a beacon... a talisman of all that is precious and meaningful in this world that awaits my return." A hint of a smile escaped the fine hairs of his blond beard.

He turned the frame over, revealing words etched in charcoal on the back. "I even penned a sonnet," the usually solemn knight jested. "Would you care to hear it?"

Likho swallowed a bitter whip of air. "My Lord... I..."

"My love, my moonbeam, salty sea air, summer breeze..." Amduat hummed in a singsong voice.

The three marshals exchanged another round of disquieted glances. Caught in a particular spectacle, Likho watched his brother with morbid fascination as he continued.

"...My love, my sunray, dawning day, sweet flower scent. My beginning, my end, my continuum—"

"My Lord." Likho finally interjected, perhaps a little more sternly than intended.

Amduat glared at his younger brother, holding the intensity momentarily before commenting: "I had fancied my penmanship as keen as my swordsmanship. Yet with your interloping, I sense their match is not in the way I had hoped, but rather in their shared capacity for bodily harm, one by blade, the other an assault on the ears. Am I mistaken?"

"I am a soldier, my Lord, not a critic," Likho replied. "And as your brother, I respect your prowess with both instruments. I interrupted because I have additional news. News... not easy for me to deliver."

Amduat cocked his head slightly and narrowed his eyes, observing his men through small, focused slits, fixating, most of all, on Likho's hand, quietly resting upon the hilt of his sword. Then, letting his demeanor sink into the shadows beyond the fire's reach, Amduat gently placed the painting back into its wooden enclosure. "What is the real news you find so hard to impart, brother?" he asked.

"News of the war's end is indeed sweet," Likho said grimly, "but it carries with it conditions we must regretfully fulfill."

"Conditions?" Amduat mocked, pivoting to face his men, his own ring-adorned hand settling on the hilt of his sword, permanently affixed to his hip. "What conditions, my loyal brother?"

Saxon and Englo immediately laid palms on their own pummels.

"Perhaps," Likho said, "perhaps it is time we convened with King Armis." With his free hand, he lifted his eye patch, revealing not an eye, but a multicolored sphere of swirling magical mist, gleaming within the fleshy cavity.

Despite being well-acquainted with gruesome carnage—practically addicted to it—Amduat shuddered at the sight of Likho's dead, hollowed eye socket. It always made his guts shrink and pickle, perhaps because it was his doing. A childhood accident, he claimed, was born of sibling rivalry and rage. But an accident, nonetheless. Amduat watched as the magical mist began to curl out, stretch into a smoky tendril that drifted downwards until it found the small tabletop. There, it coiled and thickened, gradually morphing into a four-inch likeness of a man. Once the hazy homunculus was fully formed, it twitched to life... and gazed up at Amduat.

"Amduat, my son," King Armis' raspy voice reverberated from the vapor simulacrum, "at last, this war has come to its long-awaited end. But this accord demanded a great sacrifice. The burden of my decision will remain a perpetual crown of thorns upon my brow."

The king's words became a shrill ringing in Amduat's ear. His fists clenched as a potent electric charge surged behind his expanding eyes, burning through his veins and quickening his heart into a thunderous war hammer.

"It was our last and only recourse for the survival of our nation," the wispy king continued. He glanced at the other three men, then back to Amduat. "There's no easy way to say this. I've annulled your marriage with Lianna and bequeathed her to Prince Horee in a union of our—"

"No!" boomed Amduat. He swiped his fist through the thin and smoky figure of Armis, shattering him into a million particles, quelling the king's words in a haze of color. "I will not allow this. What about her? Does she not have a say?" Amduat spat at the multicolored cloud. "She would never agree to this." He turned sharply to face his marshals. "Stand aside."

The three men held their ground.

"I'm sorry, brother," Likho said, "we cannot permit you to leave."

"Likho..." Amduat seethed through clenched teeth. The veins in his neck and temple throbbed, threatening to burst from beneath his skin. "Move aside. I don't want to inflict on my brother what I am about to unleash on that cur, Prince Horee." He squeezed the hilt of his sword.

"This is precisely why we cannot grant you leave."

"So you've chosen to protect our sworn enemy over your own kin. Your betrayal comes all too easily. I am disappointed."

"I act for your protection. And how, brother, is it so easy for you to threaten me, your own flesh and blood?"

The mist reformed, taking once more the shape of King Armis. "I share your grief," the spectral king lamented, stepping toward Amduat. "I mourn as deeply as you, but the lives of our kingdom take precedence. Prince Horee has us surrounded and outnumbers us ten to one. We had no other choice. This was the only course to salvation!"

"You have yet to truly know anguish!" Amduat hissed, venom lacing every syllable. "An honorable king would have fought to the bitter end."

"You would rather see my daughter dead than beside another man? You think only of yourself. You ignore her will."

"I know her will," Amduat said, his voice low but fierce. "As I know myself. We are one in mind and soul."

Armis hung his head. "You were never destined to marry her. She was not yours to claim."

"Her heart is a wild force, beyond any man's grasp," Amduat declared, slamming his fist against his flame-stamped breastplate.

"And yet she blessed me with it—me! She gifted me her tender nature. And I would gladly tear from my chest the beating soul of this flesh if she asked for it."

"Too many lives have already been claimed by this war. And unlike you, my daughter values your life. She has made her noble sacrifice." Armis squared his shoulders and puffed out his chest, his voice hardening. "This is my cross to bear as a father. And as your king... you will respect my decree." With that, the king's ethereal form dissolved back into a mist and receded into the fleshy hollow of Likho's eye, becoming once more a swirling sphere, now hidden beneath the patch.

The four men lapsed into silence.

The Northern Winds whipped about them, gnawing from all directions. Their eyes flickered, calculating. Their hearts drummed against their steel breastplates. Their fingers itched at their sword hilts.

"I will not ask again," Amduat said, his voice taking on a menacing edge. "Or the weight of your treason will befall your wife and children."

"Treason?" mocked Likho. "It would be treason to disobey the king's orders."

Due to his proximity, unfortunate Saxon was the first to bear the brunt of Amduat's sudden attack. He was sent squealing headlong into the searing heat of the brazier. His crash into the flames and coals whipped up a storm of sparks and smoke. Likho and Englo shielded their eyes as the cinders lashed outward. In their moment of blindness, Amduat drew his sword and drove the tip to Likho's throat.

"I do not wish to kill my brother," he growled. "Please do not force my hand."

Saxon rolled on the ground, frantically slapping at himself to snuff out the flames that clung to him. Around them, other items in the tent began to smolder.

Likho's eyelids spasmed, batting away the sting of smoke. As his sight cleared, he saw the cold steel pressed to his neck.

"Murderer. Traitor. Monster," he hissed, his throat grazing the blade as he spoke. "These will be your titles, marred and immortalized by your own hand... should you persist on this path."

With his final word still adrift in the vapor of his breath, Likho suddenly back-stepped, narrowly evading the blade. At the same instant, Englo unsheathed his sword and struck. Amduat parried with ease, then lunged, forcing Englo backward in a shower of sparks, their blades clashing in a storm of unrelenting blows. Amduat drove him off balance and sent him careening through the tent flap, crashing hard against the stones outside.

Engulfed by the North Wind's fury, the tent was rapidly consumed by a frenzied blaze.

Likho finally unsheathed his sword as Saxon regained his footing. The trio began their deadly dance, blades poised.

Saxon lunged first, his silver tip aimed at Amduat's belly. But the attack was futile, readily parried by Amduat's deft swordplay. Like a marionette master pulling strings of a puppet, Amduat manipulated Saxon into a stumble forward, drawing him nose to nose, into a lethal embrace. Amduat's blade skewered up through Saxon's jaw, impaling his tongue and embedding it into his skull. Saxon gurgled and sprayed blood across Amduat's face as the life drained from him. His body dropped like lead, crumpling at Amduat's feet with the sword still lodged in his mouth.

"Murder!" Likho roared, fire raining down around them. He charged like a madman, swinging his sword with wild abandon. Amduat moved to dislodge his blade from Saxon's corpse—but before he could, Likho rammed into him. They crashed through the burning tent wall, tearing a large swath of canvas in their chaotic exit.

Tumbling over the coarse black stones that littered the land, they grappled violently beneath the smoldering canvas sheet. At last, Amduat emerged on top, pinning Likho on his knees. Amduat stood behind him, driving a knee into Likho's back, one hand on the hilt, the other bracing the blade's tip, drawn tight across his brother's throat like a deadly bowstring. One pull, and the steel would carve straight through, separating head from body.

Their breaths fogged in the frigid night air; their chests heaved with exertion. The inferno from Amduat's tent painted them in harsh strokes of yellow and orange. Amduat bent closer to Likho's ear. "I will not kill you, brother," he whispered, "but I will not let you deny me, my wife."

The snap of taut bowstrings vibrated in the air, breaking Amduat's focus. He looked up and around, only to find himself encircled by his own soldiers. Crossbows were drawn and aimed on him. Star-tipped quarrels primed for a kill shot. A throng of blades bared, gleaming in the firelight. His once loyal men left a fifteen-foot circle around him, the eye of a tightening storm.

Amduat clenched the sword tighter across Likho's throat until a red ribbon split the skin.

Likho gasped.

Everyone stood frozen, the tension stretched to its breaking point. Even the winds seemed to hold their breath.

"You can't save her if you're dead," came a thin voice from Likho's throat, each word careful, cautious, not to strain against the blade.

Amduat took a moment to absorb his surroundings. Then, with a sharp sigh, he released Likho... and the sword clamored onto the stones. He stood upright, breath shallow. His eyes stung as they settled on the wooden crate, now succumbing to the tent fire.

In that moment of distraction, Englo—who had been creeping through the crowd—made his move. He struck from behind, slamming the pommel of his sword into the back of Amduat's skull.

But Amduat didn't fall.

He spun around, eyes blazing, nostrils flaring, confronting his marshal with the raw intensity of a cornered predator. Englo, startled, quickly retreated into the sea of soldiers, who closed in tighter around their former general.

"I've led a legion of traitors and cowards," Amduat bellowed.

From the throng, a young, pale-faced soldier was shoved forward. His malnourished frame still bore the remnants of boyish chubbiness, and he doddered up to Amduat with a pair of shackles trembling in his hands. Wide, bulging eyes stared up at the formidable man before him. Amduat examined the iron cuffs, then scrutinized the quaking boy. He snatched the bonds from him, sending the boy into a flurry of flinches before he stumbled backward into the safety of the crowd. Defiant to the last, Amduat cuffed his own wrists.

Likho finally staggered to his feet again, rubbing his throat and smearing blood across the shallow wound. He reclaimed his sword, secured it to his side, and stepped up beside Amduat. He waved off the soldiers and their crossbows. "Keep your distance," he commanded. "Tend to the fire." They obeyed. Likho reached for Amduat's arm.

"I can walk myself," Amduat snarled, yanking away.

Likho sighed, pulling his hand back. "I am truly sorry that it has come to this, brother."

"Brother?" Amduat scoffed, peering down at him. "We are nothing more than two strangers with the misfortune of sharing the same blood."

The two marched in silence toward an ancient stone tower on the rocky horizon. The structure rose from the earth, pricking the sky, which bled a foreboding scarlet. The seven Blood Moons clustered tightly, overseeing like enormous, cosmic pink eyes—eternal, mute spectators to Amduat's tragic theatre. They watched from the heavens, bearing witness to the unraveling of a great man on a shadowed, merciless stage... for their own perverse amusement.

FOUR

EVERY TIME I mention a place from my dad's story, I point to it on my map: THE ISLE OF BLACK ROCK, THE DRAGOON KEEP, THE IVORY KINGDOM, THE FERAL FOREST, THE MOUNTAIN OF BONES, THE GREAT CITY OF PANGIA.

I think the class likes the story. The few times I glance up from the page, I see them from under my bangs, paying pretty good attention. All except for Brock, Teddy, and Lucas. They just sit in the back, snickering and laughing to themselves—probably at me. Some of the kids are having a hard time seeing the details on my map. They lean forward in their creaking chairs and squint. A few moan: *What's that?* every time I point to something. I have a habit of drawing really small.

Doctor Tillman had me draw a picture of a house, a tree, and me with my mom. This was to give her a preliminary assessment of my inner workings. She didn't word it like that exactly, but by that point, I knew the type. After I drew it, she studied it for quite a while. Then, marvel at how tiny I made everything. The way she marveled made me think it wasn't such a good thing. *Isolated, powerless, overwhelmed*, all words I overheard being tossed at my mom, expecting her to catch on, which my mom desperately tried to do.

Doctor Tillman had asked me why I drew everything so tiny. I said I didn't know. But I did think, shouldn't she know? She's the doctor. Doesn't she have answers? I'm just a kid doing a stupid picture of a house, a tree, and my family. Plus, I did it in like ten minutes. I don't know much about art, but I think it takes more than ten minutes to draw something good. I don't know why my mom likes her so much. She thinks that because I draw a picture, she can understand what's going on in my head. If she has all the answers, why does she ask so many questions?

When I finish the part of my dad's story where the Ashen Knight kidnapped Zenobia's dad, and killed her mother, and left Zenobia by the big maple tree. I point to the tree on my map: *The Very Very Big Hinterland Maple Tree*. It was the only thing I drew big enough that everyone could tell what it was without groaning forward and squinting.

I stop speaking and just stare at the final word on my page. The final word my dad ever wrote. Except, really, it wasn't the final words he wrote, just the final words of the story, which was final but unfinished.

"Is that all, Bobby?" Ms. Fraser asks.

I turn my head in her direction, but I don't look up at her. "Yeah, that's it," I say.

"Alright," Ms. Fraser says, straightening herself from sitting on her desk's edge and stands next to me. "Let's applaud Bobby for his presentation." She claps really hard, directing the rest of the class to clap with her. "Thank you, Bobby," she says with a soft voice, an almost private voice—a voice meant for her and me alone. I glance up at her, and she smiles at me. I can smell her damp hair, which is tied up in a ponytail. It smells like the lavender flowers in my mom's garden. I like Ms. Fraser because she always smiles at me, and she always treats me like I'm not just some kid, but like what I say and do is important, like it really means something to her. She sent me a card in the mail—mail addressed to only me. I've never gotten anything in the mail that was solely for me that didn't also have my mom's or dad's name on it, too. The card said how sorry she was for my loss, and that I'm strong and brave and some other stuff. Ms. Fraser was really the only reason I didn't mind coming back to school.

"Are there any questions for Bobby?" she asks the class, and immediately a couple of hands shoot up into the air.

"Is that it?" blurts out Carly. She never likes to wait for permission to shout things out. She thinks just by raising her hand is her permission.

"Is that all of the story? I think there should be more to it," she continues.

"My dad sent me only a chapter at a time from overseas. He never had a chance to finish," I explain.

"Why not?" Carly blurts out; she doesn't even raise her hand this time. Once is permission enough, I guess.

I think about the answer but don't say it.

"Because he's dead as a doorknob," Brock answers for me from near the back of the classroom.

"Brock!" Ms. Fraser says. "That's inappropriate."

"But it's the truth, isn't it?" Brock looks at me. "Isn't it, Porker?"

I'm not entirely sure what's happening because I kinda just stare at my dad's last written words on the page, but I can hear a few kids laughing, and Carly says: "Oh my gosh. That's sad."

Then I sense Ms. Fraser step away from me.

"Enough of that!" Ms. Fraser says with her voice real stern. "Brock, I will not tolerate any name-calling in my classroom, and should you do it again, that'll be two weeks of detention. Do I make myself clear?"

"What?" Brock shouts. "I said, Porter."

"I have ears, Mr. Middleman, and they work quite well."

"I was only joking anyways."

"Well, your jokes aren't very funny. How would you like it if I called you Mr. Little-man from now on?"

This makes the class erupt into a burst of giggles and laughs. Even I look up from my pages to see Brock sneering at Ms. Fraser, his eyes narrow and glinting with contempt, his arms crossed.

Ms. Fraser waves her hands in the air as she turns back to the front of the classroom, "Okay, that's enough. Enough!" The class goes quiet. Then she smiles at me again and says, "Thank you for sharing that with us, Bobby, we appreciate it. You can place your report on my desk and take your seat." She moves back to her desk and sits on its edge again. "Now, I expect everyone else has chosen a book from the list that I have provided you."

I grab my map and settle back into my desk. The wooden chair creaks pretty loudly. Brock is only a couple of desks behind me; he leans over close to me and says, "Can't wait for lunchtime, Porker, oink oink." I don't look at him, but I can hear him breathing pretty hard. Why does he hate me so much?

"Well, Mr. Middleman," Ms. Fraser calls out, "if you're so interested in being heard, you'll be our next presenter. Come on up. Now!"

I keep my eyes forward, but I can hear Brock sigh pretty hard. Then as he passes me, he jabs something into my arm. I don't know what, but it stings good enough that I groan. As he gets to the front, I move my attention to my pocket, where I pull out the blue maple leaf. It's warm in my hand, but it's not glowing as bright as before. I like feeling it in my hand, all warm and soft, kind of waxy feeling.

———————

I SIT UNDER a tree for the shade, it's hot out, and I get overheated pretty easily. I rub the leaf in my hand. The glow is almost completely gone. Is it dying? I wonder. Did I kill it? I study its tiny leaf veins pretty close, but not much is happening. Barely any power cells are pulsing through them—

Something rams right into me, causing me to drop the leaf as my side and shoulder hit the ground pretty hard. Everything goes black for a second, and all I can taste is dirt in my mouth. I open my eyes and see Brock looking down at me, smirking. Teddy and Lucas are beside him, sharing the same delight in my fall. Suddenly a sharp pain streaks up my side. I curl into a ball and rock in place, moaning.

"Aw, c'mon, Porker," Brock says as if I hurt his feelings with my soft wailing, "don't start crying. Man, you're such a wimp. I'm tough on you 'cause you gotta get tough."

I'm not going to cry. Not even a punch to my gut by Brock and his goons can make me cry, but I do feel pain. I roll over onto my other side, still moaning.

Teddy and Lucas help me sit up and lean me against the tree. I hold my right elbow in my hand; it's got red scrapes down it and stings a bit, and there are small pebbles embedded in the skin. I pick them out. Brock chuckles, "Boy, you hit the ground pretty hard, Porker. Shoulda seen how you looked. You would've laughed, too."

I doubt it, I thought. I don't laugh at other people getting hurt. But seeing Brock get hurt might make me smile, though.

"Lucas and I have a bet," Brock says.

I don't care. I really don't. The pain is less now, so I start scanning the ground for my leaf but don't see it anywhere.

"Lucas says your dad died overseas fighting terrorists," Brock says pretty loudly. "But I heard he died right here in the States, not so heroically. So which is it?" Brock waits for an answer, he sounds like he honestly wants to know, but only so he can use it to make fun of me, I bet. What does he know about being a hero? He's just a bully and a coward. Does his dad have medals? I doubt it. I don't bother answering; I'm too busy on my hands and knees now, patting down the grass and dirt patches, trying to find my blue maple leaf.

"Hey! Which is it?" Brock shouts. "What, did you lose something?"

I still don't answer; I don't even look at him. I concentrate on my search. I can feel my heart pumping pretty good. The heat of the sun cooks my skin. Wet droplets roll down my forehead, neck, and armpits and collect in the rolls of my flesh; sweat rains down from me like I'm a little puffy rain cloud drenching the inside of my shirt.

"You're such a dork, Porker," Brock shouts.

I feel the bottom of his shoe press against my back, forcing me flat on my belly. I lie there. I watch three pairs of Converse shoes, one red, one white, and the other black, walk away. I listen to Brock's voice screech and snicker. "I don't know why everyone feels so sorry for that loser."

It took me pretty much the whole lunch period, but I finally found my leaf. The wind blew it into the ravine next to the school grounds. The ravine is fenced off, but there is a little footbridge that goes over the river. I lean over the railing, staring down at the leaf that is maybe twenty-five feet below me. It lies just on the edge of the bank, almost in the water. Being blue makes it easy to spot, but if I don't get to it soon, the rushing water might carry it off. I climb over onto the outer side of the railing. I grab so hard onto the metal bar that my knuckles are white as a ghost. Now that I'm over the ledge, clinging to the side of the bridge, I look down, the drop looks a lot farther than I had thought. I drool a little on my shirt because I have my mouth wide open, which I didn't realize, so I close it and gulp a hard lump of spit.

I jump. Not 'cause I meant to. I'm actually about to climb back over when my annoying, involuntary freak-out reflex kicks in. You know, the thing doctors call an "acute physiological response to sudden loud noises," but moms just call "having a nervous kid. Why am I so nervous, and of what? No one ever tells me. But it's the stupid lunch bell that sets it off. And *boom*—my nerves go all haywire and I drop like a stone off the bridge.

Yeah, it hurts pretty good. Good enough that I try to wail, but I barely have any breath in me to wheeze out a whimper. I still don't cry. Well, I don't *think* I'm crying. I do feel a bit of wetness on my face, but where it's coming from, I'm not sure. I hear the water rushing past my left ear, so I have my theories. I smell mud and wet, mossy stones. I see the sky, just a bright wash of white, and then I see a crowd of dark faces peering over the railing, looking down at me. I can't make out their expressions, but one of them, I know, is Ms. Fraser. I think she's calling for help. Another murky face is Brock. I swear it's him. I can tell by his snickering. I taste something like baker's chocolate in a tinfoil wrapper sloshing around in my mouth. I swallow a bit of it along with a hard lump. Then I'm suddenly made acutely aware that pain isn't just a one-trick pony. It's a whole class of beasts. Some fiery and burning.

Some dull and throbbing. Some sharp and stabbing, acidic and biting. Each one clings and claws at different parts of my body, all out to totally destroy me. But I have learned a trick when it comes to pain. You can't fight it, see? They like it when you struggle. But if you just lie there all dead-like... eventually, they go away. So that's what I do. I just lie there.

My mind concentrates on something warm and waxy. I manage to grasp blindly and fold it into my palm. I got the leaf back. Then I think: maybe the water will carry me away. I hope it will.

Maybe my mom is right. Maybe more noise *is* better. There's a bunch of noise floating down from the dark faces above. I don't bother making out what they are going on about. I like it down here, slowly sinking into the cool muddy bank, drowning in the noise. I think I like not thinking or feeling at all—just the sinking.

FIVE

ZENOBIA WAS knocked about hard. She had never felt such furious and vicious strikes from the winds before; then again, she had never been this high up before, either. The highest she ever climbed the Very Very Big Hinterland Maple Tree, was maybe a hundred feet or so. Now, she was three times that height and dead center in the domain of warring cyclones that thrashed and bashed in a blind madness high up in the sky.

She dug her fingers deep into the rind of the maple tree. Sap oozed in clumps over her fingertips. She steadied her footing on a branch and took a breath. Despite sniffling to herself, "It best you don't look down, less ya want yo nerves actin' up." She dropped her stare to the long plunge below anyway, putting a fist-sized knot in her stomach. She suspected it had been there from the start of her climb but only chose now, three hundred feet up and precariously latched to dear life, to rear its ugly, knotted head.

She swung her cherry nose skyward once more, still quite a ways to go. The plan meant reaching a significant height to survey the countryside to help best plot a route to her father's rescue. And she needn't waste a tick of time. She felt every beat of her heart was a beat closer to her father's end, and she was unsure how many beats were left, so every aching thump in her chest counted.

Far above her, thick clouds of charcoal sparked long bolts of red lightning before swiftly being swallowed up into the bosom of its plumed darkness, leaving the sound of distant claps of thunder in its memory. This ominous sight didn't make it any easier on Zenobia's guts.

She rubbed her wet nose across her sleeve, then continued upwards, pumping her arms, propelling herself farther up and up. Her muscles burned hot under chilled flesh. She ignored the block of ice, sloshing in a pit of acid within her stomach. Sweat droplets hardened into icy teardrops on her forehead as she dogged from branch to branch. Her hands and legs became tacky with the sticky perspiration that oozed ubiquitously from the tree bark. The sap did help give her a solid grip, but the blowhard bullies of unfettered air turned her hair loose and against her, manipulating her locks into relentless whips at her face. She had to pause every few moments to curse and brush her tresses from her eyes; her sappy fingers stiffened the tendrils, making them harsher whips.

Her heart drummed double-time, flooding her limbs with liquid fire that burned her muscles. She felt very hot and very cold at the same time—exhausted, yet jittery. Sharp pain and dull numbing ran up and down her arms and legs, every fiber of her body pulled in opposite directions. And it wasn't just her body. Her head throbbed with the same opposing extremes—half of her wanted to stop, the other half to keep going. Apprehension and ambition fought for control, each striking like a spark in a storm.

The sap had grown so thick and tacky that when she snatched another branch, the skin on the belly-side of her palms and fingers pulled in an elastic-like stretch—glued to the tree bark—until it finally snapped free, nearly tearing chunks of flesh with it. She paused to take stock of her progress and was disheartened by how much farther she had to go. Her mind dipped into the well of doubt, which ran deep and plentiful.

"Maybe thisyer's near about high enough," she reasoned, trying to land somewhere between determination and despondency. Steadying herself on the branch, she edged toward its tip. The wooden limb flexed beneath her weight. The branches this high up were thin, quick to droop, but she crept forward anyway, needing to clear the foliage.

Now, stationed long enough in one place, she could really feel the tree's crown swaying to and fro, side-to-side, in a slow, dizzying rhythm. It stirred the bungleroot knot in her stomach. No time to waste. She swallowed her nausea and cast her gut into iron. Then she looked out—far out—across the land below and before her. As if drawn by instinct, her gaze turned north first. Once she wiped the wet blur from her vision, she saw it—

Far along the ragged, murky horizon of the northern lands: A billow of blackness bleeding up into the gloomy sky, like a festering wound leaking ink into the heavens. She stared a while. Then lowered her eyes to chart the lands below. She took in the landmarks. Measured the sights. Committed them to memory, taking particular note of a sinuous line, twisting its way north toward the rot. A road, vanishing into shady hills and misty forest, where it was swallowed whole by the land.

Her eyes squinted, irritated by a glaring light in her peripheral vision. She craned her neck toward the Southlands. In the distance—closer than the big dark blot of the north, yet still far away—stood a white spike, its tip piercing the ashen clouds. Zenobia wondered how tall and wide the ivory edifice must be for her to see it from such a distance. Massive swaths of mountains and forests sprawled at its base like dirty, low-bowing peasants humbled before the majestic white scepter. Farther beyond the mountains was a narrow sliver of blue, which she was sure was the ocean. She'd never seen a real ocean. She'd only read about them, just as she'd read about the Mountain of Bones, the Tower of the Oracle Akasha to the southwest, and Fire Mountain and Dragoon Keep to the northeast. But now, she was certain she was really seeing them. And just like when she first laid eyes on the Ashen Knight in the flesh, the sight filled her with equal parts elation and dread. There was a whole world out there, waiting to be experienced—one she never thought she would.

Maybe it was the noisy storm, or dizzying wonder of the world now revealed to her from this new, heightened perspective—but it took her a moment to notice the tiny voices rising up from below. Shrill, reedy voices she knew all too well. Voices she didn't care for one bit. The boys from the neighboring farms. Four of them, always in a pack. They delighted in teasing her, calling her names, poking and taunting until they goaded her into such a fury that something—often something valuable—ended up broken.

She dropped her gaze a little too fast. The sudden height and sway hit her stomach like a punch, and for a second, she thought she might purge what little food was in there. Snapping her eyes shut, she clenched her teeth to keep from decorating the earth below with bungleroot spew. The strong sway of the tree absolutely didn't help. Not one bit. With her eyes closed, the words being hollered from below became sharper, more distinct.

"Zenobia!" they screeched. "Come down! Come down!" Their high-pitched calls carried a tone—was it worry? Concern? Maybe. But what care did they have toward her, other than making her life miserable? The thought made her skin burn red. "If them boys want me to break sump'm," she muttered, "Imma do exactly that."

Sweat-icicles on her brow melted and ran down her cheeks. She felt flushed, overheated. Was the tree... getting warmer? Or were her senses playing tricks on her? She opened her eyes—slowly—until they went wide. The sap was glowing. All around her, the tree oozed a phosphorescent blue, thick and glistening like sweat from a living, radiant giant. Zenobia bounded down the tree with acrobatic precision, leaping from branch to branch. It took her much less time to descend than it did to climb. When she dropped from the final branch and landed both feet in the dirt, the four boys backed away fast. Their faces contorted with a mix of fear and confusion. A powerful heat pressed against her back. The blinding light she'd seen from above—what she thought came from the white tower—was actually shining up from the base of the tree. Her jaw fell open. The bark had turned translucent, like frosted glass. And pulsing deep within the bole of the trunk was a vague, shadowy shape... a beating heart.

"Holy Golly," she breathed, the words falling straight out of her gaping mouth.

"Did the Ashen Knight do that?" the eldest boy asked.

"Are you a-a witch, Zenbee?" wondered the smallest and dirtiest of the four.

"She must be. That's why she's so strong," said the third boy. His blond hair was so long, and his face so fair, he could have passed as a girl himself.

"I ain't no witch!" Zenobia snapped, whipping around to face them. Though her hair was in a matted, bristly mess—she had to admit—it sure looked like witches' hair.

"We saw what happened," said the blond boy. "The Ashen Knight took your dad and killed your mom. Why'd he leave *you* alive, huh? If you ain't some kind of witch?"

"Yeah," added the fourth boy, revealing black, rotten teeth behind thin, chapped lips. He rarely spoke—mostly because no one could stand how bad his breath was—so he only opened his mouth when absolutely necessary.

"Shut your stink trap," spat the eldest, waving him off before turning back to Zenobia. "Yeah, why *did* he leave you alive? And what sort of black sorcery are you up to?" He pointed toward the maple tree, now fully aglow with a vascular network of pale blue veins that snaked and branched outward from the pulsing heart at its base. The leaves above shimmered with the same eerie light. The whole thing looked like some massive, breathing beacon—an azure torch at the eye of a dark-brewing storm.

"I gone said I ain't no witch!" Zenobia shouted. "And if y'all don't skedaddle directly, Imma knock y'all off my land myself. And you know I will." She stomped her foot and bared her teeth in a snarl.

"We don't want you here," the eldest boy cursed. "You're nothing but trouble."

Zenobia flinched a step toward the boys. They jumped back in unison. "Git off my farm! I mean it." She shook her fist at them.

Then, from over a mound behind them, more figures emerged. Adults. The boys' parents. Zenobia narrowed her eyes as they marched closer, spades and pitchforks in hand. But it wasn't until she saw *him* that the fire in her belly drained away. Her stern bravado crumbled, replaced by a creeping panic that iced the knot in her gut. Erickson. The only boy who'd ever actually been kind to her. Who once stood up for her against the cruelty of the others. And now... he was leading them. For a fleeting second, she dared to believe he might be bringing help. But that meager hope was quickly squashed when she saw their faces. Their expressions beamed with a special kind of hatred—the kind people mistake for purpose. Even his face lit up with the proud glow of shared outrage.

They came to a halt, huddling together just behind their children, ten tall faces looming above five shorter ones—all staring her down with the same sour scorn.

"You should go now, girl," said the eldest boy's father.

"Your bloodline is cursed," his mother added. "We prayed to the Plebeian Heavens that it wasn't true, but the evidence is clear. Get far away from here—and don't come back."

"What you mean, cursed?" Zenobia said.

"You're kin to the Ashen Knight," said the blond boy.

"The blood of evil runs through your veins," hissed his mother.

"We don't want to hurt you, girl," warned Erickson's father, though his hold of the pitchfork suggested otherwise.

Zenobia turned to Erickson, her lashes soaked with tears. "I ain't no devil. And I sure ain't kin to that demon. He killed my ma... n'took my daddy."

Their faces, steeped in the blue glow of the tree, only hardened. Even the boys—who she knew she stood taller than—seemed to glare *down* at her now.

Erickson bent down. Scooped up a clump of dirt—still salted with the ashes of her mother. He pitched it at her face. It struck her cheek and streaked down her chin, black.

"You better leave, devil witch!" he spat.

Zenobia staggered—just a step—but then—

A brilliant blue light erupted behind her. It flared from the heart of the tree like a divine explosion, blazing against her back, casting long shadows across the mob. The crowd shrieked and shrank from it, recoiling like demons from holiness. Eyes clamped shut, arms raised to shield against the searing light.

Zenobia stood tall in the blaze: her silhouette, a burnt matchstick before a white-blue fire. The knot in her stomach melted. The doubt in her mind dissolved. Her limbs tingled, steady and electric with resolve. A spark of divine grit surged through her. She didn't know how or why, but something deep within her—in her bones, her blood, her breath—*did know*. She would vanquish the Ashen Knight. She would rescue her father.

SIX

I LOST MY last baby tooth. Yeah, I know, I'm thirteen and *still* have baby teeth? Well, not anymore, thanks to my fall. The school nurse—who is a man—said I probably swallowed it. He said I should be fine. The fall didn't do any serious damage. The tooth should pass easily enough through my digestive system in a week or so. Then he tried to be funny, I think. The tell was his wink when he said, *The tooth will come out in the end.* I didn't laugh. But I used to make up jokes too. I used to make my mom laugh. And if I think hard enough, I'm pretty sure I used to make my dad laugh too. With jokes I made up, like: *Why did the chicken cross the highway? To keep on cluckin'.* I liked making them laugh. But that feels like a long time ago. Almost in another lifetime, even.

Ms. Fraser keeps eyeing me as if I jumped on purpose. I didn't. I tell her about my condition with loud sudden noises, she nods and says, *Okay, I understand.* Though I don't think she believes me. As we sit awkward and quiet, waiting for my mom to show up, she keeps giving me a look as if she was on the verge of shouting at me. I liked Ms. Fraser because she didn't seem like she was about to fall to pieces at any moment, like my mom. But the way she's tapping her foot and glancing at me like that, her face all red, I think she might have more in common with my mom than I thought.

My right hand is sweaty because in its fisted clutch is my maple leaf, and it's warming up like a heat pad in my palm.

I sit on the little medical bed, rubbing the leaf with my thumb. Footsteps clapping down the hall outside the nurse's office. I know it's my mom by the rhythm—short legs chopping at the floor in high heels. My stomach's been a bumbling mess all day. I'm almost used to it by now. I barely even notice the aches anymore.

Though honestly, my whole body is one big sore mess. I can't breathe without something jabbing me on the inside.

"I knew it was too soon for you to go back to school," my mom says, swinging open the door. She rushes to me. Wraps her arm around me tight. Tight enough that when I remember to take a breath, I can't. She finally lets go. I think she heard me wince. Or maybe she felt me spasm under her hug. I'm still pretty tender, but I didn't want her to know that. She'll make a big deal of it. But when it comes to pain, you can always count on your body to betray you. She starts prodding and probing, inspecting me for damages.

"They told me you jumped off a bridge," she says. "Why would you do that? Why?" Her eyes are already watery. She's gonna start crying any second. I hope she doesn't. Not in front of Ms. Fraser. She does anyways.

"I didn't jump. I fell. It was an accident. I didn't do it on purpose." I try my best to calm her down. Try to reassure her I'm okay, but I don't think it's working. She presses her cheek hard against mine, kneading her chin into my shoulder. Her tears run down the side of my face. She moans—loud—right in my ear. "Mom," I say. "Mom, please, I'm okay. I'm okay." I keep trying to convince her I'm all good, but her tears tickle my neck, soak my collar. It's real messy.

"Mrs. Porter?" Ms. Fraser finally pipes up, real soft like. She places her hand on my mom's shoulder. "Mrs. Porter, Bobby is fine. A doctor examined him just before you arrived and cleared him of any serious injuries. It was a short fall. Nothing serious."

This seems to calm my mom a little. She lets go of me. Lifts the weight of her puffy eyes, sniffling nose, and quivering chin off my shoulder. Ms. Fraser hands her a Kleenex. My mom dabs her eyes and wipes her nose. "Thank you," she says.

"Can we speak privately?" Ms. Fraser asks. My mom nods. They step just outside the door. They close it, but the door is thin and does little to keep their voices private. Adults seem to like secrets. They seem to like keeping kids like me in the dark. The thing is, they're terrible at it. They seem to like letting people know they're keeping secrets. They wear it all over their faces, hear it in their voices. Let it poison everything they do. They tell them in every way except directly. Me? When I keep a secret, I actually keep it. My blue maple leaf is my secret. No one even knows it exists. I keep secrets so well, the fact I have secrets is a secret. Sometimes I wish I could show them how it's done. But then, I guess if I did that, I wouldn't be doing it properly. Boy, the paradoxes of life.

"I can't imagine what it must be like. What you and Bobby are going through." Ms. Fraser's soft voice leaks through the door. "But, I believe it would be good for Bobby to continue attending school. To give him some sort of normalcy."

"Normalcy?" My mom's voice is shaky. Angry. "Wouldn't it be normal if he showed some emotions?"

"Everyone grieves in their own time, and in their own way. Bobby... and with the way his father..." Ms. Fraser pauses. "I believe he's processing it all the best he can."

"I'm worried. What if he's..." I think my mom is crying again. The words get kinda garbled. Then a sniffle. "...damaged in some way. Can children get PTSD?"

PTSD? I can't remember what that means exactly, but I've heard of it. Pretty sure it's not good. Pretty sure any condition that goes by letters and applies to me is *definitely* not a good thing. I'd Google it, but my mom took my computer away. I was spending too much time on it. Not getting proper sleep. She packed up all my video games—especially the violent ones—until I'm "ready to handle them again." That's when I re-read my dad's story. Worked on my map. Can't say it helped my sleep any.

My mom and Ms. Fraser sulk back into the room. I must've zoned out and missed the rest of what they were saying. I do that sometimes. It's kinda annoying.

"Come on, let's go home," my mom says. The paper lining crackles as I slide off the medical bed and follow her out of the nurse's office. Ms. Fraser smiles at me. "I'll see you tomorrow, Bobby." The way she says it... I'm not sure if it's a question or not, so I don't answer. I just look up at her as I pass. She stands by the door. Watches us leave. I watch her watching us—until my neck twinges from twisting, and I have to turn forward again. My eyes drop to my feet. One shoe pokes out in front of my belly, then disappears as the other makes an appearance. They do this, alternating and taking turns, following the sound of my mom's clacking high heels.

MRS. PALMER, OUR next-door neighbor, is a big fan of colors. She's retired and spends most of her time painting in her backyard, which butts up against ours. The fence between us is so tall that I can barely see her at all when she's outside. But somehow, she can always see me. We talked to each other through the slats in the fence. When she spoke, her mouth clicked and smacked, something to do with her fake teeth not staying in place. She smelled like peppermint. I don't have a strong opinion on peppermint, except that it's a very strong smell. Anyways, she liked to call this time of day the "Blue-Hour." Though it's not really a full hour, she said, it's only about twenty minutes. Artists like to use this term for the moment when the sun dips just below the horizon. It happens twice a day: once before sunrise and again after sunset. It casts a soft blue hue over the world. This is not to be mixed up with "Magic Hour." That's a whole other twenty minutes, sort of the opposite of Blue Hour. Blue Hour was her favorite. She told me over and over. *It's the most peaceful twenty minutes,* she clicked and clucked through the fence.

"Why do they call it *Blue Hour* if it's only twenty minutes?" I remember asking.

"Because people are really good at two things," she said, smacking her teeth. "Overestimating and underestimating time."

I'm standing a few feet from my mom's garden now, watching the end of daylight disappear into the darker part of Blue Hour's twenty minutes. My mom is on her knees, digging a hole in the dirt. Next to the hole is the cake box of gray powder and a large cup that looks like one of those big coffee travel mugs my mom gets in the morning, except this one's made of cardboard or something like that.

"Can we do this tomorrow? Blue Hour is almost gone," I say.

She stops digging. Brushes the dirt off her hands. "Come over here," she says, waving for me to stand next to her. I sigh and walk over. When I stop beside her, I kick at a chunk of dirt and send it flying. My mom gives me a grave look. I dig my hands into my pockets. I feel for my leaf and fold it into my palm. It's hard to look at her in this dim blue light. I lift my eyes to the sky, where the last of the yellow light is slipping away, casting vaporous pink smears across the dark blue sky.

"This is a Living Urn," my mom says.

I glance back at her. She holds up the big paper travel mug and unscrews the bottom from the top, separating it into two parts. Then she opens the cake box. With her little garden tool, she scoops some gray powder into the bottom part of the container.

"Your father's ashes will help nourish this budding tree into a mighty oak someday." She fits the container back together, then lowers it gently into the hole. "This way, he'll always be with us as a living memory." She looks at me. "Come down here, kneel next to me. I think it would be appropriate to bury him together."

I don't move. Her brow wrinkles. Her lips presses into a white line as she waits. I shake my head. No. She's on the verge of tears again. I can always tell. Seems like her face is always on the verge of breaking down into a flood of tears. Why does she cry so much? It's stupid how much she cries. I think she's probably so dehydrated from all the crying that she's not thinking right. Trying to turn my dad into a tree. Boy, what a stupid idea.

"Bobby, please," she whimpers. "We should bury your father together."

"Why?" I shout. Right in her face. "That's the stupidest thing I've ever heard of. You've really lost it." I can't stand looking at her sorrowful face. I can't stand looking at her on her knees in the dirt, in her stupid garden, trying to plant my dad like a houseplant. So I take off. I run to my room. I slam the door. Then I fold myself head to toe under the covers. I want to be as far away from everyone as possible. I just want to be in the dark, alone with my sore body.

With my thumb, I prod at the beast hiding in my bruises. I tease it out of my tender spots just to feel it scratch, bite, and sting. To know it's still there. I marvel at how something so sharp can leave you feeling so numb. Paradoxes are everywhere.

Life is a paradox, Mrs. Palmer once clacked her fake teeth at me and said. It was at my dad's wake. Her peppermint scent was strong, and her breath smelled of rubbing alcohol.

"It's intrinsic in all living things to self-destruct—built right into the DNA. We're born to die. We live to die. What makes it a paradox is that we can't help but fight tooth and nail against our self-destructive nature. Except some people learn over time to see past that contradiction and accept that death is natural, Greenbean."

I didn't really get what she was going on about. And before I could ask what the heck she meant, my mom came over, thanked her for dropping by, and escorted Mrs. Palmer to the door. By the next morning, she was back on her side of the fence, painting like always. And I had already forgotten about it. Until now, I guess. *We're born to die.* And we're stuck dealing with the dead like being left behind to clean up after a party—or a wake—they bailed on.

I hear my mom's footsteps stop just outside my door. I'm pretty sure she doesn't know what to do. Come in, or leave me alone. She leaves me alone. Walks to her room. I hear her crying. I feel bad for my mom. I do. She tries. It's just not good enough. It's not her fault. She's going through a lot.

It's hot under the blanket. I'm sweating. The air gets thicker with every breath, hotter—like I'm breathing in wool. It makes me yawn. I listen to my own shallow breathing, and feel the heat wrap around me like a second blanket...

———————

I MUST HAVE dozed off, because something icy and smooth touches my cheek. It wakes me. It's so dark I have to rely on my other senses besides my eyes to make sense of what's going on. But I'm groggy, the rest of my senses are slow. The icy thing—now it feels like it has slender tentacles—slips across my forehead and strokes my sweaty hair. I smell dirt. Earthy dirt and lavender. Then I feel it: my body sliding sideways toward a soft depression in the mattress. Toward the gravity of a mass that bends the fabric of my bed. A body heavier than mine. I lose to its pull.

"Bobby?" It's my mom's voice. Low and calm. I can't see her eyes, not clearly, but the shape of her head starts to emerge, haloed in the faint red glow of her hair. She must know I'm awake. "I'm going to sell the house," she says. "I think we should move. Start fresh. I think that's best."

My eyes adjust. Shadows recede, revealing familiar shapes: the glossy whites of her eyes, her pale oval face, her pink lips. But something is off. Her lips don't quite match the words, like a foreign film dubbed in English. "I love you," she says. If I move my head even a little, the shapes that make up her face shift weirdly. Her eyes, nose, and mouth seem to float on top of her face, drifting like stickers in milk. Is she really here? Am I dreaming? Still, her fingers feel real enough. The sharp tips of her nails trace my hairline gently. It feels nice.

I roll away from her, curl up in a puffy fetal ball. Makes it hard for her to continue stroking my head, so she stops. A moment later, I feel something wet drip on me. Just a few drops. Then I feel her weight leave the bed. The gravity shifts. I bounce a little as my mattress returns to its original shape. To the depression of one. I stay curled. I don't move. I face the dark wall. The floorboards creak. Almost in a whisper, like I don't even know if I'm really asking, I say, "Do you remember when I used to make you laugh?"

The floorboards are quiet for a long time. I can hear the air behind me breathe. Then her voice says, "Yes, I do." The wood creaks five more times or so, and then the door clicks shut. Everything is quiet again. I try to force myself back to sleep, pinching my eye shut so hard the blackness behind my eyelids turns white.

I'm still wearing my regular clothes. I don't bother changing into my PJs. I fish out the blue maple leaf from my pocket. It's not even squished or anything, and I've probably been rolling over it in my sleep for a while. It glows a little in my hand. It's beautiful. Like holding Blue Hour. I bring it real close to my eye, so I can see the power cells flowing through its tiny veins. I place it on my pillow, right next to my nose, and watch it with half-blurred eyes. After a bit, it dims. And keeps on dimming. Everything around me dims, until all is dark—

BANG!

I jolt up. For a second, I feel like I'm falling—but I'm not. The falling was only a sensation in my head. It's dark, except for the soft blue glow from the maple leaf on my pillow. Kinda like a nightlight. I must've fallen asleep again. I sit up and rub the sweat from my forehead with my sleeve. My clothes are soaked and cling to me like saran wrap on baked ham. My breath's all short and jumpy. I fumble out of bed and peel my shirt off. I open the window a crack to let the cool air in. My heart is really having at it inside my chest.

My window looks out over the backyard. I can see my mom's garden. There's a single lamp outside, but it barely gives off any light. Still, I think I can make out the cleared patch where the little mound is. Then I remember that dumb bird, how it talked all weird and silly. Funny how things people (or birds) say always seem to pop up in my head way later, after they've already flown off. And when it does pop in my head, it starts to kinda make some sense. I guess I'm a little slow like that. Is it strange that I never seem to remember anything my dad ever said to me?

What pops into my head now is the silly rhyme: *The prize to be buried beneath my fat feet...* or something like that. That bird was as bad at rhyming as it was at flying. I glance at the glowing leaf on my pillow. Is *that* the prize I'm supposed to bury? And if I do... what exactly will that do? I change into my PJs. They're soft, loose, and dry. They're my favorite things to wear ever. If I had to pick three things to bring to a deserted island, these PJs would definitely make the list.

I snatch the maple leaf off my pillow.

I STARE AT my feet. The cool, moist soil squishes between my stubby toes as they sink into the fresh earth. My toes—what my mom used to call her "little

Porter piggies"—point right at the low dirt mound that marks my dad's resting place. He's down there at the bottom of a paper travel mug, where he's supposed to help a seedling grow into a strong, sturdy tree someday.

I get on my knees and dig into the mound. It doesn't take long to find the cardboard urn. I twist the top away from the bottom and peer inside. The moon's pretty bright tonight, and with the one backyard lamp—and my pretty decent eyes—I can see my dad just fine. He used to be a giant. The strongest person I knew. He could sweep me up and toss me in the air and catch me all with one arm. A war hero. Now I can pick him up in one hand. Well, two hands. The travel mug is kinda the size of a Big Gulp. So to hold it properly, I need both hands. But still.

I place the maple leaf on top of his ashes. Then I twist the bottom and top back together, the seed still tucked in the upper half. I drop it back in the hole and scrape the dirt back over with my hands.

I feel like I should be feeling something. But I don't know what. I just kneel there in the garden, trying to figure out what's supposed to happen. I stare at the new dirt mound I made. Is this the prize? Why was I even listening to that stupid bird? I pick up a clump of dirt and chuck it. I get up and go inside.

———————

I WASH MY hands and feet in the bathtub. I brush the dirt off my knees, but can't do much about the dark stains. In the hall, I don't bother with the foot-prints I left behind. I sweep the dirt to the side, just enough so they don't look like footprints anymore. Now they just look like a messy trail. Good enough.

I climb back into bed. I lie as still as I can. I focus on my aches and pains as they settle into a dull buzz. My body's done for the day, but my mind isn't ready to shut up, even though I want it to. It's frustrating how nothing seems to do what I want–not even my own brain. Except crying, I guess. At least I'm not a blubbering mess. There's that.

Then something pops into my head—something my dad did say to me once. *I've lost everything. Even you,* he said, sitting at the kitchen table. "But I'm right here, Dad," I told him, staring straight into his eyes. But there was something wrong with his eyes. *I gave them everything, and they took everything,* he mumbled. There was something wrong with his voice. "Hey, Dad," I said, but he wasn't hearing me. There was something wrong with his ears. "Hey, Dad," I tried again. "Hey, Dad, why did the chicken cross the road?" There was no response; he just kept staring deep into somewhere far away and dark. "Because he wanted to be first before the egg." He got up and wandered upstairs to bed. There was something wrong with his sense of humor.

SEVEN

The Traveler's Guide To Helcyon: Sights, History, Tips
On How To Defeat the Ashen Knight

CHAPTER III: NEX

No one begins as a villain. No one is born evil. It doesn't happen overnight. It compounds with every poor, misguided choice. Each decision becomes an incremental step down a spiraling slope, plunging into the dark, cold, and dank underbelly of obscurity. The descent grows steeper with every step, slipping further from humanity, swiftly into the realm of monsters.

LONG AND UNFORGIVING WERE THE winters on the Isle of Black Rock. Spring and fall were short-lived and only slightly less punishing, while summer was essentially unheard of this far north. On the rare occasion it did appear, the sun hung dimly in the pallid sky like a sickly orange orb. For the most part, the heavens remained mired in shades of gray, deepening to purple where they met the black plains on the horizon. The dominant winds—laden with ice crystals—were a ceaseless scourge. If ever one could weaponize the gales, Black Rock would be the proving ground. This relentless, icy barrage battered against the Tower of Black Rock, but the primordial heap of stone that made up its walls had been built thick and staunch. For countless centuries, it stood defiant—an enduring monument to the damned.

Perched near the tower's summit was a turret, its sharp rooftop nearly piercing the dark ether. And its barred doors and windows housed its newest denizen, the formal General, Amduat.

His status afforded him every comfort and luxury except one: his freedom. The only thing a man of his ilk prized most. After all, no matter how gilded a cage, it was still a cage to a ferocious lion. His confinement was strictly solitary. Usually, this wouldn't have bothered him; his interest in people rarely extended beyond their strategic value in war. Solitude was preferable when the game was suspended. But this time, an absence lingered. So poignant it cleaved a chasm in his heart and split a fissure in his mind.

Anything that could break in his chamber did. Amduat smashed the chairs and shattered the tables. Every piece of furniture was reduced to splinters as he raged, spitting at the stone walls. "Betrayers! Cowards! Feed unworthy of maggots!" He hurled his bed up against the iron bars of his cell door. "I will not wither and die amongst you, putrid piles of goblin-rat excrement."

Two guardsmen watched from a safe distance, eyes twitching and throats swallowing hard with every fresh eruption of violence. Even stripped of armor, Amduat remained a terrifying and menacing figure. The cage only magnified his dangerous aura. When the storm of destruction finally ebbed, Amduat approached the bars and pressed his forehead against them until his flesh indented between the rods. He glared at the guards, face red with fury, eyes cold as glacier ice. When he spoke, his voice was disturbingly calm. "Come here," he said. Beckoning them closer with a devious grin. "Come here, I want you to deliver a message."

The guardsmen rattled their helmeted heads in refusal. They had an unspoken rule: never get too close. Rule 1 was, *don't let him escape*. Rule 2 was *don't let him out of sight*. But wedged between them was Rule 1.a: *don't get too close*. You could break your neck if you got too close, as one unlucky guard did. That fool tore up Amduat's letter to Lianna and spat at him. He made the fatal mistake of stepping within reach. Amduat's grip was still formidable. Snap. After that, rule 1.a was implemented.

"What news of my dear Lianna?" Amduat asked.

"Thereths no news," slurred one guard. A scar mutilated his upper lip, giving him a permanent lisp and a tendency to drool when speaking. "No oneth's coming forth you." He wiped his chin with a dirty rag.

"Then why prolong my miserable existence?" Amduat said, tossing a folded parchment at their feet.

The lisping guard retrieved it and cocked his head in puzzlement. "Whaths thiss?"

"A plea to have my head divorced from my heart."

The guard squinted at the heading. "Decollatio Carta Captivus Libertatum?" he read out loud; his lisp unexpectedly absent.

The charter: a clause granting prisoners of noble rank the right to request death by execution.

"Run along," Amduat said, sneering. "Deliver that to your king."

The guards exchanged a glance. Then shook their heads.

Amduat exploded—seizing the bars and shaking them with such violence that the entire cell shuddered. Sweat broke across the guards' brows as the hinges groaned and bolts rattled in their moorings. Eventually, Amduat relented and retreated back into his stone chamber, each breath a curse muttered, damning everyone and everything.

THAT NIGHT, UNDER A SKY uncharacteristically clear and potent by the tightening alignment of scarlet moons, Amduat awoke to a bitter cold. The fire in his brazier had gone out, leaving only a thread of smoke. Frost rimed every surface. The air hissed and crackled as time seemed to stutter. He rose slowly, joints stiff with ice. Each muscle coiled, flexed, and cracked as he pried himself free from the freezing rime. His ears attentive to every sound, but there was none, except his own sharp breathing. His eyes narrowed, searching the shadows for what he could only sense but not see.

Then he saw it. Floating just outside his cell door, amid the slumped bodies of the guards—sleeping or dead, he could not tell—hovered a figure Amduat knew all too well. Nex. A spectral being whose sole purpose was to sever the tenuous tether of the soul from its body. To separate the person from the corpse. Man from meat. It had been his phantom twin on the battlefields, a stalking presence he'd long sensed behind every deathblow. Perceptible only as a profound void, resonating in the deafening silence left behind when the carnage ceased. Now, it revealed itself fully. Its skull-like visage glowed with a greenish-yellow luminescence, hovering atop a flowing crimson robe. Its cowl and cloak shimmered like wet silk, glistening as if drenched in fresh blood.

"If you've come for me, I welcome it," Amduat declared.

Like a bloodstained ghost, the scarlet specter floated through the prison door, stopping an arm's length from him. Nex's face was the most flawless human skull Amduat had ever seen—immaculate, untouched by time or earthly affliction. It had no eyes, only sockets that held a darkness so absolute it seemed bottomless. Profound pools of purest black. A universe of nothingness that pulled at him, tugging at his very soul. Amduat gasped, realizing he'd stopped breathing. He inhaled sharply—air so cold it burned.

Nex spoke, its voice seeping through bared teeth like vapor.

"I bring you a gift."

"A gift?" Amduat furrowed his brow.

From beneath its crimson cloak, Nex extended a red-gloved hand, proffering a sword as perfect and otherworldly as its benefactor. Amduat studied the weapon: a dark double-edged blade forged from a mythical black metal whose provenance could only be found in dark lore. Said to be smelted in the fiery veins beneath Fire Mountain and galvanized in the Lake of Enlightened Flame. Its shadowy surface glimmered with rosy undertones, a sure sign it had been quenched in a vat of blood. A deep groove ran down the center. Blacksmiths called it a *fuller*, soldiers, a *blood gutter*. It carved so deep it nearly bisected the blade. The guard was fashioned from polished black bone—beast or man, none could say—with hooked ends that curled like talons. The hilt was bound in sinewy, blood-red fibers, more muscle than leather. And at the base of it all, in the pommel, sat a single gleaming black diamond known as *Black Star*, the weapon's namesake. This dark jewel, sourced from the nebulous realm of archaic magic, marked the sword as a product of some terrible and dark sorcery. A relic of macabre mastery.

When Amduat finally seized *Black Star*, he found it impeccably balanced and astonishingly light, feeling less like a weapon and more like a natural extension of his arm. The sword so attuned to him, embosomed between the meat of his grasp, that it seemed to antici-pate his will, guiding his hand with every cut and thrust. Its instincts harmonized more perfectly with his intention than even his own limb.

"What debt do I owe for this gift?" Amduat asked warily.

"War is inextricably twined with human nature, as veins and arteries are to the human heart," Nex's voice permeated the cell like poisonous gas. "Follow your heart, and the sword will serve your nature." The specter extended his hand, gesturing to the cell door and slumbering guards beyond.

As Amduat held *Black Star*, he could sense the heartbeats of the guards, hear the air flowing in and out of their lungs in a wheezing rhythm. One pair gasped with a slight lisp.

The electric charge of life danced over Amduat's skin. He stood tall, adding a foot or two to his stature, chest jetting outward, shoulders broadening, and teeth gleaming in a genuine grin.

By the time Amduat thought of what he wanted to do next, he had already done it. The sword sliced through the iron bars and split the spirits from the flesh of the two guards in a streak of red mist.

Amduat had always regarded killing as a necessary task—one he was adept in executing—but never a source of pleasure. It was simply a means to an end. With *Black Star*, however, the act became so facile, so mindless, that it was an afterthought, leaving no room for remorse. No tightness constricted his chest in the wake of the killings. The sword absolved him of all responsibility, transcending grave-filling into an affair of levity. It freed him to focus on his ambitions without apprehension. He smirked as he watched the dark blade absorb the sticky red fluid into its steel, restoring itself to a pristine sheen. There was no staining this sword.

Amduat looked back into his chamber, expecting to find Nex, only to see the specter had vanished and reappeared right beside him, unsettlingly close.

"Do not fear," came Nex's silent whisper, buzzing like flies on rotting meat in Amduat's skull. "I will always be with you. Even when you cannot see me, I am at your side. At your command... just as *Black Star*."

Fifty guards had been stationed within the tower's weathered stone walls. An equal number of soulless cadavers lay scattered in his wake by the time Amduat descended from the swaying pinnacle of the tower and stepped out into the crisp night air. His gaze cast their ambition southbound, toward Dragoon Keep.

But first—he needed faster transportation.

He steered toward the stables.

The doors flew open with a thunderous crack, and the horses inside exploded into a frenzy. Twelve black steeds shrieked and thrashed in their stalls, rearing on their hind legs, stamping and kicking at their stall doors. And yet, amidst the pandemonium, one horse did not stir. Fourth down from where Amduat stood, an ashen draft horse remained still. Its white coat pale as a bloodless corpse pulled from winter ice. Its eyes flared a deep, glassy red. A stoic beast among panicked fools. The choice was obvious.

What followed might have been overkill. Or perhaps Amduat no longer had full command of his actions, animated by the violent whim of *Black Star*. Or perhaps it was strategic: eliminate the herd, prevent any pursuit. Either way, Amduat cut down the remaining horses without hesitation, offering no justification.

He burst into the bitter night atop his pale steed, galloping full tilt toward Dragoon Keep. The power he commanded under him was magnificent—the massive creature moved with focused, muscular fury. The rhythm of its charge sent exhilarating surges through Amduat's own frame, making him feel invincible, unstoppable. As they carved through the northern winds, parting before him as if in deference to his newfound supremacy, Amduat savored it: he was a transformed man. And all it took was the right weapon.

CHAPTER IV: DRAGOON KEEP

Fire Mountain has always been known as Fire Mountain, as far back as the history of man can be traced. However, no mortal has ever witnessed the natural fires that made the mountain legendary. Occasionally, the ground shakes and rumbles, as though something fiery bubbles and churns deep beneath its crust. But no flames have ever erupted to authenticate the mountain's name. Despite the absence of firepower, the mountain was long recognized as a perfect natural stronghold. During an epoch known as the *Age of War Lords* in the time of the *Word Wars*, King Gilgon ordered the construction of a citadel within mountain's dormant hollows. Thus, Dragoon Keep was born. The very same stones used to build it were hewn from the mountain itself—black rock that shimmered with hypnotic specks of light, as though a starry cosmos had been trapped within. These stones became notorious for their resilience. Impervious to the siegecraft of mortal armies and resistant even to supernatural forces and weapons. It is said no force on Helcyon is mighty enough to raze or breach the fortress. With an ironic nod to its invulnerability, King Gilgon named his stronghold *Dragoon Keep*. Its construction demanded a massive labor force and spanned multiple generations, giving rise to the suspicion that it was built on the souls of ten thousand men. On the very day it was completed, King Gilgon—old and deathly ill—became the final soul to be laid to rest within its foundation, entombed deep in the vast catacombs among all those who died building his crowning achievement. Some now call this bastion the *immortal fortress*. Others, more grimly, the *immortal crypt*. Even now, after thousands of years, the shimmering black stones of Dragoon Keep remain pristine, untarnished, unbroken, and as awe-inspiring as the day King Gilgon was buried within it.

THE JOURNEY FROM THE ISLE of Black Rock to Fire Mountain spanned six arduous days, leaving Amduat and his horse visibly wearied. Without pausing since they set out, hooves thundering, spurred by the vigorous winds of rage that had now dwindled to dead air, they had borne the brunt of their relentless push forward. The white steed huffed and snorted burdensome bouts of air, its sides heaving. Amduat, who hadn't slept, slumped over the horse's broad back, his arms dangling limp at either side. He licked his dry lips, eyes unfocused, watching the blur of shadows and light race past beneath him. In that blur, he often thought he saw ghostly faces—especially hers. Lianna's face. Gentle, warm, plumb with youth and innocence. He took it as a sign. A quiet affirmation. He was on the right path.

Once the mountain finally swelled on the horizon, Amduat forced himself upright. His bloodshot eyes narrowed, inspecting the curtain wall—thick as two—and its towering gates that guarded the sleeping volcano's natural entrance, which rose, like a giant gash into the rockface, to the height of the loftiest castle, culminating in a ragged apex, and was just wide enough at the base to allow four horse carts to pass abreast. Like so much in Helcyon, it resembled a wound.

As Amduat trotted closer, the guards stationed at the gatehouse quickly stirred into formation. A dozen soldiers formed ranks; archers raised crossbows, their bolts trained on him with taut precision.

When he was fifty paces from the gate, one soldier stepped forward, adorned in ornate armor, flanked by four men bearing spears. "Hold!" the captain commanded, raising his hand.

Amduat halted, his steely gaze cast down upon the soldiers from atop his pale beast. These men looked too rested, too content, too smug. The spoils of peace, he thought, often made slop of men.

"What's yer name? And what business ye got here?" the captain demanded, advancing with a bull-legged swagger.

"I have come for private counsel with Prince Horee," Amduat replied, his voice hoarse from the journey.

"Eh, 'fraid that's impossible. Yer best be on yer way now." The captain waved him off, casual as swatting a fly, "Go on now. On yer way."

Amduat snapped the reins taut with one hand, the other resting on *Black Star*'s hilt. He nudged the horse forward, close enough that its hot, mucus-laden snort misted the captain's face. The four spearmen raised their weapons at once in warning. Amduat paid them no mind, nor did he concern himself with the gatehouse archers, their fingers itching their triggers. Leaning down close to the captain, Amduat said calmly, "But I have not given you my name."

The captain gulped, suddenly uneasy in the stranger's shadow. "What... what's yer name?"

"Sir. Amduat. Lanmarc."

The captain's eyes went wide. Flight instincts drove him to pivot— too late. Amduat seized the back of his polished steel collar and lifted him clean off the ground, his legs kicking, then flung him into the cluster of spearmen, bowling them all to the ground in a clatter, flat on their steel-plated asses.

The archers at the gatehouse tensed, fingers squeezing their crossbow triggers. Amduat swiftly dismounted and slapped his horse's hindquarters, sending the beast galloping off to a safer distance. Arrows rained down. He seized the captain again, this time using him as a shield. Some bolts whizzed past, burying themselves in the dirt; others found their mark, thudding into the captain's armor, puncturing flesh. The captain's breath turned from screams to coughs, to choking, to a wet gurgling death rattle. Then silence. Amduat dumped the body at his feet with a dull thud. He stood untouched.

The archers reloaded. The four spearmen scrambled to their feet and bolted for the gates with Amduat on their heels, *Black Star* humming in his charge.

CHAPTER V: THE DIVIDE

It had long been a deeply held belief that the supremacy of pursuing power belonged solely to men. The fairer sex, it was said, lacked the ambition—or the resolve—to attain it. But power holds no such prejudice. It is always within reach of anyone willing to do whatever it takes, by any means necessary, to seize it, shape it, or destroy it. Perhaps the greatest betrayals are the lies we tell ourselves. And when confronted with the inexorable truths of our human nature, some handle it better than others.

LIANNA STOOD IN THE MAIN hall, encircled by five silver-haired elders, all men forty years her senior. Their stooped figures hunched over an expansive map of Helcyon etched on an immense leather hide. In Lianna's delicate hand, a quill saturated with red ink. With grace and precision, she cut the map up in a score of red lines, like a butcher carving up a steer into its various parts, her hand movements as fluid as they were firm. The elders watched, their anticipation palpable, eyes hungrily awaiting their allotted fat and juicy pieces.

"Your father was right, my Majesty," one of the elders said. "You do have more to offer than just your beauty." Lianna paused, her quill poised just over the map, red ink dripping ominously. The balding elder who had spoken noticed her sudden stillness and met her icy glare. His mouth twitched, "Uh-hm, my pardon, my Majesty."

"I have many attributes to offer, Lord Byson," Lianna retorted, her lips dimpling at the corners. Resuming her task, she let her quill glide once more over the map, delineating more territories. "Although my beauty has been advantageous, it is not the feature responsible for our gathering today." The last red stroke cut decisively across the hide. "There," she announced, glaring down at her map, "our new kingdoms and states are drawn."

Her declaration was met by a sudden ripple of grumbling from the council, drawing her attention. She lifted her eyes to the cause of the disturbance—Amduat, standing at the entrance of the great hall, a black sword in his right hand and his simple clothing soaked in deep crimson.

THE WOMAN BEFORE AMDUAT HARDLY resembled the woman he remembered. Had it been that long? he pondered. Yes, time has passed, and yes, time can account for some changes. Her simple linen dress was replaced by regal attire. Her flowing hair—cascading yellow silk topped with a modest silver band—was now constrained in a caul and bejeweled gold diadem. Even her rounded sun-kissed face was transformed, revealing a chiseled jawline and pale high cheekbones. But how had time altered her very essence? The girl he knew carried herself with softness, now stood as a statue of white stone, with a long and rigid neck holding a stern and cold countenance on high. Once gleaming with wonder and love, her gaze now scanned him with cynical scrutiny. Could time have wholly erased the girl he loved?

As the room spun, he strained to understand—

No—

It was not just time; it was the world she was sold into, a world he had spilled an ocean of blood to oppose. All his sacrifices were not enough to keep her safe from this oppression. He had failed—

No—

He was betrayed. Likho, Prince Horee, her damn father—all of them, stabbing him in the back to steal her away from him to use her for their own personal gains. And pleasure.

His skin flushed red, nostrils flaring. The dark sword in his palm burned and itched—

Yet as the melody of her voice sang out in the reverberating chamber, his fever instantly broke, and he found a renewed calm.

"Love," Lianna's voice chimed, her lips ascending, eyes beaming. Dropping her quill, she rushed toward him. "I am filled with such... joy to see you, my love."

Amduat relinquished *Black Star* from his clutches, and the sword drove itself straight into the marbled floor beside him as he readied himself for their embrace.

As Lianna threw her arms around Amduat's thick neck, he drew her slender form into his pounding chest. On contact, time stood still. Her scent enveloped him with memories of blooming summer fields and honey. Her hot breath teased his chest hairs. Her voice a solace. "I've missed your strength," she said, "Your courage. Your heart is my childhood hearth."

Amduat, accustomed to having his sword express his intentions, found himself lost for words. Unable to articulate his love for her, he simply held her, reveling in their blissful embrace.

LOST IN THE MOMENT, TIME seemed inconsequential to Lianna. She was rediscovering a part of herself that she had forgotten, or pushed aside—the part that tingled in ecstasy when she surrendered herself entirely to this man. Within his massive arms, she would bury her insecurities, worries, and fears. Her life, her very being, lay bare in his enormous hands—hands capable of crushing her, but would never dare. The thought incited a giggle. He was her shield, citadel, and keep of flesh and bone, within which she could dance freely, carefree, naked, and vulnerable.

Her giggle subsided, replaced by a pang in her chest. That innocent girl was merely a memory, or worse, a dream.

Echoes of haggard breathing and murmurs brought her back to reality. Uncomfortable, bodily sounds leaking from the five elderly stewards at her back. She could sense their shock, mouths agape, eyes bulging, leering at her like owls perched in judgment, waiting for their prey to show the slightest weakness. She pulled away from Amduat's hold and turned to face her council. Their jaws hung slack as they gawked at the blood staining her side, transferred from his blood-soaked tunic.

"Let us leave this place, my love," Amduat said, gently drawing her attention back to him. "I have come to bring you home. Our home."

At first, Lianna struggled to remember which "home" he was referring to. But when the image of the blooming lilies and their lakeside cottage flashed in her mind, she smiled, then frowned. She whipped her attention on the quintet of living corpses behind her, their faces drained of life, eyes frozen in horror. "Give us some privacy," she said, at first politely. But when the stewards didn't move, she added with a firmer edge, the weight of authority pressing into her voice. "Gentlemen, if you please." After another stiff moment, the council finally mobilized into a slow procession, heads twisting for one last glance as they shuffled from the chamber.

Now, alone with Amduat, she shivered. She moved toward the large table and map, wiping the side of her blood-streaked face with a silk cloth until her complexion returned to its pale serenity.

"You *are* different," Amduat said after a moment, stalking her to the table.

Maintaining a gap between them, afraid of his touch. "I have merely grown into the person I've always been," she replied.

"They've changed you. They've corrupted you!"

"They?"

"Your father. This Prince Horee. Where is this great Prince now?" His voice rose, loud enough to rattle the crystal chandeliers.

"He is not here. He is on a hunt."

"A hunt," Amduat sneered through clenched teeth. "Indeed, he is..."

Being hunted, she was certain, was the rest of the sentence left unspoken. "Leave him be, my love," Lianna leaned into Amduat, her voice softening as she attempted to calm the storm building behind his eyes with the warmth of her touch. She placed a hand over his. "There's been no corruption. He is as innocent as a child. There's no need to harm anyone. The war is long over." She looked into his eyes, but his eyes darted like a fish out of water. When she finally caught his gaze, his jaw loosened.

"As long as I have you," he said, "no harm is necessary. Let me take you away from all this madness."

"And go where? Into the wild?" She withdrew her hand, and with it, her affection. Turning away from him, she said, "I've shaped order out of this madness. I've carved my own throne out of a mountain of madmen. I've annealed my ambition in the fires of manifest destiny. I won't abandon what I've built." Her voice struck the chamber with finality. Something in her had revolted against the childish fever dream that his return had summoned.

Yes.

She saw him now as an infection. A cunning fever that had resurfaced, rendering her naive, childish, exposed—everything she'd outgrown. Everything he represented felt beneath her. An invader. A warmonger. A man who came not to love her, but to claim her. Her heart pounded, the truth rushing unfettered from her throat:

"I wasn't taken. I wasn't sold, kidnapped, or corrupted. I chose this." She spun to face him again, posture unmoved, voice cold and even. "I made the sacrifices to get what I wanted. What we had was never stolen, because it never existed. It was a fantasy. A fleeting fancy I've gladly outgrown."

AT FIRST, AMDUAT WANTED TO mourn. Mourn how they had poisoned her mind. Mourn how he had failed to save her from putrid and vile men who'd infected her. He grieved the time lost to war, the years she had been kept from him. He wished he had stolen her away when her spirit was still unspoiled. Before the venom of her father and Prince Horee had perverted that innocence. Now her beauty—once his sanctuary—was rotting in their corruption. He shook with rage. He wanted to eradicate every man who had laid a hand on Lianna. To annihilate them—and their bloodlines—for generations in a swathe of scarlet wrath.

I don't need you.

Her words clawed at his ears,

It was my choice. I ordered your imprisonment. I'm sorry—

Then something happened.

A sound. A movement. A break.

Amduat blinked. Something had fallen. He had wanted her to stop speaking. Her corrupted words to cease their assault—their betrayal.

He noticed *Black Star* was in his hand. It had leapt from where it had been wedged into the marble floor. He hadn't called it, but it came. And Lianna... was between them.

Amduat stared at the sword. At the dark blade slowly drinking blood into the folds of its steel.

Whose blood? Had he cut himself?

His gaze dropped to the delicate crown, its golden points twinkling as it rolled to a stop at his feet. Beside it, a slender, pale hand.

She was bisected at the waist. Her upper and lower halves lay in a glossy pool of the purest raspberry jam. He searched her eyes, moist but dimming. Amber glass, reflecting the world but absent of light. They held a fixed mirror of him, her last mortal sight. A mirror he would never escape.

He collapsed to his knees beside her two halves and shattered into a million pieces. Each fracture tore through him like a thousand blades, slicing into every fiber of his being. He was stripped raw. Set aflame. His blood boiled, broiling his brain until there was a *pop*—and then nothing. He forgot his name. His history. Even how to see, or hear, or feel. Suspended in a void of numbing darkness, his existence became utterly, irrevocably nullified.

After a timeless expanse of nothing, a thought surfaced, floating through the void like vapor: *this... is what lies within the cavernous eye sockets of Nex, behind that flawless skull.* The thought carried with it a muted sensation, vague and distant. Then more sensations followed, multiplying, reassembling into a prickly awareness, like blood flooding back to slumbering limbs in a rude, jolting awakening. Words ricocheted through the dark. At first, muffled and drunken. Then sharper. Shriller.

"Who are you?" a voice screeched from somewhere, but where? Yes. Yes. The tactile world was returning. His conscience reconnecting to his rudimentary senses. The ones he could always rely on.

"You've killed my queen!" the voice shrieked, high and thin, cracking with hysteria. It came from the right—twenty, maybe twenty-five paces. And then Amduat realized: the darkness engulfing him could be lifted by simply opening his eyes. When he did, he found himself folded over Lianna's lifeless form. Her face was chalky, moist with his tears.

"Kill him! Kill him!" the same voice squealed again.

Amduat turned. Slowly. The voice belonged to a pudgy boy about eleven, swaddled in royal silks and velvet, an oversized crown sliding askew on his head as his bleated out his alarm. He stood in front of a squadron of soldiers, waving them forward with frantic urgency.

Prince Horee. His chubby cheeks were blotched red with distress, sweat beading on his forehead and rolling down his soft jowls. His small, goosefleshed hands trembled as he pointed toward Amduat, who still coveted the corpse of his queen.

Amduat rose—tall and terrible. With one hand, he raised *Black Star*, leveling its tip at the trembling boy.

"This is your fault," he growled.

"Kill him! Kill him!" the boy screamed, his voice cracking under the strain, face flushed with panic. The soldiers surged forward in a clamoring of steel, swords drawn, howling their battle cries.

Amduat stood motionless. Waiting. Let them come. He had *Black Star*.

CHAPTER VI: INGRESS DIES REDUX

O nce the novelty of bloodshed and carnage wears thin, all battles begin to look the same: a bloody, chaotic mess that ends with profound silence and stillness. A scattering of fleshy mounds. Hollowed shells. Bodies strewn prostrate all across the grounds. The specifics of one kill bleed into the next and next until the whole event is one broad crimson smear. Yet some details persist—like screams piercing the dead of night. Take, for instance, the particulars of Prince Horee's end. A child prince, on the cusp of being crowned Grand King of All Helcyon, destined to rule the known world... only to discover that his coronation would become nothing more than a phantom footnote in the history books of Helcyon.

AS THE FINAL TENANTS OF Dragoon Keep crumpled beneath Amduat's feet—soldiers and servants alike, young and old, men and women, even five lecherous lords with glances perverted with greed and power, all suffered the fatal symptoms of *Black Star*'s touch. In the chaos, Prince Horee managed to slip away, leaving him the last to die.

The massacre had not left Amduat unscathed. He bore deep wounds, draining his strength with every heartbeat. But he disregarded his injuries, setting out to hunt down the boy. Staggering through blood-slick corridors, he shouted, "Prince? Prince! Come out, you coward!" The stone walls caught him as he stumbled, keeping him upright. Torches flickered along passageways, casting shadows that danced like mocking black devils, goading him forward. He wiped the slick sweat from his brow. "Prince... Prince Coward," he rasped, struggling to breathe. Still, he dragged himself onward, leaning heavily on the walls, leaving a dark smear in his wake. *Black Star* remained firm in his grip. An extension of him now. Likely to stay there long after his final breath.

Amduat paused, sucking in ragged breaths that gargled in his throat. He dropped to one knee, his wet hair clinging to his pallid face like seaweed. His head bowed, a red string of drool slipped from his mouth to the stone below. He moaned, his voice haggard and thin, "Horee... it's... your... fault..." he stressed the final word as he forced himself to his feet. He lurched forward a few paces, then buckled again, crashing to one knee with a guttural cry. He coughed—wet and red—and slammed a fist into the stone. "Nex!" he cursed, spitting blood and fury. He rested his forehead against the cold stone wall, whispering into it. "You son of a... bitch... I... know you are... here..."

The shadows answered. From their depths came the gliding rustle of a red robe. The enormous crimson hood took shape, and from its black hollow, the pristine skull of Nex emerged.

Nex hovered to his side and laid his red-gloved palm on Amduat's head, long fingers curling over his scalp like spider legs. "I am always with you," the specter hissed through his exposed teeth.

"Give me... strength... show me... where... he is," Amduat's wheezed, breath faltering.

"You will find strength in *Black Star*."

Amduat closed his eyes. Steadying his balance, gathering strength, he inhaled once, shallow and sharp, then pried his eyes open again. He dragged the sword beneath his bent head, studying it with a sickly, fevered gaze. Sweat from his brow dripped and sizzled as it struck the blade. Within the oily gleam of the black metal, the red streaks began to move, swirling, coiling like ink in liquid. Then... they began to shape themselves. Symbols. Letters. Words. He squinted. The message slipping into clarity for a single, silent beat: *Cut thyself free.* And then it vanished, replaced by nothing but his dark reflection, wan and ghostly, staring back at him from the steel.

Gritting his teeth, Amduat summoned enough strength to peel his head away from the stone. Nex retracted his hand from the crown of his skull, leaving him swaying unsteadily on one knee, teetering at the edge of total collapse. He shuddered, gulping for air in gurgled gasps. His wounds gushed blood from them in rivulets, his heart laboring to pump what little remained of his life out of him.

With all the strength he had left, Amduat dragged *Black Star's* edge across his thigh, beside a wound so deep the bone gleamed through. Pain exploded. A gruff scream tore from his throat. But then, as soon as the blade made its incision, the sword's dark magic took hold. Both wounds sealed. *Black Star* left only a faint black scar where it cut. The agony dulled. A numbing calm spread through his leg. His lips curled into a crooked, unhinged grin. He dragged *Black Star* across his chest, arms, calves, and shoulders. Always near an exposed wound, letting the sword's dark bite pass close. And wherever he cut, healing followed. Each stroke became a channel through which pain was expelled and strength restored.

Soon he was moving—cutting, healing, accelerating. By the thirtieth self-inflicted slice, Amduat stood tall again–his shoulders squared, chest lifted, limbs sturdy and humming with violent energy. His whole figure vibrated with newfound vigor and vitality. He ran his fingers over his flesh. No damage. No tenderness. Only the etched-black lines, silent proof of his pact with the blade. He was as whole as the day he first charged into battle. Perhaps more so.

He turned his blood-lust gaze to Nex and stared directly into those cavernous hollows. And this time, he did not flinch from their eternal darkness.

"Show me where the boy is," he commanded.

PRINCE HOREE'S PANICKED BREATH CAME fast and uneven, catching in his throat until he coughed. His cheeks were wet with tears, his eyes red and puffy, and his nose dripped with a long thread of snot. The hiding spot was cramped and cold. He cuddled his golden crown to his heaving chest—the space too tight and low to wear it properly—and the pointed edges of the circlet pricked his knees. Everything about the spot was uncomfortable, and he wished he'd chosen a better one.

In his blind panic, driven only by terror, he had run and run and run. And without thinking, dove into the first hole that looked remotely safe. Now, panting in the dark, he sat hunched in a damp recess of stone, wondering what this tiny nook was originally meant for. He also wondered how long he would have to stay there.

The screams had long died out. Even the echo of his name, once reverberating through the stone corridors in a terrible, haunting bellow, had fallen silent. His stomach ached. He realized he was sitting in something wet, it soaked through his royal silks and sent a shiver up his spine. A poor choice indeed. But it was too late to move now. The beast in man's form might still be lurking. He stifled his sniffling the best he could and strained to hear anything from the narrow entrance he had crawled through. Nothing. Only the hollow hiss of sucking air.

The boy prince had burrowed deep into the bowels of Dragoon Keep, where the fortress's black stones began to merge with the primordial volcanic rock of Fire Mountain itself. Perhaps the man chasing him wouldn't come this far. The labyrinth of tunnels might be too vast to search. But... he wasn't sure he could find his own way out, either. He'd never ventured underground before; his chambers were high in the keep.

His legs had gone numb. His lower back throbbed, stabbed by something sharp. Reaching behind, he felt several oddly shaped objects pressing into his back. He pried one loose and examined it. In the dim light, it looked like a thick white stick. He cast it aside and groped blindly again. This time, his hands closed around a spherical object. He pulled it before his eyes, and after a moment's inspection, realized it was a human skull. With a yelp, he dropped it, then buried his face into his knees and sobbed.

Eventually, Horee fell asleep despite the ache in his body. He didn't know how long he was out—time meant little in a tomb—but he woke with a jolt of pain. A cramp had seized his legs and was creeping up his sides. He winced and moaned, cursing and cussing under his breath, parroting his late father's vulgar vocabulary. He couldn't bear the impossibly tight bed for the dead a second longer. It was time to leave.

He pressed his ear to the corridor outside—still nothing. Then, wiggling his way out, he scraped his round belly against the rough granite. Finally free, he stretched his limbs and rubbed the soreness from his legs and arms, working to restore proper circulation. After adjusting his crown over his sweaty hair, he peered ahead. His eyes had acclimated to the dim light, yet the corridor remained treacherous with dark, ill-defined shadows. He strained, peering deeper into the catacombs. Something lay ahead. A dark shape. About fifteen paces away. Human-shaped. Unmoving—or was it moving? His eyes couldn't decide. Could it be...? Had it been waiting for him all this time? Despite the absurdity, Horee drew a finely crafted, almost purely decorative, dagger from his belt, its hilt bejeweled with jade and opals. He slashed the short blade at the air in front of him, wildly, uselessly.

"If that's you, devil," he shouted, voice quivering, bouncing off the stone walls, "I wish to hire your services. I can make you rich if you serve me. I can even find it in my heart to forgive your murder of my queen."

The black mass moved. This time, he was certain. It advanced. Horee stumbled backward, caught his heel on a raised slab, and tumbled hard onto his soggy bottom. His crown flew off and clattered into the dark, vanishing down one of the branching tunnels. His dagger, thrown, skidded across the stone floor, disappearing into the shadows. Scuttling back in terror, eyes turning upward, just in time to meet the icy scowl of Amduat, towering over him, poised to squash the life from him. Horee screamed, curling into a trembling, whimpering ball.

"Bring the boy to the Ingress of *Dies Redux*," an ethereal whisper stirred the air around them.

Amduat snatched Horee by the back of his royal tunic, plucking him off the ground. The boy kicked and flailed, as useless as a caught mouse. With the ease of a butcher carrying a sack, Amduat hauled him off deeper into the catacombs.

THEY JOURNEYED EVER DEEPER, UNTIL the stone walls, floors, and ceiling of Dragoon Keep gave way to something far older, no longer shaped by men. Rugged, black rocks loomed around them, forming a natural underground network of gaping caverns and veined tunnels.

Amduat followed Nex, whose fluttering crimson robes left vaporous trails in the air. The specter's skull glowed with a sickly green light, casting an eerie luminescence that kept Amduat from losing his way in the vast, swallowing darkness.

At last, they reached a cavernous chamber deep within the earth. Narrow channels of glowing orange lava sneaked through fissures in the ground, accompanied by whistling jets of steam. At the center of the chamber stood a granite slab, crudely hewn from the rock as if the mountain itself had forced it upward to serve some ancient purpose. The air thrummed with a presence older than gods. It felt like a place where ancient cults had once gathered, supplicating and satiating primordial forces with blood and bone. Amduat unceremoniously dumped Horee on top of the slab.

Nex's voice hissed, curling in the steam like serpents. "Open the door."

Guided by some unseen force, Amduat drove *Black Star* into the center of the slab. The blade slid into the solid stone like a key into a lock. The granite bubbled, liquefied, and darkened into a pool of tar. Horee screamed as it ensnared him, pulling him under—limbs thrashing, clawing at the edges, trying to scramble free. Amduat held him fast. The boy prince wailed. Begged. Scratched at Amduat's arm. But the black quicksand swallowed him. Amduat kept his hand submerged, pressing the prince down until the final air bubble surfaced and popped. Then stillness. Only then did he pull his arm free.

The earth responded with a groan. Veins of orange light widened into shafts of blazing fire. The ground surrounding Amduat crumbled away, collapsing into a rising pool of eternally burning lava. The cavern floor transformed into a flaming lake, stranding Amduat on a narrow rock island where the slab had stood.

At the far end of this molten lake, the Ingress of Dies Redux rose from the undulating waves. A seven-foot arching tablet of stone framing a smooth, polished dark mirror, untouched by flame or heat.

Nex hovered beside Amduat, unaffected by the molten fury below. With a gloved hand, he gestured toward the distant mirror. The heat twisted the air, warping Amduat's vision into a wavering, dream-like mirage.

"Your final pilgrimage lies across the Lake of Enlightened Fire," Nex explained. "If your flesh bears the marks of *Black Star*, you may traverse the trench of Enlightened Fire and emerge anew."

Amduat snatched *Black Star*'s sinew-hilt and yanked the blade from the tar. The instant the sword cleared the surface, the black pool hardened again into unbroken stone. He stepped to the ledge. Flames licked his toes. Raising the blade, he dragged it across his chest, carving a fresh wound that sealed instantly, leaving behind a thin, black scar. He marked himself again. And again. And again, Then stepped over the edge into the trench of fire, scoring fresh flesh with every step. Every stroke etched a silent vow into his skin.

THERE WAS NO PAIN—ONLY THE flash of a memory.

An eleven-year-old Amduat, scrawny and shirtless, trembling under a merciless sun. His cheeks scraped and bleeding, stinging from the salty tears streaming into his wounds.

A voice boomed from above, resounding with anger and contempt: "There's no room for tears, boy. This isn't a place for infants, but men!"

Amduat didn't look toward the speaker. His gaze locked on his opponent—his ten-year-old brother, Likho. They squared off inside a four-foot-deep dirt pit, their fists clenched around wooden training daggers. Dull, but pointed. Wincing, Amduat smeared his tears across his cuts, then let out a shrill cry meant to sound like a battle roar, and he charged. Likho sidestepped, slicing the wooden blade across Amduat's belly as he passed, then swept his leg, sending Amduat crashing face-first into the dirt.

"I killed you again, brother," Likho crowed.

"Get up," the voice barked from above. "Get up. Or stay down and be buried with the dead."

Amduat rose. Grit caking his teeth, breathing hard through flared nostrils. His eyes: glassy, focused, furious. He lunged. His blade jabbed and swiped in a flurry. Likho dodged. But Amduat charged forward with feverish, manic, unhinged intensity. He drove his knee into his brother's gut. Likho folded with a wheeze. Amduat cracked a sharp elbow across the back of his skull. Likho dropped on all fours. With a vicious kick to his ribs, Amduat flipped him onto his back, gasping, stunned. Then, straddling his brother's chest, he raised the wooden dagger. And drove it into Likho's right eye.

The scream. The blood-curdling scream that followed...

The phantom of his adolescent rage and fading toll of Likho's

scream lingered, hauntingly rendered in the dark mirror's glass—
then vanished, sucked into its void. The mirror no longer reflected
the scraggy child, nor the man he had been, but something else.
Something encased head to toe in scorched metal armor, glowing
red-hot from the heat. How he came to wear this suit was a mystery.
There was the sense—vague, maddening—that he'd just glimpsed
something important in the mirror, a memory now lost forever. What
was it? Two glowing orange globes burned in the glass like embers
suspended in the black slit of his full-face helmet. He lowered his
fiery gaze to his hand: a blackened gauntlet wrapped tightly around
Black Star. That, at least, was familiar.

Nex drifted close. "Raze all armies to dust," the skull reverberated,
its jaw unmoving. "Inflict your reign of ash upon the people of Helcyon."

CHAPTER VII: THE ASHEN KNIGHT

The Ancient City of Kaste climbed the southern face of Kaste
Mountain. The southern terminus of the Dracanspyne
mountains, with Fire Mountain crowning its northernmost end.
Here, Likho had been awarded the title King of Kaste. As the
largest city in the province of Morilund—and the first civilization ever built in Helcyon—Kaste rose in ascending tiers along
the mountain slope, each level assigned to a distinct class, each
bound to its station in life. Rarely did the tiers intermingle. The
tier into which you were born dictated the life you would lead.
At the summit sat the Palace of Manifest, residence of its final
ruler: King Likho. The grand palace overlooked a city of one
million Kasteanites.

ONE EVENING, THE NEW KING was enchanting his son and daughter
with bedtime tales of battle. Projecting miniature smoky knights
from his magical eye, when the palace jolted by a severe quake. The
tremors rattled the entire mountain, shaking the city to its foundation. His children shrieked and scurried into their father's arms.
Once the quake subsided, aside from a few shattered ornaments,
everything seemed to return to normal. But the frightened murmurs
of the citizens below crept up to Likho's ear, drawing him to the

balcony. He gazed northward to Fire Mountain. There, enormous plumes of smoke and ash erupted into the heavens, marring the sky with a massive black blot that churned and spread in every direction.

Four days later, the sun was gone. The sky above Kaste had turned to ashen clouds. On the fifth day, he arrived. Amduat. Mounted on his great white steed—its coat now stained gray with soot—he approached the iron gates, the only entry through the monumental curtain wall that wrapped around the mountain's base.

From the gatehouse, the gatekeeper called down: "State your name and purpose!"

"I am the Ashen Knight," rasped the voice beneath the helmet. "I have come to kill your king."

The guard laughed. "We have the greatest soldiers and the greatest king in all, Helcyon. You'll find that task... challenging."

It was not.

As the Ashen Knight passed through the gate—tier by tier, ring by ring—no soldier, no class of people, no rank nor resistance could halt his ascent. With a single graze from *Black Star*'s edge, hundreds—thousands—were turned to ashen statues. Weapons failed. Strength failed. Strategy failed. His path was unstoppable.

From the upper palace, Likho watched the nightmare breach his grounds. He gathered his wife and children and led them to a concealed passage buried within the palace walls. It spiraled down through the mountain toward an Ingress, a portal that would carry them beyond the city. At the mouth of the tunnel, he held them close, kissed them, then removed the smoky eye from beneath his patch.

"If you ever wish to see me again," he said, placing it in his son's hand, "speak my name to the orb, and it will show you my face."

Tears spilled down their cheeks.

"I love you," Likho said. "Now go. Go—quickly."

He handed his wife a torch. Gave her one final, tender smile. She wept, and he sealed the tunnel behind them.

NOT MUCH MORE NEEDS TO be said. The victor was clear. His coronation was a five-year-long massacre. Helcyon was enslaved in fear, smothered beneath an era of ruin, shadow, and blood. Terror reigned across the world under its new overlord:

The Ashen Knight.

EIGHT

I **WAKE UP** and roll off my right arm. It's gone completely numb. I hate it when that happens. It's always the worst part when the feeling starts coming back. A flood of a trillion tiny needles pricking and stabbing my veins. I'll just have to bear it, I guess. Bear it like a man. But man, it sure sucks when it happ—

AHHH!

ARRRRG!

Darn, that's annoying.

Thankfully, my arm starts feeling better—feeling again—but my clock is dead. Nothing works. All the power is out. Sunlight blushes behind my curtains. It's morning. I recognize the tune of the birdies' *good morning* song. They're chirping their little hearts out. There must be a whole choir of them with how loud they are.

I throw my curtains open—and my mouth drops dead open. There's a giant tree in my backyard. Where the heck did *that* come from? It rockets straight up, maybe a thousand feet high. Okay, I'm not sure exactly, but it's high. Real high. Five of our houses stacked on top of each other might only reach the lowest branch. The trunk is so thick it practically eats the whole backyard. Did I sleep for a thousand years? It sure wasn't there last night. I smack my forehead against the cool windowpane. My eyes roll upward. So far, they might just roll into the back of my head. What I see could explain its miraculous appearance: This mother of all trees, blooming in vibrant blue maple leaves.

"Holy cow!"

I rush into the hall. Poke my head in my mom's room. She's not there. "Mom?" No answer. I scuttle down the stairs, hook my arm around the banister, and sling-shot myself like a bullet through the kitchen and out the back door into the yard.

I skid to a stop—inches from the tree—nearly slamming headfirst into it. My eyes and mouth are dry. I left them hanging wide open in awe. I gulp, snap my jaw shut, and rub the moisture back into my eyes. I press my palm to the tree. It's warm. Almost hot. And I swear I can feel something pulsing inside it.

"Heck of a garden your mom's got this year," says Mrs. Palmer from her side of the fence.

I jump.

The sudden movement reminds my body that it's still bruised. Everything aches.

"Sorry, dear. Didn't mean to startle you, Greenbean," she clicks and rattles through her false teeth.

I can only see slivers of Mrs. Palmer through the slats in the fence.

"Where's my mom?" I ask.

"Went to the store. Said she was getting candles and batteries. Told her I'd mind the house. Seems that mighty blue tree knocked out the power on the whole block." She pauses. "Funny, no one else seems to see it but me... and you. You know anything about it?"

I shake my head, then tilt it back to look up. My eyes scan straight up and up and up. It makes me a little dizzy, so I don't stare for long.

"How come we can only see it?" I ask, leveling my head again to the fence.

"I figure that's just as much a mystery as the tree itself."

I can barely make out what she's doing, but it looks like she's shuffling around, trying to get a better angle. I see one of her droopy eyes peeping through a knothole in the fence board.

"I'm not much of a botanist, but that's a peculiar-looking maple tree," Mrs. Palmer says.

I *know* it's a maple tree because of the multiple pointy lobes on its leaves, just like the blue leaf I buried with my dad last night. That's the dead giveaway.

"Trees are highly symbolic," she continues, "especially ones with blue leaves. Have you ever heard of the 'World Tree'?"

"No."

"Well, you can find it in all kinds of old stories. But the nut of it is the 'World Tree' connects the underworld, with its roots, to our world, with its trunk, and the heavens with its high branches reaching toward the sun. It's a bridge that ties our different worlds."

I didn't understand what Mrs. Palmer was going on about, but I figured I might as well keep listening. Sometimes the meaning hits me later—pops into my head when I least expect it. Mrs. Palmer keeps talking, but I start zoning out. Bits and pieces make it through—words like *cosmos*, *enlightenment*, and *family*—but my mind's way too full of my own thoughts to keep up. Strange thoughts, like: *could this be the very, very same Very Very Big Hinterland Maple Tree from my dad's story?* But that's impossible. Stories are just stories. Fantasies are fiction. And fiction is not real life... Yet here it is. Something pretty impossible is standing right here in my backyard. In my mom's garden. Covered in bright blue leaves. They shimmer like they've been lit with blue fire. It's beautiful. And wild. And really real.

I notice Mrs. Palmer has stopped talking. I scan the fence slats. She's gone.

I think I hear something. Tiny, brittle voices riding the cool morning breeze. They drift past my ears so lightly I almost think I imagined them. Where they're coming from, I can't tell... maybe the other side of the tree? I squint. Turn my ear toward the wind.

"We do not want to hurt you, girl..."

The voice is faint—distant—but real.

Goosebumps prickle across my arms. The hairs on the back of my neck stand up, sharp and electric. I move to investigate, edging around the massive trunk. The voices grow louder, clearer.

"I'm not evil..."

A girl's voice. Shaky. Scared.

"He killed my ma... and took my daddy."

I'm almost there, just around the bend. They sound like they should be right in front of me, but... I still don't see them.

"You better leave, witch!"

A boy's voice. Harsh. Mean.

I don't get it. They should be right here.

And then—

Bobby Porter stepped into a sudden, all-encompassing light that hadn't been there a step before. For a moment, there was only white, blinding, and endless. Then, from within the haze, shadows stirred. Blurred shapes moved like ghosts ahead of him. He crept toward them. The shadows grew sharper. One of them—a figure—came into focus. A girl. She had a delicate frame and a wild mess of red hair that looked like it hadn't met soap or a brush in years. Bobby stopped just short of her. The light from the maple tree blazed behind him, burning warm against his back like a second sun. And then—In a bat of an eye—it was gone. Light snuffed out. Warmth sucked away. A biting cold wind swept in. Bobby shivered. That's when he realized he hadn't put on his shoes. The grass under his bare feet was freezing. And he was still in his PJs. He glanced up. A small mob stood before him, gawking through their raised arms, stunned into silence.

Then an adult pointed straight at Bobby and screamed, "She's conjured a demon to kill us all. Run away!"

Pandemonium erupted. The mob, children and parents alike, knocked into each other, vaulting on their heels. Some yanked the hems of their dresses above their knobbed knees, but all tore back over the hill at a panic-stricken pace.

Standing behind the red-haired girl, Bobby watched as she watched the village fools scramble over the blue ridge. She tilted her head, seemingly bemused by the villagers' hasty and comical departure. She hadn't noticed him yet. Once the last lagging child dipped out of sight, Bobby became aware of his open-mouth breathing—

The red-headed girl spun. Fast. She dropped into a defensive stance, fists raised like a boxer.

"Think ya can sneak up on me? Yer liable to git a whoopin'," she spat.

Already whooped-stunned by her striking features, Bobby struggled to draw shut the hole in his face he left gaping wide open, let alone have it articulate any meaningful sound. He just blinked at her, doughy and dumbstruck.

"Who are ya?" she demanded.

"Uh... um... err," Bobby stammered.

"You with 'em idiots who jus' tore off over them hills?"

"What?" Bobby said, finally managing to find his voice. "No. I'm no idiot. I'm just... confused."

"Welp, if ya aim to git a jump on me, you best be beggin' Porter for mercy from the mighty pain I can snap in ya." She made a sharp breaking gesture with her hands and clicked her tongue against her teeth.

"P-Porter?" Bobby blurted. "My name is Porter."

"Who gits by namin' they sorry kid Porter?" she chortled. "I imagine you mus' have a might big ego to go with that name."

"My name is Porter. Bobby Porter."

She tilted her head again, relaxing her battle stance. "Bobby Porter?" She gave him a good once-over. "Yer thee Bobby Porter?"

"I'm a Bobby Porter."

"Imma s'pose to believe yer the son of our Lawrd Porter?" She cast a glance over his shoulder at the tree—now fully glass—its translucent trunk pulsing with the silhouette of a sizeable heart.

Her scrutiny returned to Bobby. "You came directly outta thatyer First Tree of Life. An' gone turned it to glass. Ain't that sump'm?" She began to circle him, inspecting him more closely from every angle, sniffing the air near his sweaty spots, of which there were plenty. "The Plebeian Heavens gone heard my prayers?" She asked, squinting suspiciously. "Done sent me a *mighty warrior* to help me lick the Ashen Knight for good?"

"Mighty warrior?" Bobby repeated, worried now that she was confusing him for someone he couldn't possibly live up to. "I don't... think so." He observed her as she observed him.

"Well, my mama always tol' me the Plebeian Heavens had themselves a wicked sense o' humor." She narrowed her eyes at him. "You shore don't look like no dee-vine warrior what battled a whole army o' Gigorocks an' won. The Bobby Porter I read bout in my books didn't look nothin' like a plum hawg."

"Maybe I'm not the same Bobby Porter as in your stupid books," Bobby huffed. Then trudged back toward the tree. "Where am I, anyways? How do I get back home?" He circled the glass maple. The red-headed girl vanished from his view as he moved around the wide trunk, only to reappear on the other side, watching him with renewed interest.

On his second trip around, he knocked on the glass bark, surprised to find it warm, despite its icy appearance. Still unsatisfied with seeing the girl reappear, he made several more laps around the tree. She eyed him solemnly each time he completed the loop.

By the sixth circuit, she was no longer eyeing him; she was sitting on the hill's edge, her back to him, head hung low. Tired and exasperated, Bobby approached. "Is this a dream?" he asked. "Why can't I wake up?"

"No." She shook her head. "This ain't no dream." Her shoulders trembled as though she were fighting back a rising wave of emotions. "I wish it were," she said. "I really do. If this were a dream... it wouldn't've been my fault." She buried her face in her arms and rocked back and forth, weeping.

Bobby didn't know what he said to upset her, but he was no stranger to his mouth upsetting people. All he could do was stare, frozen, as her body shook, her shoulder quaking. Her sobs seemed to fossilize him. The sound built like a storm, wreaking havoc on his nerves, rattling his bones, magnifying the pounding in his chest, agitating the tumult in his gut. His throat dried up. The back of his eyes itched. He feared his insides might rupture under siege from her distress. So, he crouched beside her. Watched her tears trickling down her cheeks for a moment. Then, in the gentlest voice he could find, he said,

"Can you please stop crying?"

And stop, she did like a switch flipped, her whole body abruptly hushed. The stillness and silence that followed hit harder than her weeping. He heard the sting of his own callousness ring in the quiet. Felt the weight of his own hushing words. And it felt shameful.

She turned and looked at him, a misty reproach in her eyes. There was a green-flecked fire behind the tears, a sharp glint that made Bobby wish he could disappear from under her flint-edge focus.

He decided it was an excellent time to look literally anywhere else. His eyes ferreting about, noting the endless pall of murky clouds hanging low and heavy in all directions. Then the ground—blue-tinged grass, and brown earth peppered with gray dust that tickled his bare feet. In the shallow valley below, he saw a modest hovel next to a tilled field. He tilted his head up again, eyes following the massive maple's sapphire crown as it arched overhead. A streak of red lightning crackled through the smoky clouds above the treetop. *Red lightning?* Bobby thought. "Where am I?" he asked aloud. He lowered his gaze, looking back to where the girl had been, but she was no longer there.

He caught sight of her storming down the hillside toward the homestead. "Um. Hey," he called out. "Where you going?"

Another flash of red lightning rent the murky skies, splitting the clouds with a thunderous crack, unleashing a torrent of fat raindrops. They came down hard, soaking everything, including Bobby.

He clumsily chased after her, one hand pulling up on the waistband of his soggy pajama bottoms, the other raised as a visor that did little to shield his eyes from the stinging rain.

The girl slipped through the doorway of the cabin, vanishing into the darkness inside.

Bobby stumbled up to the entrance, unsure if he should follow. He leaned in, poking his head past the frame. "Can I come in, please? Hello?" His voice disappeared into the gloom. He waited. No answer. Rain kept pelting his back while a biting wind nibbled at his ears and nose and snaked down the collar of his pajama top. "Please, can I come in?" His teeth chattered. His feet squished in dark mud at the threshold, going numb. Still no answer. "Oh, the heck with it", he muttered and stepped inside. "I'm coming in," he called out. But the words fell flat in the eerie hush.

It was shelter, but barely warmer than outside. As his eyes adjusted, the sound of rain pattering against clay roof tiles resonated through the cramped space. The room was small, primitive, and astonishingly sparse. Hard to imagine someone actually lived here. To his right, a narrow doorway opened into a bedroom. Directly ahead of him, a shut door. Probably where the girl had gone. The rest of the room was furnished with crudely-hewn wood furniture, hacked into shape with an ax and cobbled together with twine. Chipped clay pots, frayed and faded quilts, and braided rugs lay across the warped, grimy floorboards. The scene reminded Bobby of the Renaissance fair. His dad had taken him once and forbidden him from bringing his portable game console, saying *it would ruin the immersive experience.* Bobby hadn't cared. He wanted nothing to do with the boring Renaissance fair. His father's strictness had only fomented rebellion in his heart, making him even more determined to be miserable. He'd sulked and stomped, pulling ugly faces whenever his dad pointed at something and tried to tell him what it was like "back then."

Now, his face twisted as he stood in the tiny cabin, dripping wet. His feet stamped black footprints along the rough floor, while the sodden cuffs of his pajamas dragged behind his heels, collecting a heavy trail of soot. He slogged over to the square hole in the floor that dropped into a pit, then sloshed toward the unlit fireplace, where a cold iron caldron hung slack in its recess. He swept the austere and antiquated space with a glance. *Function over style,* he thought. A burlap sack brimming with knobby, gnarled brown vegetables caught his eye. *Bungleroot.* Everything suddenly clicked. He squatted near the pot, lifting its lid—and recoiled with a gag, burying his nose in the crook of his arm. "That's nasty," he croaked, puckering his face at the chunky greenish-brown slop that looked suspiciously like a pot of puke. "That's bungleroot stew, alright." He remembered his dad's description of it in the story.

Suddenly, a door flew open so hard it nearly flew off its hinges, shaking the entire cabin. Bobby jumped, dropping the lid back over the pot just as the red-headed girl stormed out from the back room, a sack slung over her shoulder. She stopped to give him a disapproving once-over.

Wiping his nose on his sleeve—partly for snot, partly for stew stink—Bobby said, "I think I know where I am now. You're Zenobia, aren't you?"

Her expression shifted. "Ya know who I am?"

"Yeah. I mean, kinda hard to believe, but... you're just a character from my dad's story."

Zenobia let out a bark of laughter. "Let me git this straight. Imma from some story?" She shook her head, the laugh dying quickly. "Sure, sure. I say yer from a story, now you say Imma from a-story. I ain't got no time for yer kinda bunk, boy," she said, and made for the door.

"Wait!"

She halted mid-step, whirled around, planted a fist on her hip, and tapped her foot impatiently.

"All—all I know is..." Bobby flailed his arms, helpless, "I'm not from here. I come from another world."

"I reckon yer home is yonder in the Plebeian Heavens."

"I guess? Whatever that is. We call it something else."

Zenobia's eyes danced about aimlessly as she tapped her finger on her dimpled chin, like she was following a drunken fly only she could see. "Maybe yer journey from the heavens done scrambled yer brain. Made ya plum forgot who ya are?"

"I'm pretty sure I know who I am."

"Well, as much as I'd like a demi-god to help me kill the Ashen Knight an' save my daddy, I ain't got no time to help ya remember who you used to be."

"I remember who I am," Bobby muttered.

"I gotta git goin'," Zenobia said, spinning back toward the exit.

"Where are you going?"

"Fire Mountain," she hollered over her shoulder as she stepped into the pouring rain.

Dragging a hand down his face, Bobby groaned. "Great. Just great. Out of all the mystical realms in all the make-believe worlds, I had to get pulled into this one?" He rushed after her, hoisting up his sagging pajama bottoms. "Hey!" he shouted over the drumming rain. "Hey, wait!"

Zenobia stopped and spun around, clearly annoyed. "What!"

"You can't take on the Ashen Knight alone. You know what happened last time you tried."

She didn't answer at first. Her eyes narrowed beneath wet red strands of hair plastered across her face. "You saw what happened?" she asked.

"Yeah," Bobby answered.

He couldn't tell if she was crying again. He stayed put, nervous about getting any closer. After a long pause, Zenobia marched back toward him until they were face to face. Her eyes sparkled bright against her pale, rain-slicked skin.

"You can kill the Ashen Knight?" she asked.

"Ummm... maybe," Bobby said, suddenly hyper-aware that his right eye was twitching uncontrollably with her being so close to him. Fearing she might mistake it for a wink, he slapped his hand over it. "Maybe I can... I'm pretty sure I can... maybe."

Zenobia seized Bobby's free hand and dragged him back into the cabin. She threw down her sack and shot into her parents' room. "If you got a mind to help," her voice called high from the bedroom, "you oughta wear sump'm more appropriate than them ridiculous britches you got on." She reappeared with a pile of coarse brown clothing and tossed it at him. "Thisyer's my daddy's finest. Might be a lil long in some parts but they'll do jus' fine. Put 'em on."

Bobby peeled the fabrics haphazardly swaddling around his face and head, holding up a tunic between his index finger and thumb, uncovering his winking eye.

"What's up with yer eye?"

Bobby slapped his hand over it again. "It's just a twitch, I think—can I change in private, please?"

"I prefer it. Ain't need my permission." She stepped aside, letting Bobby shuffle past her into the privacy of her parents' bedroom.

"If I ain't stress that thisyer bidness is time-sensitive," she called after him, louder than necessary, "I stress it now. Thisyer bidness is *time. Sensitive.*"

Bobby wrestled with the archaic garments, pulling and tugging the long-legged breeches over his plump thighs. Balancing precariously, he bent forward to roll the excess pant leg into thick donut cuffs, careful not to split the seat of his pants. He fought the tunic over his head, wiggling and squeezing his round face through the narrow neck hole. Just as he successfully scraped his head through the collar, he caught Zenobia watching him from the doorway. She promptly ducked from view.

He finished the outfit with boots, a belt, and a frayed jacket. A small leather pouch dangled from the belt, poking at his belly. Inside was something hard. Curious, he pulled out a silver sphere, about the size of a metal golf ball. A thin chain looped through a clasp on its edge, indicating it could be worn around one's neck.

"*Time. Sensitive,*" Zenobia reminded him from the other room.

Bobby dropped the sphere back into the pouch and stepped into the main room, vigorously scratching at his new clothes with both hands.

"Well," Zenobia said, giving him an appraising nod, "I hardly reckonize ya, now that ya kindly favor a Plebeian peasant."

"I saw you spying on me."

"It jus'—I ain't never seen someone so... plump afore is all. So kill me for my curiosity. You mus' have heaps to eat where yer from."

"I guess," Bobby scowled. "Besides, there are lots of people like me where I come from. It's normal!" He realized, just then, that he hadn't thought about food all morning. Lately, his eating had become more perfunctory than pleasurable. Especially since his mother had stopped cooking proper meals after the funeral, his diet had boiled down to take-out, order-in, drive-thru, and dine-out. Eating had become more about filling time than filling his nutritional needs. Mrs. Palmer's words clacked through his head: *The difference between being alive and being dead is this—being alive means being acutely aware of just how alone you truly are in the universe.*

Snap! Zenobia's fingers popped in front of his face.

"Hey. Ya awake in there?"

Bobby shimmied out from the lone recesses of his thoughts. His right eye quivered at her bewildered stare. Rubbing at it, he mumbled, "I'm awake."

"C'mon," she said, hoisting the sack over her shoulder.

The downpour had stopped. They stepped out into the gentler, post-storm gloom. The world was soaked—saturated, and sludgy—turning every step into a squelch. Zenobia suddenly flung her arm out across Bobby's chest, halting him before he wandered into the mire of the bungleroot field, now a mud-swamp from all the rain.

"Reckon it best you stay here a-spell."

Bobby watched as she plodded forward, her feet sinking into the muck with a gurgle, up to her shins, each step followed by a wet slurp. She made her way to a half-buried, overturned cart near the center of the field. With surprising ease, she wrenched it free, hoisting it above her head with one hand, while still hanging onto the sack in the other. Then she waddled to firmer ground on the far side and set the cart upright.

Bobby took the long way around the mud pit to join her.

"I could've looked after your bag, you know," he offered, panting slightly.

"If I done allow that, than how else I'd show off to a demi-god?"

"Well, I'm no—" Bobby caught himself. Was she being sassy? Whatever.

"That was pretty cool," he admitted.

She tossed the sack into the cart. "I gotta fetch someone." With that, she dashed toward a rickety-looking stable and vanished inside.

Left alone, Bobby scratched, yawned, then scratched again. The coarse fabric still irritated his skin, but at least he was warm and dry in his new clothes. Still, a pang of sorrow tugged at him; he'd left his favorite jammies behind.

Zenobia returned, leading a squat, bony cow. Its skeletal frame clearly visible beneath its paper-thin coat. Undeterred by the tug of the rope, it stretched its neck every few steps to nibble at sparse patches of blue grass along the way. Zenobia whispered nonstop into its floppy ear until they reached Bobby.

"Thisyer is Golly," Zenobia beamed. "Ain't she the most mighty fetchin' lady?"

Bobby watched as the cow gave him zero acknowledgment, fully focused on grazing the mud-speckled turf. He nodded a silent *hello*.

Zenobia led Golly to the front of the cart and hitched her to the harness.

"The cow is going to pull us?" Bobby asked, doubt in his voice.

"Golly is the fastest ole girl on four legs. Likely the fastest on any legs!"

They climbed onto the wooden bench behind Golly. Bobby fumbled with his hands, unsure how to keep himself from sliding off the wobbly plank. There was nothing to fasten him in.

Zenobia took the reins and gave them a sharp flick. "Git on, girl!" she hollered.

Golly didn't budge. Still grazing.

Zenobia tried again. "Git! Git girl!"

Nothing.

Bobby smirked. "Fast like the wind, huh?"

Zenobia ignored him, hopped off the cart, and strolled beside Golly. She leaned close to the cow's floppy ear, whispering something in a hushed, soothing tone. She paused—listened to the cow's tacit reply—and whispered again. Bobby leaned forward, straining to catch even a word, but the creaking of the cart made it impossible. After a moment, Zenobia strolled back to the cart, stopping short of climbing aboard.

"What is it?" Bobby asked from his elevated perch, catching her sideways glare—

FRAAAAPPPPPFFFFFFTTTTT.

A foul gust of hot wind blasted Bobby's hair straight back. Once the gas spray sputtered out, Golly lazily slumped her tail back over her blowhole, leaving behind a lingering stench.

"Gross! Are you crazy? That stinks!" Bobby fluttered his hands in front of his face, desperate to swat away the reek of rotten eggs and fresh-cut grass.

"She was feelin' a bit gassy," Zenobia said, now climbing back aboard and taking the reins. "She's shy 'bout releasin' in front o' strangers. I tol' her you ain't no stranger. She's right-good to go now."

"You could've warned me?"

"Mus'a slipped my mind," she said, smiling sweetly, as innocent as a devil.

She tugged the reins. "Git on, girl!"

This time, the cart launched forward so fast that the mud beneath the spinning wheels seemed to dry in an instant. Bobby was thrown backward, arms flailing, until he managed to cling to the sideboard and hang on for dear life.

Golly was fast—shockingly fast. A mere blur to anyone watching from the sidelines. Once Bobby got himself stable, his chubby cheeks jiggled into a reluctant smile. The rush of wind tore away the lingering stench and tousled his hair with wild abandon. The ride was thrilling. He glanced at Zenobia. She glanced back, grinning. His chest pattered rapidly, trying to keep pace with the ride. Maybe even pattered a beat or two for Zenobia, too.

NINE

KEEPING TRACK of time was proving to be a challenge for Bobby. Day and night in Helcyon felt indistinguishable—an everlasting slog of gloomy light beneath endless pewter skies. He found himself yearning for night to come. The charm of Golly's breakneck pace—once exhilarating—had waned. Now, the cart only jostled and rattled under him, battering his poor backside, making him crave reprieve.

Big oval yawns kept twisting his face into exaggerated expressions, each one drawing an unimpressed side-eye from Zenobia.

When they finally stopped, Bobby bucked upright with a jolt. Apparently, he'd nodded off. He climbed off the cart, stretching his limbs and rubbing the numbness from his butt. "Where are we?" he asked, peering around.

They had arrived in a grove of gnarled, knotted trees. Each one hunched and crooked, shaped by years of harsh living, as if bent in supplication to the harsh environment. At the grove's core lay a small, stagnant lake. Its surface, still and black, resembled a patch of liquid void.

Bobby stepped to the water's edge and peered down. His reflection—darkened, distorted—stared back. Whatever lurked beneath the inky surface, it sure wouldn't be friendly. He tried to imagine something kind, something adorable that might thrive in such dark, putrid waters, but all he could see were dangerous things with too many teeth, too many eyes—pale, slimy creatures, writhing just below the surface. Tentacles coiled in his mind's eye, slick and eager to break through, to wrap around his ankles and drag him under. He was just meat, he thought, chewed and swallowed—meat for something else.

"Thisyer's Tar Lake," Zenobia shouted over her shoulder. "I reckon it a fine spot to bed for the night."

Bobby shook his head, banishing the imagined Tar Lake beast from his anxious mind—though he still cast the waters a weary glance.

Shifting his attention to Zenobia as she tethered Golly to a crooked tree, he asked. "When does night come?"

She petted Golly rather than answering him.

As the cow noshed on a sparse patch of blue pasture, Zenobia hauled her large sack from the back of the cart and dropped it near Bobby.

"Why, it's night now," she said at last, then began digging a shallow pit near the lake's edge.

Bobby tilted his head, scanning the underbelly of the laden sky, his gaze rolling from one horizon to the other. *It's night now?* Sure, the light had dimmed a bit, and the clouds had taken on a bruised red tint, storm-like, eerie. It could pass as dusk. Maybe. But night? The Blue Hour here was really more of a Magenta-Hour, and it was lasting far longer than twenty minutes—or an hour. Possibly all night.

"Will it get any darker?" he asked, glancing toward Zenobia, only to find she wasn't there. *Boy, she can't sit still for two seconds.* She was back at the cart, rolling out a crudely stitched quilt across the back.

"Nope," she hollered as she worked. "Thisyer as dark as it gits." She paused, tipping her head back to study the roiling sky. "Strange," she mused. "Ain't never seen the night thisyer color afore."

The strange red cast permeating the air reminded Bobby of something: a night not long ago, back home. A thunderous bang had jolted him awake. He'd first thought it part of a dream, given the profound silence that followed. He'd slipped out of bed, floorboards creaking under his feet, and bellied up to his window. Drawing the curtains aside, he found himself trembling at what he saw. In the still of the night, a massive moon loomed above, casting a deep red light that bathed the world in a maroon hue. The sight made his skin crawl. Later, he'd learn it was called a *Super Blood Wolf Moon*. But something else happened that night. Something that eclipsed everything.

A metallic scraping brought Bobby back to the present. Zenobia was beside him again, fastening a scabbard and sword to her belt before stomping off into a thicket. When she returned, she dropped a bundle of branches at his feet with a pointed glance.

"S'pose you don't work much where you come from," she said.

Bobby wrinkled his face. "What's that supposed to mean?"

"It means what it means. I'm fixin' camp, and yer just standin' there, tryin' to blend in with thisyer scenery. I'm tryin' to figure if laziness is part o' yer customs or a personal choice."

Bobby opened his mouth in protest, but his words jammed up somewhere behind his Adam's apple, coming out as little more than a series of frustrated grunts.

Zenobia didn't wait. She marched over to a half-rooted, fallen tree and wrestled it free, leaving a wide divot in the earth. "Latrine's dug," she quipped, lugging the log back to the clearing and laying it on its side. "Set on down if all yer gonna do is piddle anyway."

Bobby plopped onto one end of the log, shooting her a sulky look as she settled onto the other. Methodically, she broke off dead branches into usable lengths, stripped bark into thin shavings with her sword, then gathered the materials—along with moss and brittle leaves—into the fire pit. From her sack, she retrieved a strange-looking tool: a long stick with one end sharpened to a point and a stone disc mounted at its center like a flywheel. A horizontal rod crossed the stick's middle, each end tied to a cord that looped up and fastened near the top, forming a taut triangle. She twisted the vertical stick, winding the cord until the rod lifted. A flat board with a series of burnt notches sat ready. She placed a tuft of moss in one notch and slipped the point of the stick into it. Then, pumping the rod handle up and down, the cord unwound and rewound with each motion, sending the sharpened stick into a rapid, spinning blur. A rhythmic motion, steady and unbroken, as the spindle drilled into the board.

Bobby watched, rapt by Zenobia's stern concentration as she manipulated the contraption. She pumped the handle with one hand while nestling moss fibers near the smoldering tip of the dowel with the other. Soon, thin, ropy wisps of smoke began to rise. Tossing the stick aside, Zenobia hovered low over the embers, her breath coaxing a modest orange spark. The tiny blooms of flame quickly grew under her attentive care. She nurtured the fire, gradually adding moss, dry leaves, shaved bark, and small branches. Before long, a steady blaze crackled in the pit, its warmth reaching Bobby. It officially felt like camping now. It reminded him of past camping trips with his father—wait, he hated camping. It was the worst kind of vacationing he could think of, so why was he smiling? His gaze lingered on Zenobia until she blurted, "Why don't ya make yoself a tapestry of me? It'd last longer."

Bobby's right eye fluttered. Alarmed, he yanked his ogling gaze to the lake's shadowy surface. Embarrassment washed over him, his cheeks flushed, skin clammy with beads of sweat. He made an awkward attempt to steady his fidgeting fingers. Then he froze. Locking sights on a multitude of red orbs staring up at him from just beneath the pitch-black surface. They twinkled in a nicitating fashion before fading back into the murky waters.

"Is th-there anything big th-that lives in the lake?" he stuttered.

Zenobia, surely noticing the pallor in his face and fear behind his eyes, followed his gaze to the water. "That's a tar lake," she said. "Full o' nothin' but tar. Ain't nothin' can live in a lake full o' tar. Nothin' big, anyhow." She returned to tending the fire, arranging stones around the pit. Bobby gave a reluctant nod, forcing the idea into his head that it was impossible for something big to live in a tar lake.

By the time a pot of bungleroot stew was bubbling, neither Bobby nor Zenobia had spoken in a while. Bobby gave himself a sharp pinch, wondering why he couldn't wake up. He noted the aches and pain from his fall at school had mysteriously disappeared, convincing him further that he was dreaming. However, no amount of pinching seemed to bring him back to reality. He yawned. *Can you get tired in your dreams?* he pondered. *What happens if you sleep in your sleep? Can you have a nightmare within a nightmare?* The unanswered questions played like a feedback loop in his mind, producing a headache that shot across his left brow. His right eye began fluttering again, becoming painfully aware that he was winking at Zenobia. Darn it! He slapped his hand over his eye. Either Zenobia didn't seem to notice, or she didn't care. She dished out the soft brown mush into wooden bowls and offered one to Bobby.

"Thisyer bound to turn yer stomach against ya," she said, "but it'll keep ya kickin'."

Bobby eyed the bowl for a moment, then resignedly took it. "I don't think I'm all that hungry," he said, scooping a little of the steaming slop into his spoon and pushing it into his mouth. He wrinkled his face and shuddered. "Yuck! This tastes like rotten mud." He lolled his tongue loose from his open mouth, trying to shake the awful taste from it.

Zenobia chuckled, "The more ya eat, the better it tastes."

"I doubt it." Bobby set the bowl beside him on the log.

"Alrite," said Zenobia, "only cause I don't need ya dyin' on my watch." She rummaged through her sack again and finally pulled out a short, round bottle. She waved the flask in front of him and uncorked it. "Thisyer help with the taste." She tipped the bottle over his bowl. Nothing came out at first. Then—after a stretch of time bordering on awkward—a thick, dark-golden sap finally oozed out and drizzled over his mush. She did the same to hers and stirred it in.

"Go on, now. Try some."

Bobby sighed, stirred the syrup in, and slurped another small mouthful. This time, his face didn't revolt with the urge to spit it out. But he made no utterance of pleasure either. The syrup managed to make the mud palatable at best.

"Function over taste," Zenobia said, her voice suddenly low, eyes drawn to some vague spot between her feet. A wave of melancholy passed over her. This habit of shifting moods—going from wry to glum back to snarky in the space of a breath—made Bobby anxious.

Silence descended again as they picked at their food.

Bobby found himself stealing glances at Zenobia, careful not to stare too long for fear of another involuntary wink. Each time he looked, he observed her absolute stillness. Her dimpled chin rested in the palm, her gaze vacant, reflecting only the flicker of the firelight. When she did move, it was only to feed the flames—her focus consumed by them, as they hungrily devoured each new log. *What's so darn captivating about the campfire?*

Then the breeze turned. The night air carried a scent—something like rotten flowers. Bobby sniffed the air. It was sickly sweet. Compelling in its own odd way. He couldn't stop himself from breathing it in. A faint tune followed, whistling on the wind. A melody unfamiliar but hauntingly pleasant. Then came the rhythmic thudding of many footsteps, unseen, marching past their camp.

"Do you hear that?" Bobby asked, his voice a little shaky.

Zenobia finally broke from her trance. Her head whipped side to side, trying to track the sound, her hand creeping to the hilt of her sword. "What in tarnation is that?"

And then came that darn bird. Bobby recognized Lymrik immediately. This time, gliding down from the rosy haze above, wings outstretched like someone approaching to give them a big hug. It landed gracefully on the log beside Bobby.

Zenobia exclaimed, "That's a Lyrebird!" Her eyes turned to the source of the phantom footsteps. "And them... the Pilgrims of the Dead."

"The what?" Bobby said.

"*Indeed, Pilgrims of the Dead they be.*

A soul's journey, they must concede.

Mountain of Bones.

Lured by Song of Homes.

The oracle will set them free."

The bird's dark eyes fixed on them both.

"It *is* you," Bobby shouted, leaping to his feet. "You brought me here! How do I get back home, you stinking bird?"

Zenobia moved past him, her voice thin with hope. "Is my mama here?" she called into the air. "Mama?"

Lymrik edged closer, fluffing its feathers. Its tone softened, almost mournful.

"*It aches for me to tell you.*

Your mother's fate is sadly true.

Souls stolen by the knight's sword—

Forever claimed by the dark lord.

His powers and life each year renew."

Zenobia's face dropped. She bowed her head and wiped her eyes.

The bird bobbed closer to Bobby, hopping in time with its singsong verse.

"*Delighted to see you arrive,*

In one piece, portly and alive.

Great need in bleak times,

For new paradigms,

Helcyon's glory will revive."

Bobby could have sworn it smiled at him.

"*A guide and messenger am I,*

Leading the dead, saw you from high.

Queries answered best,

May I please suggest,

The oracle's help you should try."

"The oracle can tell me how to get home?" Bobby asked.

Zenobia lifted her head again and added, "Ya reckon she'll tell us how to beat the Ashen Knight?"

"*Said to hold knowledge of the dead,*

A treasure trove in her sage head.

Enlightened decree,

Answers come from she,

Seek the white tower—South, do tread."

"South?" Zenobia cried. "We can't go south! My daddy is north. I don't even know if he's alive."

Lymrik flapped its wings, then waddled up against Bobby, pecking insistently at the pouch fastened to his belt. Bobby flinched and swatted the bird away.

"*Weep not, child, for there is Likho's eye.*
Within the boy's purse, hidden sly.
Encased silver sphere,
Lost for many years,
Shows if dad is dead or alive."

Zenobia's scrutiny dropped to Bobby's belly.

"Wha—what are you staring at?" he asked, arms instinctively crossing over his paunch.

Zenobia advanced on top of him and plucked the pouch from his belt, fishing out the silver sphere. An eye was engraved in its shell, the raised pupil protruding just enough to function as a button. She pressed her thumb to it. With a soft click, the pupil depressed, and the orb opened. Inside, a swirling, multicolored cloud glowed like a miniature galaxy. Soapy tendrils spun in opposite directions, tiny cyclones raging within a perfectly formed sphere: Likho's Eye.

"How does it work?" Zenobia asked.

"*Yes, a name's often so common,*
Concentrate on whom to summon.
And then they'll appear,
As if clearly here,
Real as though they've casually walked in."

Zenobia brought the cloud to her lips, closed her eyes, and whispered, "Daddy? Daddy, can you hear me?" She opened her eyes again. Nothing changed. The colors in Likho's Eye continued to swirl, unbothered. "Show me my daddy, Hulmick Mulhick," she then demanded. The globe lit up in response, sparkling micro-fireworks bursting within the mist. The vapor condensed and shaped itself into a four-inch gangly man who shuddered to life in her palm. Upon seeing his daughter, the figure of Hulmick gasped, then leaped joyfully.

"Zenbee! By Porter, what a sublime sight to see."

Tears spilled down Zenobia's cheeks. "Daddy! Where ya at? Are ya alrite?"

"Yes. Yes. I'm perfectly fine. But don't you dare get any ideas about looking for me, you hear? Do you understand, Zenbee?"

"Why'd he take you?"

"I don't know. But it's nothing for you to worry over. I'll get myself out. So don't fret about me, okay? You stay on the farm. I'll find my way home." He paused, looking behind him at something unseen, then turned back to Zenobia's tear-streaked face. His voice hushed. "I have to go. Stay put on the farm. I mean it. Please, don't come after me. I love you. Stay safe." His form dissolved, curling back into the misty cloud as the silvery sphere clicked shut.

Zenobia cradled it to her chest, her tears dotting its smooth surface.

The wind-song faded, as did the haunting footfalls, replaced by an eerie quiet. The kind of quiet Bobby knew all too well. The quiet of loved ones stolen into the dead of night, robbed of even their ghosts. He watched Zenobia with glossy eyes, too remorseful to twitch. His heart ached for her, understanding what it meant to feel responsible for the death of one parent and the suffering of the other.

Lymrik fluttered its feathers, loosening its joints in preparation for flight.

"Back to the skies, I do parole,
A guide for pilgrims' leaden souls.
The Oracle's gate,
Transcend, be their fate.
And their earthly knowledge, the toll."

With a majestic flare of wings, Lymrik swept the air beneath it and ascended, higher and higher, until the rose-tinted clouds swallowed the bird whole.

Bobby was struck by how the Lyrebird carried itself with more grace in Helcyon than in his world—the *real* world. He inhaled deeply. The scent of dead flowers was gone, replaced by the acrid stench of Tar Lake, a reminder of how miserable and unpleasant this place truly was.

"You ain't have any special abilities, have ya?" Zenobia asked, resettling beside the fire, slipping the chain of the silver ball around her neck.

"Abilities?" Bobby repeated.

"That's right. Like special powers," she said, looking directly at him now. "Godly stuff. You got any?"

Bobby only shrugged.

"How we gonna save my daddy? How we gonna kill the Ashen Knight?"

"Well... how did I defeat that army of..."

"Gigorocks?"

"Yeah, Gigorocks. How'd I win in your stories?"

"Them just stories," Zenobia muttered, tossing more wood into the fire.

"Maybe the stories aren't true," Bobby said, "but stories have ideas. They can still help. If I defeated a whole army, I must have done something right."

"Well..." Zenobia sighed, "you had an amulet that gone turn ya into a lion. A right big ol' lion that roared fire outta yer great big mouth. Also, you gone summoned the Meem Monster..."

"The what?"

"I said, a Meem Monster... an Element Daemon, made of sticks and stones, that directly destroys the enemies of them who summon it," she looked him over again. "Can you transform into a fire-breathin' lion?"

Bobby shook his head.

"Can you summon the Meem Monster?"

Again, Bobby could only shrug helplessly.

"Welp, I imagine some stories are only good for wastin' time." She picked up a stray branch and began poking at the fire. "What good is hope if it ain't nothin' more than fiction? What good does that do us, huh?"

Bobby watched her somber face become lost in the glow of the flames. Sensing that annoying twitch coming to his eyelid again, he spoke quickly, trying to head off an accidental wink. "Maybe we should go to the Oracle," he said. "She'll have the answers." He rubbed his eye, hoping she'd take a break from jabbing the fire and agree. But she kept stirring the coals, sending up a flurry of glowing sparks that danced briefly in the air before dying out.

Finally, she stood. "Imma off to bed."

Bobby stood too, following her.

She stopped in her tracks. "Now where ya think yer goin' to?"

"Uh... to bed?"

She narrowed her eyes. "Well, it sho ain't in the cart with me an' Golly."

"Oh... ahh... so... where am I sleeping?"

"Thereabouts by the fire, of course."

"Oh... um, by the lake?"

"Yupp."

Bobby cast a nervous glance at the dark water.

"Ain't nothin' in there that's gonna bite ya," she said. "Yer as safe as a pig-in-a-blanket."

"Oh. Sure," Bobby mumbled. "Okay. I'll sleep here. Good night."

Still standing, Bobby watched as Zenobia walked back to the cart, hugged Golly long and slow, kissed the cow on the nose, and then climbed into the back.

He flopped to the ground by the fire, leaning against the log. His eyes kept drifting toward the lake. *It's fine. Nothing can live in tar lakes. What could live in tar? Didn't the Woolly Mammoths die in tar lakes? I'm sure there's nothing in that awfully evil-looking lake that wants to kill me."*

A crunch of footsteps startled him. He spun around and felt silly when he saw Zenobia standing there with a pile of blankets in her arms. He murmured a thank you. She gave him a curt nod, then returned to the cart and disappeared under some coverings.

Bobby wrapped the blanket around himself up to his nose. It smelled like dust and old dirt. *Safe as a pig-in-a-blanket.* He doubted it. His eyes bounced between the fire and the black, glistening lake, back and forth, back and forth... until he didn't notice the moment his eyelids slipped shut and the world turned to black.

TEN

SLIMSY'S SMILE never touched his face, yet his eyes radiated a peculiar kindness. Almost too kind for his somber, deeply creased expressions, he wore. His gray skin was carved with jagged etchings, as if misery itself had sculpted his countenance with invective artistry. But those eyes—large, unblinking, and ever-vigilant—sparkled with life and hope, a sharp contrast to the rest of him. Their strange brilliance was only enhanced by the dark hollows that framed them, making them appear like glowing orbs floating in shadows. Oversized for his head, they sat wide apart on either side of his upturned, stubby nose, whose nostrils gaped with webbed snot bubbles.

With a kick from his tiny foot, Slimsy swung open the dungeon door and waddled in, balancing a tray far too large for him, laden with tantalizing food. His entire upper half was hidden behind it. He offered Hulmick a nod. Standing at four feet tall—tall for his kind—Slimsy was scrawny, even skinnier than Hulmick himself. The prisoner was already busy flaring his nostrils, sucking in the savory aroma as he rubbed his hands together. "By Porter, that smells like a dream," Hulmick said, smacking his lips. "What's on the menu today?"

Slimsy shuffled to the small wooden table and, bracing the silver tray against his chin, slid it into place. "Barbecue lamb with sweet bungleroot, and lava pudding. Which is just baked pears in custard. Plus a pile of fruit, some wine, and a cake or two."

Hulmick's eyes bulged. He licked his lips. He shuffled to the table and slumped onto the stool, salivating over the spread of flavor-glistening delicacies, gazing down at the feast with childlike hunger. "Sweet bungleroot? Who knew?" he murmured. "Every meal here is fit for a king. What's the catch?"

Once seated, Hulmick and Slimsy were nearly eye-to-eye. Hulmick, with a slight height advantage, stared down at Slimsy, his moist eyes dancing with unspoken questions.

"The master has no need for food, so why let it go to waste?" Slimsy explained, ambling his way to the cell door.

"Wait," Hulmick called, "Can't you stay a bit? I could use some company. I've been going stir-crazy down here. Heck, I've even started seeing my daughter's face speak to me from out of thin air." His smile, tinged with sadness, pulled gently across his face.

"Sure, I suppose. I've got time to kill." Slimsy returned to the table. His wide, sparkling eyes locked onto his charge with quiet fascination. As Hulmick attacked his meal, stripping meat from bone with a voracious appetite, Slimsy looked on in morbid curiosity. Hulmick's cheeks bulged as he stuffed them with food faster than he could swallow.

"Hmmm... ferry guud." He nodded, juices dripping from the corner of his mouth and down his chin. He gestured to his plate between bites, asking, "Whan thum?"

"No, thank you," Slimsy responded languidly. "I've already eaten." He watched Hulmick, puzzled by his singular focus on eating. Especially considering he'd just lost his wife to his master. Hulmick gorged as though he hadn't eaten in days, despite his stay in the infamous five-star Dragoon dungeons, equipped with medieval amenities updated for modern misery. Dragoon Keep was one of the top dungeons in all of Helcyon. The best, worst torture apparatuses ranged from "the hole," the iron maiden, and the rack to the goblin rat head-box, chest-box, and foot-box, though they were currently out of goblin rats. But what truly set the Dragoon dungeons apart, what bumped it to a five-and-a-half-star establishment, was Slimsy himself: a unique kind of dungeon accessory who brought his own bespoke brand of torment.

Hulmick gnawed the lamb leg down to the bone, polishing off the entire tray. "I've never stuffed myself with so much food before and still felt so hungry," he said.

"You've never savored anything so delicious before, so you crave more, is all," Slimsy replied, his ever-sparkling eyes gleaming with mischief. "Upon entering, I thought I did hear the voice of a young girl. Was that your daughter?"

Choking on a morsel of food, Hulmick coughed out, "Oh, no. Haha, no, I was just talking to myself." Waving the pointed leg bone in the air, he added, "Ahem, I'm not accustomed to my company alone, you see? And I'm grieving terribly for my dear Hyln. I feel I must be... er... well, having a mental breakdown of sorts. I miss my beloved wife and Zenbee so much. I must've been imitating her sweet bell of a voice, you see. Euphonious as an angel it is."

"Hmm," groaned Slimsy, nodding along with pity. "I have no clue what it's like to miss anyone in particular, especially my family. I was sold into servitude to the master when I was a boy. All I recall of my folks is the glint of silver pieces being snatched in wart-pocked hands, then thrust into my predecessor's clawed grasp. Can't say I miss him either. He was as bitter as the northern winds and twice as cruel, like blades baked into a slice of chocolate cake." He sighed, shrugged, then added, "Such is life."

As Slimsy reclaimed the empty tray—practically licked clean—he suddenly froze. Hulmick was pointing the sharpened bone at Slimsy's throat like a knife.

"I'm not... a... well, I'm not a violent man. But... in times like these..." Hulmick gestured with the makeshift weapon, flicking its bone blade dangerously close to Slimsy's jugular.

"The funny thing about being hungry," Slimsy said coolly, "is that it makes people gullible." His eyes dimmed, losing their sparkle, and he nodded pointedly at the bone.

Hulmick looked down at the object in his hand. It wasn't bone at all— just a charred black stick, crumbling in his shaky hand. His wide eyes shifted to the tray, where the remnants of his meal were now dregs of ashes. His mouth fell open, revealing a blackened tongue and teeth dusted with soot. He retched forward, spitting and hacking the bitter taste from his mouth.

"Even if that bone was real, do you really think you could escape the Ashen Knight? Of course not. Your cell door isn't even locked. You've simply never tried to open it—because deep down, you know it's hopeless." Slimsy took the tray and casually dusted off the charred residues.

Hulmick rubbed his mouth with his sleeve. "Why? Why—why did you feed me coal and make me believe it was real food?"

"Boredom?" Slimsy mused, then shrugged. "Truthfully, I don't really know." He tilted the tray longways on its edge—nearly reaching his chest—and leaned against it nonchalantly. "Food isn't exactly a necessity around here. And as a Dazzelf, I like to dazzle. Problem is, there aren't many folks in Dragoon Keep to dazzle."

"I've never felt so famished... or filthy—and I'm a dirt farmer. Why am I even here? What have I done?" Hulmick broke down in tears. "What have I done?"

Slimsy stood upright and adjusted the tray in his arms. "You think the master tells me anything? Most of what I know, I've gleaned from eavesdropping. And even then, I barely understand half of it."

Hulmick looked pitiful, his face pinched in a miserable scowl, tears sniffling and snorting down his nose. Slimsy lifted the silver tray and held it up like a mirror. "Look," he said gently. "I want to show you something."

Hulmick leaned in, peering at his warped reflection on the tray's rippled surface. Slimsy's eyes sparkled again, and suddenly, Hulmick's reflection dissolved into a sprawling darkness. A void seemed to open within the metal, a swirling black depth drawing him in. From the abyss, seven white specks popped into existence, slowly growing into luminous orbs that circled Helcyon.

"Every thousand years, when the seven moons of Helcyon align in a grand lunar eclipse..." Slimsy whispered. The moons spiraled together, merging into a single radiant orb. It pulsed pink, then deepened into a dark, blood-red glow, beaming with a visceral, ancient power. "When the Blood Eclipse culminates, in a fortnight..." Slimsy continued, "That's when it will be your time to shine." The crimson orb split into two glowing circle—eyes. Hulmick's eyes. And then, his own gaunt, confused face appeared once more in the reflection, but he didn't seem to recognize it. When he did, he flinched and recoiled from the tray. "What that portends for you, my friend," Slimsy said, lowering the tray, "I cannot say." His sparkling eyes regarded Hulmick with something close to sorrow. Pity maybe. "If it's of any comfort... whatever fate awaits you after the Blood Eclipse will likely await us all."

Hulmick sat still for a long beat, collecting himself, until finally he spoke, voice hollow. "Perhaps I should seize control of my fate... taking my life before it can be twisted into some evil game."

"Fate is immutable," Slimsy replied flatly. "Especially within these walls. Try all you like, but I guarantee you'll only find agony for your effort. The master will ensure it." He turned to leave but paused at the doorway. "Fun fact about Dazzelfs: we reveal truths by weaving lies." He gave a small shrug. "In a way, we're kinda like storytellers."

Hulmick didn't respond. He kept his eyes on the floor, fixated on bits of blackened ash scattered near his feet. The silence between them thickened with discomfort. And Slimsy finally slipped away without another word.

HULMICK'S STOMACH GROWLED like a rabid dog gnawing at his guts. Pain tore through the soft tissue of his innards. Hunched in the corner of his cell, he groaned and cursed at the lumps of coal now sitting like black tumors in his belly.

Though he'd nearly resigned himself to being cooked into gristly beef jerky, as the heat of his prison cell sweltered, he clung to the cherub face of his beloved Zenobia. Her visage surfaced again. Not with the vivid clarity as before, but as a spectral vision, beckoning. Urged on by her image, he willed his body into motion. He pushed himself to stand, though the heat drained his limbs of strength and steadiness. He teetered on shaky legs that threatened to give out, but somewhere deep within, he drew enough resilience to stay on his feet and staggered forward.

Was the vision of his daughter—whom he now followed—a heat-induced hallucination? Another of the Dazzelf's tricks? Were his delusions even his own anymore? Slimsy had unraveled his grip on reality. Had he ever truly spoken to Zenobia at all?

To his surprise, the cell door was unlocked. He poked his head into the corridor—it stretched ahead, empty and silent. Steam curled from unseen vents, but the air was cooler now, a small mercy that revived him. With Zenobia's phantom vanished the moment he stepped into the corridor, he stood there, uncertain of his next move.

Stumbling upon a narrow staircase that coiled tightly upward, he ascended in brisk, bounding steps. Each footfall echoed sharply against the black stones, convincing him more than once that someone—or something—was giving chase. He paused periodically to quell the paranoia. At the top, a low wooden door forced him to bend almost in half to pass through. Beyond it lay a spacious, long-abandoned kitchen, coated in a fine layer of ash and steeped in the sickly scent of burnt flesh. A reek that seemed fused into every stone of Dragoon Keep.

He pressed on, his long strides carrying him up another flight of stairs, through another door, down a dim passage, and yet up another set of steps. Directionless, he navigated on instinct alone, until finally a door opened onto the grand staircase of Dragoon Keep's central hall.

There, Hulmick halted—captivated.

At the heart of the chamber stood a massive geocentric model of Helcyon and its moons. Towering twenty feet high and twice as wide, the intricate mechanism ticked and hummed with the steady rhythm of iron gears. At its core lay a broad brass plate, engraved with exquisite detail to depict the map of Helcyon. Surrounding it, seven glass orbs spun on stout iron arms. The entire structure floated, improbably suspended above a steady updraft of steam rising from its convex base.

As Hulmick stepped closer, he watched in awe as the glass moons ticked toward perfect alignment. In the distance of their orbit, a larger orb emitted a fiery orange light, refracting beams through the glass moons, painting a crimson slash onto the brass plate below.

Upon reaching the mechanism, Hulmick caught the sound of whispers cascading from the chambers high above, drifting down into the atrium. Each word, delicate as a snowflake, settled in his ears, accumulating in a chilling flurry of hollow tones. Spurred by the promise of escape, he turned and sprinted toward the keep's massive double doors. Desperation surged through him as he threw his weight against them. Once. Twice. Again and again, he slammed his shoulder into the unyielding wood until a crunch reverberated in his bones, forcing him to stagger back in pain. The door remained unmoved.

He cradled his shoulder, doubt clouding his thoughts. Was it true? Was escaping nothing more than a tantalizing illusion, a dazzling daydream designed to distract him from the grim truth of his fate? The sobering realization struck: freedom was a mirage. But there was another way out. Yes. A sacrifice. One for the betterment of the world, especially for his daughter.

The murmurs continued growing more distinct as Hulmick climbed. Each flight of stairs brought him closer to the voices above. One was unmistakable: the Ashen Knight's arid timbre trickled down in fragments.

"When you first...

saw me, what...

did you think of me?..."

Another voice followed—softer, airy, and unfamiliar. A woman.

"I thought you were...

another one of...

my father's brutes."

Gasping for breath, Hulmick's ragged panting drowned out much of the exchange:

"I can—" gasp

"You are fading,—" wheeze

"Memory... time—" gulp

"Nothing left..."

At last, he reached the antechamber of his captor. Exhaustion overtook him, and he crumpled against the doorframe, barely able to hold himself upright. Through his fatigue-blurred vision, he saw the flowing sweep of the Ashen Knight's purple cloak. The Knight stood motionless, enraptured by a painting. Its frame was scorched, the canvas blistered and blackened at the edges, burned but not destroyed. The subject: a young woman of haunting beauty, rendered with vivid, radiating grace. Her skin shimmered as if lit from within. Her luminous eyes gleamed with timeless vitality.

Remarkably, she moved, turning, speaking within the frame. The portrait pulsed with life. Not merely pigment and brushwork, but something else... something alive.

———————

"I AM ALL that is left of your humanity," she said. "And time is running out. Soon, nothing will remain of me but this portrait—a face you will no longer recognize. And the man I once loved will be nothing but a destructive black hole encased in burnt armor."

"Remind me!" roared the Ashen Knight, his voice a scorched frenzy of rage. "Remind me of our days beneath Helcyon's sun! Remind me of our embrace. How tender I was with your love!"

"Our tale has been told countless times," the woman replied, her voice growing dim. "You've lost the ability to remember us. And soon, I will fade from your memory forever." The portrait stilled.

"No!" The Knight thundered. With a violent sweep of his arm, he summoned Slimsy from the shadows, stretching out his reach, pulling the Dazzelf into his iron grip. Slimsy dangled by his scrawny neck like a rag doll, feet swinging limp, gulping for air. The Knight's burning gaze seared into his popping, petrified eyes.

"Your parlor tricks grow useless."

"I..." Slimsy croaked, "I only show you what you want to see... master."

"Worthless creature." The Knight's claw tightened, poised to end him—

"Ahem!" Hulmick stepped boldly into view, clearing his throat with all the defiance he could summon. Ashen Knight and Slimsy both turned their heads slowly to face him. "I will not be a part of your evil plans," he declared, every muscle in his frail body strained to keep him upright. He puffed out his chest, raised his chin, and channeled every last ounce of courage into a final act of resistance. "I will die before I allow that."

And with that, he spun and hurled himself over the mezzanine rail, vanishing into the chasm below.

Loosening his squeeze, the Ashen knight let Slimsy slip from his grasp. The Dazzelf collapsed on the floor, panting and rubbing his throat. Intrigued, the Ashen Knight approached the edge of the balcony and looked down. There, Hulmick lay prone several levels below, levitating on a thin cloud of dark particles, sprawled out as if held aloft by smoke. Far beneath him, the grand clockwork mechanism continued its celestial ticking. Slowly, the ethereal platform began to rise, lifting Hulmick toward the Ashen Knight's flaming gaze.

Desperation cracking his voice, Hulmick pleaded, "Please... I've a daughter to protect. If you had a family, you'd understand."

"Your daughter remains alive and unharmed," the Ashen Knight retorted coldly. "Had you succeeded in your coward's leap, she would have replaced you in my plans. Henceforth, you will obey. Or she will suffer. Understand?"

The threat seared through Hulmick's ears. Tears welled. Snot bubbled. His body trembled so violently it was hard to tell if he was nodding in obedience, or simply unraveling.

"Return him to his cell," the Knight ordered, turning away and receding into his chambers. The doors slammed shut behind him.

The black cloud deposited Hulmick onto the landing, where he curled into a shaking heap.

"Get up," Slimsy said gently. "C'mon. Up you get."

It took Hulmick a moment, but he eventually rolled to his knees and climbed shakily to his feet. Slimsy led the way down, Hulmick stumbling behind him like a man half-ghosted.

Behind the heavy chamber door, the Ashen Knight's voice resounded once more, now speaking with another hidden presence. The same bodiless whisper Hulmick had heard the day of his abduction.

"Sheee is with the boy," it hissed.

"What, boy?"

"The boy from the outer world. He could disrupt your plans."

"They're too distant. It'll be too late."

"Do not underestimate their will... or their cleverness."

"...Very well. Unleash the Man-Eater."

Their voices faded into muffled obscurity as Slimsy and Hulmick descended deeper into the bowels of Dragoon Keep. Once they'd gone far enough to avoid eavesdroppers, Hulmick leaned closer and whispered, "He was about to kill you. I saved you."

Slimsy chuckled. "Kill me? Crush every bone in my body, sure. But death? That's reserved strictly for his blade."

"His blade?"

"Yeah, *Black Star*."

"*Black Star*?"

Slimsy stopped suddenly, causing Hulmick to nearly trip over him. "You've never heard of *Black Star*?"

Hulmick, caught in Slimsy's unnerving naked gaze—those bald eyes, dull and pale as blanched eggs unless they were sparkling—felt more absorbed by them than seen. He finally shook his head.

"It's what gives him immortality. Without it, he can't kill a living thing. Not even a goblin tic."

"Then perhaps we should steal it."

Slimsy burst into raucous laughter that bounced off the stone. "*Steal* it? Merely touching it spells certain death. Impossible." He wiped a tear from his eye, sighed, and resumed walking.

Eventually, Hulmick followed.

When they reached the cell, Slimsy held the door open, gesturing inside. Hulmick hesitated, eyeing it with suspicion. "It's cooler now. Trust me," Slimsy said with a sly grin. Hulmick arched a brow, then cautiously stepped in. The heat had lessened; it was, in fact, bearable.

As Slimsy prepared to close the cell door, he asked, "Any special requests for your supper tomorrow? Or just the usual?"

"Surprise me," Hulmick said, his tone flat.

"You may starve, but do not worry, death won't come. And hey, you're lucky I'm the best Dazzelf chef in Helcyon." Slimsy shut the door, locking Hulmick back in solitude.

Moments later, Hulmick tested the handle. It did not budge this time. *Lucky?* he mused bitterly. *Not the word I'd used.*

ELEVEN

**OBBY, CONFIDENT** he was trapped in a dream—a lucid one at that, found himself not floating but sinking, pulled into the bleakest depths of nothingness. Suspended in a soundless void. A space devoid of matter and light. Yet somehow, he felt himself sinking ever deeper, into an ever darker abyss.

The pressure around him escalated, like the weight of a thousand dark oceans bearing down, pushing him deeper and deeper, the pressure greater and greater. Although he couldn't breathe and had even forgotten how to, he wasn't dying. He was extraordinarily alive, every neuron acutely alarmed. As panic seized him, he noticed his heart, which should have been pounding frantically as if its life depended on it, was vacant. He'd experienced enough panic before. His heart should be wreaking havoc inside his chest. It was as if a hole replaced it. Was he dead? Was he conscience without a body? Pure, unfiltered fear without the physical symptoms? The external pressure kept building, unrelenting from all sides. The force of panic and fear swelled inside him, expanding outward. He felt like a fragile membrane caught between two colliding worlds of stress, squeezing him thinner and thinner until he would eventually be cold-pressed into zilch.

Suddenly, out from the darkness flickered a multitude of piercing red eyes—eyes he associated with the beast of Tar Lake. Though its form remained concealed, he felt its numerous tentacle-like appendages coil and constrict his limbs, torso, and neck. Tighter and tighter, they gripped, possibly the source of his suffocating descent.

"You do not belong here," it communicated, not with words but thoughts, eerily reminiscent of Bobby's own voice but with a shade of melancholy. Was he the one thinking these words? No. The thoughts were distinctly alien to him, invasive even. They wiggled and coiled around his mind like the beast's tentacles twisted around his body.

"Where am I?" Bobby questioned mentally.

"In my domain. Unwelcome."

"Am I going to die?"

"Eventually, yes."

"Are you going to kill me?"

"I do not end lives. But I can ease your suffering."

"I want to go home."

"The only way home is through the Lake of Enlightened Fire. You must pass through the Flames of Knowledge and suffer the knowing."

The creature's words coiled around his thoughts, strangling his mind as its tentacles tightened around his body. The pressure built inside and out, compressing, stretching, tearing—crushing him to his very atoms. Just when it felt like the torment would end, being obliterated into nothing, the pressure intensified evermore—pulling harder, squeezing tighter. Tighter. Harder. Tighter—

It felt like a slap across the face.

Bobby's eyes flew open, slicing through the darkness into a wash of pale daylight. Air surged into his lungs; his heart jolted into a furious rhythm. His face burned with icy wetness. Above him stood Zenobia. One hand held a cup. In the other, her sword.

"Whah—what?" Bobby gasped.

"Good, yer awake," Zenobia said flatly.

Bobby wiped his face dry with his sleeve, grumbling, "Why'd you do that? You could've just shaken me or something. Why the water?"

"Ain't no better way to rise in the morn than with a right smart splash of cold water," she replied, sheathing her sword and turning away.

Sitting up, Bobby tried to piece together what had happened. Then he spotted it—the limp end of a tentacle, hacked clean from its owner, still coiled around his ankle. He yelped and kicked it off with his other foot, scuttling backward until he was clear. He scanned the scene and realized he'd been dragged twenty feet from the campfire to the edge of Tar Lake. Springing to his feet, he spun toward Zenobia, who was already loading the cart. "There was a monster in the lake!" he cried, pointing at the oily black water. "You told me nothing could live in there!"

"I know rightly what I gone tol' ya."

"I could've been killed! Drowned or eaten!"

"Well, ya ain't none of 'em thangs 'cause I gone saved ya." She scratched Golly behind the ears. "An' I reckon that thang warn't likely to kill ya none."

"How do you know?"

"Cause when I found ya, you was wallerin' with that tentacle like ya was makin' out with it. I know what 'makin' out' is. I read all 'bout it in some of my books. Seein' ya huggin' that tentacle? A stranger might could imagine that's what ya was up to." She tossed her sack and bundle into the cart. "I cut ya free and reckoned a splash o' cold water might snap ya outta whatever trance you was in. Always worked when my Mama threw water on my Daddy when his huggin' got too annoyin' for her."

Bobby's mind boggled with questions he feared the answers to.

"Well?" Zenobia said, looking at him expectantly. "Don't just stand there with that face. Collect yer thangs."

Obediently, Bobby turned back to the fire pit. All he had to gather was his blanket. His eyes skimmed the ashy remains of last night's fire, scattered with pale chunks of charred wood. Then his gaze drifted over to the severed white tentacle. And that's when it hit him. A vision—sharp, invasive—seized his mind. Rendered him helpless in its thrall, flooding his senses, paralyzing him in that same cold numbness from the dream. He was sinking again—emotion disintegrating—adrift in the black. He saw a casket sliding into a giant oven. Jets of flames roaring to life, devouring the cheap pinewood. Through the heat-warped gaps, the bare soles of feet appeared—stark white, like bleached paper—until they, too, blackened in the fire.

He shuddered, shook it off, and snatched up the blanket. Zenobia and Golly were waiting at the cart. Golly munched lazily, utterly unbothered by anything, while Zenobia watched Bobby approach from on high her seat, scrutinizing him, as always, like she was trying to figure him out and judge him at the same time. He climbed aboard, tucking the blanket between his bottom and the bench as a cushion. With a soft snap of the reins, Zenobia clicked her tongue. Golly lunged forward, dashing into motion with a surprising burst of speed that bordered on flight.

THE MOUNTAIN OF Bones swelled in grandeur as Bobby and Zenobia drew closer, practically flying over the terrain on the delicate, winged hooves of Golly's stout legs. Though *flying* would suggest a smooth ride, no, no, no, they were more like careening and crashing against every rugged inch of trail. Bobby marveled at how such an animal as Golly could pull them at such breakneck speeds, but found himself pondering: if you could conceive a cow that ran at such soaring speeds, why not go all the way and imagine one that flew? His sore-ing butt was paying dearly for that failure of imagination. Not to mention—but mentioning—his jaw throbbed from the constant jostling, and the wind had practically sandblasted his face raw.

Zenobia, however, was unfazed. Her smile stretched so wide it seemed only a wind tunnel blasting air into her face—causing her lips to flap and bare her grinning teeth—could produce such pure exhilaration. Occasionally, she hooted and hollered, "That's my girl!"

The mountain itself was a terracotta titan, crowned with an ivory tower whose spire impaled the shadowy clouds, obscuring its apex from view. It seemed to leap toward them in jerky growth spurts, each lurch revealing more of its staggering enormity.

Finally, they came to a stop.

Grateful, Bobby dropped off the cart and immediately began plucking splinters from the seat of his britches. Zenobia trooped straight up to the mountain's base, sizing it up like she meant to wrestle it into submission. Golly wasted no time finding a patch of blue grass and started to graze.

"Welp," Zenobia announced, "thisyer's it, alrite."

Bobby glanced up from his backside, temporarily abandoning splinter extraction to take in the mountain's facade. Carved into the auburn rock was a monumental entrance resembling the classical Greek temples he'd studied in fourth grade, during that brief period he'd dreamed of becoming an architect. But this wasn't just a flat carving; it was a semi-3D bas-relief that enveloped the mountain's sheer face on all sides. The craftsmanship was breathtaking: a towering, six-story columned portico capped with a triangular pediment and a sculpted visage of grandeur stretching as wide as a city block. It reminded him of ancient rock-cut tombs he'd seen online. Grandiose mausoleums carved into the mountainsides to honor the dead, their ornate exteriors masking the crude, hollow pits within, where bodies were left to rot.

This grand temple facade was merely an elaborate imitation, offering no actual entrance at all. It was ornate in every detail, partly shrouded in shrubbery, dappled in foliage, and veined with creeping vines. At its gable end, the tympanum bore sculptural reliefs of figures poised like gods. The grandest among them sat regally upon a throne. Though too far away to be certain, its face bore a faint resemblance to someone Bobby was sure he knew. Surrounding the central figure were countless carved bodies, arrayed in rows that spanned the entire width of the mountain and stacked upon one another, climbing higher than Bobby could see. These shallow-relief figures captured the full spectrum of human activity and emotion, depicting scenes of conflict and camaraderie, individuals toiling at menial tasks, families sharing meals, others playing musical instruments, and more creating art, and writing literature. Countless effigies, young and old, embodied the whole sweep of human feeling—joy, sorrow, laughter, grief, anger, shame—on and on. Near the base, half-concealed by weeds, more unsettling tableaus emerged: scenes of war, men and women killing one another. To Bobby's horror, some of the victims were children. Other carvings immortalized the tragic act of taking their own lives.

Unable to stomach those images for long, Bobby looked upward, searching for happier stories etched into the higher levels of the mountain. The entire spectacle was like an akashic record carved in stone, a life-sized graphic novel chronicling all facets of humanity. The sheer scope of it all made Bobby's eyes sting. He closed his lids, trying to clear the overwhelming omnibus of life from his overloaded brain, before opening them again and letting his gaze settle on a frieze above the imitation entrance. Chiseled into the towering archway were the words:

ONLY THOSE WHO HAVE PASSED SHALL PASS INTO THE PAST.

"Is this the entrance to the Mountain of Bones?" Bobby finally asked.

"Imagine so," Zenobia said. "If yer dead."

"Obviously, I'm not dead," Bobby replied. Though he allowed the possibility to play a little inside his head. Maybe he was. That would explain a lot. "So, how do we get in?"

"Welp... if I recollect right," Zenobia said, pointing skyward, "we, the living, hafta climb."

Bobby pulled his head back. Way back. And farther still—until vertigo swelled and sent him wobbling. He might've fallen flat on his butt had he not quickly leveled his head and fixed his sights back on Zenobia. "How the heck do we get all the way up there?"

"You sho ain't got a grain o' sense, do ya. We climb."

Bobby staggered again at the mere thought of such dizzying heights.

"Are you crazy? I can't climb that!"

"Can't... or won't?"

"Can't. Can't. Can't! Look at me."

Zenobia didn't look. Instead, she turned and strode back to the cart. After collecting a few items into her belt pouch, she unhitched the cart and gave Golly an affectionate pat along the neck as it stretched toward a patch of grass. Then she tied the reins to a nearby tree. "Listen here," she said, her voice steady and sincere, "you can't 'cause you *think* you can't. The solution ain't never been more simple: start thinkin' you can."

To Bobby, nothing he thought of ever sounded simple. Certainly not scaling a literal mountain. "I can't climb that. No way, mon frére." He shook his head, his shaggy bangs flopping over his eyes.

"Fine," Zenobia snapped.

Bobby swept his hair aside to see her. She was hugging Golly again, breathing in sync with her pet's slow, steady chewing.

"Sorry, ol' girl, but you gotta stay here," Zenobia whispered into Golly's floppy ear. "Don'tcha worry none. Imma be back lickety-split." She gave Golly one last squeeze, pressing her cheek against the cow's warm brown coat, then turned back toward Bobby. "Okay, if ya'd mind Golly, that'd be much obliged," she said with a smile of radiant sarcasm.

But for the first time, Bobby noticed the gap between her two front teeth. There was something oddly endearing and strangely pleasing about it. His right eye twitched.

Without another word, Zenobia shot off, charging the mountain, leaping twenty feet into the air, and latching onto the rocky facade. She began her ascent with feline grace and startling agility. Bobby stepped back, eyes wide, tracking her rapid climb as she scaled the intricate reliefs. Within moments, she was already past the letter *S* in the word *pass*, gliding from one sculpted figure to the next with fluid ease.

"Can I really climb that?" Bobby mumbled to Golly. The cow responded with indifferent chewing. "Well, it's not like *you* could do it," he muttered, turning back to the mountainous wall. He ran his fingers along the grooves in the rocks and sighed. He'd tried rock climbing once in gym class. Strapped into a too-tight harness, hands awkwardly wedged into multi-colored rubber holds, one foot positioned to spring upward. His classmates watched in morbid titillation as he clung to the wall for what felt like forever, stalled barely five feet off the ground.

"C'mon, Porter." Mr. Callahan, the gym teacher, egged him on. "You can do it! Get that leg up!" Snickers and laughter punctured the silence. He gulped air, sweat rolling past his lip, his soft belly tightened as he pulled upward, pushing his foot barely an inch off the wall-grip. Just then, some-one—probably Brock—clapped loudly, startling him into a flinch. His foot slipped. His nose cracked hard against the wall, and he dropped backward in what felt like slow motion. He crashed into the mats, nose bleeding, ego devastated. Laughter exploded. Louder than it should have, like a whole stadium full of kids laughing just at him.

But that was then. Now, there were no goggling classmates. No giggling, Brock. No gym teacher shouting. Only the mountain... and its silent, unjudg-ing stone faces. They watched him, sure, but at least they didn't laugh. Still, his second fear loomed larger now: falling to his death. As he considered his next move, Golly caught his eye. Bobby gave a double take. The apathetic bovine was suddenly gawking at him, almost with a severe, casual interest. But the moment their eyes met, Golly went right back to chomping grass. That brief connection startled Bobby. He could begin to see why Zenobia was so fond of her.

Refocused, Bobby turned back to the steep mountain face. "I...probably... *can* climb this mountain," he muttered. "Why not?" He dug his fingers into the rocks, searching for stable holds and protruding crags. "If a cow can run like a race car, then I can climb a mountain," he affirmed. With a grunt, he hefted himself off the ground, clinging to the incline. He didn't dare to look up—or down. His focus remained strictly forward. Blindly, he groped for new handholds above his head. When he found one, his arms flexed, hauling him upward while his legs pushed him higher. He was doing it! It wasn't as hard as he remembered. For once, his muscles seemed to work in his favor. Energized, his limbs continued cooperating as he climbed, inch by inch, on a blind ascent.

———————

A SILVER HAZE veiled Zenobia as she scrabbled higher up the mountain. At some point during her climb, the sculptures gave way to bald red rock. Unsure how far she'd come, she welcomed a swirling breeze that parted the mist, revealing the bleak world below. Anchoring herself to a secure ledge, she paused to take in her subaerial surroundings. To her right, a shadowy hori-zon of ragged sierras jutted like saw teeth, tinged a deep purple. Behind her, thinner, ragged lines hinted at ancient forests of wild wisdom. Woods, her father, had always warned her never to enter. According to his stories, they were barbaric lands, home to tribes so ruthless they'd turn on their own kin to survive, where desperation bred a savagery that made monsters of people.

"Survival of the fittest will only make you fit for a life of loneliness," he'd once said, during one of their bedtime stories. She'd been curled against his chest, head rising and falling with each of his breaths. His long arms wrapped around her, holding the book aloft as he read. She'd felt his voice hum through his bones, vibrating against her cheek and tickling her ear.

Tears now tickled that same cheek as her mind traced the contours of his leathery, gentle face. His hollow eyes, perhaps starved of nutrition, still brimmed with soul. His smile—gap-toothed as her own—always wide and warm. A smile of her own briefly flittered across her face before she forced her lips into a straight, thin line. Why didn't memories of her mother come like this? The thought turned her heart heavy. It began to sink inside her, dragging her downward, not physically, but dangerously close. She feared it might pull her off the rock entirely, send her plummeting. She forced herself to climb. Slower now, steadier. Operating almost on autopilot.

In her memories, her mother had always been there, feeding her, dressing her, scrubbing her face clean. But it was her father who filled her world with wonder and possibilities. Who made her laugh. Who made her believe she could be anything—do anything.

Then a terrible thought struck—sharp as a needle. It pinned her in place, froze her limbs. *She was glad it hadn't been her father who died.* If one of them had to go... she was relieved it was her mother.

Her lungs shuddered. Tears stung hot in her eyes, horrified by the wickedness of her own mind. A pang split her heart like a deep crack in stone. *Not only was it her fault... but she was glad? Who was she?* One of those wild children her father warned her about? Selfish. Ruthless. She considered letting go. Just for a moment. Letting gravity do the rest. Take her where she clearly belonged. But something inside her clicked. She tightened her hold. A sudden, steely voice in her head roared louder than her guilt. *No. You have to save him.*

Wiping her eyes, Zenobia took a steadying breath. With renewed resolve, she resumed the climb, eyes locked on the summit above. The guilt would have to wait. For now, she packed it down and away.

It wasn't long before her fingers found the lip of a cliff's edge. Hauling herself over, she rose onto a ridged plateau. About fifty paces ahead, the mountain continued its steep incline, and there, near its base, began the ivory tower. Up close, the tower's whitewashed stone looked less like marble and more like bleached bone. There was no visible entrance, only a staircase spiraling around its exterior, coiling up toward the clouds.

Near the edge of the plateau, Zenobia spotted a large wooden wheel and a smaller axle were staked into the bluff. A thick rope wound tightly around a cylinder connected to a crank; the other end of the rope fastened to an elephant-sized bucket. She eyed the contraption and quickly pieced it together—likely used for lifting supplies up and down. But she realized a much better use: hoisting something far more precious.

———————

BOBBY EXHALED FORCEFULLY, blowing a gust of air that kicked up red dust into his face and got in his eyes. He maintained his grubby grip on the mountain's ruddy face, coughing and sneezing. Blindly feeling for the next crevice above him, he found a decent hold and hoisted himself up. His gaze stayed locked on the rock just inches from his nose. As for gauging his progress, well, conquering the towering escarpment an inch at a time made that impossible. In his mind, he imagined himself as Spider-Man—if Peter Parker (or Porter) had been bitten by a molasses-infused slug instead of a radioactive spider.

Then he thought he heard a voice. A tiny one. He paused, straining to listen. Muffled speech bounced down the mountainside like a loose ball of words, tumbling too fast for him to catch. He focused harder, tensing up, thinking it had to be Zenobia.

"Ketchup sounds blow!"

What? What the heck did that mean?

The voice came again: "Heads up, down below!"

Ahhhh! That made more sense. Wait—why?

He risked a glance upward. All he saw was endless rock. How the heck had he thought he could climb that? There was no way in Helcyon he was gonna make it. And then—from the silver mist high above—a dot emerged. It grew rapidly, barreling straight for him. A hard, fast-approaching something. Bobby scrambled to get out of its way. His foot slipped. His face smacked the rock. Then he plummeted.

THUD.

The ground met him hard, and faster than expected. He found himself flat on his back, heart pounding in his throat, the breath knocked clean out of him, and something wet trickling from his nose. Snapping his eyes open, two thoughts hit him at once: First, he had only made it six feet up. Second, the object was still coming. He had no time for anything but to curl up, tuck his head behind his arms, and let out a muted squeal with what little air he had left—

SNAP.

Nothing squashed him, but something *did* rattle near his elbow, grazing him as it swung back and forth. Slowly, like a flower unfurling its petals, he peeled his arms away from his face. Hovering above him was the mud-caked bottom of a large bucket. "Holy moly!" he wheezed. His heart was still racing. "What the heck!" He rolled out from beneath the wildly swinging bucket and got to his feet. His eyes darted around, half-expecting to see strained laughing faces pointing and mocking him. But there were none. Only Golly, still tending to more pastoral interests. He wiped his bloody nose on his sleeve and turned back to the bucket. It was tethered to a thick rope, swaying gently now. Cautiously, Bobby stepped closer, casting nervous glances skyward. Nothing else seemed to be falling. He reached out and stilled the bucket, halting its swing. It looked like a basket from a hot-air balloon, only shorter and more squat. Its wood was weathered gray, held together by bands of blue mossy metal.

A faint, twangy voice reverberated from inside. "If you ain't dead yet," Zenobia's voice called out, "climb on in."

Bobby stretched up on his toes and peered over the rim, half-expecting to see Zenobia curled up at the bottom with a sly smile. But the bucket was empty.

"Zenobia?" he hollered.

"Who else?" her voice echoed again, hollow and tinny, bouncing up from the bottom.

It reminded Bobby of the time his dad had shown him how to make a tin-can telephone. He remembered his father's voice, flat and faraway, vibrating along the string: *Brah-voh three, this is ex-oh, radio check, over.* Bobby had listened through the can, cupped to his ear, hearing the words fade out in a ghostly reverb. This must be something like that—Zenobia's voice traveling down the rope and collecting in the bucket's base.

"Where are you?" Bobby yelled into the bucket.

"On the mountain. Where else? Now climb in and give the rope a tug, so I know to pull ya up," her voice said.

Bobby frowned, eyeing the vessel. Sure, there was enough space for him to fit. But its sides were low, and the wood looked like it was on the verge of disintegration.

"C'mon. Git in," Zenobia barked, more impatient now.

He exhaled a jittery sigh—fast becoming his default breathing pattern—and awkwardly hoisted himself over the bucket's rim. He got stuck halfway, legs flailing outside, the bucket swinging wildly beneath him. He kicked and squirmed in panic, bouncing up and down, tugging at the rope in a frantic bid to pull himself fully inside. But before he could secure himself, the bucket lurched into motion.

"Whoah, whoah. I'm not in yet!" Bobby cried out.

The bucket jerked to a sudden halt, jolting him to tumble the rest of the way in with a crash. The boards groaned and flexed under his weight, but held.

"Jeez, Louise. Okay, I'm in."

The ascent resumed.

The bucket rocked and rattled its way up the mountainside, slamming into the protruding stone with unnerving clunks. Bobby's stomach churned, and his face drained of color as he clung to the rope with white-knuckled terror, certain each bump and creak meant the whole contraption was moments from splintering into oblivion.

It felt like an eternity and a day before the bucket finally swung to a wobbly stop at the plateau. Zenobia grabbed the bucket's rim and guided it in toward solid ground.

"You can git on out now. You ain't never been more safe."

Bobby peeled his trembling fingers from the rope and half-fell, half-clambered out, landing flat on his butt, inches from the edge and yawning drop. He scrambled backward on his palms and heels, dragging his rear across the dirt until he felt his butt was a safe distance from the precipice.

Zenobia watched him, hands planted on her narrow hips. "Boy, you sho are a real nervous kid."

"I'm a *regular* kid," he shot back, getting to his feet and brushing dirt from his hands.

"S'pose that's 'bout right," Zenobia nodded, as if confirming a universal truth. She swooped past him toward the tower's base, mounting its ivory steps with swift, deliberate purpose.

"Where you going?" Bobby called after her.

"Up. Wherelse," she replied, without looking back.

"Wait... wait!" Bobby hustled to catch up.

As they spiraled up the tower, the steps grew narrower, pressing them closer to the tower's smooth wall. Worse still, there was no railing to prevent them from plummeting back to the plateau and bouncing them farther down the escarpment to the bottom again. Bobby clung to the wall, back pressed up against it, inching up the steps in cautious, crablike movements. More often than not, he'd find Zenobia already seated on the steps above, her dour face cupped in her palms, elbows balanced on her bony knees. The moment he got close, she sprang to her feet and bounded up the steps, vanishing around the next curve. When he caught up again, she'd be waiting. Sometimes fidgeting with her sword, other times massaging her clenched jaw, or sometimes cracking her knuckles. Bobby couldn't understand why she kept waiting. He was sure she disliked him. No, scratch that—he *knew* she hated him, couldn't wait to ditch him. Yet here she was, waiting. Over and over. Letting him catch up just enough before bounding farther up... and waiting again. It went on like this for the rest of the day.

Finally, they reached the soot-dark fog that perpetually shrouded the Helcyon sky. Just beneath the heavy, leaden ceiling, Bobby found her seated again, this time chewing on a bungleroot she must've stashed in her poke. For once, she waited for him to come up beside her.

"What is it?" Bobby asked, creeping to a stop near her.

"Thisyer is plum the tallest thang in all Helcyon," she said, chewing on the bungleroot thoughtfully.

Bobby had kept his eyes diligently on the steps beneath his feet, doing his best to avoid the vertigo-inducing drop beyond. But for one foolish moment, his gaze strayed over the ledge. The dizzying view threw his balance into question, and a sudden gust of wind seemed intent on nudging him over. Reeling back, he smacked flat against the tower wall, panting. Secured again, he re-anchored his eyes to the solid steps rising before him and stayed there a good minute before lifting his nervous gaze toward Zenobia's concerned expression.

"Yep," Bobby croaked, his voice trembling. "We're pretty high up."

"It keeps right on goin' up through the sky. To where nobody gone ventured before and returned."

"What happened to them?"

"I ain't got no clue. Ain't nobody come back to say."

She finished her bungleroot and stood. "I ain't scared, but..." She paused, searching for the right words. "Where we 'bout to head to sho ain't meant for us livin'," she said, brushing her fingers through the drifting underbelly of the thick smog just overhead. "Oncet we cross thisyer cloud of death, I reckon we might could never come back."

"You're telling me this *now*?" Bobby groaned. "What about saving your dad? You want to risk never coming back?"

"A risk I gotta take to find a way to save 'em. We come this far. You ready to go farther?" she asked.

Bobby groaned again, then sighed. "I guess."

Taking one final gulp of clean air, Zenobia declared, "Onward an' upward." And she was onward and upward, bounding ahead as she had all day. Her tiny frame was consumed by the ashen mist like a ghost phasing through solid matter. Only she was the solid one, passing through a ghostly plane.

Bobby lingered a moment, trying to scrape together the courage he was sure had to be hiding in him somewhere. He sucked in and blew out quick, shallow breaths, as if he could breathe himself into bravery.

"C'mon," Zenobia's disembodied voice floated down from the soot clouds. "Hurry yer butt up."

"I've come this *far* already, I guess," Bobby muttered. "I can go *farther*." With one last inhale of clean air, he took a resigned step and trudged upward into the enveloping soot.

TWELVE

SLIMSY CLEARLY detested the beast known as Kilrok. So, when tasked with relaying orders to the creature—to track down Bobby and Zenobia—he dragged Hulmick along for company.

"What if I just ran off?" Hulmick asked, his long legs striding at a relaxed pace.

Slimsy, on the other hand—or leg—scurried on much shorter limbs, panting heavily as he struggled to keep pace. They snaked along the serpentine path of the Ashen Forest, its fog clinging low and thick like poison vapor.

"You—could..." Slimsy huffed, managing to pull even with Hulmick for a breath or two. "...try. But—it—would..." Falling behind again, he leapt forward in a burst. "It would—do you—no—good."

"And why's that?" Hulmick asked, not bothering to slow down.

"Wait! Stop!" Slimsy gasped.

Hulmick swiveled his neck nearly a full 180 degrees. His sunken eyes vanished briefly behind shadowed lids before popping back into existence, plagued with confusion.

Slimsy leaned hard against the trunk of a massive, long-dead oak. Though every tree in the Ashen Forest was lifeless and burnt, this one dwarfed them all—five times wider, ten times darker, and a hundred times more rotten. Hulmick twisted the rest of his body to match his head, squaring himself with Slimsy's uneasy stance.

"What?" he said, swallowing dryly.

"We... we're here," Slimsy squeaked. He raised a spindly finger and pointed toward a gaping hole in the base of the tree's charred trunk.

"Where's here?" Hulmick said, his eyes flicking around the dreadful grove of warped, withered trees. Each cursed into twisted shapes, indistinguishable from one another, like something clawed out of a late October nightmare.

"The beast's hole," Slimsy clarified.

"The *beast's* hole?" Hulmick repeated. "What beast?"

As if on cue, a deep, rumbling growl belched from the dark, cavernous depths of the decayed oak's rotted roots. Followed by a noisome stench that rose like a gaseous cloud. Accompanying this fetid expulsion, a bolt of red lightning slashed across the poisoned sky, and a crack of thunder rolled through the forest. Both sounds rattled Hulmick's bones. Then a stench hit him full-on, causing him to pinch his nose and cry out, "My Porter, what *is* that rancid smell?"

Despite his wide, gaping nostrils, Slimsy seemed unfazed. He merely shrugged. Another bolt of red lightning cracked and arced overhead, prompting Slimsy's lidless eyes to flick nervously skyward; his pupils quivered. "We best get this over with. Before the rain starts," he warned.

"Rain? Didn't you hear that roar? Or whiff that putrid stench?"

"Yes. But the rain here is more acid than water." Slimsy tapped the scarred skin around his eyes. "Once these peepers had hoods."

Hulmick jerked his gaze to the rolling storm above.

"Nuh—uh," Slimsy cautioned, still indicating his naked eyes. "Bad idea to look up once the rain starts falling,"

Hulmick dropped his gaze back to the black, decaying mulch beneath his worn-out shoes, feeling the bottom of his feet sink into the soggy rot. The reason nothing grew or flourished near Fire Mountain became starkly clear—life here wasn't just burned away by fire. It was eaten away by the poisonous, acidic waters.

Another red-veined thunderstrike split the sky, followed by a booming voice from the hole. Deep, rich, and deceptively gentle. A voice as soothing as a lullaby, laced with the mellifluous tones of a golden bell, meant to lull any creature into a deadly ease.

"Is that you, Slimsy, ole chap?" purred a baritone from the darkness.

"What other living idiot would dare darken your door?"

"Yes, indeed. But know this, my door is always dark, and my shadows will devour your shadows. You brought a human?"

Slimsy shot a glance at Hulmick's long, anxious face. "Yes. A friend. And I must ask that you refrain from eating him. He's *very* important to the Master."

A silence expanded between them, as if the veiled beast were carefully contemplating his reply.

"Of course," it finally intoned, with a sinister chuckle. "He is safe. But he mustn't see my true self. There may come a day when he means nothing to anyone, and he encounters me as I am... and I happen upon him as my next meal."

Hulmick began inching backward, eyes scanning nervously for an escape route.

"Yes, yes, of course," Slimsy said, rolling his eyes dramatically. "Fortunately, I have an eye for disguises. Everything will work out splendidly." Although incapable of winking—and quite unfamiliar with how to smile—he gave a broad smirk, his bulbous white eyes glittering with giddy mischievousness.

From within the tree's shadowy cavity emerged an astonishingly handsome man, standing six feet tall on two sturdy legs. His long golden hair bounced and shimmered, radiant even in this grim setting. His smile unveiled a perfect row of pearly whites. His eyes shone a vivid, hypnotic blue, his cleft chin seemed chiseled by angels, and his sharply defined features were impeccably symmetrical. Copper-toned skin stretched taut over his muscular physique, each ripple and contour a marvel of anatomical vanity. He was the living embodiment of a Herculean hero.

Hulmick stared, a blend of awe and envy stirring behind his eyes, as the beast admired his own transformed appearance.

"Bravo, Slimsy, ole boy," Kilrok hummed. "I look positively delectable. You've made me almost want to dine on myself."

"I aim to please," Slimsy said, with a little bow.

Kilrok reluctantly peeled his gaze from his own magnificent form and fixed it squarely on Hulmick, advancing toward the trembling man and bathing him in his piercing azure stare.

"So, what interest does the Ashen Knight have for this pale human?"

"Oh, something to do with his blood and the Blood Moons," Slimsy answered casually, stepping between Hulmick and Kilrok as a reminder that his charge was off-limits.

Kilrok held his devouring stare a moment longer, then tilted his head to the granite sky, and inhaled the sulfurous air with satisfaction.

"Ahh, yes. The Blood Moons return," he murmured, voice shaded with sinister reverence. "Hidden, yes. But their influence is palpable. It's been ages since I've felt their mystic alignment tingle through my veins." Kilrok dipped his head to meet Slimsy's bulging gaze. "Even you, ole boy, must feel their powers sweetening your gifts nicely, making them more potent, more vivid." His gaze returned thoughtfully to Hulmick. "A pity this one is verboten. Scrawny though he may be, the Blood Moons make the humans taste all the more scrumptious."

"Yes, well," Slimsy began, only to be interrupted by a sudden crack of thunder. It exploded in a cascade of violent red flashes above them. Both he and Hulmick flinched. When the sky finally quieted, its anger rumbling away into the distance, Slimsy continued. "I've come with orders for you. Once delivered, we must be on our way. Rain is imminent."

"And melt your delicate skin," Kilrok interjected, his silver tongue slick with sarcasm. "We must not have that. Do tell, ole chap. What dark bidding does our dark Master require of me? The Blood Moons rage, and I've little time to dawdle."

"Right, yes. Your orders are to hunt these two," Slimsy said, gesturing toward a curtain of shadowy trees. From behind them, Zenobia and Bobby materialized.

"Zenobia!" Hulmick cried, rushing to his daughter and dropping to one knee. He squeezed her shoulders tightly, shaking her gently. "Zenobia!" he shouted again. But she did not respond. Her eyes stared past him, vacant, like a doll's eyes—lifeless and cold. He shook her harder, desperate to wake her, but it was like jostling a life-sized puppet, a hollow skin casing filled with frigid air. He released her and slowly stood, still staring at her with wide, horrified eyes. "She's another one of your tricks," he hissed.

"Children?" Kilrok asked, curiosity piqued.

"Small humans I can see eye-to-eye with," Slimsy remarked.

Kilrok chuckled darkly. "The distinction between children and adults is more than just height." His grin stretched wider than any human's should, unnatural, grotesque. He sharpened his gaze on the children hungrily. "Their meat is juicier. More tender."

Hulmick suddenly erupted in high-pitched laughter, startling Kilrok and Slimsy. They turned, confused.

"You don't have her!" Hulmick shouted. "This is just another lie! Another illusion! One of your filthy tricks!" He began to hop in place with manic glee. "You'll never catch her. Never!" With that, he turned and bolted down the path. His spindly legs churned awkwardly, bony knees nearly knocking against his chin as he bounded into the gloom, fleeing Slimsy and Kilrok.

Kilrok's icy eyes followed the quickly shrinking Hulmick, then shifted to Slimsy. "Isn't he of some importance to you?"

Slimsy looked up at Kilrok and shrugged. "I'm guiding him right back to Dragoon Keep."

Kilrok let out a deep, throaty laugh. "No living soul can escape your eye, can they, ole chap?"

"No living soul can. Perhaps not even a few dead ones," Slimsy replied.

The sky detonated in a turbulent display, red lightning clawing across clouds swollen with venomous rain, ready to deliver death from above. Slimsy flinched again and tugged a hood over his head before starting down the path.

"Goodbye, ole chap. See you around," Kilrok smirked, standing beside the dummy children.

"Yeah. Sure," Slimsy mumbled.

Rain began to fall. First, a scatter of biting droplets, then as a steady, drumming deluge of poison.

The false Bobby and Zenobia dissolved into vapor. Kilrok dropped to all fours and slinked back into his decaying den within the enormous, dead oak. As he faded into the shadows, the bronze glamour of his borrowed form melted away, revealing fleeting glimpses of the monstrous shape beneath. But the darkness swallowed him before his true form could be seen. Still, his voice lingered. Rolling laughter rang out from within the tree, swelling with malevolent joy. It carried through the forest, resonating off the black trees and mingling with the poisonous downpour, as if even the storm itself now shared in Kilrok's cruel delight.

THIRTEEN

**OTH CHOKED** on the thick, poisonous gas clouds as they ascended, doing their best to tuck their noses and mouths beneath their wool vests. The leaden haze reduced visibility to almost nothing, while neck-snapping winds launched an unrelenting assault on Bobby and Zenobia, growing more vicious and vindictive with every step they climbed. A particularly violent gust swept Bobby off his feet, slamming him hard against the staircase, cracking his chin on the step's edge. The flurry continued its battery, blowing him over the tower's ledge toward certain death below. But Zenobia, quick on her feet, lunged after him and caught him by the back of his shirt.

"Hang on!" she screamed over the wailing wind.

"Hang on?" Bobby shrieked, terror-stricken as he dangled thousands of feet in the air. "You hang on!"

With one hand, she heaved him back onto the stone surface of the tower's steps. He landed with a bone-jarring thud, releasing a jarring cry.

Zenobia's eyes narrowed to slits in the swirling dark as she rummaged through her belt pouch, pulling out a piece of rope. She groped around the soft bulge of Bobby's stomach, trying to loop it around his waist. Her fingers inadvertently tickled him, and despite everything, Bobby couldn't help but let out an irritated giggle. The rope came up short.

"Yer a tick big for thisyer rope," Zenobia shouted over the gale.

"C'mon," Bobby bellowed, "I almost died and you're being mean?"

"I saved, ya. I got ya. Just sayin' the rope is short is all. Quit yer bellyaching." Zenobia quickly knotted the rope around his chest instead, securing the other end to her belt. "I got ya, I got ya good."

She shoved onward, leaning into the wind, pushing up and up with Bobby at her back, shielding himself as best he could in the slim screen of her body.

As if the raging hurricanes weren't enough, lightning began striking the tower, erupting in bursts of sparks and frying Bobby's nerves with every crackle. Several crimson bolts came so close they singed the tips of their hair, which now stood on end from the electric charge in the air. The explosive atmosphere forced them to a halt; they cupped their hands over their ears in a vain attempt to protect their hearing. But it was too late, their heads screamed with a deafening siren. Bobby shook his head to silence the piercing bells in his ears, only to find he worsened his headache. They pressed on, half-deaf and half-blind, pummeled by the ruthless storm. Zenobia had to dig her nails into the tower's stone mortar to anchor herself against the savage winds. Blindly, they clawed up the curve, inch by inch. Bobby crawled on his belly at Zenobia's heels, constantly feeling the tug of the rope pinch his armpits. He was confident they were done for. On the brink of being blasted off the tower, precariously tethered tooth and nail—

And then...

It all broke.

The hostile elements ceased their punishing assault, replaced by a disorienting silence. The air stilled, save for a soft rumble vibrating somewhere just below them. A wave of warmth washed over their wind-whipped faces, thawing their frosty noses, cheeks, and ears. They collapsed on the steps, basking in the balminess of glorious peace, and cautiously peeled open their eyes. The light was blindingly bright, burning with such intensity that Zenobia squeezed hers shut again.

"What in tarnation is that?" she asked, her voice louder than necessary, forgetting she no longer had to shout over the storm.

"It's the sun," Bobby said, sitting upright and pressing his back against the hot stone of the tower wall. He shielded his eyes with his hand, blinking until they adjusted. "Holy Moses. We're above the clouds, now!" he exclaimed, staring out across the endless ocean of smoke and ash below them. The stratosphere stretched into a boundless cerulean blue, with a dazzling hot white sun blazing high above.

Zenobia tried to open her eyes again, but instantly crimped them shut. "That's mighty bright," she grumbled. "I can't open my eyes without 'em burnin' right outta my skull."

Bobby pulled himself to his feet, feeling sturdy again. The abyss below was now shrouded in cloud, which helped settle his fear of heights. Out of sight, out of mind. He untied the rope from around his chest. "I'll lead the way," he declared, squeezing past Zenobia on the narrow steps. Once in front, he helped her tie a cloth around her eyes like a blindfold. She swayed her head slightly, testing the world through her other senses. Bobby couldn't help but giggle.

"What's so funny, wise guy?" she huffed.

"Oh, nothing," Bobby said, trying to stifle his grin. "I shouldn't have laughed. Sorry." He reached out to take her hand, but the moment their fingers touched, she jerked hers back as if burned.

"Whatcha doin' now?" she barked, startled.

"Nothing, nothing," Bobby squawked, flustered. "I was just gonna lead you so you don't walk off the stairs. That's all, I swear."

With a reluctant groan, Zenobia extended her hand, seemingly angled away from him on purpose. Bobby took it, his palms clammy and pulsing.

"Why is yer hand so wet?" she asked, grimacing.

"It's hot out. I sweat a lot. I'm sorry."

Blindfolded and impatient, Zenobia waited for him to move. Bobby couldn't help but linger, savoring the soft pressure of her hand in his. But the silence stretched too long and turned heavy. Awkward. He knew he had to keep going. Guiding her gently, he continued up the spiral. At first, the height didn't bother him. But as they climbed higher—and the clouds fell farther and farther beneath them—his fear began to creep back in. He slowed, inching upward, hugging the tower wall for reassurance.

Out of the blue, Zenobia asked, "What color is thisyer sky?"

The question caught him off guard. Grateful for the break in silence, Bobby took it as a chance to rest. He sat down on the steps, panting. "It's blue," he said.

"Blue?"

"Yeah, blue."

"Ya mean it ain't purple?"

"Purple? No. It's definitely blue."

"I always been tol' the sky is purple."

"No, it's blue. Have a look."

"I can't. Still too dang bright."

"Well, it's blue."

Zenobia tilted her head back, as if trying to sniff the sky's color. After a pause, Bobby finally asked, "Who told you the sky was purple, anyways?"

"In Helcyon yer either a Plebeian or a Patrician. That's our religion. Plebeians bleeve the sky is purple. Patricians ain't even acknowledge the color purple exists."

"And what color do *they* think it is?"

"Violet."

"Purple? Violet? That's silly. Aren't they the same thing?"

"Nope!" Zenobia cut in, wiping her cracked lips with the back of her hand. "Ain't never been more different colors. To them, violet is as pure a color as our Lawrd Father Porter hisself. An' 'cause we see it the way it is—plain ol' purple—we Plebeians are ridiculed, treated like worthless, dirty citizens. Impure, 'cause we foller a 'False Color.'"

"But that's ridiculous. The sky is blue!"

"I wish I could gander for myself."

"You will. Just wait and see. It's blue."

Revitalized by the thought of showing Zenobia the sky's true color once they reached the summit, Bobby stood and continued the climb. In all his thirteen years, he'd never climbed so many stairs. His legs burned, his lungs prickled, and his eyes ached from constant squinting. His lips were parched and chapped, and he couldn't remember the last time he had a sip of water. His swollen tongue scraped up sweat droplets in a futile attempt to hydrate. Despite it all, he was amazed at his own tenacity. Back home, he doubted he'd have made it past the first few steps. He would've collapsed and given up. But here, in this strange world, he leaned into the aches and pains and kept going, pressing ever upward.

The final steps came as a surprise. Head down, lost in the rhythm of his own footsteps, with a blindfolded Zenobia still in tow, Bobby climbed one step, then another—until suddenly, his feet landed on flat stone. He looked up. Spread before him was the breathtaking magic hour of Helcyon. The sun had dimmed from blinding white to a deep orange, now sinking low against the dark sea of clouds. Overhead, the skies shimmered with a magenta tint, painted by the magnificent moons, each casting its own scarlet glow.

"I think it's safe to take off the blindfold now," Bobby said.

Zenobia untied the cloth and slowly removed it, allowing her eyes to adjust. Her smile—bright with anticipation for a blue sky—faltered as her pupils widened, revealing a firmament no longer azure, but more purple than anything else. The crimson light of the moons bled into the sky, staining it violet. "Purple!" she blurted.

Momentarily distracted by the radiant moons, Bobby shifted his gaze to the sky and noticed it too—the purplish cast. "It is—was blue," he insisted. "I swear. The sky is blue."

Zenobia's brow furrowed as she scrutinized his flushed face and involuntarily winking eye, which made him look like a broken toy. "I reckon purple is called *blue* where yer from. Least now I know it ain't violet."

Rubbing his eye to stop the flutter, Bobby muttered, "No. Blue is blue, and purple is purple, and violet is purple. I know the difference."

"I reckon you think you do."

"Whatever," Bobby huffed. "What now?"

Zenobia strode across the full length of the rooftop—maybe fifty paces—scanning the barren space. "They ain't nothin' up here."

Bobby agreed. Aside from the chipped, weatherworn parapet encircling the roof and some faded symbols etched in the stone floor, there was absolutely nothing. Curious, he stepped closer to the markings. "Do you know what these mean?" he asked.

Zenobia joined him and stared, then shook her head. "Not a clue."

A sudden flutter and whistle cut through the air. Bobby and Zenobia turned to see Lymrik flapping toward them, landing gracefully atop a section of the parapet.

"*No living soul's been here for years.*
Surprised to find two way up here.
Since burnt Knight reined,
Enemy blood-stained—
Has your kind the courage to appear."

The lyrebird's song drifted through the open sky.

Zenobia zipped toward the bird, annoyed. "You best sing some on how we git to the Oracle. We ain't come all this way for nothin'!"

Lymrik fluttered its wings, flustered by her hostile approach.

"*You've arrived at the place you seek.*"

The bird crooned, trying to soothe her agitation.

"*From the dead, the answers speak.*
It is your shared fate,
With not long to wait—
Step on the symbols, hear them creak."

Lymrik hopped down and scuttled over to the etchings at the center of the rooftop. The intricate design depicted a large sun disk encircled by seven moons, each varying in size. The bird looked up, catching the bewildered faces of the two youths.

"The oracle you're keen to meet—
Here is where you must place your feet.
Nothing here to dread,
Many have been led—
All leave unharmed, their quest complete."

The bird paused, then added: *"More or less."*

Bobby and Zenobia exchanged uneasy glances. Then, with mutual shrugs, they stepped into the largest circle and waited.

Nothing.

"What now?" Zenobia asked, shooting a glare at the bird.

Lymrik ruffled its feathers and took to the air, lifting off as if in anticipation. Whether the tremor was triggered by Lymrik's fluttering wings or simply by coincidence, they couldn't tell. But the stones beneath their feet began to quake. The rooftop shuddered, cracked, and then gave way entirely, disintegrating into the chasm below. With the ground now gone, Bobby and Zenobia had no choice but to follow. They tumbled into the darkness. Their screams rang out, hung in the air—raw, unrestrained—then, like the rest of them, were dragged into the open throat of the tower.

FOURTEEN

THEIR SCREAMS echoed as terrible howls through the darkness as they fell—and fell—and fell into a seemingly bottomless pit... Zenobia silenced her squeals well before Bobby did, steadying her posture until she floated on her back. She gazed upward, watching the circle of red moonlight shrink into a distant red speck before vanishing altogether. Bobby, meanwhile, continued shrieking as he tumbled head-over-heels in a chaotic roll. Eventually, his throat gave out, his hollering sputtering into silence. Flailing, he awkwardly stretched out his arms and legs. The star shape helped him stabilize, shifting him from a somersault into a belly-down glide through the pitch-black void. The wind whipped past, flapping his jowls into a wet, fluttering mouthpiece. For a long time, they fell in near silence, accompanied only by the whistling wind as it slithered around them.

"Do you think there's a bottom?" Bobby finally asked, his voice hoarse, but returning to normal.

Zenobia twisted toward him. Though surrounded by impenetrable blackness, a mysterious, ambient glow illuminated them both. It lit Bobby's pallid face. His puffed cheeks, flapping lips, and hair flickering like a blonde flame atop his head. The sight made Zenobia giggle in spite of herself.

"What's so funny? We're falling to our deaths!" Bobby scolded, spittle streaking up his nose from the turbulence, completely undermining his attempt at seriousness.

"I ain't mean nothin' by it," she said, with a half-apologetic grin.

Then, through the dark, came a familiar whistling. A rising melodic tune, sharp and clear. Lymrik appeared above them, wings outstretched, feathers glowing fluorescent green, blue, and red. The bird glided downward, slowing his descent to match theirs, weaving between them.

"You stupid bird!" Bobby screamed. "This is all your fault!"

> *Much smoother it would be, your glide,*
> *If wings you both had at your side.*
> *But flap as you may,*
> *You'll drop anyway—*
> *So lay back, and enjoy the collide."*

The bird sang, snapped its wings to its side, and dove beak-first into the darkness, shooting away like a radiant, multi-colored arrow.

With little to do but fall toward whatever awaited below, Zenobia got an idea. She attempted to backstroke through the air, aiming for where she imagined a wall might be, hoping to grab hold and slow her velocity. After just two strokes, she slammed into something so hard it crushed the air from her lungs and knocked the life out of her.

BOBBY'S VISION FLASHED white. Then dissolved into black. His body went from numb to cold to searing hot as he belly-flopped into water. The first thought to flicker back into his consciousness was how miraculous it was that he was still alive; he hurt too much to be dead. Submerged in dark waters, he felt a sinking sensation he remembered from his dream at Tar Lake. But almost immediately, his direction reversed—buoyancy lifting him. His head broke the surface, and his lungs screamed for air. Gasping, he clawed at the water around him, sucking in air so wet he nearly choked on it.

As his panicked flailing eased into a desperate doggy paddle, Bobby spun in place, searching for Zenobia. She was nowhere to be seen. Just an endless expanse of black water and dread.

"Zenobia?" he cried, his own voice bouncing back, pained and scarred. "Zenobia! Where are you?" Once more, only his voice answered, mocking and hollow, parroting him word for word.

A terrifying thought struck him. He took a deep breath and dunked his head underwater, eyes wide, legs kicking as he searched desperately for her in the murk below. Nothing. He held it as long as he could. Until his lungs cried out, pulling him back up, choking for breath. In that gasping moment, he knew he was alone.

Then a whisper curled through the dark. Or perhaps it was just inside his own head. The words slithered and burrowed into the soft folds of his brain tissue like a worm: *give up,* the insidious chatter squirmed, *why bother? You're all alone. Lost, hopeless. Just lie back... and sink.*

Bobby's limbs began to slow, his automatic paddling grinding to a near stop. He whispered, "Zenobia" as the waterline crept up his neck, rose over his chin, and covered his lips, stopping just below his nostrils.

Sink.

He was tired. So tired. Ready to just let the dark waters take him.

But then, a light ignited before him. A flame, small and steady, blazed just ahead. Its glow expanded, revealing a small, slate-colored island rising from the black waters. At its center stood a statue of a woman, poised atop an ornate fountain. Bobby shook the torpor from his limbs and splashed toward the platform. Spacious enough to fit a small cottage. He grunted and groaned as he hauled his waterlogged torso over the lip of the stone ledge, clinging there, half in, half out of the water. With a final heave, he clawed his way up and collapsed onto the dry landing. Flat on his back, he lay shivering in the chill, doing little more than listening to the shudder of his uneven breathing. Above him stretched the yawning dark void from which he had fallen.

Once on his feet, Bobby turned to face the marbled goddess who had drawn him in. She was stunning. The statue depicted a divine woman, her figure wrapped in a delicate golden robe, caught in mid-levitation above a basin shaped like a pearl shell. Her arms were raised high overhead, hands cupped as if offering something invisible to the heavens. From her left palm, the torchlight that had pulled him back from the brink. From her right palm, a luminous ribbon of ropy blue water streamed out in an elegant arc, spilling into the fountain's basin and bathing it in radiant light. Her face was soft and serene, yet unyielding. Her stone-carved eyes cast downward, not at him, but toward the dark lake from which he had emerged. The longer Bobby stared, the clearer his vision became. Slowly, the cave's shadows peeled back, allowing him to glimpse the grim reality of the cave itself. The cavern walls were made entirely of bones and skulls, tightly packed and stacked high and wide, as far as the torchlight could reach, and farther still. In that moment, he understood the true horror behind its name: *The Mountain of Bones.*

"Oh boy," he gulped. Cupping his hands over his mouth to amplify his voice, he shouted, "Zenobia!" Her name rolled back, thin and eerie, repeating like a ghost caught in a broken song. Then slipped away into the stillness beyond.

———————

ZENOBIA ROUSED BACK to consciousness and sat up, a sharp pain shooting through her skull. "Mother Porter, that's right smarts," she groaned, gently pressing her palm to her forehead until the stabbing dulled to a throb.

As her senses cleared, the sound of metal skittering across stone caught her attention. She turned just in time to see the little sphere rolling toward the edge of the platform—the Eye of Likho. She lunged for it, fingers outstretched, but it was too late. The Eye tipped over the edge with a soft splash. She watched helplessly as it bobbed once on the black surface before swiftly being devoured by the fathomless dark.

"Drat dang-it!" she lashed out, slamming her hand against the stone. The jolt sent another shock of pain through her skull. "Ah-heck!" She cursed again, wincing.

After a moment of nursing her head, she took in her surroundings: a square platform of solid slate, floating in a sea of dark, glassy water that shimmered in the flickering firelight. Her gaze followed the source of the illumination, a marbled statue a few paces away. The life-size sculpture depicted a woman wrapped in a rigid, golden robe, her figure suspended above the basin of a water fountain. Arms lifted skyward, she bore an ethereal glow across her stony, cherubic face. Her hands were cupped as if offering something to the heavens, the heels of her palms nearly touching. From her right palm, a mystical fire burned, bright and fuel-less. From her left palm, a stream of soft, blue luminescence cascaded down in a graceful arc, splashing silently into the basin below her sculpted feet.

Zenobia rose slowly to her feet and surveyed the massive cave. At first, there was little more than darkness. But as she strained her eyes—willing her vision to burn through the gloom—the cave walls began to peek out from beneath their shadowy shroud. Millions of compacted skulls rose upward, stacked tight, until they disappeared again into the high-reaching dark.

"Bobby?" she called out.

Her voice came crashing back, twisted and malicious. An echo so loud and sharp it attacked her hearing like a volley of slaps. She clamped her hands over her aching ears, wincing until the assault faded into a frail, uneasy silence. Not even the stream of water from the statue made a sound. Bracing herself, ears still plugged, she yelled, "Bobby! Where you at?" Her words skidded across the shimmering lake like stones skipping over still water. But no answer came. Only the ricochet of her own anxious cry, rebounding from the dark sockets of the countless folded skeletons forming the mountain walls. The echoes returned corrupted, sinister, laden with sonic mockery, as if the cave itself were taunting her.

She flinched at the sudden, horrifying thought: Bobby might be dead. And she was probably responsible. Again. Despite his goofiness, he had started to grow on her, like an annoying habit that, somehow, becomes endearing over time. Her eyes began to water. Her heart felt mired in a vast, gloomy muck that flooded her chest, each beat becoming slower, heavier, more aimless. Overhead, the hollowed-out stares of millions of gawking skulls bore down on her. She dropped to her knees and wept. Not even when her mother was executed before her eyes. Not even when her father was snatched from her, never had she felt so bereft. So utterly abandoned.

Her sniffles and sobs reverberated outward, gathering within the reservoirs of the cadaverous walls of the cave, swelling in volume, smashing back at her like tidal waves of anguish. It was as though the skeletons were about to turn her grief against her, weaponizing her own cries to flay the flesh from her bones until she, too, was reduced to nothing but a hollow frame. But just as she braced for that emotional onslaught—a melody intervened. A song. Soft and beautiful, it blew through the space and scattered the cave's sonic daggers, transforming them into gentle raindrops that glittered as they fell onto the lake. Stunned silent, Zenobia stilled herself, listening. The music grew, blooming into the warm, familiar refrain of the *Psalm of Homes.*

Then came Lymrik. The lyrebird, radiating in an afterglow of shifting, vibrant colors, swooped down and then smoothly veered upward, gliding to a perch on the edge of the fountain's basin. It hummed and whistled the tune now permeating the air.

"Lymrik?" Zenobia called softly.

The bird gave no reply, only continued whistling, trilling with the melody that now seemed to draw something from the depths of the lake. Zenobia scampered to the platform's edge and peered over. Far below, the water began to glimmer. A parade of lights moved beneath the surface. An underwater procession. A line of spirits, marching in single file, their pilgrimage coming to its conclusion. These must have been the same spectral wanderers who had passed their camp a day ago. Each ghostly figure— man, woman, and child—radiated a brilliant, golden aura, their brightness rippling upward, fracturing across the lake's pristine surface and casting

dappled light throughout the cavern. As best as Zenobia could tell, the spirits flowed in through the cavern wall below the lake's surface, constructed
of the same skulls and bones as above. They passed, both ignorant of and
unimpeded by physical barriers, directly into the stone structure on which
she stood. It dawned on her: the island wasn't merely a platform, it was the
crowning capital of a colossal underwater column that plunged beyond the
reach of light into the loch's nebulous depths. Each soul completed their
journey in a bright flash that fizzled into bubbles as they were absorbed
into the column's core.

Zenobia knelt, lowering her head to the lake's surface, eyes scanning
the glowing figures as they dissolved one by one beneath her. The details of
their faces remained hauntingly elusive, but she froze when she spotted a boy
who looked like Bobby. Her body jolted with involuntary panic. "Bobby?"
she called, slapping the water. "Bobby!" It was pointless. The submerged
ghosts were deaf to her voice, their minds consumed by their compulsion
to march forward, always forward—into bubbling absolution.

Then came a voice, gentle and close: "The dead cannot hear you, nor
can you hear the dead."

It curled around her ear like warm breath laced with melody. Zenobia's
lips parted. *Mama?* she mouthed to herself. She turned, breath held tight
in her chest, only to wilt at the sight of the statue fountain. And Lymrik's
beady, impassive stare. The bird had stopped whistling.

"Who gone talked?" she demanded, springing to her feet.

Lymrik gave no reply. Instead, it flapped its wings, sending a burst of
colorful feathers fluttering around her. The bird took to the air, flapping
higher and higher, until it slipped out of sight into the dark shaft above.
Zenobia was left alone. With the statue. She stomped toward the marbled
woman, glaring up at her angled expression. The flicker of the torch held in
the statue's raised palm cast shadows across her sculpted features, contorting them into a grim, almost sinister visage. Yet the soft glow reflecting up
from the fountain's water softened those same lines into something gentler.
An angelic affection. Somehow, the statue seemed to regard Zenobia with
both expressions at once.

Then came the voice again, smooth and sonorous:

"Life less an echo, and more an echo of life." The statue's lips never moved.

"Yer the Oracle, ain't ya?"

"I am what you make of me, and you make me what I am."

"Sooo... I reckon that means yer the Oracle." She paused, then said more forcefully, "Tell me where Bobby is." Catching her own tone, she softened and added, "Please."

"Stand close to the spot of the boy unseen; to see the boy, a spot closer you must stand."

Zenobia inched forward, her eyes locked on the Oracle's vacant gaze. As she approached, the goddess seemed to grow, surging in stature, looming with impossible size. Her silent regard followed Zenobia until her chest bumped against the cool edge of the shell-shaped basin. The light from the fountain shimmered and shifted, luring her eyes downward across the soft ivory contours of the Oracle's face, along the delicate folds of the gilded robe, down to the levitating feet... and finally, into the sparkling fluorescent waters.

"THERE CAN BE no dead without the living, and no living without the dead," came a whispery voice, swirling around Bobby from somewhere above. At first, he thought it was his mother hovering over him as he lay semi-conscious in his bed back home, her words bleeding into his dreams. But something about the voice was off, like a poor imitation. A terrible impression. It made him doubt it was really her. Bobby turned, pushing his wet hair out of his eyes. The strands clung in heavy clumps to his face. Above him, the goddess poised over the fountain seemed to be staring directly at him now.

"Did you just say something?" he asked the statue.

"Something said is nothing until understood, and understanding the nothing said is something," the Grecian figure replied, her stone lips unmoving.

Bobby moved closer to the fountain, eyeing the glowing blue water streaming from her right palm, the flickering flame cupped in her left.

"So you can talk, huh?" he said, grabbing the fountain's edge with renewed excitement. "You're the Oracle, right? Do you know where Zenobia is? Is she all right?"

"You gaze upon the reflection of the fountain, and the fountain shall reflect its gaze upon you."

Bobby dropped his eyes to the luminous pool. Within its sparkling blue depths, he saw not his own reflection—but Zenobia, peering back at him. "Zenobia!" he shouted into the water, nearly dunking his head. "How do I get to you?"

Zenobia didn't seem to hear him. Her expression was frantic, her gestures wild but silent, trying to tell him something. Bobby mimicked her motions in response, attempting to decode the message. But he was at a loss. "I don't understand what you're saying!" he shouted into the water.

"WHERE YOU AT now?" Zenobia yelled into the bottom of the fountain, seeing Bobby in place of her own rippling likeness. "I can't hear ya!" Frustrated, she stomped and turned her nose toward the Oracle. "Where is he? How can I git to 'em?"

"You cannot go to him, but he can come to you."

"Praise Porter. How?"

"You will bring him to the waters of the fountain, and the fountain's waters will bring him to you."

Zenobia glanced back at Bobby, who returned her stare with a bewildered look. She chewed on her lower lip between the gap in her teeth and wrinkled her brow. "Is thisyer water safe? He ain't gonna die or nothin', is he?"

"The dead bring no harm, only wisdom; and what brings harm is never wise, nor dead."

"Well, that ain't assurin' none," Zenobia muttered, graduating to nibbling on her fingernail, "S'pose there ain't no harm in takin' a lil dip in a fountain," she said to herself, then shot her stare up at the Oracle, "Reckon I do got another question for ya? How can I kill the Ashen Knight?"

"The dead who know have not passed through; And those who pass through do not yet know."

"You mean you ain't got no clue?" Zenobia gripped the fountain's edge with both hands and shook it like she might rattle loose an answer. "Yer the darn Oracle. The seer of all bloody truths or whatnot. An' you don't know?"

"The child's wisdom comes from beyond this world; And the world beyond holds its wisdom in the child.

"You bring the boy to the fountain for answers hidden; And hidden answers the fountain shall bring to you"

"I thought ya could only git knowledge if them folks was dead?"

"The boy is an exception to what is known; And what is known makes an exception for the boy."

Zenobia exhaled a frustrated "Oh heck" and stepped back from the fountain to think. She tapped her finger against her dimpled chin, then scratched the crown of her red, bristling hair. Something about the Oracle set off alarms in her gut. Maybe it was the funny way she talked, or maybe it was some-thing deeper. Instincts weren't meant to be ignored. But her options were few. She had no clue how to get to Bobby—or even how to find her way out of the cave. Climbing a wall of skulls felt impossible. No. She refused to think she wasn't strong enough. She got them in this mess. Leaving Bobby behind wasn't an option. She caused enough damage as it was.

"Zenobia. Zenobia, where are you?" Bobby's voice, small and strained with panic, carried up from the basin. "Where are you? Zenobia! Where are you?"

"Oh heck," Zenobia cursed, rushing back to the fountain. She leaned over the basin. Bobby's face appeared again, breaking into a relieved smile as he waved.

"Bobby? Bobby, can ya hear me?" she shouted into the water.

His smile widened, and he nodded. "Yeah. I hear you."

"Good. You hafta climb yer'self into the fountain."

"What?"

"Climb yer'self into the fountain, an' it... it'll bring ya directly to me."

"Really?" Bobby's watery reflection leaned back, scanning his surround-ings as if hoping for another way to reveal itself. Finding none, he looked back at Zenobia. "Really?"

"Yep. Now do as I tol' ya. Ain't nothin' to it. Jus' climb on in. You'll be fine. Now git in!"

———————

BOBBY LOOKED UP at the Oracle's unyielding face. "Is this the only way?" he asked, voice low with dread. "Why can't she come to me?"

No response.

"Hey," he shouted, frustrated by the statue's silence. "You there?"

"Bobby, it's alrite. It's the only way," came Zenobia's voice, faint and urgent, bubbling up through the water. "We ain't got no time to waste, you hear?"

"Okay, okay—geesh. I'm coming, I'm coming." With all the grace and dexterity of a baked ham, Bobby hoisted himself up and over the marble rim, kicked his legs out behind him, and dove headfirst into Zenobia's rippling reflection with a splash.

This was no ordinary fountain. Beneath the unassuming surface lay the vastness of a bottomless ocean—an impossible expanse, dark as a dream-less eternity.

Why am I always sinking, falling, dying? Bobby thought, as his last breath fled from him in a stream of bubbles. He'd never been able to hold his breath for more than ten seconds—a limit he'd tested countless times in the bathtub. Panic twisted across his face. He choked, swallowing water, his limbs flailing in all directions. He fought to resurface, but the surface had already slipped too far above him, now a distant sliver of light. He was submerged. Drowning in the abyss. And he blamed Zenobia for it.

Now, all he could do was wait for the agonizing panic of drowning to give way to a slumber more terrifying in its peace. Time stretched longer, thinner, crueler. His lungs convulsed. His belly ballooned with swallowed water. He writhed. Fought. Struggled to cling to the edge of consciousness. But it was no use—overwhelmed, his vision dimmed. His eyes closed. His body went limp, eerily still, drifting downward into the dark waters.

ZENOBIA FRANTICALLY STIRRED her hand in the gloomy water of the fountain, trying to clear its cloudiness in search of Bobby. The last she'd seen of him was his dive toward her, then the water turned hazy. Now, as it slowly became crystalline again, it reflected neither Bobby's face nor her own look of alarm.

"Where is he?" she demanded, stepping back to better focus her glare on the Oracle. "What happened to him? What did you do? You best tell me thisyer instant!"

The effigy remained silent.

"Hey! Imma talkin' to you. Whadda you do?"

The water ceased flowing from the statue's palm, and the torch fire she held in her right hand fizzled into a cold wisp of smoke. If not for the faint glow of the water pooled in the fountain's basin, Zenobia would've been plunged into complete darkness. Even the, ghostly underwater procession had vanished. She shuddered, suddenly aware again of the oppressive isolation pressing against her chest, making her heart twinge with the kind of emptiness that filled from inside out.

"Hey!" she screamed at the frozen Oracle. "I asked you a question! You hear me?" Her voice came back warped with derision. Twisted by the cave into a mocking rattle, a stark reminder of how lost and utterly alone she was.

Then came a splash.

Zenobia spun toward the sound, her hand tightening instinctively around the hilt of her sword strapped to her side. Poised for combat, she strained her eyes, trying to pierce the murk beyond the platform and the limits of the dim blue glow. She couldn't see what had caused the noise— but she heard it: a sound like labored breathing, something fording the lake, moving closer. Part of her felt relieved not to be alone anymore. *Maybe it was Bobby?* But no... she sensed it wasn't. Not with that smell. A putrid stench, like rotting meat wrapped in wet fur, invaded her nostrils.

"Who's there?" she barked into the dark.

At first, silence. Then, a voice emerged, low, melodic, and unsettling. A euphonious baritone rang out from the void, each word striking like a tongue playing a carillon of brass bells, deep, ceremonial, and resounding. "I am the servant of the Lord and Master of Ash. And I have come in search of you... And the boy, my darling sweet." The voice moved like music, its tones playing harmoniously off the skull-lined walls—too smooth, too warm, too perfect. The cave, which had distorted and mutilated her cries, now amplified this voice. Polished it, gilded it, seduced her with it. She felt her muscles slacken, her guard loosen.

No—she berated herself, then tensed her body and drew her sword.

"Show yerself, stranger. Don't hide in the dark like a coward."

"With pleasure," answered the warm timbre, followed by a pair of glinting yellow eyes that seemed to float low in the dimness. At first, they hovered— eerily untethered—but as they crept into the faint blue light, they fastened themselves to the peachy visage of what appeared to be a man. Though not inherently unattractive, his features were... Off. A bristly, overhanging brow. Wide, flared nostrils beneath a long, hooked nose. A jutting cleft chin framed by thick, black sideburns. As he stalked closer, his leering face swayed from side to side with an unnatural rhythm, giving the impression that his head sat too low for a man of any real height. Then he stepped fully into the light—and the truth of his form emerged.

This was no man.

Zenobia recognized the creature immediately from her storybooks. A manticore. His lion-like body, draped in fur as black as raven feathers, was greasy from being drenched, emphasizing his gaunt, emaciated frame. His claws clicked and scraped against the platform as he prowled forward on padded paws. Above him, a segmented tail arched high, ending in a scorpion-like lance that shimmered with venom. But the most disturbing feature of all lay behind his sinister smile: Three rows of pointy shark teeth. A snaking, articulate tongue, sharp as a scholar's, slick as a liar's. And the gaze of a predator that enjoyed tormenting his prey as a way to flavor his meal. He spoke the language of reason, but

Zenobia knew at once: This thing could not be reasoned with.

As the beast approached, Zenobia stepped backward, matching him pace for pace, raising her blade in warning. "That's far enough," she warned. "Identify yerself. An' tell me whatcha want."

"A pleasure to make your acquaintance, sweet child," the beast replied. Then he began to sidle closer, circling slowly, inspecting her with unnerving delight. "The name is Kilrok. I've been sent to find you. Now, where is the boy?"

Zenobia didn't move. Her blade remained steady. "Why you want to find us for?"

Kilrok paused. His lips peeled back in a ghastly grin, exposing the shimmer of his serrated teeth. The kind of smile that didn't hide his appetite so much as underlined and bolded it. "To eat you, naturally, my darling—"

He pounced.

His tail spearheaded straight for Zenobia, but she parried the stinger with her sword. Her reflexes, swift as lightning, matched her godlike strength. She slashed at Kilrok's head, and though the manticore dodged, it wasn't without injury: his ear bore a shallow, bleeding nick. Infuriated, the beast roared. With a wide, sweeping arc, he lashed his tail. The blow struck her sword, disarming her. It clanged against the fountain, skittered across the platform, and plummeted into the dark waters. Now weaponless, Zenobia pressed her spine against the fountain. Kilrok began to circle her, purring low, swaying side to side like a predator savoring its kill. His red tongue slipped between his lips and slithered across his yellow fangs, moistening them in anticipation.

Zenobia's eyes darted frantically, searching for a way out. Every direction she could bolt to only seemed to lead her straight into the beast's snapping maw, or the venomous point of his tail, or the crushing vice of his claws. Her chest fluttered with something new. Something alien. Fear. The fountain's soft glow intensified against her back. She felt specks of refracted light scatter up her spine, as if urging her to pay attention. She peered at the water. Then back at Kilrok. And in a split-second decision, she dove headfirst into the fountain's pool, submerging herself completely.

———————

Kilrok gave a small chuckle, momentarily amused by her sudden plunge. But seconds ticked by, and she didn't resurface. His smirk faded into a thin, vile line. He lunged toward the fountain, scanning the basin. A low growl rushed from his throat, rippling the reflection of his snarled, repulsive face across the clear surface. He pawed at the surface. Nothing. Just water. Then, even that disappeared. The fountain's waters drained into the marble, as if the stone itself had drunk it down. And with the water gone went the last traces of the light. Kilrok was left alone. Abandoned. Enshrouded in eternal darkness. His growl broke into a burst of protesting laughter. A sound that twisted into a choked, bitter chortle before exploding into a howling roar. It rippled through the void, ricocheting, multiplying, folding back upon itself in a symphony of rage and hatred, a noise so sharp and resonant it could carve stone.

FIFTEEN

WRAPPED IN his burlap garb, Bobby resembled not so much a sack of potatoes as a sack of bungleroot. He sank facedown into the tenebrous waters, his limp limbs sprawled outward, drifting unconsciously. Had he been conscious, he might've reflected on the bleakness of his situation—lost in a nebulous, watery grave at the bottom of an ancient, forgotten cave, in a made-up world known to exist by only one other person... now deceased.

The seabed eventually received him slowly, almost tenderly, as though invisible arms were laying him down for slumber. First, his feet touched. Then his knees. His belly, elbows... Finally, his left cheek pressed into the sandy pillow, stirring a soft cloud of silt that resettled almost immediately.

Soon, flickering blobs of light began to dance in the watery murk. Multicolored orbs—red, white, green, and blue—glided along the ocean floor like a winding strand of Christmas lights. The twinkling, radiant whorls hovered near Bobby's head, brushing against his exposed cheek. Each touch briefly imprinted its hue on his pallid skin before fading back to icy white. Their gentle prodding began to awaken him. A jingling tune filled his ear, eliciting the spirit of Christmas. What kid didn't love Christmas? With all its candy and presents. For Bobby, it meant rocking in his dad's favorite comfy chair—which had, over time, become his favorite comfy chair—and losing himself in the glow of tree lights. Tiny flares of vivid primary colors, glimmering in hypnotic patterns, summoning warmth and wonder to the long, gloomy hours of winter nights and early mornings.

These dreamy musings tugged the corners of his lips upward, and his eyes fluttered open. As he roused from unconsciousness, the alarming sensation of water-filled lungs hit him. He couldn't breathe. He braced for panic, the sort that would normally seize his body into an epileptic fit.

But the panic never came.

The dancing lights frolicked brightly, blinking in sync with the holiday melody, which somehow imparted a strange calm. It dawned on him—almost absurdly—that he didn't need to breathe in this underwater realm. Getting used to the sensation of his chest no longer expanding and contracting, yet his heart pulsing steadily, was unsettling. Nevertheless, he pushed off the seabed, flapping his arms until he rose into an upright float.

The light orbs whisked away, darting toward a distant structure that emerged into sight from the receding shadows: a solitary three-story house, cold and dark, resting against the flat ocean floor. Moonbeams, diffused and wavering, outlined its edges in silver. That glimmer only amplified how dreary and dismal the house looked in the monochrome void.

It took Bobby a moment to recognize the building as his own home. Compelled, he swam after the lights, slogging across the porch and up to his front door just as the orbs ghosted through the walls, carrying the music with them. When he touched the handle and turned the knob, the house's dim exterior erupted into a blazing, festive spectacle. He stepped back, taking in the sudden brilliance. Christmas ornaments, tinsel, and glowing lights adorn every inch of the siding in lustrous colors. A smile appeared across his face. He rushed inside.

It was just as he remembered—except everything was submerged in water and wrapped in an eerie twilight haze. Aside from that, it felt exactly like home. Bobby drifted into the living room, where the only light emanated from a lush Christmas tree. The orbs had gathered there, dancing among the branches, kindling the evergreen into a radiant flare of red, white, green, and blue. An instrumental rendition of *Silent Night* filled the space, ghostly and warm. He floated beside his dad's old comfy chair that sat across from the 8-foot X-mas tree, becoming mesmerized by it. He reached out and touched its needles. They felt bristly and waxy between his fingers. Real.

The Christmas music cut off abruptly. In its place came a sudden *click*— a light flicked on in the adjoining kitchen. The dancing orbs scattered, as if frightened away. The house fell into an eerie dimness and silence once more, save for the pale light coming from the kitchen. A knot formed in Bobby's chest, snaking upward and lodging itself in his throat, then climbing higher still to settle behind his right brow as a dull, throbbing ache.

Dragging his feet, he waded through the shimmering water and rounded the doorway, cautiously poking his head into the kitchen.

His father sat silently at the breakfast table, staring deep into the bottom of his coffee mug, as if searching for the unfathomable truths of the universe, whispered only through the dregs of his morning brew. Bobby should've been thrilled to see him. But the knot behind his brow held any joy hostage. Instead, nausea rolled through him. The house seemed to shift—almost imperceptibly—just off-kilter enough to send his guts haywire.

"Dad?" he finally said, surprised the water didn't muffle his voice in the slightest.

Everett's gaze lifted slowly from his cup and settled on him. For a moment, his eyes looked... lost. As if straining to recognize the timid child before him. Then, his expression softened. His eyes brightened.

"Bobby," he said with a grin, "Look at you. You're practically all grown up." He shook his head in disbelief. "Where does the time fly?"

"Dad? Aren't you... are you a ghost?" Bobby rubbed his forehead as if trying to manually erase the knot of tension behind his eye.

"A ghost?" he repeated, pinching together his brow, seemingly perplexed by the term. Then. "Oh, no. No. I'm no ghost. I'm your father. And I love you." He extended his arms, inviting Bobby closer.

Bobby stayed fixed to his spot, studying his father's outstretched arms, searching for something behind the smile. Then, slowly, he stepped forward, ambling out from the doorway and into the kitchen, stopping just short of the embrace.

Everett let his arms fall back to his sides, his hands resting on his knees, coffee mug still in his hand. "There's no need to be afraid of me," he said softly. "I would never hurt you." Then something changed. His face stiffened. His eyes dropped back to the mug. "Though... I suddenly have the sense... I might have already."

"Dad..." Bobby's voice quivered. "I'm sorry... I... I said those things."

Everett went still. Unsettlingly so. So still, Bobby worried he'd fallen asleep—or worse, that he'd died right there at the table.

Cautiously, Bobby inched closer and nudged his father's arm—

Everett sprang to life. He fumbled hurriedly with a chain around his neck and unclasped it. "Take this," he said, shifting his unfocused eyes from the pendant to his son. Bobby stared down at the tiny gold medallion dangling from his father's rough, swollen fingers. It was no bigger than a dollar coin, embossed with a tiny profile of a tiger in a suit of armor, sword in hand.

"Find the Tiger Knight," Everett said urgently. "He lives in the Feral Forest. Show him this. He will help you get home."

Bobby took the chain, barely grasping what his father was telling him. "Tiger Knight?"

"In the Feral Forest," Everett repeated, helping Bobby fasten the pendant around his neck.

Just then, the house groaned. A tremor ran through it—subtle but enough to rattle them both.

"This is a strange place," Everett muttered, unease rising in his voice. "It's not our home. That's for sure." He gripped Bobby's shoulders with his brutish hands, locking eyes with him—eyes stirring with alarm. "I'm not even sure I'm your real father." As suddenly as he had seized Bobby, he let him go. He turned and dashed out from the kitchen, gliding effortlessly through the water-filled space.

"Dad?" Bobby shouted, pushing forward through the water, fighting the resistance. He caught only a fleeting glimpse of his father as he blurred up the stairs to the second floor.

Bobby rallied his strength and propelled himself up the staircase, laboring against the heavy drag of water. By the time he reached the landing, the attic door had clicked shut.

He stood before it, frozen. His heart lurched in his chest as the knot behind his brow pulsed, spiking into a sharp, stabbing pain. He reached for the brass knob with a trembling hand and, exhaling deeply, turned it. The door swung open. A flurry of floating silver particles swirled in the air. Beyond the dimly lit first step leading to the attic lay an all-consuming darkness.

Bobby stared into it—into that horrifying void. His feet would not move.

The house quaked again, groaning low. A deep vibration that reverberated throughout its slanted walls, steepening the tilt of the floor beneath Bobby's feet. His pulse quickened. Eyes clenched shut, he braced himself against the door jambs, leaning against the angle of the slant to stay upright. When he opened his eyes, a monstrous vision awaited him at the top of the attic steps. The stuff of his darkest nightmares. The giant octopian monster from Tar Lake loomed in the attic's shadows, its skin as white as bleached milk and covered entirely in a rash of red, bloodshot eyes. For the first time, the monster revealed itself in full grotesque glory—its worming mass of tentacles completely visible. All seven and three-quarters of them. Even the nubby one Zenobia had attacked. The tentacles writhed and slithered, reaching downward as if to snatch him.

Bobby squealed, expelling a cloud of bubbles as he scrambled backward. His movements were agonizingly slow in the water.

You are very welcome in my home, the monster intoned, its mental voice chilling as its appearance. *The abyss has plenty of room for you.* Its arms— rubbery and bone white—elongated as they reached toward him. Needing to think so quickly, he barely thought at all. Bobby threw his weight forward and slammed the attic door shut just as the appendages nearly reached him. He leaned into the door, bracing it with all his might. It shuddered violently against his back.

The house let out another low moan, its structure creaking under unseen pressure. The tilt worsened. Furniture, ornaments, plants, and framed photos floated free, spinning into a chaotic swirl around him. The groaning foundation pitched into a rising shriek as the walls shook and cracked. Chunks of ceiling broke loose, crumbling away and drifting off, signaling the house's imminent collapse. The angle of the house betrayed him, now so skewed that the attic door hung dangerously overhead, and gravity itself conspired against him. The door pushed open. Tentacles slipping through the growing gap. Probing. Reaching.

Needing to move fast, Bobby planted his feet against the door, squatted, and launched himself with a powerful kick. The water's buoyancy catapulted him like a torpedo down the hall toward his bedroom. Behind him, the attic door burst open, releasing the aquatic nightmare.

Clutching the doorknob, Bobby struggled to open his bedroom door. A pile of furniture blocked the other side. As the house teetered and shook, the creature surged after him, tentacles flailing in a rapacious bid to seize him. With a determined shove, he wedged the door open just wide enough to squeeze through, narrowly escaping the monster's lunging arms at his heels.

He raced to his window—now effectively the ceiling, thanks to the house's disorienting tilt—and yanked it open, wriggled through like a sailor slipping through a porthole. Once free, he thrashed and kicked with everything he had, desperate to put as much distance as possible between himself and the house. As he ascended, he caught a final glimpse of his home tumbling over the edge of a crumbling cliff, swallowed by a yawning chasm he hadn't noticed before.

His heart pounded from the daring escape. A flush of triumphant pride returned color to his cheeks and warmth to his face. A smug smirk crept across his lips. He relished the image of the monster plummeting into the impenetrable bleakness that stretched endlessly beneath his kicking feet. But the celebration was short-lived. The gulch below widened. The seabed disintegrated into the ever-expanding trenches of oblivion, erasing the ocean floor from sight. He had thought he'd reached the bottom. Now he realized: there was always a deeper low to sink to.

Panic crippled him. The knot over his brow flared with searing heat. The fear of sinking—*tiring, sinking*, slipping into the ever darker abyss so unfathomable his feeble and ignorant mind couldn't comprehend it—consumed him. A vast nothingness waited patiently for his inevitable descent. A sharp pain zipped down the middle of his skull, like his left brain tearing away from his right. Gaps opened in his awareness. Perforations in thought. His cognition leaked, draining into the encroaching void.

He blinked.

And felt a drop in altitude.

Another blink—he lost all sense of direction.

Another—his identity began to slip.

One more—and he felt himself being carried. Sharp elbows jabbing into his ribs, nearly poking through to his heart, as they sailed through the water. Warmth spread across his face. Light blazed—full, brilliant—as the silver glow of the moon intensified. His senses returned, little by little. Was he actually soaring toward the moon? No. The brilliant disk was not the moon. It was the glowing underside of another fountain.

SIXTEEN

THE WATER vomited from Bobby's lungs with a vengeance, splattering onto the dusty marble floor. On hands and knees, he found himself at the center of a rapidly expanding muddy puddle. As the purge seemed to stretch endlessly, Bobby began to fear the cascading torrent from his mouth and nose might never stop. Between the gutwrenching spasms that turned his body into one throbbing muscle, Zenobia placed a gentle hand on his little hunched nape, lending a soothing element to his otherwise agonizing ordeal.

When the retching finally subsided, Bobby collapsed onto his back, wincing with each greedy gulp of air. The atmosphere was dense, filled with drifting particles carrying the nauseating stench of rancid dust and burnt meat. He gagged and coughed, disturbing the choking haze into frenzied swirls, triggering fresh fits of painful spasms.

"I sho thought you were a real gonner," Zenobia said, wringing water from her clothes.

Regaining control, Bobby managed a weak croak, "I...thought...I was, too."

He lifted his bleary eyes, scanning the massive chapel they found themselves in. The cathedral's dome soared overhead, converging at a sharp apex far above. Along one extended wall, a row of towering lancet windows bloomed dimly with somber daylight. Each stained-glass panel told the forgotten tales of heroes and idols he couldn't recognize. Who they were, or why they had been immortalized in this colorful medium—now faded to an almost ethereal render—was a mystery. They were ghostly reflections of a time that perhaps boasted brighter years and more gallant deeds, yet meant nothing to anyone anymore. If these characters and grand exploits had ever truly existed, they'd likely been recast in heavily romanticized versions of themselves. Reality corrupted by creative license, filtered through the lens of the victors, rendered in a more righteous light.

Rose-tinted glasses, Bobby thought. The phrase flashed in his head. An enigmatic saying sparked by the ornate stained glass. He remembered Mrs. Palmer's passionate monologue about the subject.

"The past often feels like a simpler, happier, and more innocent time, but that's bull-fuddy-duddy," her dentures smacked and clicked as she spoke. "Mark my words, Greenbean, there's never been a simple time in history, and there darn well hasn't been one that's wholly innocent. That's all fat fallacies," she spat with conviction. "People get so caught up in nostalgia, always looking back through rose-tinted glasses. Or they're bewitched by the future. Always peering backward or far ahead, so much so that they neglect the present. Children, desperate to be adults, and adults yearning to be kids again. Sure, the *now* often feels like the worst bloody place to be, but it's the only real place that exists," she said, tapping her paintbrush's wooden handle sternly against the fence. "So why not treat it with a little bloody reverence?"

That sentiment—and so many other slogans, axioms, adages, aphorisms, maxims, and catchphrases—crowded Bobby's malleable mind. Implanted there by Mrs. Palmer, his parents, and practically every grown-up he'd ever encountered. Most of the time, he hadn't the slightest idea what any of it meant and had no control over when these expressions might leap from the shadows of his noggin. He figured they must have some meaning, and that one day, his jiggly brain would finally gel some sense of them. But for now, *rose-tinted glasses* still eluded him.

With *his* mind having wandered to the past, a sudden twitch in his right eye snapped him back to the present. He realized his eyes had locked onto Zenobia's back without him meaning to, as she stripped down to her one-piece undergarment, strangling the water from her outer clothes. The soaked fabric clung to her like a second skin, revealing just how delicate her bony frame was. For the first time, he noticed her fragility. How small and frail she really looked. And for some reason, the urge to hold her welled up within him.

Zenobia heard the faint squeak of Bobby rubbing his eye. "I know yer starin'," she said, squeezing out the last drops of water from her tunic before slipping it back on.

"I'm not staring," Bobby protested. "I'm just wondering... where are we?"

Buttoning up her damp—but-no-longer-soaking vest and fastening her belt, Zenobia finally turned to him. Bobby sat slouched against the fountain they'd climbed out of, still dripping wet. The fountain was the exact replica of the one in the cave, adorned with the same statue of the Oracle. But unlike the cave's version, this one held neither fire nor water in its open palms. They were empty. As empty, Zenobia thought, as the answers the Oracle had given her. But above the statue's head was a crest, carved in bold relief. And she recognized it instantly from her books: the emblem of the Holy House of Helcyon—the ancient church. They were standing in the Coronation Hall. The very place where kings of old were crowned beneath sacred arches, before the eyes of saints, spirits, and ancestors alike.

"Reckon we jus' might be smack plum in the middle of the Great Palace of Helcyon," she said.

Straining his wet arms, Bobby pulled himself to his feet. "How did we get here?"

"I imagine thisyer lady-fountain's some kinda portal," she replied, tilting her head back to glare at the marbled face of the Oracle. "You ain't nothin' but a big fat liar!" she shouted up at it.

"Who?" Bobby asked, concern rattling his voice. Thinking she meant him.

"Thisyer stupid Oracle," she seethed. "She don't know diddly 'bout defeat'n the Ashen Knight. And what really gets my goat, she gone'n tol' me if I got ya in that fountain, them answers would come. Well, she clammed right up. The charlatan."

"You tricked me into getting into the fountain?" Bobby squeaked, clearly sounding hurt. "Where that monster was?" His voice rose, shrill with betrayal.

"Whah? Wait—I didn't—Well—She done tol' me it was safe."

"I could have drowned. I did drown. I almost died!" Bobby shouted, spraying water as his head shook in fury.

"But you didn't. An' I saved ya... again," Zenobia said, trying to dislodge her foot from her mouth.

"You didn't save me," Bobby sneered, storming off down the chapel's long nave toward the exit.

Caught between her rising guilt and frustrations, Zenobia called after him: "Where you headin' to? Wait! You say ya faced that beast, too?"

She chased after him. On top of everything else, now she had to deal with Bobby's sensitive nature. Time was short. Lives were at stake. And hurt feelings had no place in a rescue mission. And yet, here she was, following him like a shamed doggy, desperate to make him understand. "I knew you'd be jus' fine. I knew it. Wouldn't let a hair top yer head git hurt. Where ya headin' to?"

"To the Feral Forest," Bobby announced crisply, not breaking stride as they moved from the spacious chapel into the gargantuan breadth of the palace.

"Why the Feral Forest?" she asked, matching his pace but consciously holding herself back to avoid overtaking him. She was more accustomed to her father's long, loping gait.

"I saw my father down there," Bobby wheezed, trying to outpace her, but she easily kept up. "He told me to find the Tiger Knight. Said he's going to help me get home."

"An' what of helpin' me rescue my daddy?"

"I don't think I can help. Sorry. I just want to go home."

"Fine!" she said, clipped and cold. "I aim to rescue my daddy myself— me n'Golly. Oncet we find a way outta thisyer royal dump, we can go our separate ways. Agreed?"

"Agreed," Bobby fired back. "I happily agree!"

Silence cemented between them as they traipsed down vast, reverberating halls and wandered the lavish remains of a palace built for gods more than kings. Room after room stretched on in baroque splendor, now faded, plundered, and hollowed out. The palace was a sprawling labyrinth of decaying opulence, so immense that neither could find a clear path out. Zenobia had never seen such superfluous excess: gilded halls and ballrooms, sweeping marbled staircases, unreasonably high ceilings, and countless columns adorned with flourishing acanthus carvings. But all that grandeur had been touched by rot, underscoring a bygone era of elegance and abundance in bold strokes, now relegated to the relics of time. Accentuating this decline was the relentless spread of Helcyon's hardest weed: the Black Vine. Its woody tendrils crept into every crevice, turning the palace's interior into a dark, overgrown wilderness.

The dull light waned as they aimlessly circled, running into one dead end after another. Zenobia's throat bubbled with curses and cusses at every frustrating turn—until a sudden pealing clang cut through her grumbling. Like startled rabbits, both froze. Only their noses, eyes, and ears dared to move.

"What was that?" Bobby whispered.

The noise grew louder, straining with the sound of something heavy being dragged across stone. Shrill whines and grating grunts bounced throughout the massive banquet hall they now stood at the threshold of.

"Yes, now," cried a voice. "Bring it closer. Closer now. This way. This way now."

Zenobia hissed an unnecessary "shush!" and shoved Bobby flat against the antechamber wall to keep them hidden. She peered around the corner, struggling to pinpoint the source of the commotion amidst the cluttered hall. The marble floor was strewn with mounds of hoarded refuse. A treasure trove of trash piled so high it towered higher than she. A gigantic banquet table dominated the center, cluttered not with food but with swords, armor, and shields, surrounded by chaotic heaps of waste. At the far end of the hall, a grand fireplace—shaped like a yawning lion—roared to life, casting a flickering glow across a small patch of the chamber. Five smaller hearths lined the banquet hall, but their mouths remained dark and cold.

Zenobia narrowed her eyes, focusing on the grisly stack of bones flanking the central hearth. She recoiled. Most appeared to be animal bones, but not all. Some remains were questionable.

"What luck now. What luck. We feast good tonight, brothers," a voice cackled. A smear of bloated shadows slithered across the lofty ceiling and crumbling walls, followed by the things that cast them. Three horrid creatures entered, hunched and malformed. Their spines were crooked and ridged, their bellies swollen, their legs wiry and insect-thin. Wrapped almost entirely in swaths of soiled, mummy-like cloth, they skulked into view. Each with a vulture's head that twitched and bobbed with erratic, jerking motions. Deep-set eyes gleamed with hunger above long, hooked snouts lined with tiny, bony barbs for teeth.

"Ugggh," Zenobia groaned. "Skulvturs. I sho hate Skulvturs."

The lead Skulvtur susurrated commands: "Bring it. Bring it here now." He guided his comrades as they struggled to haul in some unidentifiable mass.

"We do all the work now," one grumbled. "You help us now."

"Lucky for yooes now, that I found this meat. Lucky for yooes now, that I share this meat," the leader hissed in reply.

"But we are brothers," the laboring one protested.

"Lucky for yooes, to be my brothers now."

Zenobia felt Bobby edging beside her, trying to sneak a peek.

"What's a Skulvtur?" he whispered—far too close to her ear. She shoved him back. "They nasty scavengers. The more rotten the meat, the better for 'em." And then, she saw what they were dragging.

Her heart stopped.

"Noooo!" she cried, leaping from her hiding place like an arrow shot from a bow. She flew forward, darting past the banquet table. In one fluid motion, she snatched a rusty sword from the pile of junk and thrust it at the stunned Skulvturs.

"Git away from her, you tar-breeders, or Imma slice you to bits!" she screamed. Her eyes swelled with tears, her chest heaved with rage, and her heart shuddered with grief.

The creatures didn't move. They merely straightened their hunched backs slightly, startled by her sudden charge. The two, laboring over the carcass, released their hold and crept backward. But their leader clutched at his chest with a clawed hand, hissing: "Mine," he screeched, "I found it. I own it now."

———————

BOBBY SHOOK HIS head, realizing that the animal they'd hauled in was no ordinary one—it was Golly.

"That's my friend!" Zenobia bawled, swinging her blade in wide, threatening arcs mere inches from the creatures. "You vile monsters! You killed my Golly!"

The Skulvturs scuttled backward. "We did not kill it now. Only found it as is now," the leader explained.

"We know nothing of it being your friend now," the second Skulvtur added. The third one said nothing, communicating only through the rapid clatter of its beak as it nodded in agreement.

As soon as they backed off far enough, Zenobia dropped to her knees beside Golly. She draped her arms over the cow's neck and buried her face in the matted fur, near three deep gashes raked into Golly's side. Slashing wounds from powerful claws.

From his concealed position, Bobby struggled to keep eyes on her. Her sobs shook the air, thick with palpable waves of woe. Something anchored the corners of his mouth down toward his constricting chest. His heart, burdened by her grief, which seemed to carry a tangible gravity, as if the sheer force of her sorrow could pull his heart into his guts. Her broken heart reminded him of a black hole, its pull irresistible. He knew the terrifying effects of black holes from his short-lived obsession with them, before his mom banned him from the internet. The idea of being swallowed by her overwhelming sadness distressed him. For a split second, he considered slipping away. To leave her behind and find his own way out. But quickly abandoned his desertion plan. He caught a twitch of movement: the lead Skulvtur casting covert glances with the others. Bobby's pulse spiked. The trio sprang into action in a dash, skittering off to arm themselves.

―――――――――

Zenobia released gut-wrenching sobs onto her friend's cold corpse, barely registering Bobby's shrill cry behind her.

"They're gonna kill you!"

Her face transformed, burning with vitriolic rage. She seized the sword she had laid beside her and lunged at the Skulvturs with a roaring scream. The creatures instantly dropped their plundered weapons in a clattering panic and screeched for mercy.

"P-Please don't kill us now. We mean no harm now," the leader stammered.

"Only protect ourselves now," the second one added hastily.

All three stooped to a low bow, submitting to her blade.

Sword still raised, she gave serious contemplation to ending them right then and there. But after a moment, her voice seething with disdain, she snarled: "Git! Before I make bird stew of y'all."

The leader kept darting glances between the rusted blade and her fallen friend. "We regret your loss now... but she's dead now. No longer any good to you now. But we can benefit. We're starving now."

"No!" Zenobia's voice cracked like thunder. She raised her sword higher, threatening to bring it slicing down upon them. The Skulvturs immediately dropped lower, their heads nearly scraping the ground. "Over my dead body will y'all feast on her," she vowed. Then swung her blade in a sharp motion to drive them off. "Now, git!"

"Yes now," the leader croaked.

"Now!" she barked again. "Before I change my mind."

"Of course now. Right away," the second chimed in, eager to comply.

All three Skulvturs, including the silent one, hastily stepped backward, their heads still bowed low. Once they reached a safe distance, they spun on their gnarled heels and fled, their clawed footsteps clacking as they vanished into the corridor.

Zenobia only lowered her blade once the clacking of their retreat faded. As she relaxed her stance, she caught sight of Bobby ambling toward her. "I shoulda-oughta ended them nasty creatures," she muttered.

"Maybe they were telling the truth... about not having anything to do with Golly's—"

"I don't care none," she bit out, cutting him off. With a heavy sigh, she knelt beside Golly again. Her poor, beautiful pet—the most gorgeous, innocent, and loving creature she'd ever known, aside from her parents—lay so still. So cold, even with the fire nearby. Her big brown eyes were now lifeless and dark. Her tongue, limp, lolled from her mouth, never to graze on another blade of grass; her sole passion. Zenobia felt her heart bleed for her friend. All she wanted to do was hold her tight and never let go.

As night progressed, the sky deepened into an even darker shade of crimson. The passage of time became irrelevant to Zenobia. She sat consumed by her pain, barely noticing the world around her, not even Bobby, who lingered close by. Her focus remained on Golly, her hand gently stroking the cow's neck as she whispered words of remorse into her beloved friend's ear.

———————

BOBBY'S CLOTHES WERE dry at last, but the air had grown colder. Even crouched dangerously close to the fire, an icy chill pierced straight through to his bones. With his unwinking eye—the ever-vigilant one—he kept close watch on Zenobia, afraid that she'd wholly been sucked into an inert state by her pulsing black hole, ripping away any urgency to save her father. He knew he couldn't stay here forever. But the thought of leaving her behind didn't sit right either.

Suddenly, a sound from the far end of the hall caught his attention. A disjointed hissing—inhale, exhale—susurrated from behind one of the arched doorways. The crooked beak of a Skulvtur emerged, making Bobby flinch. It sampled the air with sharp sniffs and snorts before receding back into the shadows. Faint whispers followed. Too soft for him to decipher. Shooting a glance at Zenobia, he saw she was oblivious to the commotion. Her forehead rested gently against Golly's shoulder.

Bobby rose and padded over to the banquet table. He surveyed the scattered weapons and gear, settling on a sword that looked light enough for him to handle. Inching toward the source of the sibilant murmurs, he sprang around the corner, hoping to catch whatever was there off guard.

"Be still, you beasts. Or I'll cut you," Bobby warned, thrusting the sword threateningly close to the Skulvturs. The three creatures cowered, shielding their gaunt faces with clawed hands.

"We are not beasts now. Kill us not," pleaded the leader. "We are beings, like you now."

Bobby stiffened, surprised by the odd surge of power he felt wielding the weapon. Something about the sword made him feel taller, more in control. "I thought you were told to leave."

"This is our home now," the leader said, with the others nodding in agreement. "You are in our home now."

"Did you kill Golly?"

"Who now?" asked the second, his dark eyes flicking nervously toward the others.

"The cow. Did you kill the cow?"

The three Skulvturs fervently shook their heads.

"No. We only found the meat as is now. Dead," said the leader, his tone almost apologetic. "It took great effort to get it here now. What do we eat now? We're starving now."

Bobby lowered the sword, not as a gesture of trust, but because his arm was simply tired. With a sigh, he rummaged through the bulky pockets of his garb. To his surprise, his fingers found what he'd been searching for. He pulled out a small, twisted root and held it out for the Skulvturs to see. They stared at it with utter confusion.

"Well, take it," Bobby prompted.

Hesitantly, the leader reached out and lifted the root delicately from Bobby's palm. "What is it, now?" he asked, genuinely stumped.

"It's bungleroot," Bobby replied. Seeing their continued bewilderment, he clarified, "It's food."

As the other two looked on cluelessly, the leader tentatively brought the root to his beak. His slimy black tongue slid out and prodded the root cautiously before snapping off a piece. He gagged almost immediately, retching violently and spitting the morsel onto the floor.

"Poison! You try to poison us now," he spat accusingly.

"That's not true!" Bobby said, his head shaking with offense.

With a mix of fear and anger, the Skulvtur hurled the root, but it traveled only a short distance before skidding to a stop at Zenobia's feet. She stood poised, every inch of her brimming with menace, arms flexed, fists balled. Her icy glare radiated such wrath that the Skulvturs involuntarily huddled together in terror. Seeing their intense dread, Bobby felt an unexpected twinge of empathy. Almost wishing, absurdly, that he could huddle with them for comfort.

"I done tol' you bird-brains to scram," Zenobia growled.

"This is our—" the leader began, but his defiance faltered. His voice cracked. "Ho—home n—now. Y—you should—"

Zenobia lunged.

But before she could strike, Bobby stepped in—surprising even himself.

He raised his arms, placing himself between her and the trembling creatures. "Maybe we should go," he said gently, his stance wide, protective. "We still have to rescue your dad."

Zenobia froze. Her glare moved from the Skulvturs to Bobby. "Without Golly... there ain't no way to git to my daddy in time," she said. The fire in her dimmed. It was clear in her posture. Her shoulders slumped, as though vital cords holding her together had been severed. Her resolve unraveled. Head bowed, she uttered, "Even the darn Feral Forest is too far to git to."

"Feral Forest?" the leader perked up. "I know a shortcut now. Yes. A secret door that will take you to the Feral Forest in only a few steps now."

Bobby and Zenobia shot the Skulvtur skeptical glances.

The Skulvtur raised his head, tilting his nose upward, chin lifted in a mock-proud posture, as if sensing he finally had leverage.

Zenobia didn't mince words. "How? Spill it, scavenger."

The Skulvtur spread his beak in a grotesque grin. "Karcass is my name now."

Losing her patience, Zenobia sprang forward, snatching Bobby's sword, and pressed its razor-edge to the Skulvtur's throat. "Yer liable to be a carcass, lickety-split, if ya don't explain yerself. With yer vile kin feastin' on yer rotten guts."

Karcass tucked his beak toward his chest and lowered his eyes, gulping audibly.

Before things could escalate, the second Skulvtur blurted out: "He means the Ingress now."

"Ingress?" Bobby repeated, hopeful. "What's an Ingress?"

"It's a portal now. And I am named Predtork now. Yes." Predtork said, nodding earnestly. "You enter, and you'll be in the Feral Forest. No need for weeks, just steps now."

"Where's it at?" Zenobia pressed, her patience clearly thinning.

Karcass, perhaps sensing a shift, gestured past her toward Golly. "Yes. We shall show you now. But it stays behind now. Yes?"

Zenobia's fury returned with a vengeance, her voice trembling with rage. "Ain't no way in heck she'll be a meal for yer pus-bellies. I aim to bury her proper!"

Karcass inched closer, trying to appear conciliatory. "Yes, do what you like now. But we'll find the mea—the Golly—anyway now. Our noses are very good now. Why not spare us the work? You get your shortcut now, and we get... sustenance. Isn't that fair now?" He attempted a compassionate look, his brow creasing clumsily. "We respect your friend now. But she's gone. If not to us now, then the worms and critters underground will claim her now. It is the way of things. Yessss?" The protracted hiss lingered like a shrill ring in the ear.

Bobby studied Zenobia, trying to gauge her next move—but she remained inscrutable, her hardened eyes fixed on some distant point, lost in deep contemplation.

After a prolonged silence, Bobby ventured, "I bet the Tiger Knight can help us save your dad."

Zenobia didn't answer right away. Instead, she turned to Golly, kneeling once more beside her fallen friend. She clung to her with an embrace filled with immeasurable love and grief.

After what felt like an interminable amount of time, Bobby and the fidgety Skulvturs stood watching Zenobia's back in uneasy anticipation. Bobby felt a sudden urge to ask the third Skulvtur, "What's your name?" The creature looked at him, stunned, as if shocked that anyone would think to ask.

"Karnvor, is his name now," Predtork answered for him. "He cannot speak now. Bit off his own tongue now. Swallowed it."

Bobby nodded slowly, unsettled. Then the silence returned, restless, antsy, stretched thin as they all watched Zenobia, still kneeling beside Golly, petting her with care.

Then, without turning or meeting their eyes, her voice rang out, clear and commanding: "Show us!"

The Skulvturs gave a brief, excited chitter—quickly silenced by Zenobia's sharp: "Now!" They fumbled into motion, scuttling off in a clacking hurry. Heads bowed low, bobbing in rhythm with their hunched backs—a posture bent from a lifetime of sniffling and scouring the ground for rotten dead things to satiate their voracious appetites.

Chasing the quick-footed scavengers, Bobby and Zenobia moved across the palace grounds, lit by the eerie crimson glow of the night. They passed through once-magnificent gardens, now overgrown and lifeless. An expansive flora that had once been the jewel of this estate now stood like everything else in the palace: a ghostly impression, a haunting reminder of a lost opulence.

Their hurried pace led them to the very edge of the property, where towering wrought-iron gates marked the entrance to a sprawling thirteen-foot-high hedge maze.

"Just through there now," Karcass said, smacking his beak. "The Ingress is just through there now."

Bobby took in the massive hedge wall, stretching endlessly in both directions.

"Looks like one of those garden mazes," he remarked.

"It sho is," Zenobia confirmed.

As she began to caution the Skulvturs with a "You better be right...", she abruptly clamped her mouth shut, noticing the three creatures already darting into the distance, hustling back to the palace.

"Wow," Bobby said, struck by their surprising nimbleness. "They're fast for feeble-looking things." He turned back to Zenobia, catching the fury simmering behind her clenched jaw. "I'm real sorry about Golly."

"I don't wanna talk 'bout it none, you hear?" she said evenly, her eyes fixed on the fleeing scavengers until they vanished into the shadows of the palace gardens.

Wordless, she pivoted and strode through the ornate iron gates, disappearing into the depths of the hedge maze.

Bobby drew a long, measured breath. He flicked his bangs from his eyes and exhaled a heavy sigh. His heart ached for Zenobia. She had as much bad luck as he did. Unless... it was all his bad luck spilling over onto her. He tucked his head into his shoulders and sank his hands deep into his rough pockets. Then trudged onward, bracing for the many more terrible things sure to come.

SEVENTEEN

**IKE EVERYTHING** in this bizarre place, Bobby reflected, progress was maddeningly slow. Hours—perhaps days, maybe even years—seemed to pass as they ambled through the towering boxwood hedges. Thirteen feet high, the walls formed a maze of endless twists and turns. Each five-foot-wide pathway looked exactly like the last, and Bobby began to wonder if they were just retracing their steps in a ceaseless loop. It might not have been years. Or even days. But the weight of time was undeniable on Bobby's weary feet.

The hedge walls of the maze were sculpted to a sharp precision. Every bush was the same unnatural blue. Uniform in hue and form, not a single leaf out of place. Their glossy, waxy finish gave them an uncanny, almost plastic-like appearance. From the moment they'd entered this topiary puzzle, a dense fog hung low, blanketing the top of the hedges and turning the sky into a flat, nebulous ceiling of gray.

A flurry of questions buzzed through Bobby's mind. *Who does the gardening for this vast maze? How do they find their way in and out and not get lost? Do they have a blue thumb? And the gardening tools—are they anything like his mother's tools, stored in their little red shed?*

Trailing behind Zenobia, weaving through the monotonous corridors, Bobby blurted, "Does this thing ever end?" He felt as if he were starting to lose his grip on his sanity. Zenobia didn't answer. Motoring at quite the clip, she slipped around the corner at a T-junction and vanished from view. Bobby sighed and followed, entering yet another corridor identical to the one before it. Except... something was different.

Just a few feet ahead, Zenobia stood transfixed, staring at an anomaly. A full suit of armor rested on the grass, propped casually against the hedge, like it had decided to sit down for a breather and never gotten back up. Its right gauntlet still clung to a sword, the blade stabbed upright into the turf.

"That's strange, right?" Bobby said, breaking the silence. "Someone just leaving their suit of armor like that."

Zenobia edged closer, squinting for a more intimate inspection. "Yep," she nodded, "Seems like they gone left their bones, too."

"What?" Bobby hurried forward, coming up beside her and peering into the cobwebbed helmet, where a small white skull sat nestled within. The bonehead's hollow sockets seemed to stare back at him, and its jaw hung open, as if equally shocked to see them.

"That's not good," Bobby declared.

"Nope. It ain't," Zenobia agreed.

They cautiously navigated around the steel-clad skeleton, careful not to jostle its sprawled metallic limbs. The idea of disturbing the dead knight might've been silly, but a whispering voice in Bobby's head kept repeating: *what if, what if, what if it wakes up at the slightest touch?* In Helcyon, it seemed anything was possible.

Once they rounded the next bend, they pressed on—steadfast and brisk— along the unending, uniform hedges that came and went, came and went, each path mockingly mirroring the last, no matter the direction they chose. They treaded tirelessly, with no real sense of progress. Hours seemed to pass before they encountered another suit of armor positioned eerily similar to the first, resting on the grass in the exact same pose. They tiptoed past and forged ahead. But soon enough, another armored figure, casually seated on the grass, back against the hedge, legs splayed, one hand tightly clasped to its sword.

"Is it the same one?" Bobby asked, anxiety creeping into his voice. "Are we going in circles?"

Zenobia huffed a breath and leaned in, studying the knight's armor closely. Her brow wrinkled in concentration. After a long moment, she straightened and shrugged. "It's hard to tell directly."

Their initial caution for the knightly dead was visibly waning. They now hopped over the outspread metallic limbs without hesitation and carried on at pace. Not long after—in shortening intervals—they came upon yet another seated skeleton in armor. Zenobia, her patience thinning fast, gave it a swift kick. The figure, more fragile than it appeared, crumbled in a clattering jumble of metal and bone. "There," she said, brushing her hands, "now we'll know if we're goin' in circles."

But when they encountered the next knight—still upright, still pristine, still in its exact pose—Zenobia threw up her hands. "Thisyer is gettin' mighty ridiculous."

"What does it mean?" Bobby asked, rubbing the stubborn knot still lodged above his brow, which had started throbbing again.

"Means someone's havin' a right-good time messin' with us," she said, giving this one a hard kick too. It scattered into a shimmering heap of broken bones and armor. The sword wobbled for a moment, then toppled with a metallic *clang* onto the pile.

"We're never getting out of here, are we?" Bobby's voice trembled. "Those things tricked us. We're trapped in here!" He began pacing, panic creeping into his steps.

Zenobia watched him for a beat, then stepped forward, determination stirring in her eyes. Bobby was somewhat glad to see her fortitude return. He stopped pacing.

She crouched low and clapped her hands. "Hop on my shoulders."

"What?"

"Imma lift you up. Take a peek over them hedges. See if we're anywhere close to an exit. Or how far this mess stretches."

Taking her cue, Bobby placed his foot in her braced hands. "Okay." He nodded.

Zenobia stood—almost too fast—and Bobby teetered, flailing until he found his balance by grabbing hold of her tangled hair, yanking it like reins on a bucking bull.

"Ouch!" Zenobia winced. "Stan' on my shoulders. Use 'em hedges to steady yerself, dummy. Not my hair."

"Sorry," Bobby murmured, adjusting himself as he reached for the brambles instead. Even with the boost, the top of the hedge loomed just out of reach. Zenobia grabbed the underbelly of his boots and hoisted him even higher, stretching her arms up and rising onto her tiptoes. Bobby clawed toward the summit—so close now—but it still eluded him, a few teasing inches beyond his grasp.

"Anythang?" Zenobia called from beneath him.

"I can't reach the top," he reported, still grappling with the thick brambles.

"Ahh, geese," Zenobia bleated, then promptly lowered Bobby, nearly planting him on his butt instead of his feet. "Gotta do everythang myself." She lunged at the hedge, tackling it like she had the mountain, clawing her way upward. But the deceptive height mocked her efforts. No matter how well she climbed, the top just kept stretching ever higher.

Bobby had taken a seat, crossed-legged on the ground, idly plucking the pruned grass and flicking the blades aside in quiet contemplation.

Eventually, Zenobia dropped back down, a little breathless and disheartened. She rested her hands on her hips and exhaled sharply.

"I reckon them vile maggot-eaters done tricked us."

Bobby was clearing a patch of grass when he gasped, watching it regrow instantly. "Is this maze… magical?" he asked.

"Magical?" Zenobia repeated, as if he'd spoken a foreign word.

"Yeah, magical. You know, like magic."

Zenobia gave him a look, half squint, half-side-eye, that suggested she thought he might've cracked something loose in that nob of his.

"You know… Like… making stuff happen with a wave of a wand. Or mashing words together into weird phrases. 'Abracadabra!'" He waved his hands in the air dramatically.

Zenobia's expression didn't change. If anything, she looked more confused than ever.

Bobby suddenly questioned how much he really knew about magic. He wasn't like other kids who devoured fantasy books. He preferred science books. The real stuff. Fantasy? That had always been more his dad's thing. Bobby was drawn to the complexities of reality, even though they often left him feeling more lost than enlightened. Maybe that's why he pursued understanding them so much. A quest that may have led his mother to cut off his internet privileges. She told him, "Too much reality isn't healthy for someone your age. Too much reality can break you." She always talked about balance. Life needed both reality and imagination. It was as vital, she said, as a varied diet. But she was clear on one thing: don't confuse the two. Too much of either isn't good for the mind. Or the heart. As those thoughts swirled in his head, Bobby felt just as lost as he did the first time his mother tried to explain this fragile line between reality and fantasy.

Zenobia's fingers snapped an inch from Bobby's nose, jolting him from his musings.

"Hey," she said, her tone stern. "Did yer brain fall outta yer mouth?"

Bobby noticed the dryness in his open mouth and shut it.

"C'mon, git up," she urged.

In her hands, Bobby saw the gleam of the knight's pristine sword. How long had he been lost in thought?

"What you gonna do with that?" he asked, swallowing to wet his throat.

"Imma chop plum through thisyer dumb maze," she declared. Without further ado, Zenobia raised the broadsword and swung. She hacked at the hedge with fierce determination, slashing and carving until a rough path opened just wide enough for her to push through.

Bobby scrambled to his feet, eager not to be left behind. The path Zenobia had carved was surprisingly deep, resembling a tunnel more than the thickness of a typical maze bush. But then again, what was ever typical in this place? He squeezed his soft form through the narrow passage. The hedge bristled and flexed around him, the clipped branches seeming to twist and undulate as he moved. Glancing over his shoulder, Bobby's stomach dropped. The opening was sealing shut behind him. The hedge was *healing*—mending itself.

"It's growing back!" he screamed. "I'm gonna get stuck in here!" As the living hedge tightened around him, fresh tendrils wreathed forward, constricting his path, clawing at him. He chopped at them with his hand, tore, and kicked, but barely made a dent. Sweat poured from his brow, stinging his eyes, mingling with hot tears of panic. "Help!" he cried. "Zenobia!" No answer. No sign of her. Just ahead, a faint glow marked what might've been the exit—but the hedge was already closing it off. The branches bit into his clothing and skin, eager to bridge the gap cleaved into them, even if it meant impaling Bobby in the process. Trapped and trembling, Bobby screamed again. "Help! Help me!"

With a swift motion, Zenobia's hand burst through the brush, seized Bobby by the collar, and yanked him forward with force. As she dragged him free, the brambles lashed out, desperate to keep their prey, leaving deep, stinging scratches across his face. Amid the havoc, the sound of breaking twigs filled his ears, and Bobby silently prayed the cracking wasn't coming from his own bones.

Then, all at once, he was free. He tumbled onto the manicured lawn, rolling to a stop on his rear. Stunned, he sat facing the hedge he'd barely escaped. The last bit of the opening sealed shut. The living barrier was once again an unbroken wall of blue.

"Imma keep tally on how many times I saved yer butt," Zenobia said, smirking.

Still trembling, Bobby pointed to the hedge. "That's... magic. Bad magic."

Zenobia gave the hedge a thoughtful squint. "Hmm," she turned back to Bobby, shrugged. "Well, magic ain't all that special. C'mon. I reckon we found the Ingress."

Before them lay the heart of the maze: a long grassy corridor enclosed by the thirteen-foot boxwood hedges. At either end stood a door. One was a slab of polished black stone. Sharp-edged, rectangular, and gleaming like obsidian. Opposite was a rounded wooden oak door, ornately crafted with forest creatures and delicate chiselwork.

"Two doors," Bobby observed.

"Yupp," Zenobia affirmed the obvious.

Bobby climbed to his feet, flinching as he touched the scratches on his face. He wiped a thin trickle of blood from his cheek with his sleeve.

"Which one do you think goes to the Feral Forest?"

Zenobia studied both options, then pointed toward the oak door and strode toward it with purpose. "I reckon thisyer wooden door be the one."

Bobby didn't follow. "Maybe. Or maybe not," he said, lingering. "It could be a trick. Or a test."

As Zenobia approached the door, she tightened her grip on the sword, prepared for whatever might be lurking behind it. But when she swung it open, there was nothing but a long wooden tunnel, warm and hollow like the inside of a fallen tree.

She relaxed her stance and glanced back at Bobby. "Not everythang is a test or trick," she said, a hint of mystery in her voice. Then boldly traversed the threshold, stepping inside.

"Wait," Bobby yelled. But she was already gone. "Geesh," he breathed, shaking his head and muttering to himself: "My mom warned me about chasing after girls. But this is ridiculous." Brushing his shaggy hair out of his eyes, he stepped inside, too.

———————

BOBBY TRAILED A few steps behind Zenobia in silence, the tunnel stretching endlessly ahead. Helcyon, he mused, was just one monotonous stretch after another, and frankly, not even slightly amusing. In the muffled quiet of the massive log, he could hear her breathing, as crisp as his own. He could even swear he heard the faint drumming of her heartbeat. Was it fear? Or just her usual rhythm? Despite her size, she moved with the intensity of someone who had fire in her veins. She probably needed a strong heart just to pump that kind of fury. If Zenobia were an animal, Bobby thought, she'd be a dragon.

Did his father put dragons in Helcyon?

He couldn't remember.

Dim, waxy candles lined the tunnel's concave walls, flickering to life only as they passed. Each sparked a flame as they approached, then snuffed out again behind them, casting a moving halo of light that revealed only a few steps forward and back. Were these candles magical? Bobby wondered. Or just this world's version of motion-triggered lights, like the ones in fancy hospital bathrooms that flicked on when you walked in, then darkened after you left. To him, those weren't magical, just engineered. Maybe the candles, like so many other seemingly enchanted things in Helcyon, were the same. Just the mechanisms he didn't understand yet.

Curiously, the flames gave off a campfire scent. It tugged at a memory: a camping trip with his parents the week before his father's last tour. The distinctive scent of charred wood ruminated in his nostrils, lingering in a way that pulled the past to the surface, summoning that almost-forgotten weekend when he'd been nothing but a tantrum-prone burden. Blatantly discarding any interest in family traditions. Showing no reverence for the outdoors.

The last candle ignited with a sharp snap, casting sudden light on a round wooden door, marking the tunnel's end. The two paused, exchanged a silent nod of encouragement, and then Zenobia pushed it open. Outside, though brighter, the world remained cloaked in dusk. They stepped into the dense thicket dominated by strange trees. Tall brown trunks wrapped in what looked, to Bobby, like shaggy fur. Above, their branches unfurled into a wide canopy of feathery blue leaves.

Bobby reached out to touch one of the fuzzy trunks, astonished by its softness. "It's... fur?" he said, brushing his fingers along it like he was petting a giant animal. "It's really fur."

Zenobia shot him a cautionary glance. "Best to mind what you touch round these parts," she warned. "Some thangs look harmless but liable to be real dangerous."

Bobby quickly retracted his hand. "I thought you said not everything was a trick?"

"Not everythang is. But bein' in a place as strange 'n' wild as the Feral Forest, best to stay on yer toes."

"You think you know everything, don't you?" he grumbled, wiping his palm on his pant leg.

"I ain't claim to know it all. But I likely know a thang or two more than you 'bout thisyer place."

Flustered, Bobby stammered, "Well... yeah, well..." Stumped for a satisfying retort, he was grateful when Zenobia hushed him.

"Hush now." She suddenly dropped into a crouch. Her eyes sharpened, locking onto the faint sound of distant drumming. She motioned for Bobby to get down.

"What's that?" he whispered, awkwardly bending at the waist instead of squatting.

"Reckon there's only one way to find out."

She sprang up and dashed toward the noise, sword in hand—the one she'd taken from the armored corpse.

"But...," Bobby began, only to watch her hightail it through the trees, swift and fearless. He shook his head again at her constant impulse to rush into danger without a second thought.

"It's only a matter of time before you'll be chasing girls straight into trouble." His mother's voice reverberated through the gray jelly of his noggin.

At the time, he asked, "Are girls that dangerous?"

"No," she'd said. "It's just boys are that dumb."

Back then, the idea of chasing girls had seemed absurd, and the idea of girls chasing him? Even more ridiculous. Why had his mom been so harsh on boys anyway? He chalked it up to adult baggage, filtered down through parental advice. Suddenly, a pang twisted in his gut. He missed her. The ache sank him into a squat as he imagined her face. Is she looking for me now? he wondered. Is she worried? Does she even know I'm gone? Or has she already moved on, relieved to save on counseling bills?

Zenobia slipped farther from view. Bobby shook off the thoughts and moved. Chasing after her despite his mother's warnings. Despite how dumb he might be. Still, he chased her, despite the troubles ahead.

EIGHTEEN

THE VAST halls of the Great Palace of Helcyon reverberated with the discordant sounds of belches and burps. Predtork picked bits of fur between his crooked and blackened gnashers with a talon. The Skulvturs—armed with claws perfect for stripping meat from bone—now contentedly stroked their bloated bellies.

"All thanks to me now, brothers," Karcass boasted with a healthy belch. "Thanks to me, we feasted good tonight now."

"Yes, yes. You need not brag now," Predtork muttered, flicking a bone into the fire. A flurry of sparks leapt into the air.

"I believe the gratitude for your meal, gents..." a silky golden voice unfurled from the surrounding darkness, "...belongs to me."

BOO!

Suddenly lit by the firelight was the grinning face of the manticore.

The Skulvturs scrambled to the far side of the fire in a frenzy.

"There's no need to fear me..." Kilrok purred. His massive leonine form slid from the shadows just beyond the firelight and prowled closer to the flames, revealing sleek black fur and a muscular frame flexing with predatory ease. "You're too greasy and gamey for my taste."

The Skulvturs tensed, ready to bolt.

"You cannot escape me," Kilrok warned, his voice deepening to a growl. "Your foul odor betrays your every move. So there's no need to even try."

"We won't run now," Karcass said, poking his head out from their craven huddle.

"We thank you with humbleness for our meal now," Predtork added.

Karnvor, the silent third of the scavenger trio, nodded in frantic agreement, the rattle of his skull suggesting a tiny brain bouncing inside.

Kilrok's grin widened, lips peeling back to reveal a mouthful of keen, flesh-tearing daggers. He leaned toward the fire, casting great plumes of shadow up into the vaulted ceiling. "Now... have any of you seen a young redhead and her rotund friend?"

"Yes," Karcass shrieked. "We've seen them now."

"We know where they are now," chirped Predtork.

Karnvor nodded even harder, whole body rattling with eagerness.

Kilrok leaned in closer, unfazed by the flames licking at his dark fur. His shadow devoured its light. The Skulvturs huddled tighter, their wide, beady eyes fixed on his gleaming yellow stare.

"Now... tell me where they are."

NINETEEN

BENEATH THE Dragoon Keep, a primordial rage toiled and frothed from deep below. The fortress had been erected atop this tumultuous foundation, which, from time to time, unleashed roaring tremors that threatened its very pillars. As the lunar eclipse of the Blood Moons neared its perfect syzygy, these outbursts grew more frequent and more ferocious. Much of Helcyon had managed to suppress this ancient ire with layers of cool, insulating clay. But Fire Mountain stood as the lone exception. It served as a vent, a wound that led directly to the fiery core of Helcyon's storming soul, the nexus of its wrath. The Ingress of Dies Redux, crafted by clandestine Helcyonites epochs before the rise of Dragoon Keep, had been designed to pacify this eternal fury and douse its fires, empowered by the same otherworldly alignment of the Blood Moons.

Hulmick slapped a palm to his forehead and dragged it down the length of his gaunt face.

Slimsy paused his animated history lesson, noting his captive audience's evident disinterest. "This should be of some interest to you, you know," Slimsy remarked.

"I'm tired. I'm starving. And I've lost the will to go on. In short," Hulmick said bitterly. "I just don't care." He flung up his arms in exasperation and slumped onto the meager straw bedding that barely cushioned the corner of his cell.

"C'mon now…" Slimsy strolled over and gave him an encouraging nudge. "You mustn't lose your will to live. What about your daughter? Don't you want to keep fighting for her?"

Hulmick's eyes flashed. "Don't you dare speak of my daughter," he spat. He lunged. His long, bony fingers snatched Slimsy by the neck and began to throttle it. "Why won't you leave me be?" he spat. "Your constant jabbering is insufferable. I'd rather pierce my ears with a blade and pluck out my eyes than endure another moment in your company."

Slimsy's already bulbous eyes bugged out even farther as Hulmick's hands tightened. Their sparkle flickered—then shorted out—as his face drained of color.

The air crackled, dropping to a sudden frost.

The red mist of Nex materialized, swirling around them.

"Release the Dazzelf," Nex commanded in a dark whisper.

With a forceful shove, Hulmick let go, swatting Slimsy away in a desperate bid to rid himself of the pest. Then he retreated to his corner, drew his knees to his chest, and cradled himself. "Get him outta here," he shouted, madness quivering in his voice. "Take him away!"

Nex hovered above them. Its pristine skull bore deathly hollows, staring down with a gaze as cold and empty as oblivion itself. Hulmick couldn't help but study the unfathomable pits in the specter's face—abysses that glared back with the all-consuming emptiness of eternal vacuity, where memory and meaning dissolved beneath the erasure of cosmic absence. In the face of that gaze, all life seemed pitiful. Trivial.

Hulmick inhaled sharply when Nex's dreadful focus shifted away from him, turning instead to Slimsy, who lay coughing and gasping.

"It is time," Nex intoned. Then, like smoke scattering on the wind, Nex evaporated into the ether, taking the bitter cold with it, restoring the suffocating heat.

Slimsy coughed weakly, managing to pull a steady breath. "You hurt my feelings," he rasped. "I'm trying to help you see. To help you understand what this is all about. But you won't listen. You refuse to learn."

Hulmick's voice cracked with resignation. "What good is knowing the reason for my doom? How's that help me? I'm still doomed!"

"Yeah. Foresight's a cruel joke," Slimsy said, rubbing his throat. "Knowing your end when you can't do diddly-squat about it." He pushed himself to his feet. "Fate's only a gift for the lucky few. And that ain't us." Slimsy shuffled forward, offering a hand. "Now, come on. We must go."

Hulmick scowled at Slimsy. "I don't know if you're trying to help or not. But I'm not going anywhere." Hulmick curled himself into a tight ball, squeezing his eyes shut. "You can't trick me if I can't see anything to be tricked by," he muttered, tucking his head against his knees. Engulfed in darkness, he waited for some ploy or trick, anything from Slimsy. But nothing came, only a slow, encroaching stench of burnt tar, thick and noxious. The smell was strong enough to make him want to reel back and gag, but he held steadfast, grinding his face harder into his knees. Slimsy's silence gnawed at him. What was the deceitful Dazzelf plotting? Hulmick's impulse was to peek—but no. He pressed his lids tighter. "Bet you wished you could close your eyes to the world, don't you?" Hulmick taunted, hoping to goad Slimsy into betraying his scheme. No reply. "Hey, you gasbag! Why aren't you saying anything?"

Still nothing.

Only muffled groans and distant hisses; a mountain seemingly being awakened. Had Slimy deserted him? The air swelled around him, stifling and merciless. Sweat poured from every pore, only to sting his face as it vaporized into searing steam. When the heat became unbearable, akin to feeling his eyeballs beginning to boil inside their sockets, Hulmick could endure no more. He pried his eyes open—

—and found himself no longer in his cell. He was somewhere else. Somewhere worse. An unholy cavern yawned before him. Stalactites and stalagmites jutted from the ceiling and floor like monstrous tusks. The air rippled, causing the entire cave to writhe as living things.

He was bound to an iron throne that floated on jets of steam, flowing up through the cracked bedrock. Molten lava bubbled from these crevices, radiating a fever heat and painting the cavern in a searing orange glow. Hulmick squirmed against the restraints. A metal clasp pinned his head to the rigid, straight-back frame. His arms and legs were shackled, locked tight.

"Porter, our almighty Lord, please help me," he begged, tears evaporating off his cheeks as he spoke.

From the haze stepped a blackened figure. "The man you invoke," grated a fried voice from its scorched throat, "holds no interest in your fate. Why waste breath on futile prayers?" The knight's charred bulk moved into view, shadowed by a creeping mist. A red fog coalescing into the shape of Nex. But this time, Nex brought no cooling chill.

"Please," Hulmick implored, fear ravaging his vocals, "don't kill me."

"Fear not death," the burnt knight said, his assurance a herald of doom. "It is not death's inevitability that torments the soul, but the uncertainty of when and how it will come." He advanced, the clomp of his heavy steps sounding a death knell to Hulmick's hope. His burning gaze locked onto Hulmick's trembling eyes. "You are fortunate," the knight said, "for I will relieve your dread with the knowledge of your final moments." He paused, the flaming coals that were his eyes seeming to contemplate some arcane insight. Then he added, "Once you have conquered death, it is life that becomes the true horror. Haunted by the taunting warmth and light of the living. It is better to yield to death's cold embrace than cheat it, and linger in the mocking shadows of life."

The knight's glare, ablaze behind his charred visor, seared Hulmick's vision. Hulmick could endure the intensity only so long before risking blindness, yet he was compelled to stare.

At last, the knight tore his gaze away. With a swift, streaking spin, he marched to a black granite slab crudely hewn into a table. Drawing his sword, *Black Star*, and drove it down into the stone—sparking and grating—until the hilt kissed the rock. The grotto shuddered. The ground cracked open, crumbling into a widening sinkhole, birthing a maelstrom of molten lava. From that churning liquid fire, a towering mirror rose. It emerged stark and monolithic. Flames danced along the modest stone frame, but the mirror itself remained untarnished, shining crystal clear. Its surface reflected not its fiery surroundings, but an unnatural, supernatural sharpness.

Hulmick gaped, especially when he saw his own likeness trapped inside. The mirror captured him as its sole subject, adrift in a void of solid red—the color of blood. His reflection was true to life, yet wrong somehow. His gaunt face stared back, not reversed, not flipped, but as if seen through another's eyes. And within the glass, subtle lines vibrated at the edges of his visage, ghostly echoes of his face, but not quite his face. They were layers upon layers of hidden contours, ancestral lineaments etched beneath his skin; his entire lineage clawing to the surface.

"Your bloodline has run hot for thousands of years. What courses through your veins once coursed through the veins of my own brother, Lord Likho Lanmarc," the Ashen Knight said, his voice softening into something almost affectionate as he edged closer to the mirror. His own reflection in the glass was a mere phantom: faded and insubstantial. He raised a gauntleted hand and traced the vibrating contours of Hulmick's imprisoned face within the Dies Redux. "Memories of him, or of our kinship, are gone. All that remains is the faint cry he gave as he died beneath my cursed sword." He paused, almost reverently. "I made a pact long ago to destroy the world that birthed me. And now..." He exhaled, a low sound like a scorched breath. "...now I covet that life I once scorned."

"No!" Hulmick gasped. "It can't be true—It can't!"

The Ashen Knight spun toward him. "It is true." His voice was colder now, pitiless. "We are blood-fused by destiny. And you, cousin, will have the distinction of restoring my humanity."

"I...," Hulmick cried. "I can't!"

"You will," the Knight bellowed, bounding across the cavern with explosive exuberance. "The Ingress of Dies Redux reaches far into the past. Into our lineage. Back to Likho, my brother. And once the Blood Moons take their crowning perch, it shall grant me passage to that time of serenity. To my former self." He swept his arms wide, gesturing at his charred-clad form. "Before... all of this." His voice lowered, tender or threatening, Hulmick could not tell. "You will gift back to me the love I can no longer remember, but ache to reclaim. My Lianna."

Hulmick shuddered. "And what becomes of me once you do?"

The Ashen Knight loomed over him, and a chilling shadow fell over his cringing face. "You, and this world, will end," he declared, his tone final and absolute. "Once I take my brother's face, this reality will be no more."

"How can you? Where's the humanity in that?" Hulmick cried.

The Knight recoiled slightly, as if disgusted by the weakness before him. He gestured back toward the mirror. "It lies not within this realm," he said. "But beyond—there."

But Hulmick couldn't bring himself to look at the mirror. Or his reflection. He twisted his gaze as far away as he could, only to find Slimsy shrinking into the cavern's misshapen pillars. The characteristic twinkle of cunning in Slimsy's oversized eyes was absent. Their blanched, unflinching stare fixed on Hulmick.

"Help me," Hulmick whispered.

The Dazzelf, however, remained a mute spectator.

With a resolute grip on *Black Star*'s hilt, the Ashen Knight dragged its embedded blade across the stone table—a motion like throwing some ancient, primal switch. A tremor ripped through the cavern. A ceiling stone rumbled open. A shaft of crimson light burst down, igniting the mirror in a haunting violet glow. Hulmick's reflection seized. Muscles twisted into iron ropes pulled taut; lips stretched thin over clamped teeth, nearly biting his tongue; eyes flared wide into perfect circles of horror. This petrification mirrored itself onto the real Hulmick, spellbinding his body just as it had his reflection. Then his reflected image fractured, splitting into an array of pulsating versions of himself at younger and younger ages, fanning outward beyond his own birth and into a spectral throng: ghostly figures with eerily familiar faces. It was his lineage unwinding before him, a slow procession of patriarchs, each stepping backward through time. Before the mirror, the Knight's scorched gauntlet moved feverishly, rifling through the ethereal crowd, searching—and coming up empty.

"Where is he?" the Ashen Knight roared.

"The Blood Moons have yet to reach their occultation," Nex answered, calm amid the fury. "Only at their maximal celestial convergence can you bridge the distance to the one you seek."

With a snarl of frustration, the Ashen Knight flounced back to the stone table and wrenched *Black Star* free.

The ceiling slammed shut. The violet light vanished. The mirror's glow faded. The Ingress of Dies Redux sank back into the molten depths, solidifying the floor as it disappeared. Hulmick collapsed in the iron chair, every muscle slack, his body unraveling from the spell's hold. His eyes fluttered weakly; his mouth hung open, bubbling faintly with drool. Nearly unconscious with exhaustion, he still sensed the approach of a figure—small. Slimsy? Then the rough pads of fingers touched his hand.

"Return him to his cell," the burnt knight's voice commanded, distant and final. "We shall proceed again at the Blood Moons' full eclipse."

Then: muffled silence.

Then: motion.

He felt the iron chair drift through the dark.

And then nothing at all.

HULMICK'S RETURN TO consciousness was an agonizing event. His hands cradled his forehead as a storm of pain thundered behind his eyeballs. "By Porter's grace, what was that?" His groan resounded painfully loud in his cramped cell with a rhetorical question certainly not directed at Slimsy, who stood in the corner, juggling eight imaginary balls.

"That was the Ingress of Dies Redux," Slimsy answered, opening his left hand and letting the juggling balls to dissolve into mist.

Hulmick cracked his eyes open just long enough to roll them. "Why don't you leave me alone?"

Slimsy shuffled closer. "Do you know what the Ingress of Dies Redux is?"

"I don't care," Hulmick groaned.

"It's a lie," Slimsy replied anyway.

"I really don't care. Please leave me alone."

"Smoke and mirrors is all. An illusion. Which I know a lot about, you know." Slimsy edged closer again, making Hulmick shuffle uneasily on the straw bed. He tried to plug his ears with his fingers, but he could still hear the damn Dazzelf.

"There's been a shift in the paradigm of our reality," Slimsy declared, holding out his hands. Between them appeared a steaming mug of black sludge.

Sweet, glorious brew-ha-ha. Hulmick eyed it, licking his parched lips. Slimsy nodded encouragingly for him to take it. Hulmick unplugged his ears, snatched the mug, and brought it under his large hawklike nose, inhaling the pungent steam. Still determined to ignore the lecture, he took one cautious sip—then a grateful gulp.

"And with the Blood Moons influence," Slimsy continued, "my abilities have been amplified."

"Ooooh," Hulmick crooned, relishing the concoction's potency. "Ahhh-haha, now that's some brew-ha-ha."

"It's a lie," Slimsy reiterated, "but an extremely convincing one." He stepped back, watching Hulmick drain the seemingly bottomless mug. "Not only have my abilities grown. My skeptical sight has, too. I can see past the illusions riddling our world. The mirror's lore is as fanciful as your brew.

"The real concern," Slimsy added darkly, "is what happens when our master realizes the lie. We won't be free of him. Only more pain. More destruction. No escape. Only endless suffering."

Hulmick drank, letting Slimy's words wash over him like grim background noise. He nodded vaguely, caught between surrender and apathy.

After a pause, Slimsy pressed on, animated by a deeper fervor.

"I see it now. I thought I had no choice. That my story was already written in a blotch of ink on a stained parchment."

"Why must you go on jabbering?" Hulmick burst out, slamming the mug against the wall, but it passed through harmlessly. "Please," he pleaded, collapsing against the wall, "just shut up and make me see home again. Let me see my sweet Hyln and Zenobia before... before I have to die." Folding himself into a fetal position, he lay on the straw, seeking refuge in ignorance, not knowledge.

Slimsy regarded him. "Perhaps that's something I can do," he said quietly. "But first, there's something I need to do."

"I don't care what you do," Hulmick muttered, "as long as you leave me with my family."

With that, Slimsy turned away, a pip in his step carrying him off, departing the cell. Leaving Hulmick to his delusion-free misery.

TWENTY

BOBBY COULDN'T tell whether the shaggy blue fur on the trunks of the Feral Forest's trees quivered from the light breeze—or recoiled from his presence. As he hastened after Zenobia, the tree's hairy bark seemed to shudder whenever he drew near, suggesting a peculiar repulsion. Preferring to blame the rustling wind, Bobby pressed on, weaving through the thicket. Occasionally, he tilted his head back to admire the blue canopy above, which he imagined resembled the underbellies of colossal beasts, whose long legs were disguised as tree trunks, camouflaged among the foliage. Caught up in the whimsy of it, he failed to watch his step and collided straight into Zenobia's back. "Oof!" he grunted, stumbling backward.

"What in tarnation are you doin'?" Zenobia hissed, barely above a whisper. She crouched behind a bush, scowling up at him as he scrambled to his feet, cheeks burning red with embarrassment.

His mind buzzed, as he analyzed the sensory details of their unexpected physical contact. He cataloged the feel of her. Her solid, bony frame, hard as a fossilized skeleton, draped in rags, a stark contrast to his own softer, yielding flesh. His right eye broke out into its signature winking spasm, snapping him out of it, just in time to meet Zenobia's glare.

"You sho are weird," she muttered, seizing his wrist and pulling him down beside her. The spongy forest floor pulsed beneath them, alive with a dormant heartbeat.

"Look over yonder," Zenobia whispered, pointing beyond the low bluff they crouched behind, toward the valley below. "A village, I reckon."

Bobby followed her slender hand to a clearing where small wooden huts, crowned with thatch, formed a series of concentric rings. At the heart of this hamlet, a roaring bonfire blazed, encircled by figures looping and twirling in a fervent dance. About twenty villagers, each having an animal-like face, moved on their hind legs to an unheard rhythm.

Rubbing his eyes for clarity, Bobby realized they weren't beasts, but people hidden behind masks. A figure in a rabbit mask hammered on a large barrel drum. Its beat, muted only a moment before, now thumped audibly in Bobby's temples, urging his pulse to sync to its tempo. Around the fire, the revelers—wolf, zebra, leopard, giraffe, bear, panda, and more—pranced and spun with wild abandon. Their voices rose into a chant, carried up the slope where Bobby and Zenobia lay hidden:

"Raw, raw, raw.
Wild. Free. Unabashed.
Claw, hoof, paw.
Bold. Strong. Unchained.
Raw, raw, raw.
We are nature's children.
Beneath the Sun. Moons. Trees.
We are nature's children just the same.
Raw, raw, raw."

"What should we do?" Bobby whispered.

Zenobia didn't answer. Her focus locked on the scene unfolding below. The weight of her silence stifled his urge to ask any further questions, and he turned his attention back to the animal-masked dancers.

"Big. Small. Tall.
We are nature's children, one and all.
Cold. Warm. Blood.
We act on instinct and need.
Beneath the moons, stars, and sun..."

From the shadows of a hut, a man in a deer mask meandered into view, his head cocked skyward as if tasting the breeze. He moved with an odd, bouncing gait—hunched forward, drifting on the balls of his feet, wrists clasped tightly to his chest—more a mimic of a T-Rex than a deer. Threading cautiously through the revelers, he stepped into the inner circle, his movements tentative, bewildered by the chaos around him. But the dancers swept him into their swirling current, bumping and spinning him with dizzying force, until he was no longer navigating the rhythm—he was carried away by it.

"Plant. Meat. Predator. Prey.
Born free, we're nature's brood.
Raw, raw, raw.
Heed our calls. Feed our maws.
We are nature's beasts, one and all.
Raw, raw, raw."

The chant and dance halted with jarring abruptness—the rabbit's drumbeat cutting off mid-thump. A profound stillness settled over the clearing, pierced only by the crackle of the fire and the thundering thumping pulse in Bobby's chest, now filling in for the absent drum. Zenobia cast a brief sidelong glance, irritation flickering in her eyes at his audible anticipation, before snapping her gaze back to the motionless villagers.

The deer-man resumed his twitchy gait, an embodiment of dread. He edged forward, then skittered back, sniffing the air in sharp bursts, head jerking side to side like a panicked prey animal sensing danger it couldn't yet see.

Bobby was so transfixed by the deer-man that he almost missed the figure in a tiger mask—until it lunged. The tiger-masked figure descended in a blur of movement, leaping through the firelight and crashing into the deer-man in a flurry of limbs and dust.

A gasp escaped Bobby. He clutched Zenobia's arm. "It's the Tiger Knight."

"Shhhh," Zenobia shushed, peeling Bobby's hand away, her gaze never leaving the scene.

The tiger-masked man rose from the heap, clad in dulled armor that sparkled faintly under the firelight, tarnished by time, but still formidable. He crouched and nuzzled the fallen deer-man with an almost animal curiosity.

The deer-man lay still.

Then the bunny-mask drummer struck the drum again—boom—and the villagers erupted back into motion. The fire surged. They masked dancers resumed their stomping, circling the fire in a frenzy, partially obscuring Bobby's view of the two figures still entangled in the dirt. And then came the chant—this time louder, faster, fiercer:

"Raw, raw, raw.
From birth, through life, to death's embrace.
The circle never dies.
Therein lies our sacred place.
Raw, raw, raw.
Fire, ice, earth, air.

Run, fly, leap, swim.
We burn to ash to rise again.
Raw, raw, raw.
We are the meat of nature's womb.
Raw, raw, raw!
Wild. Free. Unabashed.
Claw, hoof, paw.
We will always be.
Raw, raw, raw.
Clever, swift, uncaged.
Freedom in our veins.
Raw, raw, raw.
We are the spirit of nature's brood.
Raw, raw, raw!"

The tiger-man rose to his full height, each breath heaving from his chest like bellows stoking the flames of his heart. With a mighty surge, he hoisted the deer-man overhead. The limp body, draped across his extended arms. A morbid mockery of a victory pose.

Bobby's anxiety swelled. He knew what was coming. He was about to watch the deer-man tossed into the fire—and for the second time this year, witness a body consumed by flames. A memory he'd give anything to erase. His instinct screamed: *Run.* Cry out: *Stop Him*! But he remained rooted, a frozen spectator to the emerging horror.

"Is he...gonna be okay, you think?" Bobby whispered, his voice tight.

"I can't say," Zenobia answered, just as nervous.

"He's going to throw him in. That can't be the Tiger Knight, can it?"

"I reckon we make our introductions," Zenobia said, shifting to rise. "Maybe lend that poor man a hand."

Bobby's latched onto her arm, panic in his grip.

"What if they throw us in, too?"

"That ain't gonna happen."

"Aren't you ever scared?" Bobby met her straight in the eye. His winking eye didn't flinch, holding her green-ringed stare head-on.

Zenobia's face pinched as she chewed over her words. Then:

"O'course I git scared," she said. "Every step we done took 'til now. An' every step goin' forward I'm liable to be scared. But I ain't lettin' that stop me from savin' my daddy. Besides, I'm the strongest person in all Helcyon.

Ain't no wooden-animal-mask-wearin' folk gonna toss me in no fire."

"Or me?" Bobby asked.

"Nor you," Zenobia confirmed, then stood. "Now, if we don't act, that poor man's gonna be kindlin'."

Bobby nodded. Her conviction was the courage he needed.

The drumbeat escalated. The chant climbed with it. The man in the tiger mask raised and lowered the deer-man's body in time with the rhythm.

"*Raw, raw, raw!*

Raw, raw, raw!—"

And with a climactic howl:

"*RAW, RAW, RAW!*"

He hurled the body into the fire. The blaze exploded. A cyclone of sparks and fireflies spiraling upward in a plume of smoke.

Bobby's blood sluiced, a torrent leaping from heart to head. "No!" he cried. Before his brain caught up with his mouth, his small but powerful word was piercing the air.

Everything stopped. The drum halted. The dancers froze. Even the fire's crackle faded to a low whisper. Masked faces turned toward him. Beside the tiger-man, a previously unnoticed man rose. Unmasked. Blank. His face was as expressionless as the masks surrounding him.

Zenobia emerged from their cover. "I reckon now's a fine time to say howdy." She tramped down toward the clearing.

The man in the tiger mask raised a gauntleted hand. "Halt!" he commanded. But Zenobia kept walking. Bobby scampered to her side. The tiger-masked man stepped forward, the villagers trailing him in a deliberate march to intercept. The two parties met halfway.

"Who are you to disrupt our ritual?" the tiger-man asked, voice rumbling from behind his mask.

"We're seekin' the Tiger Knight. Herd, he calls thisyer parts home," she replied.

"I'm a tiger," the masked man said simply, "but claim no title of knighthood. And your answer skirts my question, youngling."

"But you're wearing the armor of a knight," Bobby interjected, shouting over Zenobia's shoulder. Zenobia winced and turned her head from the shrill volume near her ear.

The tiger-man bent his head, surveying his weathered armor before nodding. "True. I once bore the title of knight. But now I am simply a tiger."

"What's yer name, then?" Zenobia pressed.

"Names and titles are a concern for humans," he answered, "not creatures of the Feral Forest. We are known by our essence. Our scent and our spirit. But it is you who come from the land of people. So tell us your names. And why have you disturbed our sacred ritual?"

"I'm Zenobia. And thisyer's Bobby Porter, the divine son of our mighty Lawrd Porter."

A collective intake of air rippled through the masked crowd. The tiger-man tilted his head, intrigued. "Is this so?"

Feeling emboldened, Bobby stepped from Zenobia's shadow to stand beside her. "Yes," he said, puffing out his chest. "I'm the son of your Lord Porter. And I demand to know, who did you throw into that fire? And why?"

The tiger-man's laughter boomed, cascading through the clearing for a good minute before tapering off into a snicker... then a faint cough. "A person?" he said. "No, that was no person. Merely an effigy." He gestured toward the crowd. "David!"

From the group, a man stepped forward, unmasked and calm. The same one from moments before.

"This is David. He has chosen to return to the world of people. Our ritual symbolizes his departure through a metaphorical death and rebirth. What you saw go up in flames was nothing more than a sack of sticks and leaves, bound with dung. His animal avatar was offered to the fire for good fortune on his journey.

Bobby's posture folded slightly as he sighed with relief. He took another step forward and pulled the gold medallion from around his neck, the one given to him by his father—or the likeness of him, anyway—and held it out toward the tiger-man. "Is this yours?"

The medallion seemed to mesmerize him. His gaze locked on it, statue-still. Until, without warning, he lunged, snatching Bobby's wrist. The medallion swinging in Bobby's clenched hand.

"Where did you get this?" the tiger-man demanded, his voice a low growl.

Zenobia moved fast. Her hand clamped down on the tiger-man's armored forearm, the metal groaning beneath her squeeze. "You best step back some," she warned, her tone sharp as cut steel.

The tiger-man's eyes—just two small pinholes the size of pennies within the wide painted whites of a tiger's eyes—studied her, calculating. After a pause, he released Bobby and took a step back. "You are indeed a formidable child," he said, almost with respect.

"Best believe, I ain't no girl you wanna mess with," Zenobia shot back.

Rattled from being grabbed, Bobby rubbed his wrist and stammered: "M-my father gave this to me... He said it belonged to the Tiger Knight. That the Tiger Knight would help us."

This time, a low laugh rolled from behind his mask. "Help you? And what could the Tiger Knight possibly do for you, were you to find him?"

"Save my daddy," Zenobia said somberly, "and destroy the Ashen Knight."

His laugh trailed off, but his sarcasm didn't. "Ahhh. Is that all?"

"We must stop the Ashen Knight's reign of terror," Bobby said, regaining firmness in his voice—finding a resolve that felt foreign to him. He briefly thought of Mrs. Palmer, who used the phrase—*reign of terror*—to describe the neighborhood troublemakers, including his bully, Brock. He used to think it was *rain of terror*, which made its own kind of sense. But after some internet research, he learned it was *reign*, like what a king did, not *rain*, or *rein*, like what you use to steer a horse. Understanding those distinctions had made Bobby feel grown-up. His ability to decode the covert language of adults gave him hope that, one day, he could demystify the mysteries of miscommunication. Still, those more adult-type words and phrases often tumbled from his mouth awkwardly—mispronounced, misplaced. Yet here, in this moment, he sensed his effort to sound mature was landing. The man in the tiger mask seemed to be taking him seriously. Scrutinizing him from head to gut to toe, then back again. Finally, the pinholes of the tiger mask rested on Bobby's pale, anxious face.

"I see," the tiger-man said at last, sounding more contemplative. "May I examine the medallion, please?" he asked more politely this time.

Bobby handed over the gilded piece, watching as the tiger-man studied it closely, taking in every detail from every angle.

"Well," he finally concluded, "I do recognize this trophy as something once in my possession. Something I never expected to see again. The fates, it seems, have found me and charged me with a new purpose. So I shall help you on your noble quest to vanquish the Ashen Knight and end his tyranny. And in doing so, save your father."

"So you are the Tiger Knight," Bobby said.

"I am a tiger who was once a knight," he replied. "So that's close enough, I suppose."

Relief flittered across Bobby and Zenobia's faces. Their smiles, tinged with cautious optimism, ready to vanish at the slightest provocation.

"But first," the Tiger Knight added, "we must complete our sacred ritual. And you both will join us."

And with that, their smiles fell flat.

———

IN THE HEART of Fanggul, the Tiger Knight roared with theatrical flourish, "Welcome to Faaaaangguuuulllll!"

Bobby and Zenobia were led to a large wooden table. A woman in a giraffe mask bowed low beside it, then reached into a hole in the ground and unearthed seven pieces of wood. All resembling the early shape of a mask. Still featureless and uniform, she spread them out before them: curved rectangular shapes of pinewood, each with two eye slits and a rope attached for fastening to the head.

"Choose your face," the Giraffe said, her hand sweeping gracefully over the array of crude wooden masks.

"But 'em masks all look the same," Zenobia said.

"They may appear that way now," the Giraffe said. "Choose not with your eyes, but with instinct. Then the true face of the mask will reveal itself."

Zenobia knitted her brow and pinched her chin with her thumb and forefinger, inspecting each mask thoroughly. She scanned the masks left to right, then right to left. Finally, with a mixture of impatience and resignation, she snatched one, seemingly at random. "Ahh, heck. Imma take thisyer one."

The Giraffe turned to Bobby. "Now, it's your turn."

Bobby scratched his head. "But what if I pick the wrong one?"

"The chances of that are very slim," she reassured. "Trust your body. It often knows before your mind does."

"It does?" Bobby said.

"That little tingle you get on your nose," the Giraffe said softly. "The twinge in your heart, the knots in your stomach. That's your body talking to your brain. You must learn to listen."

She took Bobby's hand; her gentle touch was warm and soft against his skin, pulsing faintly as she guided it just above the masks, then let go, leaving it hovering.

"Close your eyes and let your hand choose."

He did as told, shutting his eyes and holding his hand aloft, trembling with hesitation. Then he smacked his palm onto the table, squarely hitting the empty space where Zenobia's mask had been.

Zenobia let out a little giggle.

"Try again," the Giraffe said patiently.

After two more tries, groping at the gaps between masks, Bobby's fingers finally curled instinctively around one. He lifted it off the table.

"Perfect," the Giraffe said, clearly pleased. "Now... put on your new faces, and discover your animal."

Bobby and Zenobia fitted their masks over their heads. At first, Bobby was engulfed in darkness, his breath quickening into shallow, panicked huffs. Then his eyes found the pinholes, and a flood of blinding light poured in before the world snapped into sharp, vivid focus. Everything appeared hyper-real—crisp and luminous, even in motion or far away. The whole world seemed to shimmer with a preternatural clarity. But what really startled Bobby was the transformation of the villagers. The giraffe lady was no longer masked; her head was that of a real giraffe—surreal, yet uncannily lifelike—connected to a human body. All the villagers, including the Tiger Knight, now bore the true features of their animal masks.

"What the heck!" Bobby gasped, awestruck. Turning to his side, he found a young tortoise staring at him, wearing an unmistakable smirk. "Zenobia?" he asked, stunned.

"Yer a lion cub," Zenobia chuckled. "A mighty adorable one, too. Can I pet you?" She reached for his furry mane.

"No. Stop that," he protested, batting her hand away.

The Tiger Knight, now more akin to his namesake, approached with a bristling, whiskered grin. "Now that you've chosen your animals," he announced, "it's time for the *Zoic Gambol* under the Blood Moons." He gestured grandly towards the rosy overcast sky.

"The what?" Zenobia said, puzzled.

"The dance of fortune and unity," The Tiger Knight explained. "A celebration of the Blood Moons, and a preparation for our journey together. To defeat the Ashen Knight, we must first dance as one—tonight!"

As the Bunny pounded a rhythmic beat on the drum, others joined in, each adding their own pulse to the heartbeat of Fanggul. The village came alive with an enthralling rhythm that seemed to make the surrounding trees sway in sync.

"Raw, raw, raw," the villagers chanted, stomping and prancing, twirling and swirling in a joyful frolic, orbiting the blazing fire like planets around the sun.

The Tiger Knight waved at Zenobia and Bobby, beckoning them to join.

"I can't dance," Bobby yelled over the hum of drums.

"There's nothing to it," the Tiger Knight called back, his smile broad and fanged. "Dance with your heart, not your brain!"

Zenobia's feet caught the rhythm. Starting with tentative taps, then growing bolder. She surrendered to the beat and let it spirit her toward the gamboling group. Giddy with delight, her tortoise guise wore her signature gapped-tooth grin, the only recognizable feature from her transformation. She glided into the dance circle, becoming a vibrant link in the undulating chain of animals. Together, they moved in hypnotic harmony: hopping, shuffling, leaping in an enchanting spectacle of primal joy.

The Giraffe bent low to meet Bobby's eyes and smiled with a warmth he admired. "There's nothing to fear. Every heart is a drum, dear. If you can feel its beat, then you can dance." Then, she twirled away, merging with the swirl of dancers.

Bobby stood, tuning into the measured thump in his ribcage. His foot tapped—then stomped—in pace with the drums. At first, his awkward movements resembled someone frantically trying to squash invisible insects skittering underfoot. But soon, that ungainly dance gave way to a more fluid rhythm. His limbs found coordination with the music, and almost without realizing it, Bobby was swept into the conga line, jostling and jumping in exuberant motion, uniting with the collective.

"That's it!" the Tiger Knight cheered. "To dance is to be alive. Do you feel the rush of life coursing through you?"

"Yeah," Bobby laughed, breathless.

"Indeed, indeed," the Tiger Knight roared. "Dancing is the body's exaltation of life! To dance is to honor being alive. There's a dance for every facet of living. The Dance of Rites, the Dance of Homage, the Dance of Reverie, and the Dance of War!"

"What's this one called?" Bobby asked, his steps light and free.

"This," the Tiger Knight proclaimed, bursting into a gleeful flail of arms and skipping feet, "is the dance of Nilly-Dilly-Silly!" His wild display ended in a thunderous roar that shook the surrounding fur-trees, sending goblin-bats scattering from their branches. "Now you give it a try," he encouraged with a toothy grin.

Buoyed by the rousing atmosphere, Bobby opened his mouth to roar—but managed only a timid whimper. Less lion, more startled mouse.

"Ah, not quite," the Tiger Knight chuckled. He stepped out of the circle and waved Bobby over. Bobby bounced free from the line and hurried to him.

The Tiger Knight knelt to meet Bobby eye to eye. He gently placed a hand on his shoulder. "Your roar must come from deep inside. Not just from your throat. But from the gut..." he said, poking Bobby's belly. Then he poked Bobby's chest. "And the lungs..." Two more quick jabs. "Letting it reverberate from your heart, vibrating sound that radiates throughout your entire being."

Bobby's next attempt was louder—but still restrained by shyness.

"Close your eyes, little cub," the knight instructed.

Bobby obeyed, squeezing his eyelids shut.

"Now, focus on your breathing."

Bobby noticed it. Quick and shallow at first, then gradually deepening as he centered himself.

"Feel the beat of your heart," the knight continued. "Does it feel strong and clear?"

"Like a drum," Bobby said, awakening to the life-force thudding within him.

"Excellent. It drums the Dance of Life. With each beat, feel your blood journey from your heart to every part of you. Your limbs, your fingertips, your toes... to the top of your head, your ears, your nose. Can you feel the thrum of life within you?"

Bobby nodded. His senses felt electrified.

"Good. Now harness that energy," the Tiger Knight urged, "and channel it into a single, mighty roar."

Bobby clenched his fists, his entire being attuned to the steady throb of his heart. Each beat sent waves of energy rippling through every cell of his body. He drew a deep breath—chest out, gut tight—funneling the raw vitality to his core. It swelled, pressing outward, demanding release. And then, with everything he had, he let loose a roar. A real roar—booming, unbridled, alive. One that rivaled the Tiger Knight's own.

"Spectacular," the Tiger Knight exclaimed, clapping Bobby on the back. "That's the cry of life! Let the world hear your presence." The Tiger Knight sprang to his feet and resumed his wild dance, whooping with delight. Bobby followed, and the two made a game of it. Dancing and trading competitive roars, their voices exploding into the air.

A warmth enveloped Bobby, lightness rising inside him, fizzing at the crown of his head. Happiness—perhaps too strong a word. But it was something close, far from unhappiness. As he spun back into the swirling circle of villagers, hands clasped in theirs, the fire smearing the night in its warm glow, he caught Zenobia's gaze. Her large tortoise eyes glimmered with kindness. A gentleness he hadn't seen from her before. Moved by her attention, he roared again. A declaration of his aliveness, his spirit gliding into the jubilant chorus orbiting the gigantic central flame.

TWENTY-ONE

IT TOOK Zenobia three tries to find a lump on the ground comfortable enough to sit on. She wasn't tired—rarely did she get tired—but she did crave the cooling reprieve of the night air, a little farther from the bonfire's heat.

Settling down, she watched Bobby from a distance, surprisingly keeping pace with the Tiger Knight. His awkward movements, clumsy and comical to her, made her giggle. He looked like a sack of bungleroot came to life in a frolicking spasm. But what a joyous sack of bungleroot he was.

As Bobby jostled, his fuzzy cub face wrinkled with bursts of laughter. His little fangs—more like snaggle-nubs—peeked from his grinning mouth, and his little pink, cat-like tongue lolled to one side as he howled at the sky. An unexpected warmth washed over Zenobia then, one unrelated to the fire's intensity. She found herself smiling. A twinge of affection amassed in her chest, rising up before she could press it down. Trying her darnedest, she couldn't quite suppress it.

But then, the drumming dissolved into a dull, persistent buzz in her ears—overpowered by a sudden, stabbing pain at the base of her neck. She reached for it instinctively, but knew the ache wasn't skin-deep. It came from deeper inside. A piercing reminder: her father, still imprisoned. Likely being tortured. Her mother and Golly—still dead. Each throb scolding her: *How dare you smile? How dare you laugh?* Her joy was a mockery. An insult to the seriousness of her situation. Her heart felt like it could only beat under one condition: sorrow. Her lips pressed into a flat line. Her tortoise eyes dropped to her hands, now clawing and digging at themselves with restless dread.

"You look hungry, my child," said a gentle voice, interrupting the lashing churn of self-scorn within her.

"Yes'm," Zenobia replied softly, her voice small with shame. "I reckon I'm mighty hungry. So hungry, I mite could eat a h—"

She turned—and stopped mid-sentence. Sitting beside her was a serene woman with the noble head of a white horse, cradling a large wooden bowl of berries.

"—shoe," Zenobia corrected herself quickly. "So hungry I mite could eat a shoe, ma'am."

The horse-headed woman let out a soft whinny. "I'm afraid I don't have a shoe to spare, but I do have plenty of berries." She offered the bowl.

Zenobia dipped her hands in and scooped up a generous handful. Eating felt awkward with her new tortoise mouth and its snappy mandible, but that didn't stop her. Titling her head straight back, she opened her mouth wide and dumped the medley of berries in. She wasn't actually feeling all that hungry, but she craved something sweet, something to do besides think.

"How come Imma tortoise and he's a lion?" She asked, her words muffled by fruit. "Them masks looked all the same before we chose 'em."

"Well," the horse-headed woman nodded, "those are your Folly Animals. They reveal themselves only after you wear them."

"Foller Animal?" Zenobia said, spraying bits of berry pulp from her snapping beak.

"Folly Animals are avatars of our inner weaknesses. By wearing the face of our weaknesses, we embody it, confront it—transform it—until it becomes a strength," explained the Horse, nodding toward Bobby. "Your friend's Folly Animal is a lion, which suggests he lacks leadership, decisiveness, courage, and sunshine."

"Sunshine? You mean that bleedin', blindin' light what exists yonder, above the black sky?"

"Yes. There was a time when the black sky was unknown. When sunshine bathed Helcyon in its brilliant warmth. But the sunshine I'm referring to is the light within. Now that your friend has found his Folly Animal, he can begin his journey toward bravery, leadership, and rediscovering his inner light. And once he does, he won't need the lion's face."

"How long you reckon that'll take?"

"Everyone evolves at their own pace. Some of us have been here for more than a thousand years. David, for instance, has faced his Folly Animal for just over four centuries. A relatively quick progression."

"A thousand years?" Zenobia gasped. "I ain't got that kinda time."

"Perhaps that explains your Folly Animal," said the Horse, nodding with certainty.

"Explains *what* exactly? What's a silly ol' tortoise mean I'm weak at? Cause I'm prolly the strongest person you'll *ever* meet."

"If I remember correctly," the Horse said thoughtfully, "a tortoise indicates a lack of patience, wisdom, and support. It symbolizes one who bears the weight of the universe and all its knowledge. Supporting the world with great steadiness and grace."

"But I got all that in spades!" Zenobia said, her beak clicking in frustration. "I take on my follies head-on. An' I got a heap of smarts, too. I've read over a hundred books. Thick ones, too!"

The Horse laughed, a soft whinny threading through it. "My child, true knowledge isn't confined solely to books or intellect. Books are an integral part of knowledge, yes, but wisdom of the heart matters just as much. Reading is valuable, but it's through *living* in the world that you come to know the full shape of life: its merriments and its heartaches."

Zenobia's beak clicked softly as her frustration tempered into thought.

"There's no shame in having follies," the Horse continued. "We all do. Our Folly Animal simply allows us to recognize those flaws, so we might finally face them."

Zenobia muttered, "Well, ma'am, I reckon I know heartache all too damn well. Merriment... well, someone like me don't deserve that sorta thang."

"Oh, poor child," the Horse whispered, "joy is exactly what you deserve. It breaks my heart to meet a child who knows only sorrow, when joy should be abundant in their days."

Zenobia fell silent, her eyes drifting toward the bonfire's dancing light. She felt the urge to rip off the tortoise mask and fling it into the flames. If wearing it meant chasing after some fairytale notion of joy, she wanted no part of it. But then... she didn't. Something—restraint?—held her back. She thought about her habit of reckless abandon, how striking first always felt easier than reflecting. But all the times she'd lashed out without thinking— what good had ever come from it? She scoffed at her own thoughts. Was the mask actually working? She left the darn thing on.

As THE DANCING ended with the resonant ring of a dinner bell, Bobby collapsed onto his backside, looking up at the bright red glow veining through the thinner parts of the ashen clouds. Despite his exhaustion, he felt the electric pulse of life still humming through him.

The animals gathered around a remarkably long wooden table that curved into a broad half-circle. Bobby claimed a spot near the center of the bench. Zenobia plopped down beside him, and they exchanged goofy, pleasant grins—still enamored by their animal transformations.

Bobby, who usually had no appetite in this strange realm, now felt a surprising hunger swell within him, announced by a series of growling stomach rumbles. He looked forward to a proper feast. Until he saw what was being served.

David, now fully human and walking upright instead of the ambling deer they'd seen earlier, hauled out a massive insect-like creature the size of a small boulder. It teetered on its domed back, its twenty legs splayed in stiff, lifeless directions.

"What's that?" Bobby asked, wincing.

"That, my cub, is dinner," came the Tiger Knight's reply.

"It looks really gross."

"This meal has everything: nutrients, protein, healthy calories. It'll give you the strength we need for our journey."

The insect—something like a giant black ladybug—reeked of rotten fish. David plunged his fingers into its soft belly, as if gouging out the burnt crust of a meat pie, scooping out a steaming mess of dark noodle strands and lumpy, misshapen balls, then ladling it into a wooden bowl.

"Boy, I ain't had a mess of Beetlewurst in a mighty long time," Zenobia said, her tortoise lips smacking in eager anticipation.

"I think I'm gonna be sick," Bobby grimaced as a heaping bowl of beetle guts was thrust under his pink lion snout. Covering his nose with his hand, he gestured towards Zenobia. "You can give it to her."

David passed the bowl to Zenobia without a word and moved on down the line.

Zenobia practically buried her face into the slimy dish, slurping it up with wild enthusiasm, making Bobby gag.

"Come on now, cub," boomed the Tiger Knight. "Don't dismiss what you haven't tried. This may not be food for the gods, but it's a delicacy here nonetheless. Broaden your palate."

Bobby felt the eyes of the others pressing in. Waiting, expectant, boring into his resistance. Zenobia nudged her bowl toward him, full of the slithering black Beetlewurst. He peered into it and gulped.

"Go on," Zenobia said, pushing it even closer.

With a sigh of resignation, Bobby scooped up a small amount with his fingers. He held it beneath his nose, which immediately rebelled against the rotten gut-vapors steaming off it. Then, with a panicked flick, he threw it into his mouth and swallowed hard. His tongue instantly spasmed, triggering a chorus of hacks and coughs like it was trying to dislodge the world's worst fur ball.

The Tiger Knight chuckled. "It's an acquired taste," he said, prompting an eruption of laughter from the table.

As the crowd returned to gorging on their gross meals, Zenobia patted Bobby on the back, helping shove down whatever was still trying to escape. "Beetlewurst ain't for everyone," she said, "but I'm sho glad you gave it a try. You'll be fine."

"I feel sick," Bobby groaned, rocking gently, hoping the motion might calm his revolting stomach.

"So?" Zenobia blurted out. With slop, dribbling from the corners of her beak, she turned to the Tiger Knight. "How long y'all live in thisyer place?"

"I'm not quite sure," he replied. "Time doesn't exist in the Feral Forest. We live in the eternal now."

"I'd say about a millennium," the white horse lady offered.

The Tiger Knight scratched at the tuft of fur beneath his chin. "Perhaps it has been that long. I remember... it was well before the sky first darkened with ash."

"How can y'all live that long anyhow?" Zenobia asked, diving into another mouthful of Beetlewurst.

"The Feral Forest existed before time," the Tiger Knight explained, "and so exists outside of time. Like an island in the middle of a rushing river, time flows around us, but not through. All who dwell within its bounds are untouched by its current."

"I still don't get it," Bobby said.

"That surprises me," the Tiger Knight replied, "given you are the son of our Creator."

Bobby stilled himself, struck by a sudden thought. "Because it's written that way?"

"Perhaps," the Tiger Knight mused. "Maybe it's as simple as that. Because it is written so."

"That's just silly," Bobby muttered, returning to his gentle swaying.

Having finished his meal, the Tiger Knight leaned back. "Who am I to question the world's design? I merely make the best of accepting what is."

Brushing his shaggy mane from his eyes, Bobby pointed toward him. "Isn't pretending to be a tiger instead of living like a human kinda like not accepting what is?"

"I am no longer a man!" the Tiger Knight roared, rising abruptly with rage. The table stilled. His armored form trembled, firelight casting wild, sinister shadows across him. Then, in a flat tone laced with venom, he said, "Mankind is nothing but selfish, murdering, cowardly beasts, unworthy of this word. I think the Ashen Knight should cleanse them from Helcyon altogether."

A stunned hush fell over the assembly.

Then, Zenobia said, "My daddy is the kindest man in all the world. An' that's the truth." She pushed away her bowl, finished with her meal.

For everyone else, this marked a crestfallen conclusion to the dinner.

The Tiger Knight's fury drained from him. His fingers fidgeted with the golden medallion Bobby had returned to him. "I'm deeply sorry for my foolish words, young one," he said, his voice ragged with regret. He sat again, placing the medallion on the table and staring at it simply.

Bobby watched him—this once-mighty knight turned jovial tiger— now a solitary figure, his gaze locked on the gilded disc. It reminded him of his father, slouched in their house at the bottom of the Oracle's lake, staring into the dark recesses of his coffee mug before handing Bobby the very same medallion and telling him to find the Tiger Knight.

TWENTY-TWO

The Traveler's Guide To Helcyon: Sights, History, Tips
On How To Defeat the Ashen Knight

CHAPTER IX: THE TIGER KNIGHT

During the three-hundred-year war between Ieroland and
Morilund, the Tiger Knight was known by another name—
a name bestowed upon him by his parents at birth. That name
has since been expunged from the Records of Royal Houses of
Helcyon. Or more accurately, scratched out and overwritten with
a single word, TIGER, in crudely etched letters. Considering
there are over one hundred tigers in Helcyon, this particular
"Tiger" will henceforth be referred to as the Tiger Knight, for
clarity. Though destined for knighthood by birthright, the Tiger
Knight chose to earn his title through valor and courageous
deeds. He joined his brethren behind enemy lines, eager to whet
his blade in combat.

IN THE FROSTY PRE-DAWN OF the Monoluna—when only one of
Helcyon's seven moons dimly glimmered in the northern sky—four
hundred troops lay entrenched at the forest's edge. Their armor
emitted soft clanks while their teeth chattered and bones ached in
the cold air. With torches extinguished to conceal their position, the
faint moonlight offered little visibility for advancement. The battal-

ion remained motionless in the dark, waiting for daybreak and the warmth it might bring.

When dawn finally broke, a collective sigh of relief rippled through the flanks, their breath rising in clouds of vapor. The horizon split open like a wound slit into the firmament, pink light bleeding into the world. The Tiger Knight, training his eyes on a cluster of huts now becoming visible just beyond their cover, turned to Likho, who exhaled heavy plumes of white.

"These are the barracks?" the Tiger Knight whispered.

"Yes, my Lord," Likho replied, nodding.

The Tiger Knight turned his scrutiny back to the humble village. "Are you certain?" he asked, sensing something amiss.

Though tall and broad, Likho was still on the cusp of manhood—his fresh face betrayed only by the eye patch that hinted at his seasoned career in combat. He unfurled a leather scroll, revealing a map. "It's marked here, my Lord. Our orders are to raze it to burning cinders." His voice, still settling into a deeper register, cracked on the last word, twisting the statement into something closer to a question.

The Tiger Knight drew a deep breath, sinking into silent contemplation. They were deep in enemy territory. He was hungry for battle and thirsty for blood. Three months into his first real campaign, and so far it had yielded nothing more than fleeting skirmishes—most over and done with before he could draw his sword. This was his moment he'd been waiting for. His glory. His chance to cut down the evil enemy that threatened his homeland.

And yet... a voice within him urged him to turn back. To ride home to his loving wife and newborn son, whom he'd kissed once, hastily, on the soft spot atop the boy's head before galloping off to war.

He envisioned their faces, floating in the dim light before him, lit by the soft flickering glow of the hearth in their home. Eyes bright with love. Oh, how severely he ached to hold them again. To draw from the warmth of their embrace. But his hand found the cold hilt of his sword instead. He pulled the steel from its sheath, raising it skyward toward the dawn's bleeding sun—the signal his men awaited.

"For country!" he bellowed into the icy morning air, his breath steaming.

"For Helcyon!" he bellowed again.

And then, his blade swung forward in a decisive slash—like severing a head—its tip aimed squarely at the small cluster of huts.

"For the glory of Porter!"

A chorus of steel rang out—blades scraping free from scabbards—followed by a thunderous roar of battle cries as the men surged into a stomping march. Flaming arrows soared overhead, arcing toward the village. The small houses erupted in flames as fire rained from the sky, rooftops catching ablaze in an orange burst against the blue haze of the burgeoning day. Then came the screams—high, panicked, echoing through the frigid air in shrill, tumultuous waves.

Now, many of you might be eager for the gory details of carnage that laid waste to this insignificant village—populated mainly by women and children. Your tongues might be unconsciously tapping against the underside of your teeth in tantalizing anticipation of the lurid description, of say, a mother of five having her hair yanked back by brutish hands while hacked clean off her scalp, her piercing pleas of mercy to spare her children's lives going unheeded by the uproar of laughing invaders, who then proceed to cut her children's throat, then hers. Or perhaps you want depicted all the delicate sounds and smells of a boy, barely a man, still addled with the mind of a child, defecating his trousers as he's eviscerated, his steaming guts spilling forth over his trembling hands. Or yet, there may be interest in regaling the pain and suffering of villagers who scampered in crisp circles, aflame as screaming human torches while mocked by their attackers.

Or perhaps we should abstract this ghastly affair by distilling it to just its broad numbers: From a population of two hundred (hundred-twenty-five women, twenty men, and fifty-five children, not counting but including pets and livestock), zero survived. And out of four hundred well-trained, war-impassioned men, zero casualties. All in all, a bloody success.

Once the gruesome sounds of metal cleaving civilian flesh faded into silence, there was only the sizzle of the dying fires and the slosh of boots tramping through the blood-soaked grounds. At the center of it all, the Tiger Knight stood, shaking uncontrollably. He stilled and steeled himself only by retreating into a cold calculus, reducing the slaughter to a "victory" in numbers alone, forcing the grisly minutia of war to the furthest recesses of his mind. The shift in him ushered in an overwhelming numbness, subduing his tongue into a profound and peculiar muteness.

Rumors spread among his men that his tongue had been severed during the battle, though all scratched their heads as to how, given the minimal to no resistance they'd encountered. Some speculated that it was self-inflicted. In truth, the Tiger Knight had not lost his physical tongue but the will to use it in elocution of commanding executions. Now aphasic, his strategies were plotted and proxied through Likho via grunts and parchment. Under his tacit leadership, his battalion continued slicing triumphantly through the countryside in an onslaught of equally ruthless battles. The Tiger Knight's naive eagerness for warfare, now long disabused, was replaced with nausea and repulsion, propelled onward only by his sense of duty to country and king. He framed the entire endeavor as a statistical game, perfecting and accumulating a score that made their campaign the most successful of the whole war.

Yet, no one dared to sing his praises (not too loudly anyway), not without risking severe punishment in the form of losing their own tongue. Thus, the brutality of their year-long massacre became a collective silence, an unspoken memory buried deep within each soldier.

Upon his return to Ieroland, the Tiger Knight received a mockery of a hero's welcome—the kind of pathetic ceremony he felt he deserved. The sparse crowds that had gathered at the gates of the Great Palace of Helcyon were thinned by ongoing war, which had dispatched most of the able-bodied men to kill or be killed. Only a smattering of pitiful acclaim accosted him as he was dragged along the promenade by royal aides, their hands too soft from the luxury of court life. Their lauding of his unbreakable crusade rang hollow in his ears. The paucity of pageantry trotted out in his honor reeked of some aristocrat's desperate need to justify his own absence from the battlefields. Behind the Tiger Knight's muted facade, anger raged.

The charade culminated with the presentation of the Medallion of Tiger Knights. A depressing decoration purported to be the pinnacle of bravery and conquest. An accolade reserved for the king's most loyal and distinguished subjects. Yet, to the Tiger Knight, the token was nothing more than a disdainful trinket. He numbly went through the motions, handed off from one regent to another, accepting whatever gilt thing was proffered with a cold grip. His gaunt face remained expressionless, his eyes barely lifting past the horizon. His mind had abstracted from his flesh and sickly soul; he pondered the emptiness where his heart had once pulsed with vigor. A morbid curiosity stirred—did his blood still flow? Would it still spring forth if he opened a vein? But this macabre thought was interrupted by the cries of a child and a woman. Not cries of terror, as he initially believed, but exuberant shouts from his wife and child, who flung themselves at him and clung with hysterical devotion.

After following them home, he withdrew to his bed, where he spent most of his days. His wife, ever devoted, tirelessly tried to revive the man she once knew. Her kisses were desperate to breathe life into him. But as time passed, her efforts faded into futility, and she surrendered to simply resting her head upon his chest, wrapping her arms around his waist in silent, hopeful vigil. The Tiger Knight was haunted by the thought that his insidious apathy toward life had infected her, too. The man she once loved and yearned for had returned as a shadow—hollow and distant. Nothing more than a cruel illusion. A false promise of happiness. What she held in her warm, loving arms was the cold embodiment of the terror that consumed him.

Days and nights bled together, distinguishable only by his nocturnal screams. His tongue arched and ached, his throat cracked and croaked, his lips tore and trembled. Each night, his wife would stroke his sweaty brow until he calmed. When his fits passed, he would lie awake, exhausted, staring up at the ceiling, locked in a waking coma, paralyzed by horrors only he could see. His son's cries, which followed his own, would draw his wife from their bed, leaving him alone, vulnerable before those terrors. It was then that he clawed at his skin, scratching until it was raw. Physical pain became his grim reprieve.

"Things will get better, my love," his wife whispered into the dark. Soothing words, he wasn't sure were meant for him or the boy. "You just need some time."

Time passed. And with it, his anguish only grew more severe. His night terrors seeped into the daylight. Visions of his wife's throat opening in a glory of red, followed by his boy's ghastly demise at the same crimson-soaked blade—his blade—bled into his waking mind. He shook his head violently to banish them, only to meet the blank stares of his wife and child, their eyes, like little twin voids, black and bottomless.

On his first night empty of screams, he lay awake, staring at his wife's sleeping face. He marveled at the ease with which she slipped into dream—spiriting herself away from his torment. So far away. Any further, he thought, and she might pierce the veil beyond dreams... and paradoxically find herself closest to him there, in the vast emptiness.

Slipping from bed, the Tiger Knight felt the heaviness in his limbs—but he trudged forward, drawn by an enormous dread. His steps carried him to his son's room, where he paused beneath the cold light of the moons, watching the sleeping child. The boy lay peacefully, his tiny chest rising and falling with a rhythm as steady and self-assured as the gods themselves.

The Tiger Knight pressed his hand to his own bony chest, feeling the chill of his palm against his clammy skin. He had once believed the body would surrender to dust once the soul was extinguished. Once the inner fire, the vital spark of joy and meaning, was snuffed out. But now, he came to see a crueler truth: the body could linger, hollowed out as an empty vessel of muscle memory. In that state, the body becomes aimless and purposeless in the absence of its guiding light. A husk of hauntings, endlessly looping a phantasmagoria of horrors of its own making. The mind wandered, lost and trapped in the nightmares rattling through the corpse of its living flesh. It became clear to him then—most people lived this way: bereft of spirit, gnawing at their own rot, driven by nothing more than insatiable hunger, spreading ruin like a black plague, infecting everyone around them with the same slow agony.

Watching his son, he wondered: Did the boy carry that vital spark? Or was the idea of an enlightened inner flame just a myth? A story for children and fools? Had life ever held meaning or hope? No answer came. Only the conclusion that innocence wasn't outgrown—but beaten out of you. Brutally. By the world that fed on suffering and served only the selfish. A world he could not bear to leave to his son. And so, he saw no future for the boy. Only a continuation of the bloody past, filled with pain, despair, and screams. So many screams.

"What are you doing?" came a soft voice behind him.

He turned, slowly, his gaze like frost sliding toward her. His wife stood in the doorway, shivering. He stared at her for a long moment before answering, his voice flat: "I don't know."

"Why do you have your sword?" she asked, her voice trembling.

Only then did he feel the hilt in his hand—the weight of it tugging him back from his dark thoughts. He didn't remember grabbing the sword, yet there it was, raised. He lowered the blade. "I... I thought I heard something," he murmured. His eyes didn't dare venture above her chin. "Was checking to make sure we were safe."

"Are we?" she asked.

"Are we... what?"

"Safe?"

He hesitated, then forced a nod. "Oh... yes, we're just fine."

She swept up against him, wrapping her arms around his slender torso, her hands pressing against the sharp ridge of his spine. Resting her cheek to his breastbone, she whispered, "Everything will be fine. We just need some time. And everything will be good again." Her breath warmed the small divot at the center of his chest.

Once his wife drifted back to sleep, the Tiger Knight quietly slid out of bed once more. Moving swiftly to the dressing room, he changed into a simple outfit and paced to the front door. As his fingers closed around the door's handle, he paused. His eyes landed on the glint of gold hanging from the mantel—the tiger-embossed medallion. Despite himself, he slipped toward it and dropped it into his pocket. He could sell it for some coin. Everything else he left behind for his family, who could still live comfortably. Then he stepped out into the cool night.

He didn't know where he was going. Propelled by the urge to escape, he let his legs carry him without direction, running until exhaustion and blisters forced him to stop. When he tried to barter the medallion for a horse, every proprietor refused. The emblem marked it as royal. A token of high favor. Possessing it illegitimately risked imprisonment in the Goolog, a nasty place where delinquents, stripped bare, were bound to the trees with an adhesive sap so strong the flesh fused to the bark. The only way to break free was to rip oneself loose, skin and all. And then there were the hundreds of other horrors that went on there. Frustrated and seething, he shoved the medallion back into his satchel and counted out the last of his gold coins with a sharp click of his tongue.

He rode his newly purchased horse until it gave way to exhaustion and collapsed; it could carry him no longer. He then traded the weary steed for passage on a boat named *Riverbed*. The *Riverbed* sailed east along the Moiruh River, a sizeable snaking waterway that split the warring nations of Ieroland and Morilund. Eventually, it curved toward his birthplace: the third and smallest country on the continent, Pangul, and its capital city, Pangia.

Pangia—the largest city in all of Helcyon—was a sprawling metropolis at the eastern mouth of the river. As the Moiruh forked into three smaller channels, the city splintered into a cluster of islands packed with whitewashed adobe houses, grand civic halls, market squares, and cliffside buildings perched high against an azure sky. Its sun-bleached beaches melted seamlessly into the crystal-clear waters below. In this city, teeming with wonder, danger, and possibility, the Tiger Knight hoped to unearth the answers he so desperately sought.

After a week aboard the fiercely swaying *Riverbed*, he took to solid ground with wobbly steps. He wandered through the bustling port and drifted through the city for many restless days and sleepless nights. With each passing hour, his body grew weaker. His muscles seemed to dissolve into bone. Until at last, he collapsed, a waif of a man, upon the steps of the Great Library of Pangia. He gawked up at the colossal structure: a temple of knowledge. The largest repository of living wisdom in all of Helcyon. Its ornate marble pillars and golden-domed rooftop loomed above like a vault of infinite histories, memories, and stories.

Revitalized with a renewed promise to fill the hole inside him, the Tiger Knight dove into the library's endless collection, devouring page after page, consuming line after line with the ravenous appetite of a gundygut, recklessly feasting on every inky missive of human experience. Because no writings were permitted to leave the library walls, he concealed himself among its many rooms for weeks, stuffing his swelling cranium with reports, philosophies, and journals until his skull throbbed from the weight of it all.

"It must be in here," he muttered with each volume he flung open. And again, more forcefully—"It MUST be in here!"—with each one he slammed shut in frustration. What was he looking for? He couldn't say. Only that he'd know it when he found it. His search led him eventually to the *Occult, Candid Incantations, and Ancient Enchantments* section, where a thin pamphlet caught his eye. Wedged between two hefty tomes on dark alchemy, the tract on the Oracle Akasha at the Mountain of Bones seemed to glow with significance. It felt fated for him to find. Slamming his finger to the page, he was flooded with conviction—this was the sign. The Oracle would have the answers. Or at least the questions worth asking.

The journey from Pangia to the Mountain of Bones took four weeks. It led him back into Ieroland and its hinterlands, where the Tiger Knight took a detour to visit the Very Very Big Hinterland Maple Tree. A featured landmark noted in the Traveler's Guide as the First Tree, the original life on Helcyon. Standing at its base, he gazed up in awe, sensing a deep connection to the pulsing life force that radiated from it.

"It got the best maple syrup, ya know," a cheerful voice rang out.

He turned to see a tiny-framed girl—no older than sixteen—loping up the hill toward him, a beaming smile fixed to her face. "Wanna try some?" she asked, her lips seeming only capable of curling into joy.

"Yes," he replied, startled by her radiant demeanor.

"I've got some in my home, just down the hill. You'll hafta foller me." She skipped off toward a small hut nestled at the base of the hill.

The Tiger Knight watched her for a long moment. Then she turned and called back, "Ya comin'?"

He raised his hand. "I'm coming," he said, and followed.

The hut was larger on the inside than its humble exterior suggested. Though that was likely due to the sparsity of furnishings. A crude table, a stool, and a rocking chair near a modest hearth where a fire crackled low. On the mantel, jars of golden-brown syrup glistened. She reached up and plucked one.

"Sweetest syrup in thisyer land," she declared, setting it on the table. "Grab yersef a seat, and I'll git spoons."

"You live here alone?" he asked, dragging the stool forward.

"Been by mysef a while now, yessiree," she answered, grabbing two wooden spoons off iron hooks by the fireplace. "Ain't nobody ever come thisaway. Yer the first I seen since my mama passed." She uncorked the jar, dipped the spoons, and handed one to him, syrup dripping like amber silk. "I'm happier than a flower in a sun-shower that you came along."

"Where is your father?" he then asked, accepting the spoon.

"Ain't never met him. Reckon he passed same as my ma."

She settled into the rocking chair beside him, feet dangling above the dirt floor. She licked her spoon gleefully, seemingly unbothered by his presence. A complete stranger in her home. The Tiger Knight watched her, unsure what to make of this odd, serene girl. So trusting, so unguarded. What brilliant flame burned within her chest, beneath that dirty, threadbare dress? A light he could extinguish in an instant, if he chose. He was large enough. Monstrous enough. And she—so small, so alone, and terribly breakable.

"Ain't ya gonna try some?" she asked, smiling around her spoon. "You look like you got sump'm dark on the mind. Thisyer syrup'll cure that, I swear to Porter it will," her lips curled even higher.

The Tiger Knight nodded, trying to shake off the glum, dark expression etched deep into his face. The creases were sharp, nearly indelible. He brought the spoon to his lips, tongue tentatively reaching for the syrup's glaze. The moment it touched, a shudder of sweetness cascaded through him. It ignited a warmth in his chest. A sensation he hadn't felt since childhood. The thump of his heart slowed, its rhythm growing steadier, fuller. He slumped into a euphoric calm, his sinewy muscles unwinding like loose threads. His dark thoughts began to melt, turning into black tar that oozed from his skull, slid down his throat, and coated his heart in a slow, burning heat.

"Good idinit?" the girl grinned.

Overcome, the Tiger Knight burst into tears. He doubled over, his sobs erupting in snorting, guttural waves. The girl eased a small hand on his back, rubbing gently. "Ain't no cure for the Bitter like the sweet," she said. "Best to cry all that Bitter outta ya." His tears ran black, inking the creases in his face like a charcoal sketch of sorrow across bleached parchment. Later, the girl led him to the only other room in the hovel: a spare space with a hay-stuffed box for a bed. And a tub carved from a tree trunk. "I'll boil some water for a bath.

Inner meantime, you lie yersef down 'n rest," she said, leaving him alone, his dark tears still flowing.

That night, after bathing, the Tiger Knight lay asleep in her bed while the girl rocked gently by the fire in the other room. He awoke with a jolt—mouth wide open, yet no sound came out. His heart pounded in his ears; the room spun. He couldn't remember where he was. He fought to draw a full breath. Dragged his rough tongue across chapped lips. He crept to the doorway and spied on the girl. She rocked steadily, her back to him. A cauldron bubbled over the flames, releasing a rancid smell. The Tiger Knight crouched—poised and tense, like a cat on the verge of pouncing—consumed by an urge he couldn't define. Attack? Flee? The confusion made his skin prickle. He didn't trust the feeling. Or himself.

Then—

A knock shattered his trance.

"I reckon that knock's for you," the girl said, turning to face him with a big ole smile flashing through the doorway's crack. "I ain't got no friends nor enemies what'd come knockin' this time a' night."

He could sense her excitement by the midnight visitor, seemingly ignorant of the dangers that often came with such late-night knocks. He emerged from the bedroom, stepping cautiously to the front door. Finally, impelled by the girl's encouraging nod, he swung it open.

A young, one-eyed Likho filled the doorway.

"Likho?" the Tiger Knight rasped.

"My Lord! I cannot believe I have found you," Likho exclaimed, his voice bursting with surprise and relief.

They embraced tightly, momentarily forgetting the bite of the night air. Once inside, the Tiger Knight slammed the door shut against the cold.

"H-how? Why are you here?" he asked, gawking at his brother in disbelief.

"Your wife sent for me," Likho explained. "She feared something had happened to you and begged me to find you. I was set to leave on a new campaign, but I could not ignore her plea. So I tracked you. Though I nearly passed this place, my eye, or rather my socket"—he gestured to his patch—"began to ache terribly. The pain only eased when I stayed on the path here and flared up if I strayed. At first, I was baffled... but now I see it was Porter's grace that was guiding me."

"What happened to yo eye?" piped up the girl, now standing with her hands clasped behind her back.

Likho leaned slightly past the Tiger Knight, allowing his good eye to get a better look at who just spoke. "And who are you?"

"This is..." the Tiger Knight began, then turned to her, realizing he didn't know her name.

"I'm Hedy Mulhick," she said. "So... what happened to yo eye?"

"An accident," Likho replied curtly, his tone firm.

"Well, ya look as handsome as a reynard, even with one eye. And I've seen some pretty handsome reynards," Hedy said with a grin.

Likho let out a surprised snorting chuckle, then smirked. "Well... you are handsome as well, my lady," he said with a slight bow.

Hedy's cheeks flushed with color.

As the Tiger Knight watched the two younglings—Hedy, fifteen, and Likho, sixteen—exchanging awkward, fidgety glances, he recognized the telltale signs of youthful infatuation—that fevered state of nescient yearning. He was grateful to be long past it. Grateful that such madness had been buried in him years ago. Standing between them, he witnessed their gleaming eyes communicate in the soundless language of young love, and he felt his muscles tense and twitch. His nostrils flared, readying his lungs to launch into a lecture—for Likho's sake—on the folly of catching foolish feelings for lonely country girls. But before he could speak, a pungent smell turned his nose, reeling back in a wince.

"What is that stench?" he blurted, breaking up the awkwardness that was building.

Hedy pointed to the pot over the fire, where black oil bubbled ominously. "It's the Bitter," she said. Then, with a finger aimed at the Tiger Knight, added, "That came outta you."

"The Bitter?" Likho repeated.

"It's a res-see-doo from all the self-hate one carries with 'em on the inside," Hedy explained.

"Why in the heck are you cooking it?" the Tiger Knight demanded, suddenly feeling exposed, violated.

"Well, it sho makes for a good bond with the maple syrup," She replied plainly, "Ya can make all sorts of thingers when ya mix the Bitter with the syrup. My mama show'd me how. Turn all that bad stuff into sump'm useful."

She paced over to the fireplace, settled herself on the dirt floor, and with her fingers dug a little hollow in the earth in front of the pot.

The brothers watched, curious, as she took a wooden spoon and ladled out a bit of the black sludge, filling the small hole with it. Then she fetched a syrup jar from the mantle and upended it above the hole. They leaned forward slightly, watching the tree nectar begin to ooze out. Slow, thick, and golden.

"I reckon you'd polly like to have that eye-hole holdin' an eye again, wouldn't ya?" Hedy mused.

Likho, gently touching his eye patch, looked intrigued—though clearly skeptical. "You can restore my eye?"

"You are a witch," the Tiger Knight accused.

"Imma alchemist, is what I am," Hedy retorted, clearly offended. "Witches are nothin' but bitter ole biddies with no good for nothin' use of the thangs us alchemists make."

At last, a dollop of the maple syrup slipped from the jar's lip and plopped into the black sludge, sending up an instant plume of smoke and mist.

"Git over here!" Hedy called, waving at Likho.

Likho remained rooted to his spot, uneasy, almost afraid of the girl and her maybe witchcraft.

"I said git yo butt over here," she commanded, adopting a tone like someone's fed-up auntie. "If you wanna git an eye back, do as I told ya, now."

With a reluctant shrug, Likho moved closer and squatted across from her.

"Gimme yo hand," she said.

Likho extended it, and she took hold of it, gently spreading his fingers wide, opening his palm to her. His one hand could've swallowed both of hers whole.

The Tiger Knight shook his head at the size mismatch between them, and how his brother cowered before a figure a third his size. Watching the two hunched over a smoking pit, it looked like an ogre kneeling across from a wildflower.

Then—quick as a whip—Hedy licked Likho's open palm. Whatever spell was cast, it worked; he became pliant, letting her guide his hand into the curling black vapor. Smoke wrapped around his fingers, blackening his skin. After a few moments, she pulled his hand back and, drawing a deep breath, inhaled the rest of the Bitter smoke into her lungs. She leaned in close, flipped up his eye patch, and blew the vapor into his empty eye socket. The smoke churned and coiled until it gathered into a darkly spinning orb. Slowly, the haze condensed, draining its color into a pearly-white cloud the size of an eye, then settled into place as a surrogate eyeball.

For the finale, Hedy delivered a one-two punch: first, she pressed Likho's sooty palm over his new eye, then planted a bold kiss right on his lips. That broke the spell. Likho flinched in terror, tumbling backward onto his behind as if ambushed by cooties.

Hedy stood, arms crossed, one eyebrow raised high in disbelief. She gave an exasperated huff and scoffed at the reaction from such a big man.

Likho, momentarily removing his hand from his face, let out a small yelp and slapped his palm back over his new eye. "What did you do to me? The light is blinding."

"Well, I didn't say it'd be a *perfect* eye, did I?" Hedy shot back. "It's too darn new. Too sensitive for thisyer world. Put yer patch back over it. It'll see jest fine, even covered. Give it some time, you'll get used to it."

Sliding the patch over his newly formed eye, Likho touched his lips. "Why the kiss?"

Hedy kicked dirt back into the hole. "To seal the deal, is all? Ain't nothin' more to it. Geese. I've kiss'd reynards more grateful than you."

Likho, now towering over her, looked torn. "You put me under some kind of spell. I couldn't move a muscle. I've never felt so—"

"Helpless?" Hedy cut in, lifting her gaze from the pit to the battle-worn boy. "I reckon you've been helpless before. Maybe that's why you're so darn twitchy over a little ole kiss. Ain't yo mama ever kiss ya for luck? That's all it is."

"But it felt more than that," Likho insisted.

"That's why you don't get involved with lonely country girls," the Tiger Knight said, elbowing between them. "Especially ones who dabble in witchcraft. They're full of tricks."

Hedy, stung, kicked a spray of dirt at both of them. "I ain't been nothin' but nice to y'all! Like a proper host oughta be. Food, shelter, medicine, even a darn eye for yer troubles. If you don't like my company, y'all can leave!" She stormed off into the other room, slamming the door so hard the jars and rafters rattled.

The Tiger Knight exhaled a sigh of relief. There was something about the girl that put his nerves on edge. Whether she was grinning ear to ear or stomping up a storm of rage, her presence twisted something in his brain and knotted his gut. He turned to Likho and reached for the eye patch, curious to peek beneath it. "Do you feel like yourself? What about that thing she put in your head?"

Likho twisted away, dodging his hand and keeping the patch firmly in place. "I feel fine," he insisted. "But my vision... it's different. I see things I've never seen before—colors and lines pulsing with life. It's like I can see movement before it happens. Outlines in waves of light." A look of awe crossed his face, the marveling glow of a boy who'd stumbled into something extraordinary. "I've never seen better." His regular eye, gleaming with wonder, drifted toward the closed door where Hedy had disappeared behind. "She's given me a remarkable gift."

Remaining ever cynical, the Tiger Knight grabbed Likho's arm, pulling his attention back. "She's desperate for attention. Her tricks are a trap. Once we leave, the spell will fade, and you'll be seeing as dull as ever. We must leave."

"We can't leave her like this," Likho protested. "She helped us both. We can't repay her by abandoning her."

A tear trickled down the Tiger Knight's cheek. He wiped it away, leaving a black smear across his trembling hand. "My bitterness runs deeper than her magic can reach," he said, his voice shaking. "Only the Oracle at the Mountain of Bones can help me." He retreated into the shadows near the exit. "I cannot stay here, Likho. I cannot bear the company of others. Especially children."

Likho sighed, shaking his head. "I will go with you to the Mountain of Bones. But first, I need to thank her. Mend whatever rift we made."

The Tiger Knight sank into a wooden stool in the corner, half his body shrouded by shadow, the fire light unable to reach his face. "Do as you please," came his grim voice from the dark. "Just make it quick."

Likho approached Hedy's door and knocked gently. "Hedy?" he called softly.

A fragile, teary voice answered from the other side, "I ast'd y'all to leave. Why ain't you gone?"

"I just wanted to thank you," Likho said. "For your gracious hospitality and for everything you've done."

The door swung open. Hedy stood pale-skinned and red-eyed, her expression stern, brimming with emotion. "You wanna thank me?" she said, incredulous.

"Yes," Likho replied, nodding with genuine earnestness.

"Then face me. Eye to eye." She wiped the wetness from her cheeks.

Likho sank to one knee on the dirt floor, his gaze leveling hers.

"Now kiss me," she said.

"Kiss you?" he repeated, startled.

"Kiss me," she repeated. "I kissed ya for luck. Yer gonna re-sip-poor-cate. 'Cause I'll need all the luck I can git, gittin' over meetin' you once you're gone."

Likho gulped. But then a faint, crooked smile curled his lips. Their eyes locked, and slowly, instinctively, he leaned in. Their lips met in a soft, wet embrace.

SWOOSH—the front door slammed open, letting in a gust of icy wind that swept through the room with a rattle. The Tiger Knight's stool was empty. He was gone.

From how Likho would later describe it—after catching up to his brother—Hedy's eyes sparkled as she looked deep into him and said his new eye would guide them to the Mountain of Bones. But before she'd let him leave, she made him promise to return. And before he would go, he had to ask her if she had cast a love spell on him. She only smiled and said, "I reckon that's a spell Mother Nature cast on us both." He held her then, just for a moment, but long enough. And he vowed to return.

THE TIGER KNIGHT NARROWLY ESCAPED death five times, ascending the Mountain of Bones. Each time saved only by Likho's vigilant watch. On the fifth close call, the Tiger Knight pleaded, "Just leave me to die here. It would make entering the mountain easier."

"Not on my watch," Likho answered stubbornly.

By the time they reached the summit and tower's peak, they were deathly exhausted—nearly broken. Together, they plunged into the heart of the mountain and collapsed before the mystical fountain at the feet of the Oracle Akasha's statue.

"What now?" the Tiger Knight asked of the stone figure.

"Tolling demands a toll; only the burdened may be unburdened," the statue intoned.

"What is the price for your wisdom? I have nothing left to give."

"What you must give is what gives weight to you."

Dragging his raw and cut hands down his face, the Tiger Knight scoured his memory for what he still carried. Then, with a sudden clarity, he reached into his pouch and fished out the medallion. "This? I offer it freely." He tossed it into the fountain water. It sank without a splash, and the surface shimmered, rippling into a vision of the Feral Forest, where masked figures danced around a roaring bonfire.

"How do I get there?" the Tiger Knight asked.

"He who seeks the path to the heart must enter the fountain, and within the fountain lies the heart's path he seeks."

The Tiger Knight turned to his brother. "Will you follow me?"

"Of course," he said.

Together, they stepped into the fountain.

THOUGH BOTH THE TIGER KNIGHT and Likho stepped into the fountain, only the Tiger Knight emerged on the other side, arriving alone in the Feral Forest. Yet he did not mourn his brother's absence. He knew Likho had a different path of the heart to walk, a journey all his own. In dreams, the winds whispered and the trees murmured, showing the Tiger Knight a vision.

Beneath the vast shade of the Very Very Big Hinterland Maple Tree, Hedy worked. The tree sheltered her from the sun's brightness as she coaxed syrup from its spigots, collecting the golden nectar in her buckets. She swiped her finger along the tap and savored the sweetness clinging to her fingertip. Then, with a contented sigh, she flopped onto the grass, stretched out her legs, and tucked a blade of blue grass between her molars to chew.

Her eyes roamed the countryside in quiet appreciation—until her gaze snagged on a distant figure approaching. Her chewing stopped. She rose to her feet.

"You've bewitched me, girl," the figure called as he neared.

Hedy put her hands on her hips and squinted. "I ain't no witch. I'm an alchemist who's gotten 'customed to yer darn gruffy, boorish charm. If anythang I just alchemitched ya is all, ya big brute."

When he reached her, Likho scooped her into his arms and kissed her. In that embrace of youthful love, they folded into each other—two halves meeting in perfect contour, filling the negative spaces between them until what stood beneath the tree was no longer just a girl and a boy, but something wholly complete.

TWENTY-THREE

AS THE Tiger Knight finished recounting his story—his connection to the gilded token he never expected to see again, and his path that led him to the Feral Forest and Fanggul—Zenobia kept eyeing Bobby, who squirmed with sullen agitation. *What crawled into his britches and bit at his fleshy hinny?* She wondered.

Unable to contain himself any longer, Bobby suddenly shot to his feet and cut off the Tiger Knight mid-sentence. "You left them—y-you just left them!" he stammered, his face flushing red with anger.

Zenobia had never seen him like this before. It worried her. *Was this what she looked like when she was enraged?*

"I had to. It was necessary. For their sake," Tiger Knight explained meekly.

"No," Bobby yelled, eclipsing the seated cat. "You did what you had to do to survive the war. So you could get back to your son and his mom. You were gone so long, and they needed you. They *needed* you! And then you left them again. You're selfish. Just a selfish coward!" The last word tore from his throat with a feral growl. His new fangs flashed, spit flying. Then he bolted for the woods.

Not a creature stirred to follow him. The gathering fell into stunned silence as Bobby stumbled, then bounded past the line of Fur-Trees and vanished.

"Reckon I oughta foller him," Zenobia said, starting to rise.

"No," the Tiger Knight said solemnly. "He needs solitude. Self-reflection is part of a cub's life journey."

Zenobia shook her head. "Mister, I ain't got the slightest clue what's that's about. But we ain't got much time to waste on silly feelin's."

"We'll depart at dawn." The Tiger Knight assured her, resting a hand on her shoulder. "Patience, my little tortoise. And remember—feelings are never silly. From what Bobby has told me, I suspect you've struggled with some awful ones, too."

"What he say?" Zenobia snapped her beak. But she wasn't in the mood to dig into the emotional turmoils that had seized and spurred her so recklessly. She changed the topic before he could answer. "Never mind. Say... that girl in yer story, did you mention her name was Hedy Mulhick?"

"Yes," the Tiger Knight nodded, withdrawing his hand as she settled back into her spot.

"Well, my name is Zenobia Mulhick. And thatyer tree you mentioned? That's my ol' stompin' grounds. Figure there's any relation?"

"I have no doubt, young one. You bear an uncanny resemblance to her."

———————

BOBBY WAS NOT going to cry. And besides, why should he care about the Tiger Knight or his family, anyway? So what if he left them—that was ancient history, like a thousand years ago—*literally*, literally. His wife and son were probably long dead. Maybe it was the way the Tiger Knight didn't seem all that bothered abandoning his family that created that strange, gnawing twist in Bobby's gut, like hunger pains, but he wasn't hungry. He imagined it was a black hole, the most *deadliest* force in the universe, now burrowed inside him. He blamed Zenobia's brooding sorrow. An apparently contagious affliction now set on ripping him apart from the inside, in slow motion, nonetheless. Locking him in the eternal moment of being stretched and split for a gazillion years at the event horizon.

Dismissing the thought as ridiculous, Bobby shook his head and tried climbing a low branch of a fur-tree. After several clumsy attempts, he managed to hoist himself onto a steady perch. From there, he could barely make out the people—animals—whatever they were—clustered around the bonfire. He just sat there, letting the cold burn in his belly creep upward, its icy tendrils coiling toward his chest, strangling the heat from his heart. But he *was not* going to cry. The more he focused on the chill, the less he felt like crying. Or doing anything at all. No, he wouldn't cry. He rubbed his sore eyes fiercely, making sure they stayed dry.

"Tears are for the weak and the lame," a voice purred from nearby.

Startled, Bobby turned to look at a shadow moving within a cavity of a rotted tree trunk—the only decaying one among the otherwise lively trees—a smirking

face peeked out at him. Bobby squinted his eyes, but the face remained floating in the darkness, its yellow eyes gleaming, and a grin too wide to be friendly.

"But I see you are neither weak nor lame," the man continued, syrup-
smooth. "A brave and strong... lion?"

Bobby stared. The man's face looked wrong. Oddly placed. Odder still,
it slid up and down like it was mounted on an invisible pole, and Bobby's
mind struggled, trying to construct the hidden body it must belong to.

"Who are you?" Bobby asked, curiosity laced with caution.

"The name's Kilrok," the figure answered. "And what is your name?"

"I—I'm Bobby. Bobby Porter."

"Ahhh... not quite the face I expected from *the* Bobby Porter," Kilrok mused.

"You've... you've heard of me?" Bobby's voice quivered at the thought of
his own notoriety.

Kilrok inhaled, slowly and deliberately, drawing in a long sniff of the air.
He pushed his head farther out from the hollow, revealing locks of shimmering black mane. "I've never encountered a scent like yours," he said. "I know
the smell of all things living and dead. But you... you're entirely novel."

Uneasy, Bobby dropped from the branch, landing hard on both feet.
"Who are you, *really?*"

"I *am* Kilrok," the creature declared, emerging fully from the rotted
trunk. It skulked forward, stretching out its limbs, claws flexing as if waking
from a long slumber—or preparing for a hunt. A scorpion-like tail curled
over its back, poised to strike.

A wave of foul odor hit Bobby, so thick he nearly gagged. It smelled like a pile
of damp, moldy socks left in a musty basement, layered with the rancid stench
of green and black raw meat. It was as noxious as the creature itself.

"What are you?" Bobby asked, voice cracking with fear, and a desperate
need to understand the monstrosity before him.

Kilrok's lips parted into a sharp, menacing smile, placing rows of yellow,
fanged teeth on display. "I am a man-eater," he said with a dark delight.

A BLOOD-CHILLING SHRIEK pierced the air. Faint at first, then quickly intensifying into a high-pitched scream that Zenobia instantly recognized as Bobby's
pinched throat muscle squealing, akin to a teakettle reaching its boiling point.

"Mooooonnnnssssstttter!" Bobby bawled as he burst into the village clearing, his face flushed and contorted in terror, mouth hollerin' 'bloody murder.'

Zenobia instinctively sprang to her feet, moving with a swiftness that belied her tortoise appearance. Beside her, the Tiger Knight also leapt into action, raking the air with his nose before sneezing at the pollution that rode in on a sudden downdraft. Zenobia caught it too, an acrid stench curdling the wind.

From the treetops, the manticore descended with a thunderous crash, landing dead center in the bonfire. Flames licked its fur, but it remained unscathed, almost reveling in the chaos. With gleeful flicks of its tail, it launched flaming debris onto the village huts, setting them ablaze. The creature laughed, delighted by the crackle of burning rooftops and the scream of splintering wood.

Frozen for a moment, the Tiger Knight stood helplessly as fire consumed the huts. Around them, the villagers erupted in pandemonium, animals fleeing in every direction. Only a few stayed—the Wolf, Giraffe, Horse, and the Bear—forming a defensive ring around the manticore, readying for battle.

Bobby hit the ground at Zenobia's feet, curling into a tight ball as flaming chunks of timber rained down around them, bursting against the ground in red-hot cinders and sparks.

"Git up!" Zenobia barked, prodding him with her foot. "Don't be a coward."

But Bobby stayed curled up, shaking uncontrollably, mumbling incoherent fragments into the dirt.

"Well, well, well," Kilrok taunted, laughing as he stepped from the fire, "Do you really believe masquerading in those ridiculous masks will transform you into something you're not?"

The Wolf and Bear moved to flank Kilrok, while the Giraffe and Horse positioned themselves at the front and back of the beast. Brimming with courage, the Wolf lunged—but was easily battered mid-air by the vicious lash of Kilrok's tail, sent crashing into a thicket with a loud *crunch* of bone.

The Bear roared and charged, hand-made claws of sharpened bone raised for an attack. But Kilrok, with a deft maneuver, leapt, landing squarely on the burly man, crushing him beneath his massive weight.

Frantic, Zenobia ran to the Tiger Knight, who stood frozen. "Ain't ya gonna do sump'm?" she said, grabbing his arms and shaking him. "What the heck is wrong with you? We gotta do sump'm, right quick!"

The Tiger Knight looked down at Zenobia, his eyes wide and glassy, lost in a distant memory. Then he glanced back at the commotion—the Horse and Giraffe hurling crudely made spears, doing little to stop Kilrok, who now clawed and shredded at the Bear's mask, turning it into a bloody mess.

Suddenly coming to his senses, the Tiger Knight snatched Zenobia by the arms. "Get out of here. Take Bobby and run!" he ordered, before bolting, not toward the fight, but in the opposite direction.

Zenobia watched him run away, dumbfounded. "A heap of cowards, the lot of 'em," she cursed. But when she saw him run aplomb into one of the burning huts, she corrected herself. "Ain't a coward. Jus' plain crazy."

Spinning back toward the fray, she spotted Bobby still huddled where she'd left him, curled in a quivering ball of flesh, exposed. Kilrok's tail swept the last fighters aside like dolls. The Horse was flung into the tree canopy, landing against the branches with a bone-snapping thud, limbs askew and motionless. Kilrok advanced toward Bobby, who rocked back and forth in the dirt, oblivious to the world. Zenobia ran—fast and fierce—but she was too late. Kilrok reached him first, standing over him like a monstrous guardian over its prize. Bobby, tucked tightly into himself. Becoming so deaf, dumb, and blind to his own doom that perhaps he should've worn a pangolin mask.

"Ya think you can jus' go'n kill the son of our *Lawrd*?" Zenobia said. "Yer deader'n a corpse, beast."

Kilrok responded with a low, rumbling chuckle. "Girl, your delusions surpass even these humans playing dress up. This morsel of meat is no son of our Creator."

"Try it and see what happens. The wrath of Porter be what you git *plenty* of," she shouted, her eyes blazing with determination.

Kilrok's sheening grin withdrew into a cold, calculating look. His yellow eyes narrowed, weighing her words. Then, the beast placed a paw on Bobby's back, sharp claws dimpling the boy's skin.

"My tasty child," Kilrok hissed, "*I am* wrath."

Before Zenobia could react, an earsplitting howl split the air. The Tiger Knight seemed to materialize out of nowhere, already airborne. His blade flashing. He landed atop the manticore, driving his sword deep into Kilrok's side. The steel slid halfway in before Kilrok's scorpion tail whipped toward him, but the Tiger Knight twisted aside, yanked the sword free, and gave it a savage turn as he did, spraying black blood across his face and armor.

Wounded, Kilrok retreated, slinking away from Bobby.

Brandishing his sword, the Tiger Knight surged forward, forcing the beast back. Zenobia rushed to Bobby's side, placing her hand on his shoulder. He shuddered at her touch. His body stayed curled tight, hands clamped over his ears, eyes pressed shut, chin tucked into his chest.

"Bobby, git up," she urged, nudging at him. But he didn't move—locked deep inside his protective cocoon.

"Get out of here," the Tiger Knight implored. "Run, now!"

"I can help you fight 'em," Zenobia shot back.

"No. Go. Get the boy to safety."

Nearby, other villagers had returned, carrying makeshift weapons, helping their wounded to their feet.

"I must stay and fight," the Tiger Knight said firmly. "I'll find you again, I promise. Now, go!"

Kilrok, snarling, licked at his wound with a long blood-red tongue. The flesh had already begun to knit back together.

Frustrated, Zenobia bent low and dug her arms under Bobby's wet armpits and wrapped them around his chest, feeling his sweat slim down her forearms like a defensive goo. She scooped him up and lifted him. He stayed limp, eyes clenched, hands still covering his ears, whimpering, barely able to stand on his own. "Git yo-self together," she whispered harshly, shaking him gently, trying to pull him out of his shell.

Though she could've easily carried him, Zenobia didn't want to. With considerable effort, she got Bobby moving—half-dragging, half-leading him away from the smoldering chaos of Fanggul. As they stumbled through the brush, Zenobia cast one last glance back. The Tiger Knight, Wolf, and Giraffe were closing in around the recovering manticore, readying for another attack. Then, the trees swallowed her view. Branches whipped at them as they passed. Fanggul faded to a flickering fiery shimmer behind them, the blaze devouring the village in full.

Suddenly, Bobby tripped and slipped from her grasp, tumbling to the ground.

Zenobia skidded to a halt and turned. "You alrite?" she asked with genuine concern.

Bobby grunted in frustration, and sat up, only to slam his fist into the dirt. In one swift, angry motion, he tore the lion cub mask from his face. For a terrifying second, Zenobia tensed, half-expecting to see him peel off his skin. But no—his fur, his whiskers, the golden fuzz—all of it flattened into dull paint and etched lines, becoming nothing more than a plain wooden mask in his hands. And beneath it, the flushed, sullen face of a human boy.

"I want to go home! I want to go home!" he screamed, hurling the mask into the woods.

Zenobia reached up and touched her own face. Her finger traced the hard edge of her jawline. Then, she wrestled the tortoise mask off. A sudden pinch of cold hit her skin, followed by a rush of tingling heat across her cheeks. She stared down at the primitive carving in her hand—rough painted lines, the etched face of a tortoise—then she flung it into the trees.

Still muttering to himself, Bobby began to curl inward again, hugging his knees to his chest.

"I ain't got no clue how to git you home," Zenobia said softly. "But we can't stay here none. So c'mon."

Just then, a rustling in the bushes made them both freeze. Zenobia dropped low into a combat stance, ready to strike whatever might emerge. But instead of danger, a small figure bounded out, wearing a beautifully crafted rabbit mask. It was almost lifelike, except for the vibrant painted flowers that bloomed across the wood like springtime blossoms.

"Come with me," the Rabbit said urgently, in a hushed, breathless voice. "This way. We'll be late. We'll be late. Follow me. Follow me," and with that, the Rabbit dashed into the bushes again.

Zenobia and Bobby exchanged perplexed glances. "C'mon," Zenobia said, reaching out her hand. "We gonna be late."

They chased after the Rabbit, struggling to keep up with the nimble Fanggullian.

The Rabbit popped out from behind a shrub and waved them onward. "This way! This way! We'll be late if we don't hurry."

Feet pounding the ground, they ran. Always a few yards behind, never quite able to close the distance. Inevitably losing the Rabbit again, they stopped. Bobby doubled over, wheezing, trying to catch his breath. Zenobia scanned the area, and when the Rabbit reappeared, urging them on, she grabbed Bobby by the arm and tugged him forward despite his balking groans.

The Chase ended at a bluff overlooking the Moiruh River. A wide, flowing expanse that hugged the forest's edge like a silver-scaled serpent. Below, a wooden boat rocked violently at a small dock, barely tethered as the river's current slapped and splashed against it.

"Hurry! Get to the boat!" the Rabbit called. "It'll take you far from here."

"Where's it goin' to?" Zenobia asked.

"I've never taken it," the Rabbit replied. "But it'll carry you far away from that monster. Hurry—it's going to depart soon!"

"B-but," Bobby gasped, still trying to catch his breath, "I get—*gulp*—seasick."

"For the love of Porter," Zenobia grumbled, dragging him by the arm.

TWENTY-FOUR

THE CAPTAIN of the rickety vessel was a broad, commanding figure, perpetually drenched from head to toe. Methodical waves of river water arched over the bulwark, explicitly dousing him every few seconds, as if the river itself held a personal vendetta for some egregious past wrongdoing of his. Yet, the captain appeared utterly indifferent to the incessant soakings, as accustomed to them as a breeze ruffling the tuft of dark hair beneath his wool cap.

"Ahoy, and be welcome aboard *The Lady of the River*!" he boomed, presenting the boat with a grand sweep of his right arm, officially introducing Bobby and Zenobia to his pride and joy of his watery domain. The waterlogged timbers groaned and creaked, appearing always on the verge of disintegration. "I be Captain Knapp, master of this here vessel. Step aboard! Step aboard!"

Bobby and Zenobia stood rooted on the dock, gawking wide-eyed at the rickety, rockety, rackety contraption that barely qualified as a ship. Zenobia clung to the piling post for support while Bobby gripped onto Zenobia's damp wrist. The tempest river spray had left them wet, uncomfortable, and deeply uneasy about traveling aboard such a dubious craft. The gaps between the warped slats, the rotted planks, the sagging rails, and the gray, splintered hull made the whole thing seem less like a boat and more like a skeleton of a whale pretending to be seaworthy. Bobby chalked it up to yet another oddity of Helcyon—or perhaps just the creator's imagination failing to invent a proper boat.

Captain Knapp stood in good spirits atop the pitching deck, legs braced wide to stay upright. Another wave crashed aboard, soaking him anew.

Water streamed down his weathered, pruned face, dripping from his red-tipped nose, through his short beard, and past his crooked mouth. Still, he stretched his smile wider, his voice rising an octave in exuberance. "Heave ho and hop aboard, me hearties," he beckoned cheerfully. "She's as staunch as they come. Not once has she dipped her colors to the deep since I plucked her from Neptune's bonds!" Another wall of water slammed over the side, dousing him with a wallop across his person. Unperturbed, Captain Knapp's smile remained unshaken, his spirit undampened as he continued to wave them aboard with gusto. "Ye might be greenhorns ashore, but aboard me ship, ye'll find yer sea-legs in a jippy!"

But Bobby and Zenobia stayed fixed to the pier, unable to hide their apprehension. Bobby, especially, wore his dread across his face like a dramatic mask of distress.

Eventually, Captain Knapp let his smile sink, turning his enthusiastic wave into a dismissive swat. "Arrr, so be it. If ye be landlocked, then land-locked ye stay. I've a tide to catch and sails to set." He hauled in the gangway, battened it down, and made his way towards the bow to hoist the anchor.

Zenobia turned to Bobby with a glint of determination. "I've always fancied bein' a ship's cap'n," she declared, licking water droplets from her lips. "C'mon, I bet it looks worse than it is." Without waiting for a response, she sprang into motion. Her legs catapulted her spindly frame in an impressive arc toward the ship. Bobby, still holding her arm, was caught off guard—his grip slipped, leaving him floundering at the dock's edge, narrowly avoiding a plunge into the rushing current by dropping into a crouch and clinging to a wooden piling for support.

Zenobia landed on the deck with a wet *splunk*. The boards bowed beneath her feet, but held, resilient, if surprisingly flexible. The sudden impact sent the boat into a steep teeter. Captain Knapp, mid-step toward unmooring the vessel, stumbled with a shift in balance—just in time to be slapped square in the face with another wave.

"*Blimey*, what be this bilge?" he sputtered, spitting out a mouthful of river water. Spinning around, he spotted Zenobia stomping her boots on the deck, evidently testing the structural integrity of his ship. "Lass," he hollered. "Why be ye testin' me, Lady, like she's a bucket of leaky planks? I gave ye a fair chance to climb aboard like gentle souls. Now look at ye. Near sendin' us overboard!"

"I'm allowed to change my mind, ain't I?" Zenobia retorted. "Same goes for my friend. Now help me git 'em aboard." With astonishing ease, she snatched up the gangplank, plunked it securely on the railing, and extended the other end with a clatter on the dock, landing it just beside Bobby. "C'mon, climb aboard!" she called out.

But Bobby didn't move. The winds had picked up. The river blurred beneath him, a current of rushing white foam that looked more like smoke than water. He clung to the wooden piling at the edge, paralyzed. Deaf to Zenobia's calls, blind to everything but the river's hypnotic flow below. Something was rising. Pale, slimy, and long. At first, Bobby's panicked brain labeled it as a giant albino snake. But he knew all about snakes. This thing had no scales, just soft, wet flesh. A *tentacle*. It vanished beneath the surface— then another appeared. Then more. Multiplying. They began to coil around the dock's lower pilings below him. Bobby hugged the post tighter, pressing the side of his face into the wood so hard it left tiny splinters scratching into his cheek. The dock trembled under the strain of more white tendrils tightening around it, tugging, pulling violently. Threatening to rip the dock apart and drag Bobby down with it.

Like a host of blistering orbs, bloodshot eyes spawned into existence along the creature's pearly-white arms, each one fixing on Bobby with an unsettling sense of ownership. With every encounter—at Tar Lake, at the bottom of the fountain, and now here—Bobby felt an ever-deepening connection with the entity. Not a bond born of affection, but of something *preordained*. A primordial guilt that clung to his bloodline, tethering him to the thing. It felt like being *found* like a runaway child being reclaimed by a parent. And with that came the ache of contradiction: a longing to return to something protective, warm, familiar... and the rage of being claimed by a fate he never asked for. A fate inherited through his father's blood. A fate he couldn't escape.

Paralyzed, Bobby watched as the creature rattled the pier. But he could also feel it probing deeper—its other tentacles, the *psychic* ones, worming around inside his skull, hissing incoherent sounds, like a spell, flooding his brain with fog.

Then, through the static, the words sharpened. "The more you sssstay, the mooooore we shall become good friendsssss." Again and again, the phrase looped, laced with sinister affection.

Somehow, Bobby understood the creature's name. Or rather, the meaning of its name more than the name itself. It revealed itself not as a sound, but as knowing. A word too old, too abhorrent, to be spoken aloud.

And Bobby... was tired. Tired of being scared. Tired of feeling anything. He could sense what the creature offered: a cold comfort, an indifference to the vast, empty universe. A place inside its friendly stomach where all his fear, guilt, and sorrow would dissolve into nothing. It was not salvation—but surrender. And so, Bobby let go of the post.

But instead of the anticipated nothingness, he felt a sudden, stomach-lurching motion. In the nick of time, Zenobia plucked him from the slithering clutches of the creature, just as the pier gave way and splashed into the river. His eyes shot open mid-flight, catching a glimpse of the milky blob below still wrestling with the wreckage of the dock. Then, without warning, he landed hard on his romp atop *The Lady of the River*'s careening deck.

Zenobia swung back from the outer edge of a flying jib jutting over the boat's side and hopped down beside him, wearing an expression that sent a flush of irritation through him. It was a sardonic, smug, maybe even slightly fond. It said without words: *Yer completely helpless without me.*

The Lady of the River peeled away from the crumbling dock, narrowly escaping the aquatic monster's wrath. At the helm, Captain Knapp endured relentless splashes that targeted him alone. Undeterred, he scudded the ship downriver. "Avast ye, make yer way below. 'Tis cozier'n the hold!" he shouted, as another wave slapped across his face.

Following the captain's suggestion, Bobby and Zenobia crawled through the hatch and descended into the ship's underbelly.

The deck below was a world apart. The first thing Bobby noticed—much to his stomach's relief—was the near absence of pitch and sway. The hull's open ribs that looked so skeletal from outside were snugly sealed on the inside. No leaks. No drafts. The air was pleasantly warm and dry, offering an instant sense of calm and coziness.

The main cabin glowed in hues of red and gold, draped in silky sheets that hung from the beams like tent walls, creating a space that felt somewhere between a palace and a daydream. *Like stepping into a genie's lamp,* Bobby thought. Plush Persian rugs blanketed the floor, and oversized scarlet pillows were scattered everywhere, inviting the body to sink and stay awhile. Golden-plated lanterns, strung from the ceiling, glowed with a honeyed warmth that made the space feel alive, soft, safe, and glowing from within. A heady perfume of incense filled the cabin. Thick with sandalwood and spice, clinging to the fabric like memory. But a memory of what? His mother? Those shoddy, makeshift bedsheet forts he used to build back home, while she cleaned and burned incense nearby. This place, though—it was *more*. More luxurious. More inviting. More forgiving. More like what "home" was supposed to feel like.

Bobby eagerly plopped down in one corner, cushioned by a mountain of pillows, his crash landing softened by their embrace. Across the room, Zenobia nestled into a hammock strung between two posts, gently swaying as she busied herself with notching marks on her belt.

"What's that you're doing?" Bobby called from his pillowed sanctuary.

"Keepin' tally on all the times I saved yer lil' butt," she replied.

"Why you doin' that?" he asked, pouting slightly.

"Dunno." She shrugged. "Jus' keepin' count is all."

Bobby huffed. "Well, I didn't need you to save me, you know. Next time, just let me be."

"Maybe best I do jus' that," Zenobia sternly agreed, turning her back to him. "Let ya be with yer own damn doom!"

Bobby opened his mouth, then closed it again. No words came.

At that moment, the hatch flew open with a gust of river spray, and Captain Knapp clambered down, dripping from every fold of fabric. A final splash drenched him as he shut the hatch behind him. Too tall for the cabin, he hunched awkwardly, rubbing his hands together for warmth before exhaling deeply.

"Arr, we be at the mercy of milady's whims now," he declared, wringing out his wool cap. A surprising cascade of water hit the floor, which—somehow—absorbed it quickly, keeping everything dry... everything, that is, except for the perpetually soaked captain. He plopped the damp cap back onto his head and glanced around—at Zenobia's turned back, at Bobby's sullen expression.

"Be yer bellies hollow?" he asked, cocking an eyebrow. "I've got a pot o' bungleroot stew bubblin' away."

Receiving no response, he added, "An empty stomach makes for empty parley, and that be true as the North Star's light." Shuffling toward a narrow door at the back of the cabin, he went on, "I'll whip us up a hearty broth that'll put the wind back in your sails." With surprising ease, he squeezed his large frame through the small doorway and disappeared from view.

THE BUNGLEROOT SOUP — about as flavorful as boiled brown water served in an old shoe—was still heartily consumed by Bobby, Zenobia, and Captain Knapp. For a good while, the only sounds in the belly of the boat, aside from the creaking of its wooden frame, were the slurping chorus of their eating.

Captain Knapp, forever weighed down by his sodden wool garb and a life on the Moiruh River that seemed to hold a personal grudge against him, still hadn't dried. Huddled close around a low table, Bobby couldn't help but notice how the endless exposure to water had pruned Knapp's skin, giving him a weary, wizened look, aged far beyond what his eyes would suggest. They shone with a youthful brightness—bright as amber bolts of lightning.

"Where we headin' to?" Zenobia asked between slurps, upending her bowl and guzzling back the last brown dregs without missing a drop. In contrast, Bobby had managed to soak the front of his shirt with a steady dribble of soup down his chin.

"Arr, we be settin' full sail for the Great City of Pangia," Captain Knapp answered, grinning.

"Pangia?" Zenobia spluttered, spraying a bit of soup. "They got the biggest darn *liberry* in all Helcyon!"

"Aye," Knapp chuckled. "Sure as the tide's ebb and flow, they do. If ye've a thirst for the written word, that'll be the place to quench it."

"Reckon it holds the secret to dispatchin' 'the Ashen Knight. It gotta."

"Settin' yer sights on battlin' the Ashen Knight, are ye?" Knapp's grin faded. His tone shifted, quiet and grave, and he squinted one eye at Zenobia, realizing she wasn't joking.

"Got meself no other choice," Zenobia said plainly.

Knapp turned to Bobby. "And what about you? Ye plannin' to cross swords with the Ashen Knight, too?"

Bobby wiped his chin and frowned. "What's the point? I'm not brave enough. I'm too scared. I'll just ball up and do nothing but wait for my end."

"Brave enough, ye say?" Knapp pondered, pulling a damp smoking pipe from the inside pocket of his coat. He fell silent, mulling over the words with a series of thoughtful grunts. Then he fished out a spindly stick, set it aflame on a lantern dangling precariously close to his head, and lowered the tiny torch to his soggy pipe. "Too scared, ye say?" he murmured, trying to puff. "Bravery, lad..." he muttered from the corner of his mouth, but the wet tobacco refused to catch. The pipe wheezed, producing a choking puff of smoke before the flame fizzled with a crackling sizzle. After several more futile attempts, Knapp cursed, "Ye scurvy rat!" And stuffed the pipe back in his coat. "Ye don't know bravery without a dose of the jitters," he declared. "So, ye quakin' in yer boots is the sea tellin' ye, you're ready to brave the storm."

"That doesn't make any sense," Bobby objected.

"It makes all the sense in the world," Knapp avowed, leaning in closer. "Bravery's not the absence o' fear, lad. It's the musterin' o' courage in the face of it. If ye weren't afraid, ye couldn't show true bravery. Now could ye?"

"Well, I don't do anything but be scared. That's not brave!" Bobby said dejectedly, glancing at Zenobia for support. Her complacent silence miffed him. Of all their disagreements, this would be the one thing she wholeheartedly agreed with him on.

"Halfway there, ye be, with the scared part nailed down." Knapp leaned back, his towering height making his distant gaze seem judgmental as he stared down at Bobby and Zenobia. He scratched at his damp beard and added, "Not that I be encourgin' ye to face off with the Ashen Knight, mind ye. That'd be madder than a drunk rat ridin' a cat."

Zenobia, probably sensing Bobby's slow descent into self-loathing paralysis, finally spoke up. "Ya gone done lots of thangs, even though you was scared," she said, her voice lifting with a spark of encouragement. "Ya climbed that mountain. Ya stood up to them Skulvturs. Ya done plenty brave thangs."

Bobby took Zenobia's pity about as well as he took Brock's punches—with gritted teeth.

"I jus' wish you'd stop catawaulin' bout it," Zenobia chortled.

Bobby shot her a stern look, one he hoped had a cutting edge to it.

Zenobia reached over and smacked her hand on his shoulder. "I'm jus' ribbin' ya some. Geesh. Bein' the son of our Creator an' all, I ain't want yo big ol' head gittin' too big, now."

"Offspring of the creator, ye say?" Captain Knapp perked up, intrigued.

"Yupp," Zenobia nodded, removing her hand from Bobby's shoulder, "Yer in the presence of ah-dahity."

Knapp slapped his knee with glee. "Well, blow me down! Here I be, sailin' with a child o' divine!" His amusement suddenly took a somber turn. He leaned in again, lowering his voice to a confiding whisper. "Aye, I've heard tales... murmurs among the water spirits of the briny deep. Speak o' a savior. A savior, mind ye, who might also herald our doom. One who'd cast out the Ashen Knight from Helcyon, sure as the tide... but in the same breath, might just scuttle Helcyon to the forgotten deep." He narrowed his eyes into slits, polished black half-circles that bore into Bobby. "If ye be the very savior them sea yarn spins... then ye might also be the squall that sinks us all."

A heavy silence settled over them, filled only by the creaking and squeaking of the vessel and the dull wash of water sloshing against its side.

Then, Captain Knapp's face brightened, revealing his wooden teeth in a broad grin. "The way I reckon it," he said with a glint of optimism in his eye, "the end of this here world's just the birth of a finer sea to sail. So, don't ye fret none, lad." He let out a hearty guffaw—which promptly caught in his throat, sending him into a hacking cough before recasting into a fit of hiccups.

TWENTY-FIVE

THE **ASHEN** Knight's activities during his boundless, brooding downtime are seldom—if ever—a topic of interest among his subjects. Yet, to grasp his singular motive over the past few centuries, one must briefly examine the remnants of his earthly desires. This man—who traded his humanity for blood-soaked supremacy—had paradoxically relinquished all value in its spoils. The world lost its meaning to him. And so, in gaining everything, he gained nothing. His thirst for revenge lost its value the moment he dispatched his blade, *Black Star*, against his enemies. The memory of them faded almost instantly as soon as their lives were severed from this worldly plane. The bloodletting had rendered him a rotten, hollowed-out shell. Animated by wrath for wrath's sake. Eternally rapacious, driven by a hunger whose origin he could no longer recall. After all, what are we without our memories? Without the virtuous and traumatic events that shape us? In that sense, the Ashen Knight was no longer a man, but a shapeless mass of killing impulse, cloaked in the silhouette of one.

And yet—within the vast emptiness—he would catch fleeting glimpses of who he had once been. These nebulous shadows compelled him to claw desperately at the ghosts of his past, haunted by the misguided belief that something precious—something long lost—could still be reclaimed. Something that might rekindle the true fire of life within him. A flame snuffed out the moment he was set ablaze. To the Ashen Knight, that elusive spark of humanity—once reignited—was his only chance at salvation. And it had a name.

Lianna.

Though he could no longer recall her as the person she once was, or the love he once held for her, she remained his ultimate prize. The key to becoming human again.

For this purpose, the Ashen Knight kept the Dazzelf close at hand, using him to conjure Lianna's likeness in the vain effort to preserve her gentle essence fresh in his memory, sharpened for his schemes. The reanimated portrait had an uncanny ability to coax the faintest tingling sensations from the deepest recesses of his worm-eaten mind. Yet it was never enough. He yearned for her in full—her scent, her touch, the heat of her heart. Only her flesh could bring him back from the brink of total annihilation. Only she could prevent the collapse of the thin contours that still defined him as something *more* than a monster. The mystic alignment of The Blood Moons' millennial eclipse, in conjunction with the Ingress of *Dies Redux* and the presence of a descendant from his own bloodline, offered a single, long-awaited chance to pierce the veil of time. To go back. To retake all that he had lost.

Standing before the portrait of his desire, the Burnt Knight waited eagerly for the Dazzelf to arrive. Each day, Slimsy was charged with rousing the image of Lianna to life, but now the little trickster was late. Nowhere to be seen. Just as the Ashen Knight prepared to summon Nex to retrieve the slippery confidence-man, he froze. A pale woman entered through the chamber wall beneath Lianna's portrait, gliding forward, bathed in an angelic blue light. Her skin shimmered with an icy radiance. A pearlescent silk gown flowed around her form, accentuating the statuesque beauty of her once-living shape.

The knight's rigid posture softened. He gave a dry gasp.

"Lianna..."

"Amduat," she said softly, her voice carrying the amiable sorrow of an ex-lover guilty for breaking a heart. "You've changed so much. I barely recognize you."

"Is this some trick of the Dazzelf?" He spun, scanning the chamber for the spineless trickster—but found only her, glowing.

Lianna stepped to the burnt knight's chest, her hand rising to trace the charred edge of his helmet, a lingering gesture, tender and commanding, meant to soothe the bull raging inside him.

"I followed the sweet melody of the Psalms of Homes," she said.

"From where?" he demanded, his fiery orbs flashing heat. "I've scoured the depths of the Enlightened Fire, seeking the truth of the dead to bring you back to life, only to learn, as things stand, it is impossible."

"You can't bring me back," Lianna said, withdrawing her hand, realizing her touch had done little to temper his rage. "But I've never truly left you. Not since I became a victim of that damned blade of yours."

"*Victim?*" the Ashen Knight repeated, shaken by the suggestion that he had harmed her—*victimized* her.

"You don't remember?" she asked, narrowing her gaze, trying to read him through the twisted armor. She stepped back, taking in his full, scorched form. "That explains your foolish quest," she said, letting out a bitter laugh. "Let me enlighten you, my dim darling. *You killed me.* Which, on its own, wouldn't have been so bad, except being slain by your accursed sword bound me to you even in death. I'd say I hate you for it, but hate is too kind a word."

"No!" He lunged and seized her wrist, shocked to find her tangible. He held her in place, his molten gaze locked onto her icy composure. "I *can* undo what I've done," he insisted, though his voice quivered with doubt.

"No," she said simply, unshaken, "you can't."

Her cold indifference extinguished the last embers of his anger. He released her and stepped back, almost cowed by the delicate ghost before him.

"You seek to reclaim your humanity. To flee from the monster you've become," she continued, her words now cutting with surgical precision. "The Enlightened Fire showed you what you are. What you've always been. It revealed how immutable the past is. Destiny shaped by your actions cannot be undone. It called you what you are: a *Destroyer*.

"But you refuse to accept these truths. You cling to man-made lies, to the child's fantasy that time can be changed. But what truly troubles you, Amduat, isn't the monster you are. It's the splinters of humanity you still cling to. Let go of those splinters. Pluck them out, and you'll find the peace you seek."

Her tone shifted, mocking and cruel now. "You, my poor dearest, can never return to the past. It's etched in the indelible blood you've spilled. And that mirror—the *Ingress of Dies Redux*—holds no real power. It's not a portal. It's a cruel reflection of a rosy past that never truly existed. A dream, designed to entice fools into wasting their lives in a haze of nostalgia.

"So what use is there," she asked with sincerity, "in being enslaved to a past you can't change?"

The Ashen knight listened, barely breathing, as his sizzling stare studied the soft face of the woman he only vaguely remembered—but knew he should love.

"You're trapped in this hell as much as I am," Lianna said, punctuating the silence with a step forward. Her tone turned unexpectedly friendly again. "I suppose even the vilest among us need a sense of purpose. A reason to endure. And that's where there is hope, my belligerent *amour*, not in the past, but in the future. There is freedom in the world beyond Helcyon. For the first time, there is freedom from the dreadful story that is your tragic tale."

"What world is that?" he asked, flaring with intrigue.

"The world of gods."

"Gods?"

"The creators of our prison. The ones who condemned us. You—the love of my life and bane of my existence—can break free from their control."

"How?" His voice rose with eagerness. "How do you know all this? Why return to me now, like this?"

"Everything changed with the arrival of the Creator's son. He's the key to your salvation. Through him, you can transcend the burnt corpse of your tormented existence. You could do more than just rule over blighted lands, but *create and destroy worlds* at will."

"But..." He hesitated, reaching out his blackened glove, gently tracing her ephemeral cheek. "That will mean abandoning the little humanity I have left? It means... losing you?"

With the grace of a saint, Lianna placed her slender hands around his massive gauntlet. She gently guided it away from her cheek and laid it over his hollow chest that once held the pulsating muscle of sympathy. The Ashen Knight did not resist. His hand remained, still and heavy, pressed against the metal plate.

"You'll forget everything in the realm of the gods," Lianna said. Her voice, cooling again with a waning fondness. "Forget me. Forget Helcyon. You'll be free from pain, longing, and frailty."

She paused.

"And I, at last, will be free from *you*." She bowed her head and turned, gliding back toward the spot she had first appeared. As she passed through the solid castle wall, her voice still rang clear, cold and unyielding: "I was never the real prize you sought, my darling. Your true desire has always been to rediscover meaning in your vengeance. That can only be achieved through the boy." Her words lingered long enough to pierce the fortress of his mind—before absorbing into the silence of the black stones of the Keep. Erasing all trace of Lianna, save for the sensation of a splinter—small but sharp—lodged in the void within his chest.

Slimsy marked his arrival with ill-timed cheerfulness and a broad grin. "You ready for your daily lover's quarrel, my Lord?" he quipped.

The Ashen Knight remained motionless. The sound of his jaw grinding within his helmet signaled a tempest brewing within him. He then called out, "Nex!"

"I am here, my Lord," came Nex's whisper, slithering through the air. The crimson shadow hovered just behind Slimsy, as if it had always been there, its pale-green polished skull set arrogantly atop his bundle of fluttering, blood-red robes, clearly relishing the opportunity to startle the Dazzelf.

"Was what I witnessed the truth?" the Ashen Knight demanded.

"And what did you witness, my Lord?"

"Lianna!" he roared. "Was that truly her spirit speaking to me?"

Nex was silent. The pits of despair where its eyes should have been drifted toward Slimsy, studying his craven form for a moment or two before finally replying with a hissing, "Yes."

The Ashen Knight fixed his searing focus on Nex. "Was her revelation truthful?"

"Indeed. The boy holds the key to your liberation," the shade confirmed, cryptic as ever.

"Does the boy comprehend his own power?"

"Not presently. But he will, in time."

"How do I use him to access the world of gods?"

"That knowledge lies beyond my reach," Nex replied, drifting past Slimsy as it approached the Burnt Knight. "Only the Enlightened Fire can provide such an answer. A burnt offering of great significance will be required for this wisdom."

"Of course," the knight muttered. Then, his fiery gaze dropped down onto Slimsy, who was already sweating profusely. "Bring him to me," he commanded.

Before Slimsy could manage a meek nod, the Ashen Knight stormed off, departing the chamber in an earthshaking stride.

SLIMSY'S FREQUENT FORAYS across the boundary between truth and invention had become all too effortless. The more he manipulated this line, the more its borders blurred into obscurity. And now, with the Blood Moon's eclipse nearing its zenith, his deceptions were taking on such uncanny veracity that he began to doubt their falsity. His fabrications had grown so potent they seemed to transubstantiate into fact. Lianna's apparition left him uncertain: was it a figment of his own conjuring, or had it truly been her spirit that swayed the Ashen Knight to change course? In any case, this new turn of events conveniently aligned with his own objectives. Besides, so much of the lie had germinated from truth that he wondered if the fib even mattered. Especially since Nex hadn't seemed the least bit perturbed. Could it be, Slimsy wondered, that he had made a fool of the formidable specter just as easily as he had duped the Ashen Knight?

A shiver ran through him. An internal chill that clashed sharply with the infernal heat burning beneath his cracked feet. He knew what must come next. Deep down, he knew it. But he felt just awful about it. Profound sadness and sympathy welled inside him for Hulmick. Slimsy's throat tightened as he swallowed the arid air, trailing behind the forlorn lump of a forsaken figure that was his new friend, as he now guided him step by step through Dragoon Keep's labyrinthine depths.

They passed from scorching tunnels to cool corridors, through icy passages, then back again into sweltering subterranean canyons. A steady descent, spiraling ever deeper. At last, they neared the Cavern of Enlightened Fire, suspended above an immense underground sea of flames. This was the same cavern of the mirror. The same chamber that had borne witness to so many deaths and sacrifices.

"Is this the end of me?" Hulmick asked, his voice calm with resignation, his head bent sharply, eyes fixed on his dragging feet. "What will become of my sweet Zenbee?"

Wiping the cold sweat from his brow, Slimsy took a moment before answering. "She'll be just fine," he said. Though the weight of uncertainty throttled his voice.

Suddenly, Hulmick stopped in his tracks, and Slimsy tumbled into the back of his gangly legs. The Dazzelf, distracted by staring at the glittering diamonds within the black rock beneath his feet, was not paying full attention to his charge. Then Hulmick spun around, crumpling like a man whose bones had shattered all at once. Prostrating before Slimly's heavily crusted and callused feet, groveling.

"Please," Hulmick begged, "I don't want to die. Please. I want to see my little girl again. Please! I don't want to die. I don't want to die!"

Slimsy said nothing.

He stood motionless before the trembling gape of Hulmick's despair. His own bright, all-consuming eyes swept over the broken man with practiced detachment. He walled off any path to clemency within himself, fully aware that any act of mercy could jeopardize the grander design. The larger plan had to prevail—by any means necessary, even if it meant facilitating the end of the blubbering, broken man who knelt at his feet.

"Daddy?"

The faint, youthful twang of a voice rolled down the stone corridor, seeming to spill forth from a gap in the wall about fifty paces ahead. Hulmick abruptly ceased his snorting pleas and veered his head toward the delicate sound. "Daddy, where are you?" the voice came again. Leaping to his feet, Hulmick called out, "Zenbee?" His voice lifted with hope. "Zenobia!" He bolted toward the archway leading into the Cavern of Enlightened Fire and slipped through.

Slimsy gave a half-hearted chase. When he reached the entrance, he found Hulmick embracing Zenobia and Hyln, clinging to them desperately, pawing at their faces, weeping and laughing in ecstatic madness. He kissed them with ferocious joy. The passion of a father granted a miracle. A second chance to prove just how severely he loved them.

Slimsy stood watching, his throat constricting as if a spiked stone had lodged in his Adam's apple, producing a strangled croak. Perhaps this was a subconscious attempt to warn Hulmick of what he failed to notice:

The Ashen Knight, looming behind this blissful reunion. *Black Star* was already embedded in the altar, seething with bubbling black tar. This was the sacrificial site for opening the Trench of Enlightened Fire. The Ashen Knight snatched Hulmick by his scrawny neck and hoisted him in the air. And yet, even this did not efface the elation from Hulmick's expression. Slimsy's gift, empowered by the Blood Moons, was indeed an unbreakable illusion. In Hulmick's mind, he stood in the idyllic setting of his little cabin, beneath the giant maple tree, in the arms of his loving family. Blissfully unaware of his true predicament, deep within the molten bowels of Fire Mountain, suspended above the churning tar pit, nearing his end.

To the Ashen Knight, it seemed Hulmick's giddy ignorance was mockery. Without further delay, he plunged him—from crown to toe—into the tar bath. There came no cry, no burbling screams of pain. No recognition at all that Hulmick suffered as he was swallowed by the dark, viscous liquid. In an instant, he was gone. Digested and absorbed into the stomach of Fire Mountain, dissolved into core minerals and recirculated among its twinkling black rocks.

Slimsy shuddered to find Zenobia lingering near the altar, waiting for her father to return from his dip. Hulmick's illusion should have vanquished with him. Except—there she was. A fragile girl, as solid-looking as any natural person, staring at the altar in quite bewilderment. Slimsy's instincts were to shut his eyes in an attempt to dismiss the vision, only to remember that he had no eyelids. So he clumsily covered his eyes with his hands. When he looked again, she was still there—and this time glaring right at him.

"You," she accused, her voice sharp with rage. "When I git my hands on you, I'm gonna strangle yer noodle neck till yer eyes pop outta yer skull!" With a shriek, she bolted straight for him. Slimsy yelped and flung his hands up in defense just as she leapt. But the moment she touched him, she vanished in a puff of colorful smoke.

"Holy Porter," Slimsy gasped, his heart a pick hammer chipping at his ribs.

"Silence," boomed the Ashen Knight. His eyes—like burning coals— berated Slimsy as he retracted his arm from the tar, now free of Hulmick.

The cave then threw itself into violent tremors. The ground cracked wide into jagged fissures, venting gouts of scalding steam hot enough to boil flesh from bone in an instant. Chasms yawned into existence, radiating pits of liquid fire. The earth fractured further, widening into an expansive, fiery gulf, its flames burning an unnatural white-blue. Brightening the cavern were arcs of lightning flashing across its swirling surface.

With *Black Star* returned to his blackened grip, the Ashen Knight stepped to the edge of the fiery gorge and plunged into the infernal abyss.

Slimsy found himself stranded on a narrow outcrop of the cave's edge barely large enough to stand on. He clung to the stone wall, flames licking at his toes on all sides.

"My Lord," he called anxiously into the abyss. "Uhm, my Looorrd?"

The heat bubbled around him. His eyeballs smarted from the sting of sweat that poured from his brow into the basin of his deep-set sockets. Across the blazing divide, Nex materialized, undulating in a slow, dreamlike way, entirely unaffected by the searing heat. "Hey! Can you help me?" Slimsy shouted, frantically contorting his form, trying to wedge himself deeper into the crevices behind him.

Nex remained silent and reticent.

However, its vacant hollows seemed to settle on Slimsy. But it was hard to tell whether the death-wraith even saw him. Or whether Slimsy existed at all to the thing.

Ridiculous!

Of course, Nex was acutely aware of him. Nex was aware of everything. The specter was keenly attuned to all life, no matter how trivial or insignificant. It *delighted* too much in ushering each creature to its final breath and into the stillness beyond. Nex was the ultimate equalizer. In its numbing embrace, every soul—king or slave—was just alike, destined for the same intimate journey through a maggot's belly. And in time, Nex would offer the same impartial attention to Slimsy as it would to his master. All of them—*all of them*—reduced to worm fodder.

Wait.

Was his time at hand? *Was that why Nex was here?* Was he to meet his end in the eternal flames of the Enlightened Fire? A new panic overtook him. Slimsy heaved serrated, dry breaths as he clung to the cavern wall. His body trembled uncontrollably. Fear reached its fever pitch. Then—abruptly—a wave of calm broke over him. It was as if a lever had been pulled in his mind, releasing a torrent of clarity and stillness. His thoughts aligned like tumblers in a lock. The panic was gone, swept away by something deeper, something that inoculated him against fear. Understanding had arrived.

The Enlightened Fire gnawed at his flesh, searing a trail of transparency through him, like burning dead brush from the cluttered corners of his mind. Connections he'd never seen before began clicking into place. Thoughts raced through his head, opening to profound truths, like discovering that the secret to making the perfect cup of *brew-ha-ha* was explicitly linked to the meaning of death itself. The more paths lit up, wending down occult avenues and hidden streets, the more acutely he felt his ignorance. It was like learning and unlearning all at once. Each filled gap only emphasized the sheer vastness of what remained unknown. A creeping numbness spread through his toes. He looked down to find himself standing at the edge of a black sea that now stretched endlessly before him. Lapping waves kissed the skin away from his feet. Yet he felt no pain. He stood at the border of utter darkness. On the brink of a tiny island of sparkling light that encompassed all of life. On that freezing shoal, Slimsy peered beyond the light's reach into the bleakness... and saw a boat adrift in the waves of impenetrable shade. Its lone occupant: his master. Rowing steadily back to shore.

The ground shuddered and thundered. Slimsy jolted back into his physical body. He lost his footing on his tiny patch of solid ground within the Cavern of Enlightened Fire. Screaming, he tumbled toward the fiery lake.

Thud!

The cavern floor jutted upward in a chaotic heave, rising in broken, disjointed slabs. Slimsy landed, curled into a fetal ball atop one such ascending segment. He lay still, stunned. Then slowly, he unfurled, testing his limbs. His feet were blackened and blistered, but he still felt no pain. The cave floor continued its grinding ascent, each slab locking back into place, sealing the trench once more.

At last, as the final sliver of the gulf began to close, the Ashen Knight emerged from its diminishing blaze. For a moment, his body armor glowed in lustrous, molten hues of red and orange—then cooled swiftly back to its familiar, blackened shade. Nex drifted silently to his side as the last stone clicked into place.

"I know what must be done," the Knight declared, a stone grinding inside a furnace. From behind his iron helmet, his eyes blazed, hotter, brighter, and more focused than ever before.

TWENTY-SIX

BOBBY'S SLUMBER was interrupted by a sensation of something
kneading the soft, doughy rolls that padded his body—affectionately known, in his mother's words, as her "lovable little bakery."
In his sleep, whatever was prodding his flesh seemed to dig all the way into
his dreams, where he found himself on a baker's table—not quite as himself,
but a version of himself with no arms or legs, his body made of uncooked
pizza dough rolled into a flat disk. His head, however, remained its usual
spherical shape, protruding from one end of his pancaked form. In this
surreal bakery, a hundred arms with a thousand fingers—all belonging to
Zenobia—patted, rubbed, and molded his soft body. Despite the nightmare
logic of it all, Bobby wasn't afraid. He felt a peculiar comfort in the swarm
of nimble fingers and thumbs that pinched and massaged him.

Then the dream took a turn. Zenobia began to weep. Her thousand fingers
kneaded a deluge of tears into his doughy bulk, soaking him into a soggy,
gooey paste. Pieces of him began to separate. Soft hunks of dough sliding
off the table and slapping the floor with wet splats. His form was rapidly
decomposing into puddles of goop. And soon, his head was rolling toward
the edge of the table, toward the gutter below. Panic rose. He tried to call out.
Tried to tell her to stop. But his voice was too faint, drowned by her sobs and
the squelching noise of his disintegration. More of him spilled off the edge...
slopping down the drain—

BOBBY WOKE UP. But not with the usual jolt that followed his nightmares.
Instead, he opened his eyes slowly, gently. Feeling the rhythmic sway of the boat

and a quiet, steady pressure squeezing his rib cage. He peered down. A tangle of fiery red mane was sprawled across his belly—the source of the muffled sniffling. Reaching out, he touched the hair. Despite its wiry appearance, it felt soft, like steel bristles spun from cherry silk. The mop of hair shifted. Zenobia turned her face upward. Her pale cheeks were tear-streaked, her emerald eyes shimmering. Her tiny nose rubbed raw. She had her arms wrapped tightly around his body. Was she... hugging him?

"I... I feel..." she sniffled in a small voice, "like there's a big hole in my chest. Like when my momma died. 'Cept bigger. I'm real scared sump'm bad happen'd to my daddy." Tears shuddered down her cheeks. "It's too late," she moaned, burying her face into the comforting softness of Bobby's body—just like he used to bury his own face deep into his pillow back home, trying to escape the world. Now, Bobby understood what it felt like to *be* that pillow: damp, a little sore... but deeply wanted. *Maybe even needed.* There was a certain solace in soft things. Malleable materials you could bend to suit your needs, wrap around yourself like padded armor. They couldn't stop swords, or hammers, or bullets. But they could protect you from the things that really hurt. The kind of pain that didn't just end with you, but used you as kindling. Spreading its anguish like a wildfire, fanned by ferocious winds, devouring everything around you. A searing pain that could reach even the lives of strangers, carried on as poisoned skies of choking smoke. That kind of hurt was boundless. But it could be smothered before it ever had a chance to ignite. Quelled by something as simple, as powerful, as the soft press of a pillow like Bobby's.

Then his thoughts shifted to the limits of the pillow. It was passive comfort. A softness that *suffocated* rather than alleviated. It offered no resilience, no toughness to meet the world's sharp edges. It dulled, rather than sharpened. It could soften his mind, depriving the brain of fresh oxygen, turning it into putty, when what he needed most was the opposite. He didn't want a putty brain. He wanted one *ballooned with fresh air*. Filled with empowering ideas, encouragement, and hope. He needed his parents to lift him from his suffocating pillow and give him that flow. That vital, productive, profound breath of life. Air that would expand him from crown to sole. Air that would lift his thoughts, stretch his spine, and fill him with enough strength and courage to be something more.

However, Bobby had long accepted that his parents did their best. Capped by their own shallow and stunted breath, unable to transmit much more than their own aching air. There had been fleeting moments—slim breaths of warmth—carried by his mother's loving smile and playful nicknames, in his father's supportive hand lifting Bobby's frame from the cold muck, hoisting him high on his shoulders to soar among the birds and sun. But those moments thinned quickly. And Bobby learned to pad himself against the inevitable fall back to the hard clay of earth, into the deep trenches where his parents' gaze remained perpetually fixed, trapped in a solipsistic worldview that life had a personal vendetta against them. In their eyes, bad luck afflicted *them* alone. And Bobby was more than just a chip off the ole block—he was a chip on their shoulders. A burden to neglect, yet impossible to escape. After each emotional crash into the muck, he would crawl on his belly, seeking inert soft things to exhale his aching air into. Smothering himself in the toxic exhaust—thick and choking—immobilizing him from moving toward anything of real meaning.

Bobby processed all of this in just a few seconds of awkward silence, in his own straightforward way. And now, with Zenobia pressed to him, he wanted to offer her something more than just a soft thing to cry into. He wanted to *breathe*—the hope and encouragement he felt were lacking in him.

"I don't think your dad is... gone," Bobby said gently. "My dad wouldn't have written the story like that. He'd have made it so you and your dad would beat the bad guy together."

Zenobia's shivering body seized at his words. Much like it had during their first encounter by the Very Very Big Hinterland Maple Tree, where he'd foolishly opened his mouth to voice his opinion. But this time, when she looked up at him, it wasn't with a scowl.

"You mean I'm bound to save my daddy?" she asked softly, rubbing her knuckles across her cheek to wipe away the tears. "Like it's my *des-ta-knee* to slay the Ashen Knight and save 'em?" She sniffled, drawing the runny mucus back into the tiny, flaring nostril of her cute nose.

"That's how my dad would've written it, yeah," Bobby said, nodding.

"I sho wish we had that dang eye, so we could be sure," Zenobia said, sitting up, combing her fingers through her wild hair, repeatedly snagging on knots, which she powered through with brute determination.

Bobby, meanwhile, was reluctant to rise. He'd forgotten about Likho's eye. That strange little orb might've helped with the question of whether her father was still alive. But part of him was quietly glad they no longer had it. Sure, there was uncertainty without the eye, but it also brought a belief that he was right. The comfort he'd felt lying there in that cradle of warmth and quiet, with Zenobia kneading him, had vanished, replaced by a creeping nervousness. He sat upright, stretching the uneasiness from his limbs.

"Sorry for makin' a mess of yer tunic," Zenobia said, glancing at the wet patch on his shirt. She let a coy smile slip past her lips for his benefit. Then returned to a frown. "Yo daddy's the Creator... so that means mine's still alive? That's how it's s'posed to go, ain't it?" She stared at Bobby, eyes glassy, her face on the verge of crumpling.

"Why do I still feel thisyer black hole in my chest?" she whispered. "Like a big ol' piece of my heart's been stolen away when I think of him?"

Bobby brushed his bangs from his eyes and saw it in her—the fragile way her body folded inward. The air of hope had already left her. Maybe she'd seen through his optimistic bluff. Seen that he didn't really believe what he was saying. His words, too light, too fluffy; they dissipated quickly against the weight of her dread and sorrow. After all, *he* was the one who said it. And what power did his word really hold? Still, he wanted to say the right thing, to lift her out of that growing hollowness. But his mind came up empty. He knew the danger of silence in moments like this—how it could amplify, expand, and feed the void inside. His father's silence had done the same. It wasn't just the absence of words. It was how it hushed his entire being. Like those monks Bobby had read about. So devoted to their meditation, they began to mummify themselves while still alive. In his father's case, it wasn't devotion. It was surrender. His eyes hung low, glazed and distant, locked below the horizon—already fixated on the worms writhing in the soil beneath his grave.

Bobby shook his bangs from his eyes, pushing away the thought. He didn't want to leave Zenobia in that kind of quiet. He kept digging through the folds of his mind like a treasure hunter forging through murky brain matter, searching for any gem of comfort or wisdom. The right spell to make everything good.

"Your daddy must still be alive. I know it," he finally said. But he didn't really know it; he should've said that he *hoped* it was true. But he didn't. Zenobia's face brightened some, but a strained silence settled between them, threatening to shake his conviction. Just then, the hatch above creaked open, and a misty spray of morning air raining down.

"Land Ahoy!" Captain Knapp's voice boomed as he poked his head through the opening.

Zenobia wiped the river spray—and her lingering tears—from her face, her response tinged with irritation. "Ain't we flanked by land?" she said. "We're on a dang river, after all."

Knapp met her retort with a brief contemplative pause, then announced with gusto, "City Ahoy!" He withdrew from the hatch, letting a wash of pale daylight flood the space below, momentarily blinding them.

Climbing up onto the deck, Bobby and Zenobia drew deep breaths of the cool, breezy air. They strolled toward the bow and leaned over the railing, absorbing the grandeur stretching before them. The City of Pangia unfolded in a sprawling urban tapestry of vibrant color and ceaseless activity. Thousands of multi-hued buildings stacked vertically across rugged terrain, clinging to the pronged banks of the Moiruh River. The river split into three winding tributaries, dividing the city into distinct boroughs—each crowned by mountainous hills brimming with homes and tenements that spiraled up to the peaks.

The ports buzzed with a frothy swarm of ships. Even at this early hour, the docks pulsed with trade and motion. A clamor of commerce and conflicting ideas. Voices drifted on the wind in a cacophony of bargaining, haggling, and high-minded pontificating. And with the sound came a pungent odor.

Bobby crinkled his nose in disgust. "Pee-yew, what's that stink?"

"Aye, that be the foul stench of the Great City of Pangia," Captain Knapp exclaimed, clomping up beside them, as soaked as ever, his gaze fixed on the nearing skyline. "They'll crow 'bout their high civility and forward ways, but mark me words, don't go stickin' yer noses too close to their gabbin' traps." He leaned in, wrinkling his own nose. "All rotten, they be. From feastin' on too much bloody meat and confectionery treats. Nary a soul there gives a hoot 'bout scrubbin' their chompers, least of all them high-and-mighty Patrician folk. That stink? That's the minglin' of all their endless yappin' and espousin' foul rot." His weathered face grew serious as he eyed them both. "Ye sure ye be wantin' to disembark in such a place? Pangia ain't for the faint of heart, I tell ye."

"It holds the biggest liberry of livin' knowledge in all Helcyon," Zenobia answered, her face set with a hard-edged determination. "Reckon it might have answers we're lookin' for. It ain't a matter of want, Cap'n—it's a mus'."

"Aye, I reckon so," Captain Knapp nodded, a wry smile flitting across his face. "But mind ye, that place might be teamin' with more riddles than solutions."

His words were cut short by a slap of cold river water that narrowly missed Zenobia and Bobby. Shaking off the splash, Captain Knapp burbled, "Settin' course for shore, it be!" He spun on his waterlogged heels, his boots squelching and chorking as he made his way back to the helm.

Bobby watched him go, thoughtful. He suspected the liquid lashes weren't by chance, but the doing of some water spirit. Apparently, Captain Knapp was serving penance for something bad he'd done long ago. Penance meant ferrying those in need up and down the river. Bobby had overheard him the night before, when he was supposed to be asleep. He was speaking to someone, or something, well late into the night. Creeping above deck, Bobby had found Knapp swaying in a hammock fashioned from a fishing net, holding what looked like a one-sided conversation with the river itself.

Hidden behind a few barrels, Bobby had listened closely. Eavesdropping was a skill he had honed over the years of listening to his parents during their fights, when they cried, or later, when his father slunk through the house like a ghost. Or zombie. Or some alien impostor who'd come back from his tour in place of his real father. Despite his clumsy bulk, Bobby was surprisingly good at disappearing into the shadows of furniture. Becoming invisible. Or maybe, as he sometimes feared, simply being invisible.

"What other choice had I?" Knapp's voice had been quiet, but firm. "The lad would've been taken. Maybe worse."

"He is not meant to be here," a voice had replied, melodic, disembodied, like fingers dancing across harp strings. "The Fates can no longer see what's meant to be."

"What's that supposed to mean?" Knapp had asked.

"The boy brings uncertainty. Instability. A disruption of the natural order."

"Is that truly such a bad thing?" Knapp chortled in a seafarer's gruffness. "The world we sail ain't exactly a catch of fish. Seems we're caught 'twixt the devil and the deep blue sea."

"This is serious," hissed the thing in the river, and with a swift deluge, it hurled a cascade of water down upon him. "Even the Oracle has gone silent. And she's a chatterbox. The boy stirs chaos in our world."

Listening to the clandestine exchange between the captain and the mysterious river entity, Bobby felt a profound heaviness descend upon him, making him acutely aware of his ugly, awkward body. He longed to climb out of his flesh and run. To be something else. Anything else. With no desire to hear more, Bobby slipped back down the hatch, undetected.

AT PRESENT, WITH the ship docked, Bobby followed Zenobia down the gang-plank. His eyes drifted to the dark waters below, half expecting to see the river spirit's face staring up at him with a disapproving glare that said: *You don't belong here.* Or worse—the bloodshot orbs of the albino mollusk rising to say: *You very much belong here. You belong to me.* But he saw only the rippling dark, slapping gently against the dock's pillars.

"Don't ye be mindin' her words, lad," Captain Knapp called out, drawing Bobby's heavy gaze upward. The old sailor's soaked face broke into a smile, a twinkle in his eye. "Aye, I know ye were eavesdroppin'. But don't mind the likes of her—she's bound to her own briny depths, spinnin' yarn of doom and gloom like them immortals always do. Don't let her tales anchor yer spirits to the doldrums, lad."

Bobby hesitated, then asked, "What did you do? To be..."

"Shackled to this here river?" Knapp interjected. "Well, lad, the Sea—she were where I first cast me heart. But I was lured away, bewitched by this beauty." He gestured to his ship. "It were love at first sight, lad. The moment I found her restin' on the sea floor, forgotten to the ocean of time. In rescuin' her from her watery grave, I'd wronged the Sea herself. An affair that set me adrift on these very currents, tryin' to curry favor from the Sea, to free me *Lady of the River* from her watery bonds." Knapp raised his pruned hand and gave a hearty wave. "Keep ye sails set to positive winds, lad. They be the winds that'll carry ye to fairer shores." With that, he hoisted and fastened the gangplank and swiftly set sail back down the river. Despite the wave's endless assault on the thoroughly soaked captain, his cheerful voice rang out over the splashing current. A melody carrying over the water like a half-sung legend:

"*I'll be sailin' on the waves o' me love, true and bold. I'll be soaring on the wings o' me love—SPLASH—evermore. I've been searchin' every shore. Seekin' every fair— SPLASH—face. And in the eye of every storm. It's yer calmin' love I'm bound for— SPLASH—I've sailed the briny seas. Searchin' every port—SPLASH—and bay. Seekin' every graceful face, fer me bonnie—SPLASH—bride. When the tempest blows it's gails—SPLASH—The mighty waves makes a sailor quail—SPLASH—But in the eye of every storm, It's yer calmin' love I'm bound—SPLASH—for. I'll be gallopin' on the gallantry o' love. Meandering on foot and boat, in the woozy wend to me love...*"

SPLASH...

...I go...Yo ho! Yo ho! To me love we go...

Bobby watched the boat disappear into the distance, the burbling croon of Captain Knapp fading slowly in from earshot.

"C'mon," Zenobia called at his back.

Turning around, Bobby saw Zenobia already being swallowed by the dense crowd swarming the harbor and markets. He was losing sight of her in the churning mob. "Wait!" he shouted, rushing after her. He plunged into the heavy tide of foot traffic. A chaotic clash of people surging in opposing directions, like two rivers colliding in a whirlpool of chaos. Struggling against the crush of bustling bodies, Bobby pushed his way through. Being shorter and smaller than most, he was easily jostled, knocked, and spun about by the mass of indifferent patrons, his cries for space lost in the commotion. The air shrieked with sharp calls of vendors hawking their wares, their voices clanging against the hollers of buyers haggling over prices, many of whom dressed in expensive-looking purple robes.

Bobby kept calling out Zenobia's name, but his voice was overpowered by the discord of merchants around him. Competing with its volume was like trying to be heard over the thunderous crash of Niagara Falls while standing on the trading floor of the New York Stock Exchange.

Bobby clawed his way through the throng of self-absorbed consumers until, finally, he caught a bit of red— Zenobia's hair, a fiery flicker in the fog of people. It bobbed in and out of view, vanishing, then blipping back to life just a few yards ahead. She moved effortlessly through the crowd, her elbows met with scowls and vitriolic hexes from those too zealously narcissistic to yield.

At last, Bobby broke free from the madness, emerging into the wide-open space of the vast town square. The frantic press of the harbor crowd gave way to a more contemplative buzz, but Zenobia was nowhere to be seen. He took a deep breath, then instantly regretted it. A noxious blend of odors assaulted him: rotting fish, moldy bread, and the rank stench of body odor fused into one lethal fragrance. He cupped his hand over his nose and mouth, leaning hard into mouth-breathing as he scanned the square.

The plaza was surfaced in majestic white marble, littered with men in plum-colored robes milling and mulling about in animated conversation. Myriad groups of gentlemen gathered in small islands. Some laughed over idle gossip, others perched atop crates, haranguing their followers in a passionate spray of speech. The square was a sea of purple, rippling with ideologies, opinions, and judgments.

Dominating the center of the plaza was an imposing seven-tiered fountain. Streams of water arched gracefully into the air, descending in cascading layers into terraced pools below. Atop the grand spectacle stood an *acrolith* statue: a man, chiseled from black stone, triumphantly mounted on a white marble horse, caught mid-gallop. The horse's carved expression was one of panic and strain, contrasting the rider's confidant glee. In one hand, the man held a gleaming golden book aloft, while in the other, a bronze sword hung low in a posture of submissive repose.

The fountain—an elaborate celebration of the power of prose over brute force—was both eye-catching and unavoidable, a shrine of ideological pageantry. Bobby reasoned Zenobia would surely spot him if he stayed near it.

But as time ticked on with no sign of Zenobia's fiery, folksy charm, Bobby grew more uneasy. His fidgeting drew unwanted attention from several purple-robed men strolling about. Their sideward glances held a silent kind of contempt, as if children didn't belong in the public square. The most unnerving attention, however, came from a patrol of the Pangian Peoples Guard. Six square-jawed soldiers in purple military cloaks, each emblazoned with the unit's insignia, trooped past the fountain in disciplined formation. But as they marched, their eyes sharply focused on Bobby with overzealous attentiveness. Heads twisted back to maintain their stare, even as their bodies moved forward in perfect step.

Bobby swung his sweaty bangs from his eyes and tried to deflect their focus by feigning to study the fountain with scholarly interest. "Hmmm," he murmured aloud, nodding studiously to no one. "Now *that's* quite interesting," he added, gesturing vaguely. The charade seemed to work—partially. A pair of men nearby noticed him, looking on with open skepticism, but the guards' heavy boots finally receded into the distance.

Bobby's false fascination slowly became real. The fountain's detail was extraordinary. Every sinew and muscle in the rider and horse was exquisitely rendered. As he stepped closer, he noticed an inscription chiseled into the book held aloft:

WORDS SOW DISCOURSE; SILENCE SAYS PLENTY; SEEK FACTS
IN FICTION; WORDS SHIFT MEANINGS, IDEAS DO NOT.

The final line, squeezed along the bottom edge of the golden book, struck something deep in him:

WE ARE HEIR TO OUR FATHER'S STORIES.

"There you are!" shouted a shrill voice behind him, making Bobby's shoulders jerk up in surprise. He spun around to see Zenobia standing with her hands on her hips, glaring at him like it was somehow his fault they'd gotten separated. "Why you pinchin' yer nose like that?" She asked, her face twisted in confusion.

Realizing he was still holding it, Bobby answered in a nasally tone, "It stinks."

"What?" she barked.

"It stinks," he repeated.

"I got that. *What* stinks?"

"The whole city. It just smells really bad here."

This drew the full attention of two nearby men, who'd been eyeing them with idle curiosity—until now. The younger one, clean-shaven, with sleek, raven-feathered hair, watched with a neutral expression. The older man, his face veined like marbled glass beneath translucent skin, sneered. Twisting his long, wild white beard, he clucked, "Pangia is certainly the cleanest city in all of the world." His jaw creaked as he added, "And additionally, its people, the purest populace."

"It still smells kinda funny to me," Bobby said.

The old man scoffed. "Obviously, your nose knows no better." He sniffed haughtily. "Evidently, you're not from here, so I'll allow such a slight to slide this time."

He turned to leave, but Zenobia piped up bluntly, "Thisyer city does reek sump'm awful like."

The old man's eyes flared in disbelief. His bushy white brows arched like cats hissing at full height. "Young girls should keep their tongues tied tight in the public forum," he fumed. "Where are your parents?"

"An' what if I don't?" Zenobia shot back. "What'll ya do 'bout it? I reckon that awful stench is comin' straight from yer rotten mouth."

The man grabbed Zenobia's wrist. "As a proud pedigree of Pangia, I cannot allow a transient *fopdoodle* to insult me. Or my city! You're coming with me, you little brat!" He yanked hard, clearly expecting her to budge, but she didn't. Not even an inch. He added his other hand and tugged harder. Nothing. Zilch. Zenobia stood planted, smirking.

Then it was her turn.

She seized the front of his velvet robes and hoisted him above her head.

"Put me down! Put me down!" the old man screeched, legs kicking in the air. "Roman! Do something. Help me!" he cried out to his younger companion. But Roman just stood there, frozen, mouth agape.

"Put me down now!"

A crowd began to gather around them.

"Put. Me. *Down!*"

"A'rite," Zenobia said coolly. "Down you go."

She chucked him into the fountain. He hit the water with a cold, hard *splash*, resurfacing in a spluttering thrash.

"Best not fight the water, mister," Zenobia called out. "It's yer friend. Might help warsh that awful smell off ya some."

As he flailed in the shallow basin, Zenobia turned to Roman. "Where's this Great Liberry of Pangia at?" she asked.

Still shell-shocked, Roman nodded slowly, lifting a trembling hand and pointing toward a golden dome rising in the distance, set above the dense, urban sea of buildings.

"Much obliged," Zenobia said, winking. Then she grabbed Bobby by the arm. "C'mon. I ain't losin' ya again." She dragged him off toward the library, leaving behind a sputtering elder, a bewildered crowd, and a ripple of whispers in their wake.

TWENTY-SEVEN

THE **G**REAT Library of Pangia—also known as the Capital of Living Knowledge—spanned eight-city-blocks and towered like a cathedral built in worship of wisdom itself. Constructed in the style of ancient temples, it soared thirty stories high, with its massive central dome, parodying the grandeur of Babylonian aspirations. A sweeping flight of marble steps led to an expansive portico lined with thick Ionic columns and adorned with statues of unnamed gods and goddesses representing the humanities.

Upon pushing through the monolithic doors into the inner rotunda of the main lobby, Zenobia and Bobby were immediately enveloped in a profound quiet. The raucous din of the city vanished the moment the doors shut behind them. Inside, sound seemed to be vacuumed up and swallowed by the very architecture, leaving only the muffled tap of their footsteps on polished stone as they wandered in open-mouthed awe at the conservatory's sheer scale and beauty.

Still catching his breath from their sprint, Bobby wheezed—only to be swiftly shushed by Zenobia. "Thisyer's a *liberry*, so hush now."

Dozens of oak tables, polished to a fine gleam, filled the circular room. Velvet-upholstered chairs invited visitors to settle in and lose themselves in the boundless text that lined the walls, like sacred scrolls.

"Well, ain't this jus' the purtiest thang you ever saw?" Zenobia exclaimed, her voice bursting with delight. Her outburst drew a wave of disapproving glares from nearby readers, who turned their heads with tight-lipped frowns and irritated scowls.

"I know, I know," Zenobia shouted back. "I know where I am. Ain't no need for yer guff. I *know* how to be quiet. My daddy taught me good how to read all quiet-like."

The annoyed expressions twisted further, now red-faced sneers of disdain streaked across mouths too disciplined to speak.

Then a calm, clear voice cut through the tension: "May I help you?"

Bobby jumped, while Zenobia spun around to find a middle-aged man with a polished bald head standing behind her. He was completely hairless, no beard, no brows, no lashes. His yellow-brown eyes were sharp yet warm, set symmetrically in a square, composed face. He stood tall, poised, his green tunic neatly belted beneath a dark gold cloak and diagonal sash of fine green silk.

"Who are you?" Zenobia asked.

"I am the Librarian-in-Chief of this grandiloquent establishment," he answered, his voice somehow full-bodied yet soft enough not to disturb the quiet. Unlike Zenobia's earlier outburst, his words reached their ears without drawing a single irritated glance.

"And may I ask," he continued, with a courteous incline of the head, "who *you* might be?"

"I'M—" Zenobia began to blurt out, only to be silenced by the librarian's ink-stained index finger pressed softly to his lips.

"Please," he said, "speak *sotto voce,* so as not to disturb our readers. This is a library, after all."

"I'm Zenobia Mulhick," she said again, this time in a lower voice. "An' we're lookin' for some information."

The librarian tapped his smooth chin with his inky finger. "What kind of information are you seeking? Subject? Title? Author? Date of publication? And does the boy speak?" His warm, tawny gaze shifted to Bobby. Without eyebrows, his face looked oddly naked, yet the smooth ridges above his eyes rose high in curiosity, lending him a kindly expression. "Not that I mind quiet children," he added. "They often prove to be the best readers and writers."

"I can speak," Bobby said. "I'm Bobby Porter. And we've come to find out how to defeat the Ashen Knight. Do you have a book on that?"

Surprise flickered across the librarian's naked face. "P-Porter, did you say?" he murmured, fingers once again tapping thoughtfully at his chin.

"The son of our Creator, if ya can bleeve it," Zenobia hollered, her voice rang out. She slapped her hand over her mouth, trying to contain it, but it was too late. Her words had already ricocheted across the rotunda, eliciting another rumble of irritation from the readers.

"Yes. I see. I see—of course," the librarian muttered. "Remarkable timing, indeed. To arrive today of all days." Then louder: "A *divine* kind of timing.

Please, follow me." He scooted behind them, gently ushering them toward one of the many corridors branching from the central space. Zenobia and Bobby exchanged a look, shrugged, and let themselves be led.

"You liable to have that sorta book?" Zenobia asked as they slipped deeper into the library, passing a long hall lined with stern-faced marble busts of old men.

"Defeating the Ashen Knight?" the librarian whispered as if he were wary that the marble figures might overhear. Once they passed the hall of stone faces of yore, he quickened his pace, taking the lead. "It's a topic with scant literature. However, I believe I know of a unique book that may contain relevant information. A very rare piece indeed. A real *sui generis*."

As they hastened through the library, each room they passed resembled a vast warehouse, stacked with towering bookshelves that reached several stories high. Every shelf crammed with seemingly infinite volumes. Bobby struggled to keep track of the sprawling maze of chambers they sped past, each marked by etched placards mounted above the entrances, declaring a wild array of specific and often baffling subjects:

ARTS OF SCIENCE; HISTORICAL FACTS ON FICTION; FICTIONAL FACTS IN HISTORY; EVERYTHING WRONG WITH THE WORLD (*a notably massive chamber*); WARFARE AND UNFAIR WARS; REMEMBRANCES OF LOST AND FORGOTTEN THINGS; PANGIAN LAW; DISAMBIGUATING PANGIAN LAW'S AMBIGUITIES; HOUSE OF ROYAL FAMILIES; AMUSING MUSINGS OF MUSES; HILARIOUS DRAMA OF UNFUNNY COMEDIES (*a puzzlingly specific section that especially baffled Bobby*)

And on and on it went, as they went on and on and on through this truly great library. Just as Bobby felt certain they couldn't possibly pass one more room without his feet falling off, they finally came to a stop before a placard that read:

UNFINISHED WORKS IN PROGRESS.

"We have arrived," the librarian announced, a trace of mystery curling in his voice. "Here, every unfinished story resides. The pages update themselves as they are written. Sadly, many remain incomplete." With a dramatic sweep of his cloak, he pushed them into the section, adding that his office was just beyond.

This room—possibly the largest of them all—stretched on before them, seemingly with no end in sight. As they made their way through this section, the librarian stopped abruptly. "We have a leak!" he declared. Bobby watched as the librarian hurried down an aisle of high-reaching shelves. At first, he didn't understand what he was looking at. Then he saw it: a puddle on the marble floor—not water, but words. Actual handwritten letters flowed in looping over-laps, pooling into a small mound. Tracing the source, the librarian scooted a roll-ing ladder along a rail, ascended thirty feet or more, and plucked a single book from its place on high above. The one responsible for the leak.

"This happens frequently," the librarian said as he descended the ladder, holding a book titled: *Why Me?* "When a work is overwrought with waxing verbosity, filled with loquacious lamentations, and rampant with prolific paeans of grandiloquent misery. Prose so poorly produced, it begins to leak. The book is practically crying out to be edited. Edit, then cut in half, then edit again. Trim, tweak, rewrite, abridge, set aflame, and edit once more." He stooped over the word puddle on the floor, rummaging through it. "Let's see what we have here," he mumbled to himself. "Anything good?—aha!" He held up a word triumphantly. "*Pusillanimous.*"

"Sometimes, you can find a gem among the disregarded trash," the Liberian said with a smile.

Bobby looked at the word curiously. "What's it mean?"

"It's an adjective to describe someone timid or fearful," the librarian explained. Standing upright, he tucked the leaky book under one arm while holding the word between his forefinger and thumb.

"A-coward," Zenobia added bluntly.

"Yes, in crude terms," the librarian agreed. "A cowardly type."

"Lily-livered," Zenobia continued, "Chickin'. Yella. A real pus—"

"Yes, yes, a real pussyfoot," the librarian interrupted quickly. "Now, let's continue. Someone will clean up this mess later."

After a considerable trek deeper, they arrived at a tall, slender green door, distinguished by a brass plaque that read:

OFFICE OF THE LIBRARIAN-IN-CHIEF.

Still juggling the leaky book and his word, the librarian retrieved an enormous brass key ring from beneath his sash. He thumbed through the tangle of keys until he found the right one. Just before unlocking the door, he turned to them with a small, apologetic smile.

"How rude of me. I haven't properly introduced myself. In my role as librarian, I often forget my own name. I am Bobble Gentles. Delighted to make your acquaintance." With that, he turned back to the door. The key slid home with a satisfying *click*, followed by a symphony of mechanical sounds—clicks, clanks, and a long, hollow *thunk* as ten bolts unlatched and allowed the door to swing open.

Bobble Gentles' office was high and deep, though made cramped by teetering stacks of plain, leather-bound tomes arranged in labyrinth rows. They followed a narrow, zigzagging maze of medieval manuscripts deep inside, the stack. At last, they reached a cozy nook: a fireplace crackling with a low flame, a broad oak desk and stool, and a plush armchair nestled amid more manageable piles of books.

As soon as he laid eyes on the inviting, overstuffed armchair, Bobby made a beeline for it and collapsed into its cushioned embrace with a deep, relieved sigh.

Bobble Gentles, meanwhile, glided to his desk, leaving a trail of dripping words behind from the leaky book wedged under his arm. "The only remedy for a leaky book," he said, rummaging across his cluttered desktop for parchment and a quill, "is to pen a scathing critique of the work in progress. That's guaranteed to terminate the whole ill-conceived endeavor and stop the leak." He brandished a pre-written review with dramatic flair. "Fortunately, I keep a few on hand to expedite the process."

"But... how do you know if it's bad if you haven't read it?" Bobby asked.

"The book itself is the testament to its quality—or lack thereof," Bobble Gentles replied. "It bemoans its own existence. A cry for mercy from a hapless author. Sadly, not all who wish to write *should*. Desires and dreams do have limits." With a final scribble and signature, he slapped the critique between the book's weeping pages and snapped it shut. Instantly, the book shriveled, compressing into a small, inky husk in his palm, a sad, sticky wad of failure. "It's quite the sad affair," he concluded, woeful of his task, "to witness someone's dream die in your hand." He lobbed the wad into the fireplace, where it hissed and vanished in flame. Then, from the top of a neat pile, he retrieved a clean, unmarked volume and gently placed the rescued word inside.

Zenobia, her curiosity piqued, plucked up a book from a nearby stack and flipped it open to a random page.

"Whadda all thisyer books, anyhow?" she asked, squinting at the first word she saw.

HIPPOPOTOMONSTROSESQUIPPEDALIOPHOBIA.

The word twisted around her tongue as she attempted to pronounce it. "That can't be real."

"Oh, but it is," Bobble Gentles declared. "This is my life's work! A project so innovative and revolutionary, I'm certain to have my likeness immortalized in the Hall of Knowledge, right beside the busts of esteemed librarians." He stood tall, chin lifted, attempting the stoic gaze of a marble head. After an abstract pause, he returned to the moment with a snap of his fingers. "These volumes contain the breadth of our rich language, from erudite terms to parochial patois, quotidian quips, and everyday slang. I've amassed them all throughout my prosperous tenure as Librarian-in-Chief. I am a linguistic scavenger. A logophile. A word-hoarder. A vocable virtuoso." He beamed. "My goal is to create the first comprehensive compendium of our tongue. *Bobble Gentles' Word Omnibus*. Say you come across a word you've never encountered before, and with a quick glance through one of my handy Word Omnibus volumes—presto! You've got its meaning. A genius, ground-breaking endeavor, don't you think?"

"A dictionary?" Bobby said innocently.

Bobble Gentles' self-congratulating grin deflated. "A what?"

"A big, thick book full of words and their meanings. We have it where I come from. It's called a dictionary."

The revelation hit Bobble Gentles hard, a blow right to the soul. He went eerily silent, all color draining from his face. Then, like firecrackers popping in rapid succession, the room erupted with crackling. All around them, the unmarked manuscripts began to shrivel and contort, setting off a domino effect among the towering stack. Bobby and Zenobia watched in stunned silence as the room transformed into a collapsing heap of withering pages, the devastation even reaching the book in Zenobia's hands.

Once the tumult subsided, an utterly destroyed Bobble Gentles sat among the ruins of his life's ambitions. He slumped over, his voice barely above a whisper as he lamented. "So I suppose—*ahem*—my idea is not as original as I believed." His tone was steeped with despair. "My life's work... it's meaningless." He buried his face in his hands. "I only wanted to create something transformative. Something to benefit humanity. And now, my dream is as dead as that poor drip whose prose I just edited into oblivion. Thirty years... wasted. I'm a fraud," he said.

Hoping to offer some comfort, Bobby said, "You can still make your own dictionary. It'd be the first of its kind in Helcyon."

"That's a stupid idea!" Bobble Gentles shot back, slapping his hand against the desk. The last pile of decrepit books, barely clinging to their stack, toppled over in a dusty collapse. "I aspired to be remembered as a true innovator. Someone my predecessors would revere. But now? I'm nothing but a copycat, a plagiarizer—*a phony*!" He emitted a whine so pathetic it wilted in the air around him. "Tis the curse of knowledge, I suppose," he muttered. "To understand that nothing created, nor anyone who creates it, is truly original anymore."

Bobby sank into himself, silently berating his big mouth. He always said the wrong thing. Always made it worse. His stupid words ruined lives.

Zenobia, unfazed by the growing pile of melodrama, continued flipping through the shriveled wordbook in her hands. She held up a wrinkled page filled with curious entries: AEROPHOBIA; MALEDICTAPHOBIA; PHALACROPHOBIA; POGONOPHOBIA; OMPHALOPHOBIA; TRISKAIDEKAPHOBIA—and so on, all in different handwriting styles.

"Whadda all theseyer words mean?" she asked. "An' what tongue is they even written in?".

Rubbing his red, damp eyes, Bobble Gentles croaked, "That's Inglish," the bitterness in his voice unmistakable. "They're phobias. Types of fears that afflict us. And now, I'm afraid I find myself confronting my own *kakorrhaphiophobia*."

Zenobia snorted. "That word sounds mighty made-up to me."

Bobble Gentles looked at her, solemn and slow. "My dear child, in a sense, all words are made up. Language is a collective fantasy we pretend is real. Words are plucked from the capricious air, shaped by our tongues to agitate the mind, or inked into existence to disrupt the placid vacuity of the lazy thought. And now my worth, like the words I once revered, has—*poof*—vanished into the prosaic oblivion of *hoi polloi*." He slumped onto his stool with a defeated thud, chin sinking into his palm.

Zenobia shut the book with a sharp *snap* and tossed it onto the nearby pile. "We didn't come all thisyer way to hear ya mope cause someone else beat ya to thinkin' up a word book. Ya s'posed to git us that information we came for. So quit mopin' n'give it... please."

Bobble Gentles exhaled, so long and loud it seemed to deflate him entirely. He slid from his stool onto his knees and reached beneath his desk, dragging out a small chest reinforced with brass corners and sealed with a thick padlock. With a soft *click*, the lock released. He paused, glancing up at Bobby and Zenobia.

"What I'm about to reveal is sacred," he said gravely. "Known only to myself and the Librarians who came before me. This morning, I dared to consult it, against tradition, against sense. And now... I understand the warnings. The power it has to stain the soul." He opened the chest with a creak and carefully lifted out a plain-covered book. Its title glinted in bold silver: THE TRAVELER'S GUIDE TO HELCYON: SIGHTS, HISTORY, TIPS ON HOW TO DEFEAT THE ASHEN KNIGHT.

Bobby recognized the book straight away—it was his father's. But how? Wasn't he inside his father's story? The thought bent his mind in a disorienting way, like asking if you could dream within a dream.

"My Porter, what sorta writin' is that?" Zenobia gasped, gobsmacked by the book's title.

Bobby realized her astonishment wasn't at the words themselves, but at how they appeared, printed in precise, uniform letters. In this quasi-medieval world, where all writing was scribbled by hand in illegible script by the literate few, such clean typography was a shock. It seemed divine. To Bobby, it was a reminder: the difference between magic and mundane was often just a matter of what technology a world did or didn't have.

"And now that you two have shown up," Bobble Gentles went on, "claiming to be the son of its author. Proof which is still pending. But I can't ignore the curious timing of it all." He laid the book affectionately on his desk, opening it to reveal more of its sacred print.

Bobby and Zenobia crowded around the pages, inadvertently elbowing the librarian in their eagerness. Bobble Gentles stepped back and allowed them space.

"I'll leave you to study the text," he said, his tone regaining a shade of its earlier dignity, though his movements still sagged with resignation. "But, bear in mind, like all volumes in this library, unless claimed by the rightful author, this manuscript must not be taken beyond these walls." He pointed at the book with grave insistence. "This one, in particular, is expressly *verboten* from leaving my office."

With that, Bobble Gentles turned away, wading through the scattered remains of his now useless wordbooks. Reaching the doorway, he paused. Glancing back at the children lost in the sacred scripture, he murmured, "Henceforth, I shall let all leaky books lament and leak unchecked. Let every sorry syllable spill freely into the void." Then, without another word, he stepped through the door. It closed firmly behind him with a solid *thunk*, followed by the measured clicks of ten bolts sliding back into place.

Zenobia and Bobby barely noticed. The librarian was gone. Their attention was fixed on the strange, perfect pages before them, searching for answers in the printed words.

Bobby, catching the clack of bolts sliding home, said with concern, "I think he just locked us in." He watched, uneasy, as Zenobia hunched over his father's book, her fingers tearing through the pages in a frantic search. Then, all at once, she froze. Her body stiffened, as if she'd hit something. Some truth, some horror. The pinch in her brow eased; her narrowed eyes widened into slack disbelief. She turned a few more pages, and something in her expression curdled, shock giving way to fury.

"Poppycock!" she yelled, slamming her fist down on the oak desk, splintering a chunk of its edge clean off.

Bobby flinched. "What's wrong?" he asked, already fearing the answer.

"It ain't here!"

His gaze dropped to the open page. The header, set in crisp, perfect Times New Roman, read: CHAPTER XXVI: HOW TO DEFEAT THE ASHEN KNIGHT ...but beneath it, the page was stark white. Blank. Turning the next, and the next—nothing. Page after page of empty promise.

"It's not finished," Bobby said. A fact he'd already known in his bones. But still, part of him had hoped. Hoped his father had left behind some final clue, some hidden wisdom waiting to be deciphered. Instead, only absence. Only the shape of what wasn't there. Disappointment.

Zenobia stomped her foot, hard. "Useless. Utter useless!" she cried, her rage boiling over into tears. "Not even yo daddy knows how to kill the Ashen Knight." Her eyes found Bobby's, wet and burning with anger and grief. "He made him. Can't he jus' unmake him? Why can't he help us?"

Bobby swallowed. The answer thudded in his chest like a truth too large for his lungs.

Because he can't.

Because he's gone.

Because your god is dead.

The words wouldn't come. His tongue felt thick and numb. The air was too thin and hollow to carry sound. What alchemy could turn that dust into words anyways? He didn't have it. Not now.

"I hate thisyer world," Zenobia muttered, swiping the other books off the desk with the back of her hand. "Ain't nothin' but misery. Ain't nothin' more I want to do with it."

"There's gotta be *something*," Bobby insisted. He flipped through the pages again, forcing a surge of determination into his search, desperate to find anything that might help—

Until he stopped. There it was. His drawing. His own map. The one he'd made for school. All his familiar doodles: squiggly roads, small, crooked buildings, curled symbols representing portals—and there, clearly marked, the location of the *Sword of Aegis*. Helcyon's most powerful weapon.

He stared, stunned. It was impossible. And yet, there it was.

"Holy moly," he exclaimed.

"What?" Zenobia looked up.

"There are more portals like the one we used to get to the Feral Forest."

"Yeah, so?"

"There's a bunch more shown on this map. In my dad's book."

"Big whoop," Zenobia sniffled.

"One of them leads to the most powerful weapon in all Helcyon. The Sword of Aegis."

Zenobia stood straighter. Her skepticism gave way to a flicker of hope. "Can it kill the Ashen Knight?"

"Of course—well, I think so... I'm not sure. But I'm pretty sure it can."

She fixed Bobby with her now-infamous probing gaze, the kind that dissected his confidence like a scalpel, leaving him anxious, exposed, and awkwardly winking in its wake.

"Fine," she said, straightening her tunic. "We git thisyer sword n'plunge it straight into the heart of that demon. If he's got one. Best we take the book with us."

"But the librarian said we can't take it from his office or the library. And... we're locked in."

"We need it!" Zenobia said, her voice firm. "It's life or death."

Before Bobby could protest any further, she charged the tall green door. Her shoulder slammed into it with a thunderous crack, blasting it apart into a shower of splinters and broken wood. She darted into the room beyond, scanned it quickly for danger, then glanced back. "C'mon, it's clear. Grab the book!"

Heart thumping fast, Bobby snatched the book and tucked it under his tunic without thinking. The hardcover pressed uncomfortably against his bare belly, chafing him as he chased after Zenobia into the adjoining chambers. Together, they fled like a pair of scrappy, childlike thieves ducking down passages, darting between towering shelves, dodging every distant footstep. Their escape was a breathless crawl through an endless maze of chambers and corridors. From section to section, Bobby's pulse pounded with each turn. He kept expecting Bobble Gentles to leap from the shadows or emerge around the next corner. But the librarian never came.

By the time they reached the library's main entrance, Bobby was drenched in sweat, the book clinging to his torso like a second sticky stomach. They burst into the open air, hit hard by the stench of rot and the rattle of city noise. Without pause, they flew down the front steps and slipped into the crowd. But just before Bobby could disappear into the flow of bodies—

Two large hands clamped down on his shoulder.

"Hold it!" barked a man.

Bobby spun to find himself seized by uniformed guards wearing the insignia of the PANGIAN PEOPLES GUARD. Warmongering brutes not to be underestimated, they were as disciplined and ruthless as the ancient enforcers of Rome.

Bobby yielded at once. A life conditioned to obey authority abdicated his freedom in favor of unquestioning surrender.

But Zenobia didn't yield. She unleashed a fierce defence. She sent the guard grabbing her arm flying, tumbling down the steps and vanishing into the chaos of the streets. More guards charged her, only to be thrown off with explosive strength, colliding into carts, columns, and startled bystanders. The street churned with alarm. Steel hissed from scabbards as a half-dozen more guards surrounded her, blades drawn, treating her like some dangerous animal. Her growl, low and feral, curled from bared teeth, along with a sharp whistle that escaped the gap in her snarl, taunting. She was gearing up to take them all down, wild-eyed and fearless.

"Zenobia!" Bobby's scream tore through the noise, raw and pleading. "Please stop. We're caught."

Her eyes shot straight to his.

There he was—cuffed, restrained by two guards. One of them held the book in his filthy hands.

And just like that... she stopped. The fire drained from her in an instant. It gutted him. Watching her forfeit so easily—*give up*—he felt the shame crash into him. His weakness had diluted her strength. His stubborn frailty had doomed them both. Her submission, so sudden and complete, confirmed the burden of his presence: a weight too cumbersome for even Zenobia's strength and resilience. Now, she was suffering the great hushing of his intrusive existence. Bobby's congenital bad luck, etched deep in his network of unwise blood, coded in his DNA by the misfortunes of his ancestors, only reinforced the truth: stories already written cannot be rewritten.

That revelation was written across Zenobia's face. The moment she realized her fate was not the heroic adventure of rescuing her father as they once imagined, but a tale of epic tragedy. And she reacted as any sane person would when confronted with such cruel clarity. She gave up.

The encircling guards closed in swiftly, locking iron manacles around her wrists and fastening a collar around her slender neck. A thick chain linked the collar to a guard's command—her leash.

From the top of the library steps, Bobble Gentles stood, his expression unreadable as he observed the chaos below. His gaze wandered until it locked on Bobby. A guard returned the book to him, and Bobble secured it beneath his cloak with a curt nod of acknowledgment.

Then came a familiar shrill voice. "That's the little bilious brat, alright!" shrieked the white-bearded old man, shoving through the crowd for a better look. He jabbed a bony finger toward Bobby and Zenobia. "You two will pay proper penance for your misbehavior. I'll see to it! I'll personally see to it!"

"Let's move," ordered one of the guards, yanking Zenobia's chain.

She resisted at first, her body locking in defiance as the collar snapped taut. "Don't give us any more trouble, girl."

But then, her resolve dissolved quickly. Eyes lowered, she fell into step with the guards.

Bobby, lacking a collar—being too meek to mandate one—was shoved into the ranks of the Pangian Peoples Guard, marched along like a prisoner of war. Together, they were paraded through a gauntlet of bile-spewing citizens. Bobby looked back once more to the library steps, searching for Bobble Gentles, but the librarian had already vanished behind a wall of jeering bodies. It was a spectacle of sanctimonious outrage and public shame. A perp walk down a cobbled throughway. As Bobby was pushed forward through the spit and scorn, he imagined a day when he might stand tall enough to meet the world's judgment eye to eye—unflinching, unapologetic before his ignorant accusers. But for now, he had to stomach being forced to walk beneath it, face to face with the lint-clogged navel of a world that had already decided what kind of person he was.

TWENTY-EIGHT

IN **THE** sprawling expanse of The Great City of Pangia, its denizens towered like giants. Their faces were contorted in apoplectic rage, a lifetime of self-righteous indignation having carved deep creases into their skin, engraving their disdain in indelible scratches of vehemence.

Bobby noticed the absence of other children in the crowd. It was all old people, and younger old people, draped in various shades of purple, or violet, or something in between—or neither. Perhaps the color that swathed the citizens of Pangia wasn't quite the piety of purple, nor the validity of violet, but something closer to overripe red, the color of bruised blood.

The commotion outside the library had stirred these bruised-blooded hoi polloi into self-satisfying outrage. Any excuse to vent the bitterness of their own joyless lives on any convenient target. And they found easy targets in children, especially ones like Bobby and Zenobia.

Faces passed in a smearing blurs, strained and swollen with contempt and age. They spat: "Damn children, always causing trouble!"

"Where are their neglecting parents?"

"Riff-raff begets riff-raff."

"I hope they punish you good!"

They hurled their ire and wagged their accusing fingers, offering no specifics for the supposed offense. Bobby couldn't understand why taking a book merited such public scorn. In Pangia, it seemed, simply being a child was treated as a kind of sin, inviting endless pillory and castigation until, somehow, you emerged from the other side of youth, transfigured into an acceptable adult.

He remembered something else his father once said: "Hard work makes a hard man." Back when his voice still filled the room, before his body went quiet. He said it to motivate Bobby to shed his baby fat by working the fat of the land, which was their backyard, and later, his mother's garden. Sometime after his return, his father said something stranger. It'd be some of the last words his father ever spoke: "Holes just lead to more holes. Deeper, darker holes." It had nothing to do with anything. It just came to him in that moment.

Stalking through the frenzied mob, Bobby tried to catch a glimpse of Zenobia, who walked a few feet ahead, surrounded by guards. He searched for any sign of how she was holding up, but all he could see was the frizzy fray of her red hair, her head perpetually bowed low toward the ground. The clink and rattle of her chain marking her steps.

Their march through the agitated mob ended at the foot of a stately building, not unlike the Great Library of Pangia, though smaller. Its architecture mimicked the prestige of ancient Greek and Roman constructions, as all official government edifices that came after would do, as if to imply that all truths and laws must be enshrined in this sacred geometry of straight lines, right angles, and perfect circles.

As they mounted the steps, the sea of discontented, bruised-blooded citizens began to dissipate, retreating into the shadows of their mundane and self-important lives, already forgetting the commotion, forgetting what they were so outraged about. All but the old white-bearded man, who still hovered nearby like a pest. His shrill voice distinct from the dwindling buzz of the crowd. "These monstrous mudlark miscreants should be punished to the fullest extent of the law!"

Crossing the threshold into the building, Bobby and Zenobia were thrust into a narrow cage whose tight dimensions forced them to stand.

Once more, close to her, Bobby felt a stir of conflicting emotions. Part of him wanted to take comfort in their closeness. But any joy he might've felt was dashed by the severe gloom stamped on her face. She looked broken in her subdued demeanor. Her once-bold fire dimmed. The fierce spark in her eyes that scolded and challenged him with every look now seemed extinguished. He knew what he had done to her. He hushed Zenobia—just as he'd hushed his father. If only he could learn to hush that part of him. The part that ruined things, maybe then, he could preserve whatever shred of Zenobia still remained. Maybe he could cling to whatever piece of her still needed him. Still wanted him.

"I'll get us out of here," Bobby whispered. "We'll save your father."

Zenobia didn't respond. Her stillness was so complete she could've been mistaken for a sad puppet whose strings had been cut. Her eyes focused on the floor, and whatever lay beneath it. Just as his father used to. With the same grave contemplation.

The forum into which their cage was rolled and locked into place was an enormous, opulent oval arena—more a circular circus stage than a court of law. Stadium-style seating wrapped around the stage in thirty rising tiers, offering onlookers a clear, voyeuristic view of the tribunal spectacle about to unfold. A low partition of marbled balusters marked the divide between the audience and the courtroom floor.

At the far end of the stage stood a throne, silent, yet commanding. Crafted from pure gold and plush with cushions of deep purple velvet, it rested upon a platform that raised it high above all else. Ten sentries stood in perfect symmetry—five to a side—while two more stood guard near Bobby and Zenobia's cage.

With a ceremonial strike of spear butts against the marbled floor, a resounding knock signaled the beginning, triggering a flooding of the chamber with the stampede of feet and the clamor of conversation. The bruised-blood citizens of Pangia poured through the many arched entrances, scrambling for seats with feverish excitement.

Then came four sharp knocks. The crowd stilled, first to a murmur, then into tense silence.

"Court is now in session," announced the sentinel to the right of the throne, his voice booming off the domed ceiling. "The Honorable Judge Draconis King presiding."

From beneath the throne, a trapdoor opened, and a figure emerged. He wore no purple nor violet, unlike the rest of Pangia, but robes of gleaming gold. Small in stature, scarcely four feet tall, he nonetheless radiated authority and gravitas. In one hand, he held a bejeweled scepter that glinted with gems and diamonds as he ascended a narrow staircase that slid out from the throne's base. Once seated, he lifted his scepter high. A wave of thunderous applause erupted. Then, with a flick of the rod, silence returned. Then Judge Draconis King turned his bulging eyes toward the cage, pointed his scepter at the accused, and, in a voice deeper than expected, demanded, "State your names."

"I'm Bobby Porter," Bobby answered, clear and steady.

The name *Porter* spread like a spark across dry tinder—sneering whispers rippled through the spectators. But a sharp motion from the judge stilled the stir once again.

"Porter, you say?" The judge's voice carried a clear note of irritation and impatience. He jabbed the sharp point of his scepter toward Zenobia. "And you, girl. Your name?"

Zenobia, face downcast and despondent, offered no reply until a guard rattled his glaive against the bars and shouted, "Tell the court your name!"

"Zenobia," she finally whispered without looking up. "Zenobia Mulhick."

"Do you both plead guilty?" the judge asked, already sounding as if he wished to be elsewhere.

"Guilty of what?" Bobby yelled. The retort shocked even him. There was boldness in his voice, a new self-confidence, summoned from somewhere he couldn't explain.

"Guilty of what!" the judge mocked, visibly taken aback. His whole face twitched with annoyance as he scanned the chamber for the prosecutor, eventually spotting him buried nose-deep in the gutter of a book. "Ahem!" the judge prompted pointedly. The prosecutor jolted upright, his small, dark eyes blipping in and out of existence, dumbfounded and confused. Then he stood up from his chair. "Yes, your Honor?" he stammered, flustered.

"What are these two being charged with?"

Floundering through a tangle of papers, the prosecutor muttered, "Ah, yes... well... they are being charged with..." His fingers fumbled uselessly through the mess. "It's a very serious charge indeed, Your Honor. A very serious charge..." He stalled, buying time, then finally abandoned the pretense. He straightened and gestured vaguely toward another figure near the dais. "Allow me to introduce the plaintiff and key witness in these proceedings... a Mister Sir..." He trailed off. By now, it was clear he didn't know the name, the charge, or much of anything.

With theatrical purpose, the white-bearded man, whom Zenobia had dunked in the fountain earlier, shuffled forward and bowed deeply. "Paterfamilias, Your Honor. Lord Sir Paterfamilias."

The judge turned to him. "And what do you charge these two with, Mr. Sir Paterfamilias?"

Drawing himself tall and sucking in a deep breath of self-righteous indignation, Sir Paterfamilias launched into a shrill performance. "Your Honor, what *aren't* these two nasty little ne'er-do-wells guilty of? And where do I even begin? They are guilty of the most grievous and grotesque crime of assaulting and insulting a pious Patrician priest!" He clutched at his chest, indicating himself as the noble victim. "Furthermore, your fair and fortuned Honor, they've slandered and defamed the good people of Pangia and, by extension, the Crown itself—calling us 'smelly' and 'dirty,' claiming our mouths and minds are full of rot!" He edged closer to the cage, his voice rising with each accusation. "And—yes! They uttered an ungodly curse. A vile hate crime!" His hands trembled in dramatic fury. "They said all Pangians should be burned alive!"

Bobby objected with a resounding cry. "We didn't say that! That's a lie!" But his protest was drowned out in jeers and boos from the onlookers.

"Silence!" the judge bellowed, rapping his scepter against his throne. "Quiet!"

Paterfamilias, not missing a beat, added in a tone now low but laced with malice, "And of course, these villainous vagrants demonstrated their devious, demonic tendency by violating our most sacred law: pilfering a book from the Great Library of Pangia." He then collapsed in a dramatic heap, as if the weight of the accusation were too much to bear—though the smugness curling on his lips betrayed his performance.

With a sigh bordering on apathy, the judge turned toward the defense. "And what says the defendant's counsel in response to these charges?"

The counselor—who somehow represented both the plaintiff and defendants, a conflict as blatant as the unlawful possession of the book he held in his lap, titled *The Dunce's Guide to Disambiguate the Ambiguities of Pangian Law*—hurriedly tucked the volume under his tunic and stammered as he was called upon. "Ah... well..." his eyes darted around in search of an escape. "We have no further questions or witnesses and, therefore, rest our case."

The judge's gaze pivoted back to Bobby and Zenobia. "What faith are you?" he asked.

Bobby . "Faith?"

"Do you follow the Patrician or Plebeian doctrines?"

Bobby scratched his head, baffled. "What's that got to do with anything?"

"It'll determine the severity of your punishment, boy. So which is it?"

"I follow the Plebeian faith," Zenobia said firmly, lifting her head and meeting the judge's expectant gaze for the first time.

The crowd burst into disapproving boos. The judge raised his scepter once more, quelling the unrest.

"And you, boy?"

Bobby's confusion deepened. "But that's unfair?"

"Answer the question," the judge said.

"I'm not any!" Bobby said flatly.

"Impossible! You must be either Patrician or Plebeian. Do you believe the sky to be the hue of violet... or purple?"

"The sky is blue. Not violet or purple. Which are basically the same color anyways," Bobby declared.

This invoked a collective gasp, sucking the air out of the chamber.

After a heavy pause, the judge rose and pointed his scepter at Bobby. "Clearly, the verdict is self-evident," he announced, swinging his scepter between Zenobia and Bobby as if it were the scales of justice. "You are both guilty of corrupting the impressionable youth with your dangerous lies and falsehoods.

"What youth?" Bobby scoffed, "I don't see any kids—"

"As well!" the judge shouted over him, "as well as thievery, assault, and public disorder!" His scepter leveled straight at Bobby. "And you, mister, are doubly charged with heresy, for denying the State-sanctioned truth of the sky's color, and taking the Lord's name in vain. Ignorance may be a Plebeian's plight, but conscious rebellion is heresy. For these crimes, you are both sentenced to the Isle of Black Rock for one thousand years of hard labor." The judge raised his scepter, poised to deliver the final blow—

"The boy speaks the truth. The sky is blue!" a bold and clear voice called out from the gallery.

Every head turned toward the clatter of metal rattling down the aisle. A man in a heavily tarnished suit of armor advanced toward the court. His face was hidden behind a carved wooden mask crafted like a tiger's snarling maw.

Bobby's hand found Zenobia's arm and squeezed it. A smile broke across his face. "It's the Tiger Knight," he whispered.

Zenobia, however, remained despondent.

The Tiger Knight was halted by three sentries before he could step onto the court floor, but his presence alone commanded the attention of the entire room. The judge stood on tiptoe, straining to peer at the interloper. "And who might you be?"

With a resonant clang of armored fist against his breastplate, the man declared, "I am the Tiger Knight!"

A shrill shriek erupted from the white-bearded accuser. "Madness! There hasn't been a knight in a thousand years. Not since our ruler reaped his reign over all Helcyon! It's preposterous. Inconceivable!"

"Yet here I stand," the Tiger Knight said, unmoved. "Alive. A knight who became a tiger, and now returned a knight once more—though still a tiger." He spun to address the gallery. "I once was like you. A proud Pangian, born in a time before the sky was blotted out by ash. And I'm here to testify that

I've seen with my own eyes the boy's truth. The sky is blue."

Another collective gasp overtook the room.

"Words of a madman," squawked the old man. "Made madder still by that ridiculous costume. Lies from behind the wooden mouth of a beast! Ha! Are we to believe he's older than a millennium? He's a blasphemer. An accomplice in this cabal of conspiracy criminals!"

"I have caressed many sins," the Tiger Knight said calmly, "but my lips have never embraced a single lie."

The judge, now seated again, lifted his scepter and gestured. "Bring this man forth."

As the sentries escorted the Tiger Knight forward, he passed Bobby's cage. Though the mask gave nothing away, Bobby offered him a hopeful grin.

The judge leaned forward, resting his chin atop his clenched fist, studying the knight as if trying to place him from some long-forgotten school days.

"Sir," he said at last, "the court requires your identification and declaration of faith—Patrician or Plebeian?"

Holding his head high, the Tiger Knight proclaimed, "I am kin to Mother Nature, and her children bear no names. It is only Man who, in his vanity, foolishly claims the exclusive right to significance and supremacy, dividing himself into factions with labels of 'us' and 'them.' But, for the convenience of those insular minds who cannot conceive a world without titles, categories, and borders, you may call me the Tiger Knight. My allegiance lies with the earth and her azure skies."

"Enough," the judge slammed his scepter against the palm of his hand. "Your testimony only brings you closer to imprisonment alongside these heretics and thieves. State your true name and faith, or join them in punishment."

"Tiger Knight," came his unwavering answer. "My allegiance is with the Earth and her—"

"Spare us," the judge cut him off, springing to his full diminutive height. He struck the throne's arm with his scepter. "Take him into custody."

Guards closed in and seized the knight. He gave no resistance as they bundled him into the already cramped cage with Zenobia and Bobby.

Bobby gawked at the knight now wedged beside him. "I thought you were here to rescue us."

"All is as planned," the knight said.

"So... what now? What's the next part of your plan?" Bobby asked, eager for the action to begin.

"A tiger moves through time moment by moment, guided by instinct," the Tiger Knight said cryptically. "Any long-term plan devised by man is bound to fail. The world moves too quickly for variables to hold. Entropy makes fools of forecasters. Only short-term goals can be trusted. Being in here with you was my goal. And I've succeeded."

Zenobia snorted. Her scoff was biting with disdain. But there was something in it. A kindling sign of her former fiery self. A reprieve from the shadow of defeat that had claimed her.

Their awkward reunion was cut short by yet another voice cascading across the chamber. "Your Honor, I have something to add. If the court permits." Bobble Gentles stepped into view with long, deliberate strides. His scholarly grace carried him swiftly to the marbled railing that marked the court floor.

On the brink of retreating down the staircase of his throne, the judge groaned and rolled his eyes. "The hour of my supper has long passed. If you must speak, do so quickly. Name and faith."

"I stand before you, your humble Honor, as Bobble Gentles, Librarian-in-Chief of the Great Library of Pangia. Raised a Plebeian, but practicing as a Patrician."

The judge's sour expression softened into a mild curiosity. "Ah, the esteemed Librarian-in-Chief. My father once held your post. How can the court assist such a fine and reformed gentleman? Has the library recovered its stolen tome?"

"It has. And that is why I am here," Bobble replied. "May I approach your honorable and gracious court?"

The judge plopped back into his throne with a dramatic sigh, his stomach punctuating the moment with a loud grumble. "Proceed. But be warned, my patience wears thin as my hunger grows dire, and no amount of fawning or flattery will satiate it. So take pity on my empty stomach with a pithy plea."

Bobble Gentles stepped before the judge. "Your venerable wisdom knows well the law prohibiting the removal of books from The Great Library of Pangia, ensuring access to all Pangian citizens—"

"Yes, yes," the judge interrupted, nodding vigorously. "The court is well aware of all laws. On with it."

"Of course. My apologies," Bobble said without hurry, his patience undeterred by the judge's urgency. Taking a measured breath, he continued, "So, as you, a knowledgeable magistrate, surely know, only the author of a book may reclaim possession of their written work from the library."

The judge leaned forward, his irritation surfacing beneath his smile.

"Get to the point, librarian."

From beneath his cloak, Bobble produced a book—the perfect text—and held it high for all to see. "There was a misunderstanding, your equitable and munificent Honor. The author of this book," he declared, "*is* this young man right here."

"Which, young man?" the judge asked, brow raised.

Bobble stepped squarely in front of Bobby. "This young man—Bobby Porter."

Caught off guard, Bobby looked up at the librarian with utter confusion.

Their eyes met. Bobble's gaze was warm, his knowing smile a quiet aura of reassurance.

The judge directed his scepter at Bobby. "Is this true?"

For a moment, he looked every bit the dumb, mouth-breathing dolt Zenobia often teased him of being. He didn't know how to respond.

"Well...?" the judge barked, nearly drowned out by another growl of his gut. "Are you the author of the book you're accused of stealing?"

Bobby's mind scrambled. Could he be the author? His map was in it. The Sword of Aegis, his creation, was right there on the page. Maybe that counted. Bobble nodded at him, slow and steady, like a ticking of a metronome. Almost involuntarily, Bobby nodded back.

"Yes," he squeaked at last and at first, then continued with growing conviction. "I am the author of the book."

The judge ballooned his chest with a skeptical breath, then deflated it with another sigh. "While your word alone carries little weight with me, the endorsement of the Liberian-in-Chief cannot be easily dismissed. You may return the book to its supposed rightful author. However, let this be clear: this does not absolve all charges. Court adjourned. Lunch awaits." With a sharp whack of his scepter against his throne, the judge hastened away, disappearing down the stairs and through the tiny door at the platform's base.

Bobble Gentles slipped the book through the cage bars to Bobby, who hesitated to take it.

"But... I'm not its real author," Bobby said.

"It appears you are now as much the author of the *Perfect Text* as your father. Turn to the front page."

Bobby opened the cover. On the first page, it read:

COPYRIGHT © BY EVERETT PORTER AND BOBBY PORTER.

Bobble's smile warmed. "Unlike your father, though, you can be present for your creations, to guide and protect them."

Feeling Zenobia and the Tiger Knight's eyes on him, Bobby clutched the book tightly. Its weight seemed to increase the moment he took full possession of it. "What about your life's work?" Bobby asked, averting his eyes, ashamed. "I'm sorry I ruined it. And your door."

Bobble Gentles' smile broadened, serene and sincere. "Though I was disappointed that my project didn't become the pioneering work I'd wished for, and my name shall not be inscribed into the annals of librarian history, nor my likeness immortalized alongside the greats in the Hall of Knowledge, this ordeal has inspired me. My love for letters is personal, and the joy of collecting words doesn't require recognition. I've decided to devote myself to supporting all those leaky books. If I may be so bold, and invent a wholly novel concept: not a critic, but an *editor-in-chief*."

He waved a hand before him, as though the title were being spelled out in the air. "I shall help all those voices whose articulation might falter, whose piddly prose may grate the eyes and ears, softening their offense just a smidge when read. Perhaps through some budding wordsmith, I'll find a different kind of legacy. One, just as meaningful. I am grateful to you, Bobby Porter, for expanding my worldview."

Bobby had to stifle his urge to tell the librarian that *editor-in-chief* was already a thing in his world. But seeing how excited Bobble was about his new purpose, he didn't want to spoil it. Maybe he wasn't a total ruinous mess-up after all.

The moment was cut short by a sentinel rapping his glaive against the bars. "Let's move!" Another guard elbowed Bobble Gentles aside as they shuffled the prisoners into another cage set atop a wagon. At least this one had more room.

Despite their grim departure, Bobble Gentles offered a piece of parting inspiration, raising his voice above the clank of wheels and creaking wood. "The *Perfect Text* will do more good in your hands than it ever could locked away in a chest! And when you've finished the book, it will hold a place of honor in our library for all to treasure."

The wagon, with Bobby, Zenobia, and the Tiger Knight inside, rumbled from the courthouse and onto the main streets. Bobble Gentles followed a short way, his figure trailing until a guard stopped him at the archway. His last words lingered for a moment, then were drowned by the knocking trundle of wheels over cobblestone, and he disappeared from Bobby's view.

TWENTY-NINE

BOBBLE **G**ENTLES'S words rattled around Bobby's head: "The Perfect Text can do more good in your hands..." Bobby doubted that. Locked up and carted off to the frozen tundra of the Isle of Black Rock made the book feel useless in his hands. It might help kill time, but indulging in its pages seemed frivolous given the urgent need to escape and save Zenobia's father.

Zenobia's silence at the far end of the cage made his gut ache. He attempted conversation, but each time he spoke, the sentries struck their polearms against the bars. Even an involuntary sneeze earned a jarring clang against the cage, loud enough to ring in his ears. The guard followed with a sheepish glance, acknowledging his overreaction.

"I don't believe they want us to speak," the Tiger Knight said, earning another clang. "No talking!" barked the sentry. The knight nodded, as if confirming a theory.

As the wagon rolled toward the city outskirts, it turned onto a broad cobbled street that cleaved two vastly different worlds. On one side, ornate homes in vivid hues stood proudly, with vibrant bazaars and bodegas over-flowing with expensive-looking food, drink, and vice. The city's wealthiest reveled without a care, oblivious—or indifferent—to the somber procession of prisoners passing before them.

On the other side: harrowing devastation. Although the stench of rot permeated the entire city, this side was particularly pungent. This, it seemed, was where the children of Pangia had gone. They milled about in filth, their skin blotched by pestilence, their ragged clothes darkened by generations of soot. They spoke only in groans and moans, living among trash and decay. Discarded barrels, hay, and other debris served as their makeshift homes. A group of five children with threadbare cloth wrapped around their skeletal-thin frames thumped crude clubs at a pack of goblin rats. One child, no older than seven, snatched a stunned rodent and bit into it with blackened teeth.

Bobby turned away, nauseated, and cast his eyes back to the other side, where a man covered in musical instruments played an upbeat tune while a young couple danced in ignorant joy. Rage simmered within Bobby. How could these people ignore the misery just steps away from them? Neither side acknowledged the other. The road was a unspoken divide, an invisible wall that neither dared to cross, while their prison wagon rolled straight down its center.

The guards ignored the contrast entirely, their focus locked ahead. Zenobia remained pensive, her expression unreadable. The Tiger Knight sat curled up in his corner, his painted tiger mask hiding any clue of thought or whether he was even awake or asleep. Feeling hopeless and alone, Bobby turned to the book, hoping with all hope to find something—anything—useful.

He flipped to the last page before the blank ones, and his eyes widened. A new chapter had appeared: THE TRAVELER'S GUIDE TO HELCYON: SIGHTS, HISTORY, TIPS ON HOW TO DEFEAT THE ASHEN KNIGHT—CHAPTER XXIV: MAHRS STREET.

This chapter detailed Pangia's rise from a humble village into a city renowned as the birthplace of written language. A history previously unwritten by Bobby or his father. It chronicled Pangia's pivotal innovation: the invention of recorded keeping, which catapulted the settlement into a booming center of trade, serving as a key gateway along the Moiruh River. But with growth came conflict. As diverse peoples flooded the city from all over Helcyon, they brought with them their own languages, creating confusion and frequent misunderstandings among merchants and officials. To resolve this, the Pangians developed a standardized language system known as Common Language or Lingua Franca—abbreviated as CLLF and pronounced "CLIFF." Though intended to create clarity, the strictly enforced system instead ushered in cultural erasure. Other languages were deemed obsolete. The resulting tensions sparked the War of Words.

Despite its name, the war wasn't fought with clever insults or scornful slurs, biting wit, or cutting slights, but with blood and steel. A century of brutal fighting decimated the population, leaving only a fraction of the city's former glory. When peace finally came, with no victor declared, the survivors began to rebuild. Embracing a new trend of the era, they fortified their city with a massive stone wall. Amidst this reconstruction, a new sanctuary emerged: the Great Library of Pangia, a monument to knowledge and texts.

In the years that followed, the Pangians refined their language, naming their dialect "Pancliff." Pangia's strategic position at the mouth of the Moiruh River helped reestablish it as a commercial hub, and Pancliff, later dubbed "Pancliffish", spread through the trade routes to the neighboring hamlets and villages across Helcyon.

As the War of Words faded into lore, Pancliffish evolved into the region's dominant tongue. Over generations, its name was shortened: from "Pancliffish" to "In Cliffish," and eventually to "Inglish", now the universal language of Helcyon.

Bobby lifted his nose from the pages of the book, a question nagging at him: *What about Marhs Street?* Massaging moisture back into his eye, he peered down again—and as if to answer his question, new text suddenly appeared onto a blank page before him.

To the west of Pangia lay another small settlement, a village named Mahrs. It was older than Pangia by centuries. But unlike what would become the Great City of Pangia, Mahrs remained small, its growth stunted by customs that prohibited change, which kept its population low. As Pangia expanded, pushing toward every corner of land along the forking Moiruh River and the sea, it eventually collided with Mahrs' borders. At first, an agreement preserved each community's territory. But with Pangia's relentless growth, Mahrs soon became enveloped entirely, turning it into an enclave within towering city walls, choking it off from the rest of the world like a massive open-air well. Cut off and isolated, Mahrs was forced to survive on scraps and waste discarded over those fortified walls. Over time, this relegated the area to little more than a dumping ground. More years passed, and as peace settled and trade flourished, the city walls were razed to allow for freer movement. But now, the roads that replaced those walls served to underscore Mahrs' segregation even more starkly. The city turned a blind eye to the eyesore at its heart.

These were not the children of The Great City of Pangia, as Bobby first assumed. They were the victims of centuries spent living in a sewage dump. In The Great City of Pangia, children grew up too fast. Most looked like adults by the age of thirteen. But in Mahrs, a malnourished diet of refuse and rubbish, compounded by poisoning and disease, had a devastating toll. Few survived to adulthood. The community had withered into one made up almost entirely of children, their parents bedridden with illness by the time they reached the ripe old age of twenty-five.

Bobby closed the book, his frustration audible. "Geesh, why doesn't anyone help those poor people?"

A sharp *clang* of the guard's polearm silenced him. The Tiger Knight stirred, snorting himself awake.

"Quiet!" the guard ordered.

Bobby reopened the book, facing the next blank page. He focused, his thoughts repeating silently: *Someone needs to help. Someone needs to help. Someone needs to help.* As if summoned by that inner plea, more words began to materialize:

Marhs existed as an overlooked blemish on the tapestry of the prosperous and progressive "shiny city on a hill" for far too long. The turning point came unexpectedly. A single Pangian woman, dressed in a striking yellow silk gown, responded to a mysterious internal call. She looked up from her five-tiered, double chocolate cake and saw, really saw, the children of Mahrs. Moved by a pang of sympathy, she crossed the road and knelt in the mud beside them. She shared her food. Her presence marked the first moment someone from the city truly acknowledged their suffering.

"How have I never noticed you before?" she asked aloud.

Inspired by the encounter, she founded an organization devoted to lifting Mahrs out of neglect and poverty.

Bobby felt a phantom tap on his shoulder, which prodded him to crane his neck once more toward Mahrs Street, now dwindling in the distance. He caught sight of a figure in yellow crossing the road. She became harder to see as she knelt among the children.

A smile broke across his face, a sense of optimism bubbling within him. Zenobia, catching the change in his expression, looked at him questioningly.

"I think I just—" he began, only to be cut off by another jarring *clang* of the guard's staff.

"Quiet!"

THIRTY

AS **THEY** plodded deeper into the maroon shadows of Morilund, the lively bustle of the Great City of Pangia gave way to the bleak expanse of hardscrabble prairies. Having left the last tendrils of the Moiruh River behind hours ago, the three prisoners cast their solemn gazes toward the ominous silhouette of the dark, saw-toothed mountains cutting a formidable swath across the northern horizon. The onset of night became distinct to Bobby for the first time, marked by the darkening and reddening of the otherwise gloom of the thick coal clouds, and the biting chill of the winds began their nightly feast on his flesh. Bobby breathed the bitter, cold air, somewhat relieved to be far away from the pervasive stench of Pangia.

Night in Morilund in particular brought a curious silence, not for the absence of sound but for the isolation of each noise sounded—the metallic rattle of the marching sentries' armor, the sporadic snorts and rhythmic clomping of horse hooves, the creaks and thumps of the wooden wheels against the rocky terrain—all resonated separately, yet together, against the backdrop of the ubiquitous wailing of the Northern winds. These forlorn sounds made their clamoring expedition seem lost against the vast, lifeless plains, emphasizing their lonely existence as the only signs of life in the unwelcoming region of Morilund.

AS THE SHADOWY, pointed peaks clawed higher into the laden sky, Bobby, after poring over his book, confirmed they were nearing the southern entrance to the hostile Dracanspyne mountain range. There, embedded within the range's first notable summit, Kaste Mountain, sat the Ancient City of Kaste, a marvel of ancient ingenuity. It was the first city ever built, hewn directly into the rock. Now, a ghostly ruin of its progressive past, it marked the onset of the imposing ridgeline that stretched northward like a colossal, crooked spine, terminating at the hellish crown of Fire Mountain.

Their current trail would hug the western flank of the mountains, steering clear of Dragoon Keep to the east and leading them north toward the Isle of Black Rock. According to Bobby's calculation, it was a daunting five-day trek along the mountains, then five days more to their dreadful destination. However, a closer inspection of his map unveiled a hidden, quicker route that could drastically cut their travel time, promising a direct line to Dragoon Keep within mere moments. Moreover, nestled within the Ashen Forest bordering Fire Mountain lay the Sword of Aegis, the mightiest weapon in Helcyon. A plan was taking shape in his mind, but he needed to act soon before the variables shifted, and they would be doomed. The first step was clear: they needed to escape. Dang it—he was already stumped.

That evening, as the convoy encamped near a cluster of massive boulders, tucking the prison wagon between a band of three such colossal stones, a single sentry settled near the wagon to watch over them, leaning up against one of the natural giants for comfort. The rest of the guards distanced themselves, kindling a fire and rolling out their goose feather blankets in preparation for sleep.

"Did you kill the beast?" Bobby whispered, scuttling as close as he could to the Tiger Knight, though his chains limited his mobility.

"Alas, no," the Tiger Knight responded gravely, "But we gave him a darn good fight. Unfortunately, once he got wind that you two were gone, he retreated. With a limp, I might add."

For the first time, Bobby took in the extent of the battle's toll on the knight's armor. The most severe damage was evident in three long gashes that mutilated his armor down one side of his breastplate.

"I'm glad you didn't get hurt," Bobby said.

"I wish I could say the same for some of the others," the Tiger Knight replied, lowering his mask's pinholes to his scarred hands that trembled slightly.

Breaking her long-held silence, Zenobia spoke, "Why come for us?"

The Tiger Knight lifted his pinholes to her.

"Why ain't you jus' stay back in yer forest? Why bother comin' after us?" she pressed.

"Because..." he started, pausing as if his wooden facade hid the eyes that darted back and forth, searching for a suitable answer. After a moment, his mask jostled by the agitation of an unseen jaw as he started again, "Because I was compelled. That beast—the manticore is pure evil. It lives for nothing more than to gorge on the flesh of the innocent. It delights in the destruction of all living creatures. Knowing it pursued you, I could not stomach the thought of you two falling victim to its appetite. I had to come and protect you. I made a vow." His last words resounded in the empty air.

The nearby sentry banged his polearm against the boulder. "Quiet down in there! No more talking!" he barked.

The three lapsed into silence, listening to the distant chatter from the campfire.

"It came out of nowhere," one of the sentries, his voice gravelly, shared with the group. "Straight from the treetops it was—"

"The Roc. A giant eagle," another guard interjected, his tenor reedy and eager.

"A giant eagle, the Roc," the first continued, undeterred, "Its wingspan was as wide as a... as a—"

"Three Draco-Elephants, lined up end to end," the reedy and eager voice chimed in again.

After a contrived throaty cough, the storyteller resumed, "Yeah. It was really big."

"So what'd ye do? How'd ye kill it?" a third guard asked.

"As it swooped down and snatched up one of my men, tearing him asunder with its mighty talons, I notched a golden-tip arrow blessed by the Patrician well of holy strength. Well, it started straight for me, I steadied my breath, our steely eyes locked, and with a precise aim—"

"Got 'em right between the eyes, and it dropped dead straight away," the eager guard cut in again.

Armor rattled in frustration, "C'mon!" cried the raspy raconteur, "I'm trying to tell it! You're ruining the story, you idiot!"

After a long, silent beat came a shamefaced apology, "I'm sorry."

"Go on, tell us another," encouraged one of the other guards.

"Ahh," grumbled the first guard, "No. Time for rest. Tomorrow holds another long day for us."

The night settled into a deep quiet, the earlier conversation fading into silence. The air grew still, the winds whispering themselves to sleep. All

that remained was the crackle of the dying campfire, the occasional huff
from the horses, and the emerging buzz of the snoozing guards. Even the
sentinel tasked with watching them had succumbed to slumber, leaning
heavily against his boulder.

Amidst the profound quiet, Bobby, Zenobia, and Tiger Knight were still
quite alert, their minds alive with contemplation. Seizing a moment he felt
was safe, Bobby cautiously presented his book to Zenobia and Tiger Knight,
splitting it open to the map that splayed across both pages. He tapped his
finger on the dotted spirals that detailed a network of shortcuts connecting
key places all over Helcyon.

"Listen," Bobby whispered, tracing a route with his finger. "If we can
escape and get to the Ancient City of Kaste, we can use the Ingress to the
Sword of Aegis. And with that, we can go to Fire Mountain and into Dragoon
Keep and defeat the Ashen Knight."

"The Sword of Aegis?" Tiger Knight inquired with a curious tilt of his head.

"It's only the most powerful weapon in all of Helcyon," Bobby explained
with a hint of pride. After all, he created it.

"I understand," the Tiger Knight nodded. "We definitely need to have
that if we are to slay the Ashen Knight."

Zenobia said nothing as she merely glanced at the map with little interest, then scooted back against her side of the cage.

"So," Tiger Knight urged, "what is our escape plan?"

Bobby had no idea about the specifics of their escape plan. Until now,
Zenobia had shouldered their planning, driven by the deeply personal
mission to rescue her father. Now, as Bobby mulled over their situation,
he felt the weight of leadership suddenly descend upon him and, with
it, the understanding of the enormity of the burden Zenobia had borne.
Trying to save a parent, even for a person as strong as she, was a herculean
task—akin to ascending a storm-lashed mountain while carrying a titan
determined to resist, digging its heels deep into the earth in defiance of help
and rational self-interest. The question that haunted him was poignant:
How do you save someone who seems hell-bent on escaping salvation?

"I tried to save my father," Bobby confessed in a soft, quivering voice,
"but I couldn't."

Zenobia met his eyes for the first time since her hushness, her green
gaze soft and full of mournful understanding. And he was grateful to bask
in her pity.

"I tried my hardest," Bobby continued, "but I couldn't save him. Back where I come from, I didn't have any power. But here... I think maybe I do. And I swear I'll help you save your dad. With all my power I've got, I will." He marked an invisible X over his chest and pressed his fist to it. "I swear it."

"The lion's heart of truth and passion indeed roars strong within you, cub," Tiger Knight remarked, his tone imbued with respect.

Zenobia regarded Bobby with a lengthy silence as if trying to read the lines in his face for the validity of his sincerity. Though Bobby couldn't imagine there were too many creases in his swollen face, the dark circles under his eyes surely spoke the truth to his hard and troubled life.

"OK," Zenobia finally spoke, "What's yer big plan, big brain?"

The playful challenge sparked a touch of joy in Bobby, and the corners of his mouth leaped upwards. He bucked into action, jerking his head about in a frantic search for inspiration. "Okay... okay... if we..." he sputtered, examining the tight grid of iron bars and the multiple iron locks on the cage door. "Can you bend the bars? Or bust the locks?"

"Iron bars's too tough, even for me. Maybe if I had some tool or anuther, I might likely bust 'em locks to bits."

Bobby explored their caged transport. The heavy iron chains latched to their ankles were anchored to the metal part of the cage, but the floor beneath the thin layer of hay they squatted on was just the wagon's thick wooden flatbed.

"I got it!" Bobby whispered excitedly. "The bottom—it's just wooden boards. Zenobia, you could rip those up, and we can sneak under the cart."

Zenobia jangled her shackled ankle. "What 'bout thisyer chains?"

"I've got an idea on those," Tiger Knight added confidently. "Just get us to the campfire, and I'll deal with our restraints."

Zenobia leaned into the bars with a determined sigh, surveying the surroundings. The guards lay snugly in their sacks arranged near the crackling warmth of the fire. The two horses stood not far off, tethered to a gnarled tree. The closest guard to them teetered between half-wakefulness and sleep, his head drooping in a dance of drowsiness before eventually coming to a rest on his chest.

"Okay," Zenobia whispered, shuffling to one side of the wagon, wrapping her fingers tightly around the bars. "We ain't crawin' under the wagon with a whole cage latched to our legs. I'll rip this whole thang free from the wagon-bed itself."

Bobby and Tiger Knight offered silent nods of agreement as Zenobia positioned herself, feet apart, knees bent, readying to engage her extraordinary strength most effectively. Bobby kept one eye on the drowsy sentinel as Zenobia was just about to pull up hard. The guard's head sprang awake, and Bobby signaled her to hold. The guard swiveled his head in a nervous scan of his surroundings, seeming more worried with whether anyone had seen him doze off than checking for trouble from his captives. Satisfied he was in the clear, he scratched his gruffy face, and then peered over to the prison wagon, only to find the three prisoners staring at him from the darkness of their cage.

Rattling his armor, the guard shuffled his wooden stool closer to the wagon, positioning himself to maintain a clear line of sight on his prisoners while seeking a more private spot away from his companions. "I suggest ye be quiet and get some shut-eye," he grumbled, settling into a more comfortable repose, laying his staff weapon across his lap. "You won't get much rest at the Isle of Black Rock," he added with a grim chuckle that sounded like he was gargling stones.

Ignoring his warning, Zenobia fixed her steely eyes on the guard and began to sing. Her voice produced a most angelic tune of melancholy as she wove words into a mellifluous melody:

"*In the season of crimson moons.*

"*When the wind blows, sweet flower bloom.*

"*I'm reminded of my sweet, sweet love.*"

The guard burst into a mewing wide yawn, overwhelmed by the lullaby. Zenobia continued, her scowl never leaving her face as her voice softened to a hypnotic lilt:

"*In the days that shone its golden light.*

"*Atop the silver seas and down below the blue ocean deep.*

"*I'm reminded of my sweet, sweet love of halcyon days of yore.*

"*The faint calling of the Palms of Holmes.*

"*Drifts on the breeze of the avian tongue,*

"*To march the dear departed souls.*

"*Past the great living tree and to the mountain of bones.*

"*Where their earthly wisdom is set in stone.*

"*I'm reminded of my sweet, sweet love of halcyon days of yore.*

"*I pine for my sweet, sweet love evermore in those halcyon days of yore. Halcyon days of yore...*"

There came a *clunk* as the guard's helmeted head rolled back against the rock. His mouth falling open to the sky, he was snoring like a buzz saw.

Marveling once more at yet another of Zenobia's unexpected gifts, Bobby watched in awe as Zenobia resumed her stance. Her delicate hands gripped the bars with unyielding strength. She leveraged her muscle against the cage, channeling all her might into a forceful pull upwards. At first, the cage resisted with a threatening groan, loud enough to risk rousing their captors, but with a persistent effort, Zenobia overcame its stubborn hold. The cage's base gave way with a loud cracking snap of splintering wood and explosive release of iron rivets, unmooring it from the wagon bed.

The sudden noise startled the immediate guard into snorting wakefulness; his beady eyes flitted about in a scramble to understand the meaning of the disruption. Eventually, he fix his gaze upon the wagon and its shadowy occupants. Bobby, the Tiger Knight, and Zenobia continued their disquieting stares from the darkness of their captivity.

The guard rose from his station, wielding his polearm. He edged closer for a better inspection of his prisoners, just as the fire crackled and popped, swiping his attention toward the flames.

It's just the fire you heard. Bobby silently willed the thought into the guard's head. *It was just the fire; go back to sleep. Go back to sleep, you idiot.*

However, the trooper turned his watch back on the wagon, his scrutiny intensifying as he neared the bars Zenobia clung to.

"Git ready to move," she whispered from the corner of her mouth.

"You three don't like to settle down, do ya?" the guard said as he leaned close to the bars. "That's the problem with ye kids." He paused, shifting his eyes to the tiger-masked knight before adding, "And weirdos. Yer too rowdy, ye need that rowdiness whipped out of ya." The guard's gaze dropped, landing on the gap between the splintered base and the iron cage.

"Now," Zenobia commanded.

For an instant, the guard's face twisted in shock and fear. A reaction most satisfying to witness. The cage was suddenly thrust forward, the entire iron frame tipping over the edge of the wagon. The ensuing chaos was a blur of motion and noise; the guard was caught off guard and pinned beneath the cage, unconscious as it crashed to the ground on its side. Once Bobby, Zenobia, and Tiger Knight gained equilibrium from their hard landing, they swiftly maneuvered the cage upright, rolling it off the guard and allowing their feet to shuffle along the ground. Taking a moment, they studied the supine stillness of the guard whose armor they had flattened like a tin can.

"I hope we didn't do any permanent harm," the Tiger Knight said as he stooped to relieve the fallen man of his sword and dagger. Then, gesturing to Bobby, he said, "Arm yourself with the staff, cub. Zenobia, if you can, please carry the cage to the fire so it is enclosed inside with us."

With the polearm in hand and his book secured, Bobby followed Zenobia as she plucked up the cage, and together they hobbled toward the campfire. Their shackled feet moved in unison, the clinking chains dictating their pace. Their approach was masked—remarkably—by the chorus of snores and nighttime flatulence emanating from the circle of slumbering soldiers. It even seemed to cover the sound of their earlier tumble.

"What now?" Bobby whispered, his words nearly lost in the buzz and tooting.

"We slip over them," proposed the Tiger Knight. "Likely to ensnare one or two in the cage with us."

Zenobia nodded and effortlessly lifted the cage high enough for them to maneuver over their oblivious jailors. With cautious steps, they crossed the narrow maze of sleeping bodies and scattered gear, making their way to the fire's center. At one point, Bobby yelped in silent alarm as the hem of his tunic caught a stray ember. He frantically patted it out with his book, smothering the spark before it could spread.

Once positioned around the campfire, they found a guard sprawled half-in, half-out of the cage's perimeter. The Tiger Knight yanked the man fully inside, and Zenobia lowered the cage to the ground. The guard groaned dreamily, eyes still shut. "Whaa—what is it? Time to go?" he mumbled. Then, upon sitting upright, he blinked in confusion as his gaze met the three captives. Zenobia promptly bonked him back into unconsciousness with a quick bop of her fist. He flopped flat on his back, a few strands of hair sizzling as they brushed the fire.

By then, another guard had already sprung to his feet, bleating the alarm. "Escape! They're escaping! Wake up! Wake up! Escape!"

"Quickly," urged the Tiger Knight. "Lay the chains across the fire—we must heat the metal until it yields."

Together, they stretched their bindings across the blaze. The Tiger Knight stoked the fire with fresh wood, intensifying the flames. He relieved the dazed guard of his sword and offered it to Zenobia. "We'll break the chains once they're red hot," he said. "Until that time, we may need to defend ourselves from in here."

Zenobia accepted the sword with a crooked smirk. "Pleasure doin' so."

The rest of the guards, now wide awake and bristling with weapons, converged on them under the command of their captain. His grogginess undercut his authority as he stepped forward, sleep still clinging to his eyes. "Ain't no escaping. Unless your aiming to... aiming to..."

"Making peace with yer maker," quipped the guard with the reedy voice.

The irascible captain stomped his foot, shooting a fierce look at his interrupting subordinate. "I didn't ask for yer help in finishing my sentences!"

"Yer long pause seemed like a call for it," the guard shot back.

Face boiling with frustration, the captain raised his blade threateningly at the guard who'd been a thorn in his temple all evening. "I really can't stand it when you do that."

The junior guard, undeterred, squared up with his sword raised. "Maybe, don't start a sentence ye ain't gonna finish."

"I'll sure finish this fight ye started, if that's what ye're after. Your wife'd be plenty pleased if I did," the captain added with a sneer.

The other guards nervously peered amongst themselves with half-shrugs, unsure how to respond to the escalating infighting.

Meanwhile, the Tiger Knight focused on his task, raking the coals with his blade. A whirling shower of sparks and embers danced through the air as he heaped more coals over their chains. The iron began to glow orange.

"Why'd ye have to bring my wife into this?" grumbled the junior guard, his voice high and furious.

"Because if she weren't sister to my wife, you'd be scrubbing dungeon latrines instead of serving in my squadron," the captain seethed.

Taking advantage of the distraction, the Tiger Knight dragged Zenobia's red-hot chain from the fire and braced it against a large rock beside the pit.

"Hit it now, with all your might," he said.

With a mighty swing, Zenobia brought the blade down. The glowing chain links burst apart in a spray of sparks, setting her free.

The squabbling guards didn't notice.

"Ye take that back! I earned my position here on my own merits," the junior guard insisted.

"Ha! Don't make me laugh," laughed the captain.

Next was Bobby's chain—shattered clean by another brilliant strike. Tiger Knight's own bonds proved more stubborn. It took a second blow— this one so forceful it fractured the blade in two as it severed the final link.

"Umm... guys..." another guard spoke up, pointing emphatically toward the action, "the prisoners?"

Reacting too late, the captain turned just in time to see Zenobia lift and hurl the iron cage toward him and his bickering subordinate, flattening them both beneath its crashing weight. Her warrior cry ripped through the clearing at a deafening volume as she lunged toward the nearest guard to her right.

Spotting the charging terror—this demon girl with hair red as fire and eyes like a dragon's glare—the guard bolted in blind panic, his fear outrunning any shred of duty or dignity.

As Zenobia wildly chased her prey, the Tiger Knight faced off against the last two soldiers still standing. Their blades sliced and thrust in a frantic show of skill, aiming to intimidate him.

"Let us see what mettle you possess, sirs!" he called out, raising his own blade, balanced and calm.

The two guards rushed the Tiger Knight, and three steel blades clashed, swords locking in an entangled clinch.

Zenobia ceased her pursuit of the fleeing guard near the tethered horses, who stood unbothered by the chaos. Hawking up a wad of mucus, she spat it into the dust like a hex upon him and all his cowardly ilk. Convinced he wouldn't be coming back, she turned her attention to the horses. Her voice softened as she approached, hands raised to the bristling creatures in a show of peace. "Now, easy," she cooed. "All I'm gonna do is set ya loose. Maybe ride ya a littl'. If that's alrite with you beauties?"

The Tiger Knight spun and shifted with fancy footwork, blending battle and ballet. He danced circles around his opponents. "Alas, your first error in your training," he taunted mid-parry, a hint of laughter in his voice. "True swordplay is not merely brute force—it is rhythm. It is elegance. They ought to teach you boys how to dance."

Bobby stood outside the fray, awkwardly gripping his polearm and book as he watched in anxious awe. His eyes darted between the Tiger Knight's fluid combat—prancing energetically around the two tiring guards like a cat toying with its prey—and Zenobia's tender communion with the horses, her hands stroking their necks, her voice soothing their ears. It made Bobby think of Golly for the first time since the Great Palace of Helcyon, where they had left her with those ruthless vultures. Though Golly had never touched him personally, he remembered the depths of Zenobia's grief over the loss of her beloved pet. Poor Zenobia, she'd lost her mother, her only friend, and now he feared she'd lost her father too. He knew how the story was supposed to go—her reuniting with her dad—but he also knew how unreliable his own father had become in recent years. How he'd sometimes tell Bobby that the world, in truth, was indifferent. That people were cruel. That endings were rarely—if ever—happy, so why pretend otherwise?

"I'm not being pessimistic," his father would say. "I'm being realistic."

Bobby spun to his left and saw the subordinate guard wriggling free from under the cage. The guard stood up on unsteady legs, zeroing in on Zenobia. He staggered toward her, raising his blade in a stealthy arc, readying for a sneak attack from behind.

Panic surged through Bobby, his throat constricting around an urgent warning that escaped as no more than a feeble squeak. The adrenaline struck like lightning, spurring him into a dash forward. The polearm clanged to the ground, forgotten, his book still clenched in his hand.

The guard closed in on Zenobia, the tip of his blade just heartbeats from piercing her back.

Bobby's second shout tore from his throat, raw and primal: "ARRRRRRGG!"

The guard turned just as Bobby launched himself into the air, the heavy book raised high. With a spirited downward swing, he slammed it squarely against the guard's helmet, sending it spinning askew. Temporally blinded, the guard stumbled in circles, dazed and directionless.

Zenobia, alerted by the cry, spun around to witness Bobby's daring move. Without hesitation, she delivered a finishing blow, driving the helmet deeper into the guard's skull and knocking him out cold.

Bobby doubled over, gasping, hands braced on his knees, trembling from the aftermath. The adrenaline that had ignited his courage now left his limbs weak, his head swimming, chest heaving with a wild, erratic heartbeat.

Zenobia gave him a tight, approving nod. "That's one notch for ya."

He winced through a breathless smile, every muscle aching from the burst of action.

The two guards the Tiger Knight had been toying with now slumped against one another, too exhausted to continue. The knight, still as light-footed as ever, circled them, extolling the virtues of dance. "Dance," he lectured between pivots, " is the best exercise you can offer your body— bestows agility, sharpens minds, sustains stamina!"

"Let's git movin'," Zenobia called, motioning him over.

With a last graceful bow to his opponents, the Tiger Knight offered them a final thought: "Consider this, sirs—your loved ones may very well

be overjoyed by an unexpected dance. Swept up in a whirlwind of passion."
He then turned and joined his companions, smoothly mounting one of the
steeds, while Zenobia helped Bobby clamber up onto the other. The Tiger
Knight then extended his hand toward Zenobia, inviting her to take it and
ride with him on his horse. She regarded the gesture with mild surprise,
then took it, swinging up behind him.

Bobby, perched uneasily on his horse, began to whine, "But I don't know
how to ride a horse."

The knight's reply was simple but essential: "Don't fall off. The horse
will handle the rest." With a click of the tongue and gentle nudge of his heel,
his horse burst forward, kicking up a cloud of dust.

Bobby's horse, taking its cue from its partner, bolted after it, prompting
Bobby to cling on for dear life, his screams swallowed by the thunderous
thumping of its hooves.

WHEN CONSCIOUSNESS RETURNED to the captain, it was through the grating
persistence of his brother-in-law, who was trying to rouse him with repeated
slaps. "Wake up. Wake up. Wake up," the reedy voice nagged.

"Alright. Alright," the captain grumbled, swatting his hand away. "Stand
back! Give me room."

Once given space, the captain sat upright and caught sight of the lingering dust trail fading in the distance.

"Ahhh heck!" he groaned. "Just great! They... they... they—"

"Kicked our butts," his brother-in-law cut in.

THIRTY-ONE

EFORE HIS tour, Bobby's father was a talker, often espousing his reflections on life during their nighttime ritual of being tucked in. "The world belongs to no one," he would proclaim fervently. "Yet we act like it does. We harm in the name of that belief. It irks me that people don't see that. Everything under the sun—plants, animals, insects—we're all part of one system. Where's the empathy in the world?"

Even as a child, Bobby found himself nodding along, absorbing his father's worldview during those precious moments before sleep. Everett Porter's philosophy, shared in the quiet of Bobby's room, wasn't just fatherly wisdom but the seeds of Everett's literary musings.

"There are two kinds of power in the world," he'd explained to his wide-eyed boy. "Whole-sum Power, which the people wield for the people. And Abject Power, pursued by those who seek absolute dominion for their own ends. That kind of power corrupts, divides, and controls through fear and isolation." He punctuated the thought with a finger shot to the ceiling. "That kind of power is often stronger than any single person. That's why people are kept scared. Alone. Divided against their neighbors. But remember, united people hold the true power."

Leaning in close now, Everett spoke in a low, soft voice. "If Whole-sum power is greater than Abject-power, then why does Abject-power sometimes win?"

In the pause that followed, Bobby stared blankly, unsure how to answer. His father answered for him.

"Because people forget," he said. "In times of peace, they forget the pain of despair and oppression that comes with Abject Power. They become too content, and when they become content, they grow restless. Resentful. Reckless. There's a crisis between the collective and the individual. And that tension creates gaps. Gaps for those who hunger for Abject Power to slip through."

He paused again, the spark of urgency returning in his voice. "That's why stories are vital," he said. "They remind us of the pain. The world forgets its history too easily, which is how darkness comes back. But storytellers are the keepers of truth. A bridge across the gaps in memory."

And, as he always concluded. "Without them, humanity is doomed to repeat its mistakes."

Bobby, barely grasping his father's words, nodded in acknowledgment anyway.

"Do you know who one of those sacred scribes is?" Everett asked, then answered himself with a grin, tousling Bobby's hair. "Your old man. Well, I hope to be someday."

His father's sharp optimism about the power of the pen was soon blunted during his time on tour. The constant concussive explosions seemed to knock out of him any hope he held for humanity. Far from optimistic, his writing was abandoned at a grim juncture—a purgatory of a tumultuous and troubled world left for his son to navigate alone.

Bobby had come to believe more in the power of words for ruin than inspiration. The evidence surrounded him in the desolate landscape, its harsh, unforgiving terrain devoid of life and beauty. This burnt and barren country, sick and toxic in the wake of conflict, was supposedly meant to belong to everyone. A world beyond redemption. The collapse of the human condition—conjured by the darkness that hemorrhaged from his father's pen—now leaped from the pages into reality.

Was Bobby capable of mending such a world? The doubt plagued him, heavy as iron, visible in the way he slouched, head low between his stooped shoulders, the slight hump at his nape pronounced. He rode glumly through the wasteland, a solemn silhouette against the backdrop of devastation.

Their progress was slow, the horses clomping forward in a lazy rhythm, lulled by fatigue. While Bobby and the Tiger Knight conserved their dwindling energy in quiet vigilance, Zenobia had succumbed completely to her exhaustion. She was slumped against the knight's back, mouth slack, a slight snore escaping her nose. Her gapped tooth peeked out as her face softened in sleep. In that moment Bobby saw past her hard edges, saw the child beneath the warrior, vulnerable and delicate in repose.

The Tiger Knight's wooden gaze stayed fixed ahead. The long-held hush began to press in, crawling under Bobby's skin like an itch, until he finally spoke, his voice flat with drowsiness, "How can you see through that mask?" he asked.

"What mask?" the knight replied, equally low and weary, his gaze never shifting.

"The tiger mask you're wearing."

A dim chuckle rumbled from behind the wood-and-paint. "Ah, yes. I have worn it so long, it feels like my face." He tilted his head and scratched his furry painted-on chin. "Strange, I find it hard to recall what I look like underneath."

Their conversation lapsed into another stretch of silence before the Tiger Knight spoke again. "Where are we headed, young cub?"

Bobby gestured toward the distant peaks of the Dracanspyne Mountains, their serrated silhouettes piercing into the murky sky. Brief flashes of red lit the clouds, followed by the dull roll of thunder. "To the Ancient City of Kaste," he said, patting the satchel at his side where his father's book lay nestled. "There's a portal there. It'll take us straight to Fire Mountain and Dragoon Keep, so we can save Zenobia's dad."

"Ah. Heading straight into the monster's lair, are we? Out of the skillet and into the fire?" the knight said, half amused, half solemn.

"Umm... yeah, I guess," Bobby answered, not loving the sound of that.

"It will be a warm reception, I'm sure," the knight added, and the silence returned.

Eventually, the Tiger Knight broke it once more. "You showed real courage back there."

"I did? How?" Bobby asked, surprised.

"You intervened when danger was near. You protected your friend without hesitation. And you're still riding beside her, even with peril ahead."

"Oh." Bobby scratched his nose. "Well... she's saved me more time than I can count. Though *she's* been counting." He chuckled. "She's the brave one."

The knight reached beneath his breastplate and pulled out the medallion Bobby had returned to him. He extended it forward. "I want you to have this."

"But... it's yours," Bobby said. "Because of your bravery."

"It was your father who gave it to you to give to me, wasn't it?"

"Yes. Or... someone who looked like my dad," Bobby clarified.

"Whoever he was, he understood its meaning to me. Though it may be a symbol of valor, to me, it stands as a mark of shame."

"But you survived so many battles, and the war, and fought courageously for your people," Bobby insisted.

The knight exhaled deeply. "To outlive war is not the same as to survive it, young cub. I've drawn breath all these years through endurance, not triumph. In truth, my survival came at the cost of my courage. Trading bravery for cowardice in the moments when I failed to raise my voice against wrong, when I lacked the will to stand for what was just. And I have spent all these years seeking to redraw the moral lines I once allowed to blur in the fog of war."

Bobby often found adult words wrapped in riddles, laden with irony and contradiction, to be frustrating. This moment was no exception. Maybe it was his tiredness, but the knight's confession left him bewildered. "What?" he asked.

"I've been hiding a long time," the knight said, giving the medallion a slight shake, "from this. The prize for my atrocities. I came to your aid, hoping— perhaps foolishly—that I might reclaim some scrap of redemption. I don't want this token of heroism. I do not deserve it."

Bobby looked at the medal still offered to him. "Your mask... it's about facing your weakness, right?"

The knight's shoulders tensed slightly. He considered the question, then nodded. "Indeed. That is well said."

"You wear your weakness. Accept it. And because you accept it, it makes you stronger.

"By acknowledging your weakness, you can begin to turn it into a strength. It does seem you've been paying attention. Very good, young cub," the knight said, a tinge of pride in his voice.

"Then maybe you should keep your medal and wear it until it becomes a symbol of bravery again."

A chuckle vibrated behind the knight's painted fur. He withdrew the medal and tucked it back beneath his breastplate. "Spoken with such persuasive conviction, I find I cannot possibly part with it now. You've reminded me of an old saying in Fanggul: *There is great strength in vulnerability.* You are a most precocious cub."

Bobby gave a small smile. He thought of how clear things could seem when you let them be simple. *Kid-logic.* He hoped he wouldn't grow out of that. Looking at the knight, he asked another question, "But what does it really mean to be a survivor, then?"

The knight paused for a long, lamenting breath. "I believe all three of us carry the shadow of death in our hearts. It leaves no visible mark, but the scars run deep, etched into the flesh of our soul. So you'll understand when I say this world is broken and filled with broken people. To witness, or fall victim to—or worse, to take part in—the cruelties of such a world can strip away the very essence of hope, goodness, and meaning. What's left is often anguish, apathy, and despair.

"Yet, if we can manage to wring meaning from the meaningless, find compassion amid the chaos, and somehow grow from our terrible losses— much like a flower sprouting from the ashes of a burnt forest. If we can endure such harsh realities and emerge resilient against the cold hollowing of grief and sorrow, then in my eyes, we are survivors.

"It is not an easy thing to acknowledge the presence of profound pain and darkness and still tend the inner flame of hope. However, doing so reveals a wondrous truth: having faced the darkness without letting it consume us, we affirm that pain and loss are not all there is to life. Life holds more, much of it good."

Bobby nodded. He'd never had trouble acknowledging his pain and darkness, or so he thought. Now, all that remained was to see what more life held for him. He just worried it held nothing but more darkness and pain.

Their conversation faded into a pensive quiet. The three riders, saddled on two hobbling horses, traversed Morilund's bleak and battered landscape. The lands bore the scars of ancient upheaval, its treacherous surface shattered by apocalyptic eruptions and hardened by the bitter northern winds into ridged fields of volcanic glass. It was a realm forged in extremes—of heat and cold, fire and ice—an open antagonist to life itself.

As they rode, the Dracanspyne Mountains loomed ever nearer, their sharp peaks and sheer cliffs spiking black against the sky. Silent and watchful over the travelers' path, bearing witness to a world hellbent on testing the limits of their endurance.

———

BY THE TIME the Tiger Knight, Zenobia, and Bobby cantered up to the outskirts of the Ancient City of Kaste, night's ruddy hue had paled into the gray wash of day. They halted before the towering dark wall of stone—thirty feet high and stretching endlessly around the mountain's base, with no visible entry point in sight. The trio scanned the wall's expansive length, bewildered, searching for any sign of an opening.

Perched atop his horse, Bobby craned his neck to take in the city's strange beauty. An ancient metropolis that seemed to crawl up the mountain's face, its tightly packed blocks clinging precariously to the cliffs. Aware of the history of Kaste Mountain and the ruined city of antiquity that clung to its basalt rocks, he couldn't help but wonder out loud, "Do you think they called it the *Ancient City of Kaste* when they first built it?"

"As far as I'm aware," the Tiger Knight replied, "it's as if it has always been here. Timeless. Without a beginning, only a past stretching into oblivion."

Zenobia, more concerned with the challenge of finding the entrance to the walled-off city, dismounted and paced up to the massive stone wall. She recoiled as she touched the surface, slick with a glistening black mold

"Ugh! Ever'thang in thisyer place is disgusting," she grumbled with a grimace.

"What does your book say about finding a way in?" the Tiger Knight asked.

Bobby dug into his satchel, pulled out the volume, and flipped to the section on the Ancient City of Kaste. After scanning the text, he reported, "It says we need the Eye of Likho to reveal the gateway."

Zenobia threw up her hands in frustration. "I ain't got that damn eye, no more. That oracle prolly got it stuffed in her greedy no-good-for-nothin hands at the bottom of the dang lake. Useless know-nothin'n'all!"

Diving back into the pages, Bobby stumbled upon another passage he swore hadn't been there a moment ago. This addendum offered an alternative method. Shaking his head in disbelief, Bobby called out excitedly, "Wait—it says we can *make* our own eye. We just need syrup from the Very Very Big Hinterland Maple Tree, some earth clay, wall mold, and boiled Bitter. But it has to be done by the hands of an alchemist." Looking up from the book, a grin spread across his face as he glanced between the Tiger Knight and Zenobia.

The Tiger Knight, amused, said, "I believe our dear turtle dove here is our alchemist."

"I ain't got no clue how to do alchemy!" Zenobia said. "And I ain't no *turtle dove* neither."

"It don't seem too hard," Bobby said. "The book gives all the steps. I can read them to you."

Hands on her hips, Zenobia blew out a dramatic huff. "Fine. But why ya lookin' so dang happy? "

As she moved to peek at the book's instructions, Bobby clutched it protectively to his chest. "I'll read them out loud. Step by step."

Zenobia narrowed her eyes at Bobby, a penetrating glare he nearly missed. Despite her unsettling scrutiny, Bobby tightened his hold on the book.

"Oh, fine," she said, spinning away. From a little sack tucked in her vest, she pulled out a little jar of syrup. "Alrite—who's got any Bitter?"

The Tiger Knight admitted, "I ran out long ago." Then his pinhole eyes shifted to Bobby.

Feeling the weight of the knight's gaze, Bobby blurted, "What? Me?"

The knight explained, "Bitter drawn from the Son of the Creator may yield a powerful eye."

"But I can't cry," Bobby protested. "Isn't that how you get Bitter? By crying it out? Well, I can't."

"Could you at least try?" the Tiger Knight asked.

Bobby gulped and muttered sourly, "I guess."

He endeavored a dismount, but the maneuver went sideways fast. As he swung his leg over the horse, he tipped awkwardly, teetering precariously half off the saddle. Off balance, his flailing limbs spooked the horse, which kicked its hind legs, sending Bobby tumbling off in a clumsy somersault. He landed hard on his backside with a loud *thud*. "Ow!" he groaned.

Zenobia snorted, doing her best to stifle a giggle.

The Tiger Knight, in contrast, dismounted with effortless grace and offered Bobby a hand. "You can't make Bushbeetle Booblia without cracking a few giant Bushbeetles," he said jestingly.

Zenobia bent down, peering into Bobby's wincing face. "Any tears from that littl' tumble?"

"Just pain," Bobby moaned. "Lots of it.".

As the sting in his tailbone receded, Zenobia muttered curses while scraping a layer of slimy mold from the wall. She clawed out a small divot in the dark clay and smeared the slime inside. Bobby knelt beside her gingerly, still cradling his bruised behind, while the knight busied himself building a small fire nearby. Zenobia passed the tiny syrup jar to Bobby. He peeled back the cloth lid and dipped his finger in. One sticky slurp, and a warmth bloomed through him. The tip of his nose tingled. The air filled with the scent of honeyed spring. If happiness had a flavor, this golden molasses was it.

"Okay," Zenobia said, eyeing him, "how we s'pose to extract thisyer Bitter from ya?"

Bobby shrugged helplessly. "I don't think it's gonna work. I've been way sadder than this, and still—nothing."

Zenobia tapped her chin, lost in scheming thought, before snapping into action. She pinched and twisted a bit of flesh from Bobby's side—hard.

"YEEOWW!" Bobby squealed, high-pitched and indignant, but no tears came.

Zenobia's hand darted behind her back in shame. "I'm sorry. I'm really sorry. I figured it might trigger somethin'."

"What the heck!" Bobby yelled, whimpering without weeping.

It was a special kind of torture for Bobby—pain without a release. The physical sting evaporated as quickly as it struck, but the deeper wound lingered. The Bitter, bottled up and burbling in his guts, a dark turmoil he couldn't name or measure. He feared that without some remedy, some release, the havoc inside him would soon eat him whole. Memories of that night at Tar Lake surfaced, along with the dream—so vivid in its despair and sense of suffocating pressure—that it threatened to dissolve his very essence, leaving behind only the faint outline of a boy who had once been Bobby Porter.

A new sound yanked him back: Zenobia's sobs. She was hunched over, face in her hands, black-streaked tears spilling between her fingers—Bitter tears. She must have tasted the syrup too.

Alarmed, Bobby leaned toward her. "Why are you crying?"

"I—I don't mean to hurt n—no one," she stammered. "I—Imma gist so darn impulsive." Her voice cracked. "I ain't worthy of thisyer maple syrup. Not with all the people I've done hurt." She flung the bottle away.

It clinked against the knight's armored toe. He picked it up, then came to her side and placed a steady hand on her shaking shoulder. "We all bear moments wherein we cause pain. Be it by intent or by folly," the knight said with quiet gravity, gently returning the jar of syrup to her hand. " Such moments are lamentable, yes, but more grievous still is when we turn that cruelty inward. This syrup is not merely sweet, it is a medicine. I entreat you, let it do its work. Allow yourself the grace to heal."

The knight collected Zenobia's Bitter tears with an iron bowl he retrieved from a saddlebag. "Your gifts transcend mere strength of muscle," he said, positioning the bowl beneath her bowed head to catch the trickling Bitter. "You descend from the First Family. You are no ordinary alchemist. You can transmute this despair into hope."

Zenobia's inky deluge gradually ebbed. She rubbed the oil-slick Bitter from her eyes, smearing streaks across her cheeks. Ever prepared, the Tiger Knight produced a handkerchief with a magician's flourish, as if conjured from air. After a reserved pause, Zenobia accepted it, scrubbing her face clean until pale skin reemerged. She blew her nose with gusto, then returned the soiled cloth. "Thank you kindly," she sniffled.

"But of course," the knight replied, his voice warm, the faintest smile hiding beneath the mask. With delicate care, he pinched a clean corner of the cloth and dropped it over the fire. It crackled and sizzled, curling in on itself before burning up into black smoke. Then he set the bowl of Bitter over the fire to boil.

The process of crafting Zenobia's Eye didn't unfold as expected. Though they followed the instructions closely, one minor detail was omitted—one that had made Bobby smile earlier but was promptly dismissed the moment he said it out loud. The result was... peculiar.

Instead of an enchanted, mist-filled orb similar to Likho's Eye, what wobbled in Zenobia's open palm was a milky, drooping marble—a flaccid, congealed egg rather than a magical object. An abomination of alchemy, raised by the impatient hands of a girl who was ready to punch magic into submission.

"What good is this to anyone?" Zenobia scoffed, examining the sad little lump with frustration.

The Tiger Knight snickered. "As I foretold, the enchantment requires a seal-ing kiss."

"I can't imagine why sump'n so darn nasty as a peck is so importin' to creatin' an enchanted item?" Zenobia sneered.

It had been the one neglected instruction—a kiss to seal in the charm. To Bobby's own dismay, his lips had poised and pursed themselves the moment he read it, his heart aching with anticipation. He'd leaned forward, offer-ing his first kiss like it was a sacred act. He wasn't sure when he'd fallen for her. Maybe he'd always had. But in that charged moment, when the world seemed to hinge on one small gesture, he realized his feelings were real. And for a breathless second, he thought—just maybe—she might feel it too.

But nothing came. No kiss. No spark. Just dry air between them, chapping his lips. His heart squeezed into palpitations so cutting and sharp, it chopped his hopes into pulp. Of course, she didn't feel the same. Not Zenobia. Even for the sake of the mission, she still shut it down. He would've followed her to the ends of the world, through Hades' fire and ice, to his own ruin. Now he understood: his ruin didn't lie in some distant fate. It was here, in the soft collapse of a boy's stupid, fragile heart. Maybe that's what his mother had meant when she warned him about chasing after girls: not because they were dangerous, but because he was an idiot.

"Alrite, I think I got it," Zenobia said, a glint flickering in her eyes. With sudden conviction, she slapped the gooey orb against her forehead. It stuck like a gelatinous third eye. By some mystic miracle, it held fast. She spun toward the stone fortification, pacing left and right, her jiggly eye twitching with each sharp scan of the wall. Then she halted a few yards to their right, hopping in place and jabbing a finger at the wall. "Hot dang! Look right there. I gone and found it!"

Bobby and Tiger Knight hurried after her, but Zenobia was already sprinting full tilt at the wall, shoulders down like a battering ram. It appeared to them like she was about to collide with the large stone barrier.

"Zenobia!" Bobby called. "I don't think that's a good—"

A loud *crack!* And a burst of splinters cut him off. Zenobia vanished into a cloud of dust and debris, slipping clean through the wall. When they reached the spot, they found only solid stone, the wall untouched. But shattered wooden fragments lay at their feet.

"Zenobia?" Bobby shouted at the wall.

Two hands burst through the wall and grabbed their wrists. Before either could react, they were yanked straight through the fortification as if it were smoke. Bobby stumbled into a field of tall grass and regained his footing in time to see Zenobia glaring at him. Her face was now splattered with goo; the mystic eye broke into a slimy mess across her dour face like a broken yolk. Now, it was Bobby's turn to poorly stifled a snorting giggle.

"Looks like you've got egg on your face."

Zenobia crossed her arms, issuing a seething huff that blew a big bubble in the slime before it popped with a wet *plop*.

The Tiger Knight, ever composed, produced another handkerchief and offered it with a gallant flourish. "This one you may keep, my dear hatchling."

Zenobia snatched it and scrubbed furiously.

Bobby eyed the knight. "Where do you keep getting those?"

The knight bent toward him, voice low and knowing. "A noble animal never travels without handkerchiefs. Something a young squire would do well to remember."

"But where do you *keep* them all?"

The tiger mask's pinhole eyes held on to him for a blank moment before the knight turned his head away, surveying their surroundings.

"A gentleman never tells," he simply said, peering across the golden fields that carpeted the mountain's base.

"I thought you were an animal, not a gentleman," Bobby retorted.

"Well..." the knight murmured, his gaze fixed on the view. "Well..." He left it at that.

They stood in silence before the open pasture, the curtain wall rising behind them. Its wooden gates were now visible, one sporting a busted hole like a grinning mouth with a tooth knocked out.

The wild, yellowed wheatgrass scratched at Bobby's armpits, its fat kernels tipped with bristly hairs. At his feet, the ancient dirt road had nearly been reclaimed by nature, marked only by a pressed flatness in contrast to the clumpy hillocks to either side. The path stretched straight up the piedmont toward Kaste Mountain, where another wall ringed the mountain itself.

All around them, the fields were mottled with bald patches—charred black circles where nothing grew. Bobby knew the story of Kaste's violent end. He imagined the human kindling, bodies scorched into the soil, their last moments seared into the earth. Statues of ash, frozen mid-stance, scattered like dust across the mountainside by a single, wrathful storm of soot. And when the blustering squalls had finally spent themselves, they too fled the city, leaving behind a vacuum-sealed graveyard.

Upon entering the city's outskirts, the air thickened with dust—a heavy choking fog that hung like a gauze over everything. They pushed through the tall grass, trespassers in a tomb, time abandoned. Ages had passed without a living soul stirring; the atmosphere was so dead-still, even the ghosts had long since absconded. There was no wind here. No breath of time. Only the cold, unyielding solitude of basalt and stone. A deep shiver coursed through Bobby as an acute loneliness possessed him, squeezing at his very bones. It brought an eerie sensation that his flesh no longer belonged to him—sliding over his skeletal frame like a suffocating wrap. He and his companions trudged on, forging through the heavy air and rigid terrain toward Kaste Mountain, each step a slow, dragging effort, as if they were wading through a dense body of water.

THIRTY-TWO

THE MOUNTAINOUS city stood as a fossilized imprint of a once-thriving hive. Rudimentary buildings clung to the slope as well-preserved husks, clustered like the dead cells of an open hornet's nest stretching up and around the mountain. The stone structures were packed so tightly atop each other and jammed next to each other, the individual buildings melding into one massive edifice, half-grown from the black rock, as much a part of the mountain as apart from it. Four great stone belts encircled the city, carving it into five stacked districts. These rings, like inner ramparts, were secured with gateway buckles—the lone central passage from one tier to the next, its broad thoroughfare winding its way to the very top. From base to summit, each layer bore its own distinct chromatic range: dark grays at the base, rising through tawny-brown, silver, ivory, and finally crowning in a dull, tarnished gold at the mountain's peak.

Zenobia darted ahead, rustling past Bobby and the Tiger Knight, slicing a path through the wheatgrass toward the first inner wall.

Once more, Bobby chased after her, this time with the Tiger Knight at his side. *A wingman*, he thought. He remembered the term, though not what it meant. Right now, he figured it meant *the man who kept you company while the first love of your life runs as far and as fast from you as she possibly can*. But was it really love? What did he know about love, anyway? How could he tell the difference between the ache of love and the ache of loneliness? One just seemed sharper, that's all.

Mrs. Palmer once described her love for her late husband as something more profound than aching infatuation. *Romantic love*, she said, was a delightful thirst—okay for a while but unsustainable. *True love*, she explained, was like growing into the half of yourself you never knew was missing—a better angel—until, one day, you became a single being with two minds, two hearts, four arms, and four legs. Stronger. Brighter. Wiser. Satiated and whole.

It was, Bobby decided, kind of a high bar.

He also suspected, even at just thirteen, he was doomed to that age-old realm of unrequited love. His heart limped on, stumbling over itself as he fought to keep pace with her.

When he finally caught up, she was standing still, fixed in place before a pair of lofty lead gates. Gigantic double doors sealed tight. Her head bent back as she studied the strange inscriptions etched thirty-five feet above. "Ain't got the foggiest clue what it says," she said, puzzled.

Unlike the cloaked outer wall, these doors were richly adorned with bas-relief tableaus. The one they stared at showed masses harvesting crops, tending cattle, laboring in fields. The writing above was in a long-forgotten tongue, yet Bobby could read it.

"Strata of the Serfs," he said between breaths, mopping his brow with his coarse sleeve.

Zenobia tilted her head. "How the heck ya know that?"

"He is the Son of the Creator," the Tiger Knight answered. "He understands all languages in our world, both ancient and new."

"Oh. Guess that makes a lick o' sense." She ambled up to the oversized doors and planted her palms against the gate. Digging in her heels, she tensed her wiry arms, elbows clicking into place. With a grunt and a long exhale, she pushed until something heavy cracked behind the gate. A moment later, it creaked open without resistance. She clapped the dust from her hands and smirked. "Ain't met a door yet I couldn't bust open."

"Until this day, I had never met such an enchanting hatchling whose strength is equaled only by her charm and wit," said the Tiger Knight with a delighted bow.

Bobby rolled his eyes as he moved on, leaving them to their banter. He stepped through the first inner wall and into the district beyond.

The city's oppressive stillness made his forehead bead with sweat. Though they were outdoors, the air refused to move. It hung dense and stagnant, like woolen cotton caught in his throat. With no breeze, the stifling atmosphere of preservation clung to him, thick with the scent of mold and long-dead life. The entire city held its breath, so long that it had forgotten how to breathe.

On all sides rose squat, blocky structures, solid in their original stone forms. Their edges, slightly dulled by the boredom of time, remained largely undamaged. The dumpy clusters of cubic houses were laced in soot, grime worked in from the squalid, crowded lives of long-lost occupants, who might've fled only yesterday, so well preserved were their belongings. Amid the buildings' monochrome palette, the only splashes of color came from faded rugs and tattered clothes festooned between homes on sagging lines. Frayed curtains still hung in the narrow rectangular cutouts in the brickwork, and barren doorways offered glimpses into dark, vacant voids. The facade of homes still stood, intact in form, but anything truly homely—movement, warmth, laughter—had long since been hollowed out.

The archaic impression of human life played tricks on Bobby's mind. He swore he could hear faint echoes: wares jangling in a busy marketplace, the clatter of leather soles hurrying along cobbled streets, the whispers of voices. But none of it was real. Not a single acoustical blip nor bleep pierced the heavy stillness. Bobby noticed more black smears marking nearly every stone lane, doorway, and alley. It appeared the people of Kaste had abandoned their shadows, too. They strode onward in studious silence, climbing the abandoned thoroughfare and mounting the first of many stair flights on their upward journey.

The second barricade, Bobby read aloud, "Strata of the Artisan Merchant." His voice felt distant, choked in the thick air.

Zenobia muscled the gate open, and they continued. The buildings in this level were taller and more ornate, yet just as tightly packed. Storefronts and shops were just as they left them, their contents preserved and untouched, but as lifeless as the strata below. The narrow streets were littered with clay trinkets and wooden toys, scattered among countless pottery jugs and vases, each one beautifully decorated with hand-painted patterns.

They passed a quaint, circular park centered around a giant stone monolith, overwhelmed with stenciled handprints in every color, pressed there by hands so tiny that only children could have made them. Ten large totem posts lined the perimeter, each carved with a different animal facing inward. One post depicted a life-sized human figure, and something about the man's face seemed vaguely familiar to Bobby, though he couldn't say why.

As they continued to move up the silent streets, the Tiger Knight picked up a deep clay bowl half-filled with water. He sniffed at it, recoiled, then hacked out a cough. "Putrid," he declared, setting the bowl back down.

The third barricade read: STRATA OF THE SOLDIERS. This section displayed a relief of an army in motion—marching, battling, defending, and slaughtering. The streets were broader, flanked by open square lots likely used as training grounds. Imposing rectangular structures, barracks, and temples stood every few blocks, mute and hollow. Statues of stone warriors, clad in full battle regalia, stood sentinel at every corner. Swords, spears, armor, and shields lay scattered in heaps across the streets, tossed haphazardly atop dark stains marring the otherwise bright stone road.

The Tiger Knight and Zenobia rummaged through the discarded weaponry, inspecting their quality and craftsmanship before casting them aside. Strangely, none of the weapons rang or clanged against the ground. Each struck with a muffled *thud*. For several minutes, they flung swords and gear against stone, steel, and wood, fascinated and puzzled by the dulled response.

Exhausted, Bobby welcomed a stone bench and dropped onto it, grateful for the rest. He swung one heel onto his opposite knee and dug his thumb into the aching meat of his foot. "My dogs are really barking," he sighed, quoting Mrs. Palmer.

While massaging his feet, Bobby studied a nearby warrior statue. Its eyes, deep-set and distant, held a vacant, unfocused look. And suddenly, he recognized it—*the thousand-yard stare*. Mrs. Palmer had described it when recounting her late husband's return from Vietnam. She'd said Bobby's father wore that same look once. How hadn't he seen it before? The statue resembled his father. Bobby sprang to another statue across the street. Same expression. Same eerie emptiness. All of them bore his father's face. He said nothing. He didn't want to explain his father's long stare or the long story behind it.

As they continued their ascent, his feet had stopped barking, but still whimpered with every step. Higher up, the air thinned, easing the cottony resistance in his lungs. Yet the stillness held thick, immovable, and unnatural. Every motion pressed against an invisible mass, the air resisting their passage.

The fourth gate's tableau depicted a posse of nobles in opulent robes, draped in jewels, caught in static scenes of leisure and excess. "Strata of the Nobles," Bobby read from the arcane script. Zenobia wasted no time. She smashed open the sealed doors, and they proceeded through.

As they climbed toward the summit, the tiers narrowed, but the posh neighborhoods widened in space. Large villas perched precariously along the cliffs, while vast, vacant spaces once hinted at being parks and public plazas. They marched up wide, smooth avenues, passing mansions hidden within sprawling estates, their borders marked by extravagant rock gardens, parched fountains, and still more stone figures of his dad. Bobby now realized the totemic figure on the second level had worn his father's face. Even the rug patterns on the first level—those swirling lines—traced the contours of his father's features: the same hollow eyes, the same distant stare. And the fountain back in Pangia? That was him, too. His likeness had been here all along, stamped in cold stone.

Reaching a high outcrop that jutted from the mountainside, Bobby spotted a lonely marble bench overlooking the gloomy lands below. He decided it was a good place as any to rest his dogs again. But when he peered over the edge, his stomach lurched. It looked to be a trillion feet to the bottom. He staggered back, grabbing the bench and collapsing against it, hugging the seat as his pounding heart pressed tight against the cool slab of marble.

"Ain't this a sight to make even angels cower?" Zenobia quipped, plopping down onto the sliver of marble Bobby wasn't already clinging to.

Her comment sparked something hopeful in him—if he was the coward... that meant he was also the angel. Perhaps—just perhaps—Zenobia held a twinkle of interest in him after all. Or at least, started to see *something* in him.

Bolstered by that fragile scrap of hope, he straightened, slowly forcing himself upright beside her. They sat quietly. Bobby stole glances at her as she stared out over the wasteland they had crossed. Her soft, indrawn smile caught his attention. Gapped front-tooth gently biting her bottom lip, green eyes gleaming with thought. The constellation of freckles on her nose and cheeks shimmered faintly, like stars dusted across her face. She looked like someone caught between memory and dream, as if the ruined land still held the trace of something beautiful, or maybe the promise of what it could be again.

Without warning, Zenobia stood. Still not looking at him, she said, "Welp, I sho' glad yer eye don't twitch no more." Then, she returned to the main road.

The fifth and final fortification stood before them: a massive stone wall, forty feet high, stretching across the craggy crest of the mountain. Here and there, sheer cliffs dropped dramatically into oblivion. Bastions jutted from the wall, their connecting walkways once alive with patrolling guards, now silent, cold mementos to the city's long-dead defense. The gatehouse was ornamented with a bas-relief, wrought in bronze, silver, and gold, and mounted across the gilded portcullis. It depicted the kingdom's social hierarchy as a segmented pyramid. Each tier aligned with an elemental symbol. At the base, the Earth layer showed laborers and farmers. Above them, Water held craftsmen and merchants. Ascending further, Fire was the domain of soldiers and knights. The Air level, just below the peak, housed the nobility. And crowning them all, in the Sun segment, sat the king and queen on twin thrones, gazing over their realm. Between them stood a radiant Tree of Life, binding all layers into one, unified order.

"Lemme guess," Zenobia said, squinting up at the tableau. "Stratus of ye Olde Royal-pain-in-the-Butt?"

"Close," Bobby said. "Stratus of the Majesty."

"Same difference," she scoffed, and promptly tore the gate down.

Bobby gasped at the splendor that broke open before him. A massive garden spanned the mountaintop, manicured with uncanny precision. The ground was carpeted in sky-colored grass so vividly blue it seemed to glow. Wide marble boulevards climbed the slope, flanked by thickets of oak trees whose broad golden leaves still gleamed in the dull light. Rocky grottoes dotted the landscape, their walls sparkling with inlaid diamonds. At the garden's heart was a stout topiary maze, peppered with dry gold fountains, each embellished with intricate arabesque floral patterns. Long flowerbeds lined the paths, their petals frozen in full bloom, glinting like shards of stained glass. A narrow creek snaked through the garden, slipping under three wide bridges of gold brick and pooling in mirror-clear ponds. As Bobby crossed the central span, he paused, noticing the water below didn't ripple. It wasn't water at all. It was some crystalline medium, unmoving and silent, deepening the unnatural tranquility that blanketed the place.

Now it was clear: this wasn't a real garden. It was a jewel box. A preserved illusion of life. The golden leaves, the shimmering flowers—everything had been forged, sculpted, cast from precious metals and stones. Nature's beauty immortalized in deathless, opulent artifice.

Above it all loomed the golden chateau, perched on the mountain's peak like a gilded tomb. The fortress boasted a towering ten-story keep and twin five-story wings, each lined with bulky towers and piercing spires that soared even higher than the summit itself. Once the pinnacle of masterful masonry and regal craftsmanship—a shining emblem of supreme royalty—it now stood as little more than an elaborate sarcophagus, embraced by the indifference of a barren mountain.

The final climb to its doors was like scaling a Mayan temple. Bobby's legs screamed with every step, dragging the corpses of his own feet. When they reached the top, Zenobia—undaunted and untired—threw open the towering doors. A torrent of hot, fetid air surged outward, striking them like the breath of a cursed tomb: thick, humid, and ancient. The stench of sealed decay washed over them in an asphyxiating wave. Yet even in that putrid gust, Bobby felt a fleeting relief, a momentary breeze against his sweat-slick face. But the sensation turned quickly. The air settled heavier and stickier than before. Sweat poured anew, crawling down his limbs in rivulets, pooling in the creases of his flesh, soaking through the pits of his clothes. Still, he trudged forward. Numbed feet lugging him into the dark, cavernous interior.

THIRTY-THREE

THE DIM span of the castle's grand halls enveloped them as they stepped inside. With the little light there was, Bobby flipped open his book and buried his nose between the pages as they wandered aimlessly through the enormous corridors, weaving between rows of fat columns that stretched far above their heads.

"Where is this Ingress located?" the Tiger Knight inquired, his voice trailing behind Bobby in the eerie stillness.

The scant light made reading difficult. The text blurred as the book wobbled with Bobby's every step. He was further distracted by the muffled footfalls and the strain of trying to hear his friends. Their voices seemed to evaporate before fully forming, absorbed by the airless void that amplified the deeper they ventured into the palace.

"It's somewhere in the Ancient City of Kaste, but it doesn't say where," Bobby called out. Yet his voice came out muted and distant.

"That year book's as useful as a melody to a tone-deaf choir," Zenobia mocked.

The sound grew so thin Bobby could barely register anything beyond the pulsing, sluicing, and gurgling of his own squishy innards, which clogged his ears. He jammed a pinkie into one ear, wiggling to clear it, but only stirred a dull, grating scrape inside his skull. The need for his ears to pop drove him mad.

"Is anyone else having trouble hearing?" he bellowed, though the words seemed to reach him only through the vibrations in his bones.

So attuned now to his inner thrum, Bobby's mind was dragged back to a memory he wanted desperately to avoid—his house, the attic, a suffocating silence shared only with the hushed bodies of the dead. The silence had been so pure, so utterly devoid of sound that only the scratching of his own neurons seemed to exist, clawing madly through the dark corridors of his mind.

"Bobby!" Zenobia's voice cut through the muffle. "Bobby, you okay?"

He felt slight pressure on his arm, which he gradually recognized as her fingers gripping him. Shapes swam into form, and his vision refocused to find Zenobia's face waving before him, her bright eyes locked on him with concern.

His lungs burned. He gasped, realizing he hadn't been breathing. Air rushed in, slaking his aching chest and carrying the foul tang of moldy cheese across his tongue. His ears flushed with heat, and only then did he know why: his hands were clamped tight around his head. He pried his palms away, easing the pressure. Relief came almost instantly.

"You alrite?" Zenobia asked again, her expression turning stern.

"Y—yeah, I'm fine," Bobby said, wriggling free from her hold. "I'm fine."

They found themselves in a large chamber Bobby couldn't recall entering. The Tiger Knight handed him his book—apparently dropped during his

light filled the space, reflecting off stark-white marble walls, a polished floor, and a vaulted ceiling that soared far overhead with heavenly illumination. The room's immense scale suggested some ceremonial or royal purpose.

At the far end, a series of marble statues lined a long marble plinth, immediately drawing their attention. Each figure displayed the same vacant expression Bobby had come to recognize as his father's. Except every statue was dressed in a distinct set of garments, each representing a different role in society. From left to right: his father as a laborer, bearing a hammer and scythe. Then a priest or holy man. Next, an artist, with a lyre, pen, and brush. A knight came next, clad in armor with sword and shield. Beside him, a nobleman clutched a heavy sack of coins. The sixth figure portrayed a crowned king holding a scepter, and last of all, a man of science burdened with an armillary sphere, scrolls, and thick-bound books.

"Them faces all look the same," Zenobia said. "Even got the same odd stare you jus' had, Bobby."

Bobby twitched his head, almost like a tick, as he brushed his bangs from his eyes. He was momentarily taken by her casual use of his name. Had she ever said his name out loud before? If she had, it hadn't sounded like this. This time, it seemed to carry warmth, a trace of familiarity. He savored the sound of his name spoken in her soft voice.

"They all look like my dad," he then said, shame and confusion curling together in his throat.

Suddenly, a powerful voice boomed through the chamber—a chorus of seven voices announcing in unison.

"We are the Stations."

The three jumped.

"Who said that?" Zenobia demanded, scanning the room.

"We did," came the reply, now clearly emanating from the seven marble figures.

Bobby squinted at them. "What... are you?"

"We are the council known as the Stations," the voices explained. "We assign titles and purpose to all who reside in the city of Kaste."

"Who created you?" the Tiger Knight asked, stepping closer.

"The architects of the first civilization. Men and women who emerged from wilderness and chaos to raise the walls of order. We were crafted to preserve that order. For Kaste to endure, every soul must know their place. Now: what are your titles?"

"I'm Bobby Porter," Bobby said, pointing to himself.

"We do not recognize such a title."

Bobby exchanged shrugs with Zenobia and Tiger Knight.

"I am the Tiger Knight," said the knight, squaring his shoulders.

"Greetings, soldier. Welcome to the city of Kaste."

"Imma dirt farmer'n syrup maker," Zenobia declared, arms crossed.

"Greetings, laborer. Welcome to the city of Kaste."

After a beat, the voices turned again to Bobby. "And you, young man— what is your title?"

Bobby frowned. "Do I need one? We're not staying. We just need to find the Ingress to Fire Mountain. Do you know where it is?"

"All inhabitants of Kaste must possess a title. Without one, we cannot assist you."

"Then can you answer me?" the Tiger Knight asked. "As a knight?"

"A soldier is not privy to such information."

Zenobia stepped closer. "What 'bout a farmer?"

"A laborer, certainly not," answered the voices, this time with a note of offense—as if the very notion that someone like her might be worthy of the answer was absurd.

Zenobia snorted, cracking her knuckles. Her glare narrowed to a focused wrath. With fists clenched, Bobby half-expected her to knock the whole council down right then and there.

Bobby's mouth opened to ask if a deity might be privileged to know its location, but only an idle drone escaped his throat.

"If you lack a designated station," the Stations offered, interrupting Bobby's throaty buzz, their tone shifting towards helpfulness—perhaps sensing their imminent threat in Zenobia's menacing snarl—"one can be assigned. That is our purpose."

"Ah. Okay," Bobby said. "How?"

"With a simple test."

After a dramatic pause, a deep grinding and rumbling erupted beneath their feet. A single tile loosened in the floor, and a marble pillar ascended, shaking off eons of dust. It groaned to a halt at around Bobby's height.

"Choose the symbol that most appeals to you."

Bobby strolled over to the pillar and examined the five stone tablets stacked from top to bottom. Each bore a unique etched symbol: the topmost showed a heart at the center of a cross; the one below it, a square with a heart, spade, club, and diamond at each corner, like of a playing card; the middle tablet featured three parallel zigzagging lines; then, a circle bisected by a vertical and horizontal line; and the last, at the bottom, a crown resting atop of a short iconic column-like pedestal.

He tapped his chin, groaning in concentration as his finger crept up to scratch his blond head. Absentmindedly, he began to nibble his thumb.

"Okay," he squeaked at last. "I pick..." He paused, then pointed to the tablet that displayed the square containing the heart, spade, club, and diamond. "This one."

The moment he chose, the remaining four tablets disintegrated into dust.

"Now choose the maxim by which you live, "the Stations boomed.

"One: 'See the way, go the way, show the way.'

"Two: 'Know thyself.'

"Three: 'Others before thyself.'

"Four: 'Steadiness, fortitude, and consistency are keys to success.'

"Five: 'Once you find faith, you find the answers.'

"Which words do you embody?"

A hefty silence followed as Bobby rifled through his thoughts. The maxims had wedged themselves in his mind with surprising clarity, word for word. He turned them over carefully, chewing on their meanings, testing their fit. He gnawed his thumb to the edge of raw before finally declaring, with uncertain conviction: "Umm... 'Others before thyself?'"

As soon as the words left his lips, the unchosen sayings vanished from his memory. Try as he might, Bobby couldn't recall a single word of the other options. Only his chosen motto remained, acutely etched in his mind like a scar: *Others before theyself.*

"Now for the final question: answer this riddle, and we shall know your station.

"How are reality and fantasy the same?"

Bobby whipped his head toward his friends, but their emphatic shrugs and reticent stares made it clear—he was on his own. He dug through the mushy gray matter squatting in his skull. *How is fantasy the same as reality?* Oh boy. Did they have something in common? There had to be an answer. There's always an answer to a riddle, isn't there?

He turned back to the Stations, studying the ossified blank gazes. A gaze that wasn't just the unraveled, despondent look that had haunted his father's sallow face in those last days. No, it was also, to Bobby's sudden horror, the exact same expression that had seized Everett Porter when Bobby spoke his final, most damning word to him—the one that hushed his father forever. That hollow stare had been captured in stone, immortalized in chilling detail across every statue.

Then, a clacking voice whispered—not in his ear, but in his head. Mrs. Palmer. His ever-wise neighbor, his personal oracle.

"That's an easy one," she clicked breezily in his mind.

Sure, easy for her maybe. Bobby wasn't so sure. He wasn't smart like she was.

"Sure, you are," her voice replied, firm and insistent. "You really think I'm talking to you right now? You think I'm something outside your silly little brain?" She chuckled. "And *that's* your answer, my boy."

"I've got it!" Bobby blurted, startling Zenobia and the Tiger Knight. "You can mistake one for the other."

A weighted silence stretched.

"You can mistake reality for fantasy... and fantasy for reality?" he added, his voice dipping into the register of doubt.

Still, the silence held.

"Is that it?" Bobby asked. "Did I get it right?"

"There is no single correct answer," the Stations finally declared. "Based on your choices and responses, we have determined your station to be that of a bard, scribe, and storyteller. A station not permitted access to the Ingress."

Zenobia pushed up her sleeves past her knobby elbows, revealing flexed sticks that were her arms, ending in punch-bound mitts. "Alrite, they ain't no need for these bozos no more," she spat.

Before she could charge, the Tiger Knight gently placed a hand on her shoulder, restraining her from turning the Stations into rubble.

"What Station is required to access the Ingress?" he asked calmly.

"Leader, Nobleman, or Clergy," the Stations replied.

The Tiger Knight paused, then said, "I am a Nobleman." He drew the medallion from beneath his armor and held it up for them to see. "Behold my coat of arms—the Noble House of Lanmarc."

"As a Noble, you are not permitted to associate directly with Laborers," the Stations intoned. "You would no longer know who this Laborer is, was, or will be. If you accept these terms, you will be blind to the Laborer's very existence. Do you accept?"

"That's crazy!" Bobby burst out. "Why should he have to do that? It makes no sense."

"It is as it's always been," the Stations replied, their voices unmoved. "The order of society must be preserved."

"It's alrite," Zenobia said, grinding her jaw. "We're practically strangers, anyhow."

"But I would never get to know you, hatchling," the Tiger Knight lamented, his timbre similar to the same flattened tone Bobby remembered in his father's voice after returning home from tour. A tone flattened by endless grief and self-loathing. A voice that mirrored those same lost, stony eyes.

"I feel denying myself that honor would be something I would regret for the rest of my days," the Tiger Knight continued, his words trembling with fear of losing something irreplaceable.

"I reckon you won't remember me none anyhow," Zenobia said. "So I figured they be no regrets. And if we don't do this, there ain't no gettin' to Dragoon Keep. And my daddy's life depends on it."

There was no mistaking the dire exuberance in her reasoning.

The Tiger Knight straightened, his posture as rigid as his wooden mask. "You are right, hatchling. We must save your father," he avowed with solemn resolve. He bowed low to her and took her hand gently. "Zenobia Mulhick, it has been an honor to know you. Brief though our acquaintance has been."

He released her hand and turned resolutely toward the Stations.

Bobby tugged at his cuff. "Is this really the only way?"

"We have no time to search for another," the Tiger Knight said. "The Blood Moons near their tipping point, and whatever plan that demon has set in motion will soon come to its dreadful fruition."

Bobby let go. His hand dropped limply to his side.

"Don't fret, my cub," the knight said, resting his hand on Bobby's shoulder. "I will never forget you."

Bobby said nothing more.

Turning to face the statues, the Tiger Knight declared, "I am ready. Do what you must."

"It is done," the Stations thundered in unison. "Welcome, Noble, to the city of Kaste."

Tiger Knight remained still for a long moment, facing the statues, as if his mind had been wiped clean.

"Tiger Knight?" Bobby asked, gently shaking his arm.

The knight turned to him. "Yes?"

"Are you okay?"

"I feel as right as a tiger in the jungle," he said. "Though it's strange—I know the location of the Ingress to Fire Mountain, but I cannot recall why we seek such a ghastly place."

"You don't remember anything about Zenobia?"

"What is a Zen-o-bia, young cub?" the knight asked, tilting his head in confusion.

Bobby pointed at Zenobia's bemused face. "She's Zenobia!"

The knight scanned the space where Bobby pointed, but his eyes seemed to pass over her as if she weren't there.

"He can't see me none," Zenobia said flatly.

"But she's right there! Can't you see her?" Bobby cried, gesturing more emphatically.

"It appears to be just us two formidable felines, young cub."

Zenobia folded her arms. "The dumb animal can't even hear me," she muttered. "Jus' git 'em to take us to the portal already."

With a big sigh, Bobby gave up trying to make Zenobia visible to the Tiger Knight and shifted tactics. "We must get to Fire Mountain now, to save my best friend's father from the Ashen Knight. We're running out of time. It's life or death!"

"Then we must move swiftly," the Tiger Knight said, suddenly sprinting into action. He rushed to one side of the long marble podium, where the Stations were mounted, and pressed his hands against the stone edge. With a growling grunt, he shoved with his legs—but his feet slid out from under him, nearly sending him sprawling face-first on his belly against the marble tiles.

"Th...the en...trance..." he groaned, forcing himself upright again. He braced and heaved with all his might, boots screeching on the spotless floor, leaving black marks as he struggled for traction. "...is... under... this..." he panted.

Zenobia joined him, gliding to his side. She dug in with both hands and pushed. At first, the base groaned and grated. Then—with a pop—it gave way, sliding more easily than expected. A plume of dust burst into the air as the podium shot forward. The slab moved so fast, the Tiger Knight nearly lost his footing and tumbled down the opening now revealed beneath it. But he caught himself just in time and sprang up straight.

"Ah-ha! I knew I would prevail!" He exclaimed, admiring his own biceps with what seemed like mild surprise. "I feel I've gained strength since our little adventure began, cub."

Zenobia rolled her eyes.

The three gathered around the rectangular opening in the floor. A narrow spiraling staircase dropped into shadow.

"Guess we go down," Bobby said, his voice carrying slightly into the depths.

"It leads deep into the mountain," said the Tiger Knight. "We best get moving." He descended first, clinking and clattering down the steps until he disappeared below the marbled floor, swallowed by the dark passageway.

Bobby hesitated at the edge, staring deep into the black. He wasn't scared of the darkness—no. The dark often comforted him. It was what waited beyond it. The stark, unforgiving light that might expose what he truly feared he was: the villain of the story. That's what filled him with dread.

He raised his head and found Zenobia's pinched face. She was biting her bottom lip, clearly lost somewhere in her own head. Still, her presence gave him hope. Maybe, with her beside him, he could survive whatever truths the light would burn into view. Or maybe... once she saw what he was really capable of, she'd recoil in horror, just like everyone else probably would.

"Be warned," intoned the Stations in an ominous, bodiless chorus. "Neither Scribe nor Laborer is permitted to use the Ingress."

Bobby's face twisted into a full-body grimace.

Zenobia caught it and smirked. "Pay no mind to 'em stupid statues," she said with a sneer. Then, without warning, she snatched his arm and yanked him forward."Now, c'mon!"

And just like that, they plunged into the hole, into the dark, and presumably toward the cruel light waiting on the other side.

THIRTY-FOUR

**HE DARKNESS** persisted, hardening into deeper shades of black. Bobby, Zenobia, and the Tiger Knight moved cautiously, blindly feeling their way down the narrow staircase. Bobby kept his arms outstretched, elbows bent to accommodate the tight passage, his fingertips grazing the slick, damp blocks on either side. Stone sweating with cool, mucous mildew. With his vision rendered useless, his other senses sharpened. His nose twitched at the high-gagging-fidelity stink of sickly rotting fruit that slimed the spiraling passage. His feet thudded step by step in reverberating clomps. Below, and sometimes disorientingly beside him, the Tiger Knight's voice bounced through the corridor, distorted by the tight acoustics as he occasionally grumbled:

"Does this passage have a bottom?" or "I can't make hair or tail of either my hair or tail." "Cub, are you still with me? I think I can hear your heart tapping. And your breath rasping."

"I'm right here. Right behind you," Bobby answered each time.

Zenobia would chime in, "Don't forget lil ol' me! Oh, never-yo-mind, ya already did!" Her comment always met with silence. Then giggles from her and Bobby.

And inevitably, the Tiger Knight puzzled, "What is so humorous, cub?"

To which Bobby replied with a shrug in his voice: "Oh, nothing. Never-yo-mind."

This strange little ritual was repeated in various playful ways as they descended deeper.

Then the wall changed. Under Bobby's fingertips, the smooth stone gave way to bumpy, porous edges. The surface grew wetter, gooey, and drippy, and whatever was seeping from the ceiling kept landing squarely on the back of his neck, sending fresh shivers down his spine.

And then—suddenly—the left wall was gone. His hand swept through empty air, nearly pitching him sideways into nothingness. He froze, dropping into a squat to steady himself. Reaching out, he confirmed it: the wall had vanished. A gulf had opened at his side. A gaping void of unknowable depth.

In the dark, his heightened hearing picked up the distant *drip-drip-drip* of water to his left. The sound was so precise, so persistent, it mimicked the patter of rain, underscoring the perilous abyss yawning beyond the stairs' edge.

"You ain't fallen off yet, have ya?" Zenobia's voice bounded up the stairwell.

"Of course not," Bobby answered, doing his best to hide the tremble in his voice. He'd already fallen into one dark pit and wasn't in any hurry to repeat the experience.

"What did you say, cub?" came the Tiger Knight's voice, distant and delayed. He was far below now.

"Never mind," Bobby shouted.

"All right," the Tiger Knight called up. "Careful not to fall off the ledge."

Bobby stood and moved forward slowly, keeping his right hand against the remaining wall. The steps no longer spiraled but dropped in a steep, straight descent. His feet felt for each next ledge like testing ice.

Eventually, they all collided at the bottom in a tangle of limbs and apologies. In the pitch dark, Bobby had no idea what part of Zenobia he'd touched, but his face burned hot enough he worried it might glow. "Sorry," he mumbled, not entirely regretful. Even mortified, he cherished any excuse to be near her.

"Yer steppin' on my dang foot," Zenobia grumbled, her breath warm against his ear, intensifying the flush already rising in his cheeks.

"Sorry," he repeated, shrinking back and pressing against a moist, rugged wall.

"No need to apologize, cub," said the Tiger Knight somewhere in the dark. "It's dark as a mountain's bowels down here. There should be a doorway somewhere around here..." The sound of his armor clinked and clanged as he felt his way around. Then came a grunt, followed by a creak.

"I think I found it."

A burst of blinding light exploded into the chamber, slicing the blackness in half. From one blinded state to an even more painful blinding state. Bobby flinched, throwing his hands up and pinching his eyes shut. His vision, steeped so long in absolute darkness, stung from the brightness. But gradually, the glare softened into a blood-red bloom behind his eyelids, and after some time, he could finally see. The chamber was dimly lit now, just enough to move forward without groping the dark or flailing their hands in front of their faces.

They entered a cavern so mountainous it could easily fit a small town, streets and all. Its far walls lost in the gloom. As they ventured deeper into the mountainous hollow, a wall of sound assaulted their ears: chipping, clanking, rumbling, the constant roar of machinery, and the hiss of steam. Rows of red rocks fell like curtains of rubble across the breadth and length of the cave, raining down from above onto an elaborate network of steam-powered conveyor belts embedded in the ground. The belts shuddered into motion, carrying the rocks off toward some distant, unseen place.

Bobby peered upward. Above them spanned another dizzying web of conveyor belts, crisscrossing in three dimensions all the way up to the cave's red ceiling. There, high above, tiny figures—thin, monochromatic versions of his mother's garden gnomes—chipped away at the bedrock with minuscule pick hammers.

"What are those?" Bobby shouted over the mechanical din, pointing skyward.

Tiger Knight turned his head, his wooden mask searching but failing to focus. "What do you mean, cub? The falling rocks?"

"He's jus' as blind to them laborers as to me, I reckon," Zenobia said.

The Tiger Knight waved them on. "This way. We must keep moving down!" he shouted over his shoulder.

"Down?" Zenobia groaned. "Now jus' how far down we gotta go?"

Bobby pulled out his book and flipped to the chapter on the Ancient City of Kaste. "Well," he began, scanning the page, "there are as many Sub-Stratases underground as there are levels on the mountain." He shut his book and brushed his bangs out of his face. "So if I were to guess, the portal's probably at the very bottom. That means... yeah, we're going all the way down." He tucked the book back into his bag.

"Oh—and the book says those little guys are Kastites. They're made from the same red rock as the mountain itself. Looks like they survived the Ashen Knight's destruction by staying hidden in here all these years."

"You mean these lil' guys been hidden in thisyer mountain for a thousand years?" Zenobia asked.

"Yup. I don't think they're interested in anything beyond what they were built for."

"An' what's that?"

"The last queen of Kaste, Queen Hedy Mulhick—your great-great-great, great-great—

"Git on with the point already!" Zenobia cut in, clearly annoyed.

Bobby cleared his throat and hurried on."Your ancestor was a queen. You come from royalty!" He paused, waiting for some reaction—surprise, disbelief, anything. But Zenobia just crossed her arms and squinted at him, unimpressed.

"Well, anyways," he continued, deflated a bit, "she used the last of her special maple nectar to make 'em. They're golems—built to raise the serfs out of the slums, revolutionize Kaste's economic and social structure, fix class inequality." He grinned, proud of the words he'd memorized, even if he only half-understood them. But Zenobia still looked at him like he'd just spoken in tongues mid-stroke. He dropped the grin and added. "Before she could put them to use, the Ashen Knight came. And the Kastites have been mining ever since, just... mindlessly working." He gestured toward the industrious little clay-bodied workers, clinking and hammering, their centuries-old toil uninterrupted.

From up ahead, the Tiger Knight's voice bellowed: "Hurry up, cub. No time to waste!"

"C'mon, let's keep on movin'," Zenobia said, heading toward the sound of the knight's call.

Bobby trailed behind, still baffled by how little she seemed to care about the fact that she was royalty.

They chased the Tiger Knight's voice as it boomed and bounced through the vast caverns, making him seem everywhere and nowhere at once. Again and again, he called, "This way, cub. Come this way." Bobby and Zenobia dashed down steps and staircases, slipping through a series of old, unmarked wooden gates. Each threshold led them deeper into dank, rocky passage-ways. No matter how hard Bobby tried, the knight's ricocheting calls kept eluding precise direction.

As they descended into the mountain's depth, each level narrowed, form-ing a kind of inverted mountain—a pyramid tipped upside down and buried in the earth. Every sublevel was inhabited by its own distinct class of pottery-molded citizens.

The second sub-stratum bustled with clay people managing the torrent of red rocks cascading from above. These workers crafted everyday objects from raw materials, placing them on conveyor belts that whisked the finished goods to lower levels.

The third sub-stratum housed the Kastites' inspectors and record-keepers, who appraised and cataloged each item in clay ledgers. They sorted everything—books, weapons, pottery, and effigies—into neat piles, each group shipped off via conveyor belt for the next level down.

Sub-stratum four unfolded into a wide thoroughfare, split between two wildly different camps. On the right, miniature clay soldiers marched through endless battle drills, their clashing weapons breaking again and again. They discarded the shards onto a belt, then picked up new ones and resumed training without pause. On the left, clay artists and performers staged a hypnotic spectacle—ballerinas twirling in perfect rhythm. At the same time, sculptors, mimes, jugglers, and actors cycled through silent renditions of life's tragedies and comedies in an eternal loop.

To Bobby, it all felt surreal. Then again, everything in Helcyon operated like a dream. A part of him wanted to stay and watch the odd terracotta gnomes at their crafts, but there was no time. His legs pumped harder; his thighs chafed raw against the coarse fabric of his pants.

Sub-stratum five opened into yet another, slightly smaller, bisected cavern. On the left, clay nobles lounged in lavish feasts, gorging from large plates and gulping wine from goblets bigger than their heads, though the food and drink, like everything else down here, were made of clay. Some read books, others gambled or debated, mouthing sentiments without sound. All of them were wrapped in layers of indulgence and apathy. Opposite them, a congregation of clay clergy knelt in rows before altars, solemn in their silent devotion. One by one, they prayed to small idols and figurines— then, just as easily, swapped them for others and tossed the discarded icons onto a conveyor belt that passed by.

The entire spectacle was a mimicry, a hollow imitation of life where nothing held genuine substance or meaning. What had once been designed to bridge the chasm between social classes had, over a millennium, calcified into a rigid, atavistic hierarchy. The artificial bourgeoisie now emptied goblets, scraped clean their plates, flipped through meaningless books, won or lost pointless games, or out-prayed their idols, only to facilely exchange one ideology for another. All the while, they discarded their broken weapons and used-up goods, which gushed through storm-drain-like vents, cascading downward toward a final terminus below.

The final sub-stratum assaulted Bobby and Zenobia with a wave of heat and a dense curtain of steam, thick with a sulfurous stench of scorched earth and singed hair. Gagging, they clamped their hands over their mouths and noses as they made their way down a towering staircase carved into the raw stone of a vast chasm. There were no walls, no safety railings, just open stairs and the horrifying notion that a single misstep would send them plummeting five hundred feet into a bubbling lake of lava that churned at the cavern's base. Here, all discarded items from the levels above rained down in a relentless torrent of terracotta debris, dissolving back into the molten core of the mountain.

Rising from the heart of the roiling lake of magma was a small island, upon which the facade of a palace, with ornate columns, tall windows, and anterior steps, had been carved directly into the rusted floor of the bedrock. The structure was fully visible only from the landing at the top of the staircase, where, looking down from such height, the illusion was that the palace stood upright, as if facing it head-on. But as they descended and reached the bottom of the stairs, arriving at one end of a long, arched bridge stretching precariously over the steaming lava toward the island, the palace's perspective flattened, becoming flush with the ground and nearly vanishing from view.

They paused intermittently as they crossed the bridge, feeling it sway under their feet. With nervous glances exchanged, they quickened their pace—only to slow again each time the bridge shuddered beneath them. Concerned that their footfalls were exacerbating its instability, they decided to pussyfoot it the rest of the way.

Upon reaching the solid footing of the islet, they approached the flat-tened palace exterior embedded in the ground with caution. Its windows and doorways, now recessed voids, resembled freshly dug graves dipping into the dark. Helcyon, as always, distorted Bobby's sense of direction—up or down was purely a matter of perspective. Had the palace stood vertically, like a normal palace, the stairs would've ascended toward a grand entrance. But lying flat as it did, those same steps now seemed to lead deeper into the earth—into the very heart of the planet itself.

"Seems like we're either goin' up or goin' down," Zenobia observed.

"I guess," Bobby said as they continued, step by step, sinking into the enormous grave of an entryway.

Navigating the tomb-like palace felt like exploring the great pyramids of Egypt, or at least how Bobby imagined them. Grandiose pillars, thick with dust, supported the low ceilings, their surfaces chiseled with more semi-3D carvings depicting occult rituals and scenes from a lost civilization. Torches mounted on the walls cast a murky golden light that bathed Zenobia in a warm haze, softening her features and giving her a healthier, more luminous look than the stress of their journey had lately allowed.

They moved ever downward, through narrow corridors choked in silence. The thick stone walls—and the packed rock beyond—muffled all outside noise: the churn of the lava, the cacophony of laborious golems above. The palace felt entombed in its own pocket of time.

Eventually, they emerged into another sizable chamber hall. A dark twin to the white-marble gallery of the Stations far above. But where that place had shimmered in sterile light, this one was cloaked in gloom and suffocating haze. Sparse torches sputtered and smoked, casting long, quivering silhouettes across the damp stone.

"Tiger Knight!" Bobby shouted.

At the sound of his name, the knight turned from where he stood, facing a massive bronze statue of a three-headed serpent. "Bobby Porter, my cub," he said with a chuckle. "You've finally caught up."

The statue's coiled body rose like a squat column, twelve feet high and sixteen wide, from which three discrete serpent heads unfurled. Each bore a calm but ever-watchful gaze, the flickering torchlight glinting off their polished eyes in a way that made them seem almost alive.

"This is the Ingress," the Tiger Knight said.

"The snakes?" Bobby asked with some concern.

"We are Trilogy," came a susurrating trill from the bronze effigy. Like the voices of the Stations, the words were intoned by three distinct entities speaking in harmony: one a bass, one a tenor, and the third a soprano. "You have traveled far. We know you seek passage to Fire Mountain."

"That's right!" Zenobia said, stepping before the snakes.

"Where is the Ingress?" Bobby asked.

"We are them," said Trilogy, their voices blending into a harmonious chorus. "We are the earth, water, and firmament; the body, mind, and spirit; the past, present, and future. We embody animal, insect, and plant; the Suns, Moons, and Planets; mother, father, and child; birth, life, and death. We represent the beginning, middle, and end; the dream, the real, and the belief. We are the trinity of the cosmos. The ingress, egress, and passage between. But above all, we are the keepers of knowledge, wisdom, and truth. We are Trilogy."

"Great! Can ya git us to Fire Mountain, or what?" Zenobia pressed.

"We are three gateways to three destinations," Trilogy answered. "But our passage is closed to your kind. Your place is here, among the laborers."

Suddenly, a dry patter rose. Hundreds of hardened mud boots marched in tight formation as a legion of clay soldiers poured into the chamber, surrounding Zenobia, Bobby, and Tiger Knight. Though only a foot and a half tall, the Kastite warriors looked menacing, armed with pointed swords, arrows, and staves fashioned from hard, cutting clay.

"What is the meaning of this?" the Tiger Knight demanded.

Another platoon streamed in behind the first, bearing an iron cage shaped like a giant birdcage.

"I command you to tell your soldiers to stand down and explain what is going on!" the Tiger Knight said, striding toward the Trilogy. But his advance was cut short by a wall of spearpoints jabbing toward his chest. The snakes stood unmoved, their cold, indifferent gaze locked on them.

Then the army surged forward in a coordinated attack, swarming Zenobia. She fought back ferociously, her fists shattering and smashing the little terracotta troops like fragile ceramic dolls.

To the Tiger Knight—oblivious to her struggle—it appeared the soldiers were simply bursting apart in a bizarre, inexplicable spectacle.

"We need to help her!" Bobby screamed, yanking at the knight's arm.

"Help, who cub?" the knight asked, his head swiveling wildly in confusion. "Far as I can tell, the threat is taking care of itself."

Zenobia continued her flurry of kicks and punches, even throwing in the occasional head-butt. Nicks and scratches bloomed across her knuckles, arms, and face like a wild rash. But there were too many. For every soldier she shattered, another two swarmed in. Overwhelmed, she was driven back against the cage. The miniature clay soldiers finally managed to shove her inside, slammed the door, and locked it with a harsh clang before carting her off.

Bobby lunged after her, but a phalanx of soldiers snapped into formation, their interlocked spears forming a barbed barricade. He spun back to the snake heads.

"Where are they taking her? And why?" he demanded.

"Her place is among the workers," came the cold, harmonious reply of Trilogy. "She will mine with the rest of the Laborers."

"How come?" Bobby cried.

"Because she was born a serf and Laborer. That is her destiny."

"But she's the great-great-great-great-granddaughter of Queen Hedy Mulhick—the last queen of Kaste. She's not just noble, she's royalty!"

"Her lineage is neither royal nor noble," the snakes answered firmly. "It is the bloodline of a simple worker. And she would affirm it."

"Release my friend. Right now! You dumb, stupid thing!"

"We cannot."

"Cub," Tiger Knight said gently, stepping beside him, "I must admit, I am... perplexed. What is happening? What can I do?"

Bobby rubbed his burning eyes. A dark pressure was building inside him, pulsing with the intensity of a caged animal trying to break free. He tried to calm it with deep, rapid breaths. Slowly, his shaking eased, replaced by an eerie stillness. A quiet rage settled behind his heart, a heavy smoldering core. His head swam. Then, in a voice suddenly composed, he asked, "What about us?"

"The Noble may use the Ingress to Fire Mountain freely," Trilogy said. "Though stationed as a scribe, you, Bobby Porter, are something more. Your essence transcends our worldly conventions. You may move as you wish, provided you remain within the city's bounds."

"I need to think," Bobby muttered, scuffing at the shattered remnants of clay soldiers littering the ground. He squared his shoulders and fixed Trilogy with a hard, steady gaze. "Where can I go to rest?"

Without a word, the guarding soldiers shifted. Their formation parting to form a narrow pathway, allowing Bobby and the Tiger Knight to pass. Free to wander within their strange new prison.

Bobby turned to the Tiger Knight. "C'mon," he said. "We need to think."

"Yes," the Tiger Knight agreed. "Thought shall be our north star amidst this madness of confusion."

THIRTY-FIVE

BOBBY AND the Tiger Knight roamed restlessly, their footsteps ringing through dim vestibules and calcified corridors, until they stumbled into a perfectly cylindrical room. Its elevated cathedral dome ceiling concluded with a circular opening at its apex, the size of a large dinner plate. Mirrored by an identical hole directly below, in a floor dipped in a smooth, convex surface. The curving walls were decorated with ancient graffiti, depicting a looping narrative of a giant monster made of detritus wreaking havoc upon various groups of people with no clear beginning or end.

"What is this room?" exclaimed the Tiger Knight, his voice resonating against the curved walls, amplifying until it spiraled into a grating feedback. Bobby and the Tiger Knight clamped their hands over their ears, wincing until the echoes dwindled and the drain in the floor swallowed up the last reverberations of the knight's question.

Bobby quickly dug out his book and flipped it open. Before his eyes, ink began to bleed onto the once-blank page—words forming in perfect script, assembling a coherent narrative about the MEEM MONSTER.

"Aha!" Bobby shouted, his voice building upon itself, rising into a sonorous assault that crescendoed into a sharp pitch before diminishing and swirling down the chamber's central hole. Realizing the nature of the room's special acoustics, he whispered, "This is an Echo Chamber. We can summon the Meem Monster here to help us get Zenobia back."

The Tiger Knight remained utterly still, giving the impression of bafflement behind his mask. After a pause, he whispered, "What is a Zenobia?"

Bobby slapped his forehead in frustration. "Never mind. Just repeat everything I say. Okay?"

The Tiger Knight nodded, cautious.

Bobby closed the book. He didn't need to read further. He knew the workings of the Meem Monster, written in the newly inked chapter of The Traveler's Guide To Helcyon: Sights, History, Tips On How To Defeat the Ashen Knight, just as well as he knew the rage boiling inside him. He knew now that he was the one filling those blank pages. All he needed was to unleash the meanest, most hateful thoughts he could muster against those he despised. His words, weaponized, turned into a chaotic being whose sole purpose was to annihilate his enemies.

Shutting his eyes tight, Bobby envisioned the bloated, spiteful faces of the bruise-blooded adults from the Great City of Pangia, their disdain punching down on him. He let the bitterness saturate his heart, fueling his rancorous throat. He began to scream, "I hate!"

Reluctantly, the Tiger Knight echoed, "I hate."

"I hate those soulless, stupid, stinking, stubborn Kastites!" Bobby shouted, his voice oozing with venom.

The Tiger Knight repeated, and the chamber viciously amplified the words, twisting and mutating the sound into a chaotic caterwauling.

Bobby's shouts grew louder, battling the rising storm of his own hatred. "I hate how stupid they look! How selfish and ignorant they are! They're empty, useless waste of space. They're a mistake. They shouldn't exist. I wish they were never made!" At the center of the chamber, a cyclone of blustering wind began to form, the force pressing Bobby and the Tiger Knight against the wall. The wind howled and hissed, yet Bobby didn't relent. He screamed over the roar with intensifying desperation and vitriol, "I wish they all would die. Die. Die!"

His hateful words, parroted by the Tiger Knights, fed the cyclone's fury. The air grew thick and electric as if the chamber could barely contain the raw, malicious energy they had unleashed. A dark storm cloud formed in the center of the windstorm, quickly growing and darkening the room until it was illuminated only by sporadic crackling of electricity. The force of the raging storm intensified. The room vibrated, the walls shook, and the graffiti almost appeared to leap to life in the flickering shadows cast by the sparks of energy. Small debris discharged from the ceiling's circular opening, shaken loose by the quaking room.

Suddenly, a bolt of lightning burst from the storm's center, blinding Bobby with its flash of pure, white-hot light, searing the silhouette of a massive ogre into the back of his eyelids. Stones and sticks cascaded from the ceiling, swept into the ever-growing vortex. Bobby and the Tiger Knight pressed themselves against the wall, trying to avoid the swirling debris. Bits of whirling sand nicked Bobby's cheeks and chin, leaving small streaks of blood.

The churning debris began to coalesce, piece by piece, compacting into a single gigantic shape. The very outline Bobby had seen behind his eyelids. The giant creature took form at the cyclone's heart, starting with a torso that sprouted limbs, oversized hands, and feet. Its spine hunched and bristled with barbs, a thick neck anchoring to a blocky head. Its cracked mouth yawned wide, sucking the violent cyclone into its chest, which now pulsed like a heartbeat with the contained storm's power. Lightning flickered through the stone golem like luminous veins throbbing with life. The Meem Monster bellowed with rage and pain as it gained consciousness, opening its black diamond eyes.

The entire chamber seemed to shudder as the Meem Monster dropped from its levitation, crashing to the ground. Everything was eerily quiet, with the storm now inside the beast. It left only muted air in the space. Sound no longer resonated but was silenced as soon as it hit a surface. The Echo Chamber was now a dead room.

Gaping up at the towering twelve-foot behemoth, Bobby felt a pang of regret settle in the pit of his stomach and heart. As the thing's bulky frame shifted about, taking in its surroundings, seemingly confused, its joints grinded like nails on a chalkboard. Then the creature turned its gaze upon him, dark stone eyes locking with Bobby's half-hidden behind his mussed hair. At that moment, Bobby felt the weight of his words—the hate and devastation—as they flowed directly through the Meem Monster.

Did he really want this? Did he want to destroy every Kastite? He suddenly felt emptied, drained of all his fury. The force that had kept him standing until now was gone. Bobby collapsed, his body giving out as he stared up at the monster. It watched him back with a hateful glare. With Bobby's rage exhausted, there was nothing left but shame and regret, which he imagined his parents might have felt when they got to know him, the oddity they crafted.

The Meem Monster seemed to sense Bobby's change of heart, aware of his regret. His shame of it. It hesitated, then abruptly turned, wrenching itself away from its creator, and burst out of the room.

"What was that thing?" the Tiger Knight asked in a small and shaky voice.

Bobby managed to drag the back of his hand across his nicked face, smearing the blood across his pale cheek. "A bad mistake," he said.

A sudden crash boomed from beyond the room, followed by more smashing and shattering, which reminded Bobby of the saying, a bull in a China shop. "C'mon," he said, forcing himself to stand. "We have to try and stop it."

"Stop it?" the Tiger Knight repeated. "But we just invoked it?"

"Yeah, I think I made a mistake." Bobby grabbed Tiger Knight's arm, pulling him forward, and they set off after the Meem Monster.

The noise of destruction guided them as much as it taunted them. They chased the ghostly sounds of violence pealing through the passageways. The swelling clamor of shattering glass and cracking stone seemed to blend into something alive, something screaming. They had to double back more than once, deceived and misdirected by the labyrinthine passageways and the strange way the underground palace carried sound until they finally found a stairway leading up.

They halted in horror at the threshold when they emerged on the upper level. The aftermath of the Meem Monster's rampage lay before them. A field of broken terracotta soldiers shattered into countless sharp fragments. Bobby stepped carefully over the lacerating shards. Occasionally, a Kastite was still partially intact or split cleanly in half, invoking a memory of a priceless porcelain heirloom he had accidentally broken a year ago, marking his inaugural year of bad luck. The lifelike figurine revealed its hollowed insides, and now Bobby felt the same hollowness within himself. He was overcome with a sort of empathy for the soulless beings. Though the Kastites were nothing more than animated pottery—mindless, empty, yet obedient homunculi eager to perform their duties—seeing their broken forms scattered across the ground still filled Bobby with guilt, each fragment a reminder of his own destructiveness. It made his already heavy heart feel even heavier. He was responsible for this damage, his words having further shattered an already broken world.

They continued upward, passing through level after level of utterly obliterated Kastites. With every step, Bobby felt his body grow heavier and heavier, his breath shorter and sharper, and exhaustion pulled at him. His legs burned, his lungs felt like they were on fire, and his heart pumped molten acid through his veins. Still, he pushed on—harder and harder, faster and faster—until everything that could ache did so to its fullest. He had to find the Meem Monster. He had to stop it.

At last, he reached the topmost level. The entire cavern stretched before him, a sea of barbed red shards. The remains of every last Kastite the Meem

Monster had destroyed. In the distance, Bobby saw the monster hammering at a cage on the ground, Zenobia trapped inside.

"There it is," Bobby wheezed, turning to the Tiger Knight, but the knight was nowhere to be seen. Somehow, he had lost him along the way. Unsure when, where, or even how it happened, Bobby knew he couldn't afford to stop now. He had to save Zenobia alone.

"Zenobia!" his voice cracked as he screamed her name. Pain shot through his legs as he hobbled towards them, his feet getting cut by countless razor-sharp chunks of Kastites littering the floor.

Zenobia fought back as best she could from inside the cage. The Meem-Monster's fists savagely pounded down on the enclosure, rattling the bars with each crashing blow but failing to damage the strong metal rods. Despite being trapped with this craggy beast, Zenobia did not cower; she was not easily intimidated and was not as easily defeated as the Kastites. As the creature swung at the bars, she managed to grab one of its massive fingers, twisting it until she dislocated it, leaving it at an unnatural and painful angle. The creature recoiled with a child-like whimper, cradling its injured hand before popping the finger back in place. And when it stepped too close, Zenobia punched its big toe, sending the monster roaring in pain as if it had fiercely stubbed it. Though her strikes were small compared to the monster's massive form, they were still effective, causing it immense distress.

The Meem Monster let out a frustrated bellow, finding the cage an obstacle between its fists and its infuriating target. It gripped the cage and shook it violently, tossing Zenobia around inside. She clung to the bars, her eyes blazing with determination. The longer the struggle went on, the more enraged she and the monster became.

The Meem Monster raised the cage high above its head, preparing to smash it against the pointed boulders below. Zenobia thrust her arm through the bars, aiming for the creature's eye with her fist, but she fell short. The monster shook the cage again and readied to slam it down hard. Zenobia braced herself for the impact.

Bobby collapsed at the creature's feet, utterly spent. "Stop!" he shouted between ragged, wheezing breaths, positioning himself between the cage and the ground. The Meem Monster froze, staring down at Bobby's crumpled form as if recognizing its maker.

"Stop!" he wheezed again, "I... I don't want you... anymore." He gasped for air, then with firmer resolve, exhaled, "I don't need you anymore."

The monster cocked its head, emitting a pitiful whine like a child whose toys were being taken away.

Bobby extended a trembling hand, placing it on the Meem Monster's stony foot. "You did it. You killed them all. There's no more use for you. Please don't hurt her." As the words left his mouth, a bitter, oily darkness seemed to seep into him. His lips quivered, and sweat—or maybe tears—ran down his cheeks. He still couldn't cry, so it was probably sweat.

The Meem Monster's obsidian eyes stared, sadness clouding them momentarily. Then its expression twisted, rage igniting once again. It let out a horrendous roar that shook Bobby's bones. Its malevolent intent shifted to its creator. With a swing of its massive arm, it tossed the cage aside, sending Zenobia crashing to the ground. The Meem Monster raised its foot, ready to smash Bobby into the earth.

"Halt, you maledictive monster!" a voice hollered. Bobby and the Monster both turned to see the Tiger Knight approaching, holding Bobby's book high, its pages splayed open to the section on the Meem Monster. The Tiger Knight held the book out, pages facing the creature. Instantly, the monster shrank back, a whine escaping its maw as it retreated, clearly fearful of the book's power.

The Tiger Knight tore the pages free, ripping them into strips and then into smaller squares. Each tear made the stone beast shudder, its form shrinking with each rip. The Tiger Knight knelt by Bobby, thrusting the scraps into his hands. "Quick, cub, eat the paper."

"Eat the paper?" Bobby repeated, dumbfounded.

"It's the only way to destroy it. You must eat your words."

Bobby hesitated, staring at the knight, then at the pile of torn paper in his palm. The Tiger Knight nodded, urging him on. "Eat them."

Resigned, Bobby shoved the scraps into his mouth, chewing on the expanding wad of wet paper. He swallowed, coughing as the stubborn mass fought its way down his throat, threatening to get stuck at every moment. He groaned in disgust, forcing himself to take more, shoving it into his mouth. The paper was dry and rough, the ink bitter and acrid, exactly how he imagined ink would taste. It turned into a hardened paste as his saliva dampened it. Four rounds of chewing and swallowing later, something began to happen. The Meem Monster bellowed in agony, clawing at its stony flesh, then clamped its head with both hands. Its cries rose to a high pitch, shattering several of the Kastite's lesser damaged clay bodies into smaller bits. The monster's screams became the howling of winds, rising into a raging storm, until finally, a crack like lightning erupted from its chest. The Meem Monster was blasted backward, its body crumbling into a pile of rubble. The force of the blast sent particles of Kastites hurtling through the air. Bobby curled into a ball, shielding his face with his arms.

A dust cloud billowed up, swirling in rust-colored spirals. As the storm finally dissipated, a red haze hung in the air, stinging Bobby's eyes. He coughed, trying to sneeze the dust from his nostrils; thick drool with tiny fragments of the book pages oozed out of his mouth. He then dragged himself over to where the cage lay on the ground, upended.

"Zenobia?" he called, his voice hoarse. "Zenobia, are you okay?"

He saw her lying on her back amid the rubble, half in and half out of the cage. The door had busted open with the crash. Bobby's heart thudded as he reached for her, desperate for any sign she was still breathing.

When Bobby touched Zenobia's arm, she jerked away, shaking off his touch. She groaned in a faint but sweet drawl, "What in Port-nation was that thang?" She sat up, cradling her head in her hand. "Imma getting mighty sick of being put in cages, I can tell ya that much."

Seeing she was alive and seemingly unharmed, Bobby slumped onto his back, exhausted yet relieved. He lay across the uneven heap next to her, ignoring the pointy pieces that pricked painfully into his back. They both rested in silence for a few minutes, breathing big, irregular gasps.

"I'm sorry," Bobby said after a while.

"What for? That ain't for everthang," Zenobia replied sardonically.

"I made that thing."

"You made it?"

"I think... I think I can use words like a weapon. To destroy things."

"Ain't that so?"

"I've hurt a lot of people with words," Bobby admitted, his voice trembling.

"Well, I hurt plenty of folks with my bare hands. And I don't feel too good 'bout it neither."

"I think..." Bobby forced out his words between stifled hacks, making it sound as if he were crying, "I think I might have killed my dad."

Though Bobby wasn't crying, he desperately wanted to. He wanted to bury his face in Zenobia's arms, like she had buried her weeping face into his belly on the boat. He wanted her to squeeze him so tight she'd squeeze his tears out. But he knew that no matter how tight she held him, she could never squeeze out the pain that lived and thrived inside him, and so she would have to hold him forever. At that moment, he knew, beyond a doubt, that she was his only salvation.

"I don't ever want to lose you," Bobby said.

Zenobia remained silent for a long time. Bobby imagined the debate warring in her mind: Do I dive into thisyer confession or leave thisyer can-o'-worms sealed like a chest of plague-infested blankets?

"Did you hear what I said?" Bobby asked, his voice thin and fragile.

"Yeah," she finally coughed out, then fell silent again as if suddenly realizing how wounding her words could be. It might have struck her then, the power her tongue held, equal to her fists in the harm they could do. Anticipating a response, Bobby understood how deeply she could hurt him, depending on what she chose to say next.

"It's jus'..." she began, but then her voice trailed off, her presence growing so silent that her breathing seemed to cease. Instead of finishing, she stood up and walked away.

Zenobia's wordless departure wounded Bobby badly, and he let a dull pain spiraling in his spine snake up and spread outward through his torso, settling heavily in his chest. His right eye twitched. He ached at the thought of how deeply he believed he knew Zenobia as if she had been inked to life from the spilling of his own unwise blood. But for her, he was nothing more than a stranger, a burden, a portly nuisance that was more trouble than he was worth and which she was stuck with. The dull pain sharpened into a focused, intense cramp within his chest and gut.

"Cub?" Tiger Knight's voice sounded over the wreckage and was soon followed by his fixed tiger face hovering over Bobby's view. "Cub, are you hurt?"

"No," Bobby said with a whine.

"Good to hear," The Tiger Knight said, helping Bobby to sit upright, and returned his book to him. "You left this in the Echo Chamber."

Bobby took his book, placing it on his lap. Struck with a thought, he perked up and looked at the knight, excited. "You think we could just destroy the Ashen Knight by ripping out his chapter and burning it in a fire?"

"I fear not, young cub," the Tiger Knight replied. "Gaze upon that chapter on the Meem Monster, and you shall see it remains. Once penned, it appears it cannot be undone. Much like history itself."

"But we destroyed the Meem Monster," Bobby retorted.

"Yes, by reclaiming your words, indeed. Yet, the Meem Monster shall endure as long as hateful words do." The Tiger Knight stood up. "Come now," he reached out a lending hand to Bobby. "It seems the portals have opened for us. I caught sight of them during my return to the chamber, where I sought to learn how to vanquish the Meem Monster."

Bobby uprighted himself with the knight's help and exclaimed, "How?"

"I'm afraid I know not the reason, young cub. But we shall find out."

BY THE TIME Bobby, Zenobia, and the Tiger Knight returned to the lowest chambers of the inverted mountain, Trilogy was no longer the hardened effigy of three snake heads atop a coiled pillar. It had shed its bronze exterior like a snake sheds... well, sheds its skin. The remnants of its hard casing now lay in crumbled heaps beneath the giant, hissing, three-headed serpent before them, now a very alive creature. Its coiled bodies with their entangled ends were still rooted in place, but each of the Trilogy's heads swayed slowly to and fro, and each was distinct in its own glistening hue of red, green, and silver reptilian flesh. Forked tongues flickered from between their thin, frowning lips in rhythmic darting motions—tasting the air—before retreating again.

"Bobby Porter, you have razed the last visages of civilization from the Ancient City of Kaste," it spoke, in its familiar chorus of voices, intoning from somewhere deep in their long throats without any movement of their lips. Bobby, Zenobia, and Tiger Knight were little more than dark blurs reflected in Trilogy's six black orbs, as its large eyes glared down at them.

"I didn't mean to... I didn't think..." Bobby stammered, "I didn't—"

"We are not here to judge you," hissed the serpent chorus. "We merely record the past, reflect the present, and forewarn the future. Now, with the hierarchy obliterated and the Ancient City of Kaste relegated to history, the Ingress is open to all." The three massive snake heads bent low, jaws unhinging wide in a gaping yawn like a Venus flytrap awaiting its prey. "Enter the Ingress of your choosing," the moist pink muscles of each snake's open throat flexed as it spoke, tongues flicking.

"We have to crawl into your mouths?" Bobby groaned.

"Appears so, young cub," the Tiger Knight answered for them. "I shall go first and ensure all is safe."

The Tiger Knight took hold of one of the long fangs curving down from the roof of the green snake's maw, steadying himself as he began his awkward climb into the creature's opened throat. He folded onto his hands and knees, crawling deeper into the reptile's pulsing gullet. As soon as he was fully enveloped, the green snake clamped its jaws shut and lifted its head back to its original position. A red glow began to burn beneath the scales of the green head, like vents of a stoked kiln, until, in a flash, the entire head hardened back into bronze.

"Hey!" shouted both Bobby and Zenobia in unison.

"What did you do to 'em?" Zenobia said, giving the snakes a dirty, menacing look.

"The Noble is safe. There is but one Ingress per traveler. Choose your Ingress."

Bobby and Zenobia faced each other, their expressions glum. "I reckon I'll see that sorry face of yers on the other side," Zenobia said wryly.

Bobby gave a grim nod.

Zenobia's mouth twitched into an uneasy smile, and she winked. "See," she said. "Even my eye is inclined to git all twitchy sometimes." Then, true to her reckless nature, she plunged headlong into the silver snake's maw. It snapped shut, swallowing her, its head rising with a flash of internal fire that quickly solidified it back into a bronze cast.

The only Ingress left open was the red-skinned snake head. Bobby inched closer to its fanged threshold, slick with milky drool.

"The living exists on the lean margins between the hot fires of light and the cold void of darkness," declared a single serpentine voice, presumably that of the red snake. "Fire will illuminate but burn, as the void will numb you into blankness. Do not let either light or darkness wholly devour you, for it will destroy you. The mind requires a centering balance between these forces, for they give each other meaning: as hot does cold, as night does day, as life does death. Be warned, Bobby Porter, you approach the unbending brink of no return. Cross it, and irrevocable change will follow."

Bobby waited for something more. Something encouraging, something not quite so doomsday-like. He listened in vain, staring into the now mute, gaping mouth of the Ingress, which only continued to fill with more milky drool. Yuck.

Bobby tried to exhale all his nervousness, but it clung to his shaky limbs. He clambered forward, entering the mouth of the red snake head, doing his best to avoid its flicking tongue, though it grazed him a few times. But, there was no escaping the viscous slime coating the entire oral cavity. He crawled farther down into the ribbed darkness, feeling the breathing, pulsing life force beneath his palms on the spongy, organic membrane. The light swiftly squeezed into a narrow white slit behind him before snapping to pitch black.

He froze, stilling his body in hopes of stilling his panicked heart. Miraculously, it worked. Despite being entombed in the belly of an oversized snake, Bobby was unharmed and felt... okay. Darkness was once again his comforting friend. What he could not see could not harm him. As the last of the panic-flushed blood drained from his ears, it was replaced by a soothing whistle of wind coming from somewhere ahead, along with the faint scent of burning wood.

He crawled blindly forward, slipping along the moist, squishy tunnel until his hands and knees scraped against a rough surface. Pain shot through his kneecaps as the warmth and softness of the snake's flesh gave way to the cold, hard surface of stone. He didn't think he would miss the coziness of being inside a giant snake's throat, but he kinda did. Focusing on something spotty in his vision, it became clear that it wasn't just his mind playing tricks on him in the dark. A small orange light glowed far ahead. He shuffled onward, pushing through the sting in his knees, watching the light refine itself into a rigid half-oval hole, large enough for him to squeeze through.

Finally, Bobby made it to the other side, slipping out of the opening with a small jump. He paused, rubbing his aching knees. A warm breeze slithered over him, carrying the strong scent of burning wood, and an eerie, pervasive sound of crackling. He took in his dire surroundings, finding himself in the middle of another forest, but this one looked to be set aflame. The trees, pale and smooth as albino skin, towering like bone columns into the thick, hazy air. Their crowning branches blazed with fiery leaves like flickering wicks. The entire forest glowed beneath a canopy of perpetually lit flames.

"Zenobia?" Bobby shouted up at the burning treetops, "Tiger Knight, where are you guys?" No answer returned his call. He was alone again. Bobby shivered, pulling his bag and the book it held close.

He spun back to where he'd emerged and found the giant snake head carved from the bole of a tree. He considered passing back through the Ingress but quickly dismissed the idea. His friends had to be here somewhere. With a determined kick of his heels, he strode forward, taking the first path he faced.

"Zenobia!" he yelled, creeping farther into the burning forest.

THIRTY-SIX

THE **HARDEST** thing about living as a human, the Tiger Knight often thought, was living with the dead. He had his bouts of obsessing over his wife, Aurora, and his son, Aborealis, whose fates had long since faded into obscurity. But it was the death of strangers that haunted him most; their ghosts clung to him like stubborn ticks, buried deep beneath his thin, pallid skin, pulled taut over a rickety bone scaffold. He lived in a constant state of shivering, itching, and welting hives, all concealed beneath his tarnished knight's armor and scuffed tiger mask. As it had been for a thousand years.

The knight took the awkward twenty-foot drop from the Ingress (now the egress), attempting a graceful landing like a cat on his hind paws, but instead crashed hard in his steel boots at the bottom of a dim, cavernous space. Pain shot through him like long blades stabbing up through the soles of his feet, splintering his shins, knees, and tendons. The knight screeched like a wounded animal, falling back with a clanging thud against the rocky ground, immobilized and splayed on his back. He gazed helplessly upward, and into the yawning mouth of the stone serpent that had expelled him. The giant snake head appeared frozen mid-attack, its jaws open, ready to swallow him whole once again. Cold sweat trickled down his clammy flesh, mingling with hot tears as he winced beneath his mask, his breath vaporous and ragged.

With no choice but to wait in stillness for the pain in his lower extremities to ease, his thoughts drifted through patchy, long-buried memories, shaken loose by the agony. Disjointed fragments of bloody battles. But no, battles implied proper combat. These had been slaughters, nothing more.

That was the trick with war: every heinous act was buried under its chaos, every cruelty vindicated in the name of victory. He had obliterated his fragile, small, defenseless enemies as if they were nothing. All in the name of what? His name? A name he forbade himself to remember. He closed his eyes, his body shuddering, this time not from physical pain but from an agony that sprang from within. He quivered at the screaming slaughters that played against the inside of his eyelids. A nightmarish montage of humanity's worst impulses. A mosaic of senseless carnage.

The Three Hundred Year War had elevated his family from farmers to nobles through generations of campaigns, but he alone had swiftly razed that nobility with his bloody commands. "Nobility" was a meaningless word to him. Even "farmer" was too honorable a title for him to reclaim. Only humans felt entitled to titles, he thought. Beast was the most fitting moniker for his primal, uncouth nature. He had cast himself far from civilization, deep into the Feral Forest, donning a tiger's face, and it had been the best decision he had ever made. Yet, for the first time, as he lay against the cold, wet rocks of the cave, he wrestled with the notion of appropriating the honest nature of the majestic tiger. A splendid creature, always unapologetically itself. Dangerous, certainly, crude perhaps, but never cruel, not like he had been. Only the beast of man possessed the capacity and appetite for the enormity of evil. Only humans chose wickedness, eagerly casting aside mercy to hone their tools of malice.

The Tiger Knight felt a cold emptiness spread within his chest. A gap in his heart he had thought long repaired. It was the unsettling realization that the Tiger Knight could be no other being but himself. Human.

"No!" he cried, shaking his head, trying to dislodge the splinters of horrific imagery of his past barbarity from his mind, to rattle them back into the depths of his mental penetralia. He could lie there, wallowing in self-repugnance over his past wicked deeds, or he could get his ass up and find the boy. Yes, the boy needed his help. An unshakable feeling grew within him. He was forgetting someone important to the boy. He knew part of his mind was missing. Memories mired in a dark haze, beyond which he was certain lay a treasure trove of answers. But he'd have to move on without that part of him; the boy needed him to help crush the current evil of the world: the Ashen Knight. He would give his life for it. If it came to that, giving his life wouldn't be a sacrifice; it would be atonement. But would his ghosts accept his lifeless offerings?

He finally grunted to a feeble stance. The ground prickled beneath his feet, and his legs felt like two heavy logs as he slogged toward a naturally formed archway leading deeper into the cavern network. Mazarine-blue light bathed the walls, and bioluminescence lent a mystical glow to the space. He paused beneath the chiseled text carved into the stone arch: CAVE OF LOST ECHOES.

Drifting on the breeze that flowed through the passage was the faint, indefinable noise of battle. As the din grew louder, the Tiger Knight began to pick out the clink of swords, shrill cries, boots pounding on muddy ground and bone, and the hollow sound of final, lamenting breaths. Beneath it all lay the crackling fire, a constant reminder of its relentless purpose to consume everything. Amidst the chaos was the legacy of the knightly order he once belonged to, the Order of Fire.

An orange glow appeared at the far end of the tunnel. The Tiger Knight advanced toward it, sensing that his internal nightmares were connected to the sounds now accosting his ears. What lay ahead, the knight worried, was the merging of horrifying image and sound into a complete, gruesome picture—one he dreaded but felt compelled to witness. He trudged on, thinking about calling out for the boy, but something in him told him that the boy wasn't anywhere near. This place seemed empty, except for the ghosts he brought with him. Ghosts more numerous than he could remember. This place drew them out of the shadows, and they oozed from every chink in his armor like a mist. The presence of his ghosts seemed to solidify, taking on a weight that grew ever more oppressive.

As he hobbled toward the light, the ghostly reflections of battle merged into an indistinct, muddy soup of sounds that sloshed in his ears, muffling his hearing as if he were underwater. He shook his head, trying to clear his ears, but the muffled underwater distortion remained. Moving forward, the tunnel opened into another chamber, larger than the previous one. Here, the obsidian rocks sparkled with the flickering dance of orange light and the mystical shimmer of a starry night. Only one place in Helcyon possessed such shimmering granite. He was deep in the bowels of Fire Mountain.

The air was cool above his head, but the ground beneath his feet burned hot. Gazing up, he beheld an impossible sight: it was as though he stood at the bottom of a lake, staring up through the rippling underbelly of the watery surface, with glimpses of flames licking the sky at the edges of the shoreline. Was he truly underwater? Had he drowned and was too stupid to realize it?

Suddenly, he found himself unable to breathe. Then it registered—he was submerged in water, which hadn't been there a moment before. The crushing weight of the depths now pressed down on him, squeezing the air from his lungs. His throat clamped shut, and he jerked in a panic. His mouth opened wide, bubbles bursting in a frantic ascending flurry as he gulped uselessly, like a fish out of water—or a man drowning. Adrenaline surged, and one thought screamed through the chaos: "Get topside, you fool!"

He lurched upward, but something held him down. He kicked and thrashed, yet he remained anchored. It was his armor. The metal was too heavy, and his mobility too restricted for him to swim to the surface. Quickly—though it felt as if it all played out in slow motion due to the resistance of being underwater—he unburdened himself of his plated armor, stripping off his chain mail until he was left in just his padded jacket and leggings. His heart thumped wildly, his vision growing blurry, his lungs threatening to take in water, crying out for air. He thrashed his once more, and finally, he began to rise, buoyancy taking hold. Kicking and flapping, he swam to the surface until he broke through, gasping for air.

He waded, disoriented, in the shallows. His vision refocused, and what he thought was a pond turned out to be a large puddle. Through the pinhole view of his tiger mask, he tried to grab hold of the shifting reality around him. A world that seemed to change on him instantly, like a dream. He sat upright, legs splayed in water, now barely a few inches deep, soaking his backside. The palms of his hands pressed into the muddy bottom, and when he lifted one, chunks of gray clay clung to his skin. His hand dripping with crimson liquid. The shallow slick wasn't water—it was blood. His surroundings were pocked with similar bloody pools. He shuddered, the sudden waft of the vile stench of burnt flesh filling the air.

A thick black smoke blotted out the sky, with only a clearing to the south on the horizon, where a sliver of sunlight seemed trapped amidst the pink fringe. He turned his attention back to where he sat, mired in blood and mud, and saw the raging fires burning the huts of the simple village. Though the flames roared, they consumed no more than they already had, leaving the structures half-blackened, perpetually burning as if caught in that frozen moment. He lumbered out of the crimson puddle, staggering along the muddy ground toward the center of the ravaged village.

"Hello?" he called out aimlessly, his voice raw from the increasing smoke. "Is anyone here?"

The air grew dense with smoke along the path to the village's epicenter, flanked by burning huts, and small, body-sized knolls dotted the muddy lane.

As he moved onward, the mounds began to double in frequency, becoming more distinct from the grayish mud of the ground. The Tiger Knight now followed a legion of boot and hoof imprints stamped into the earth. Farther along, the clay mounds transformed from amorphous shapes into more defined figures, as if he were following the discarded prototypes of a sculptor, whose tool was a sword, refining his craft by cutting rigid clay into the final shape of a lifelike, yet lifeless, human child, face down in the muck.

He halted before this final figure and crumpled to his knees. He grasped at it, trying to turn it over while bursting into sobs, muttering, "I'm sorry... I'm sorry..." When he managed to turn the child over, her partly burnt and mutilated face stared up at him. Her gray eyes were wide, yet blank and cold. "I'm sorry... I'm sorry..." he repeated in agony.

Staring into the child's face, smeared in mud and blood, a long gash across her cherubic face—a vision broke through, a memory of that day many years ago. It was the day he had ordered the extermination of the enemy village, the day his tongue had stopped working, leaving him mute, until his return home. At dawn, he had stormed the village, meeting almost no resistance, until a single attack came from behind. He spun around, instinctively swinging his sword, and as the spray of blood cleared from his vision, he saw her: his enemy. A lifeless child no older than ten, a small rock still in her hand.

Now, clutching this lifeless child to his chest, sobbing uncontrollably, he heard a wet, sloshing sound coming from behind. Something rising from the mud. He turned to see them. A horde of clay figures, moving. Some shaped like people, others horribly deformed. They were all covered in dark goo that dripped like melting wax, twin dots glinting from the shadows of eyeless sockets that glared at him. The knight could feel their silent judgment.

"Take me!" Tiger Knight screamed, "Take me so I may atone! Tear me limb from limb! Hack me until I am naught but pulp for the worms!"

They did not move.

"I've damned myself!" He wept, his voice cracking. "I have rent my own soul asunder with guilt and remorse for the wicked deeds I've wrought unto you. I offer whatever scraps are left of my tender spirit, that thou may exact thy revenge and justice!"

They said nothing.

A sensation of thick, oily sickness rose from deep in his gut and filled his chest. He could swear his blood was solidifying, clogging his veins. Was he becoming one of these mud corpses? Surely, he had entered the serpent's

mouth and was now being digested by hell itself, tormented by the reckoning he deserved but had never received from those he tormented. He
had once been eager to prove his prowess as a killing machine for the war
cause. But with each swing of his blade that sliced flesh and nicked bone,
he had imbibed metaphysical acid, eroding his soul until only his unwell
conscience remained to live with his barbarisms. To him, there was nothing
left in humanity but to kill or be killed. This very village. It was here that his
seminal atrocity had been enacted. And now he had finally returned after
spending a millennium stitching together a new soul in the Feral Forest,
fashioning something majestic, worthy of his ghosts, something they could
sink their teeth into and wrench from him, like tearing skin and meat from
bone. Yet here he knelt, unpunished, surrounded by victims who stared at
him, their silence like pity.

"I am here for you to obliterate, you idiots!"

Nothing.

From behind came another squelching movement. He did not need to turn.
He knew it was the child, the one he had murdered. When he finally dragged his
eyes back onto her, the child stood before him, her features obscured by a crust
of filth and hacked flesh, her body dripping with mud. A vile stench of rotten,
burnt meat emanated from her.

The child clawed at her face, tearing away the muddy, bloody exterior.
From beneath the dark mess emerged the soft, fresh glow of an angel's face,
clean and unmarred, along with vibrant red hair bouncing free.

The entire group of figures followed her lead, tearing at their bodies,
swiping away the heavy clay, revealing human faces beneath. Men, women,
boys, and girls, all bearing their very natural features, moles and all. They
became whole again, unsullied, unmutilated.

The child, shining bright, stood close, eye-level with his kneeling position. She no longer smelled vile. The knight resisted the urge to hold her
in joy that she was alive again. He remained still, not wanting to scare her
away. Her sparkling green eyes held his gaze, and then, with gentle hands,
he removed his tiger mask and smirked at the face behind it.

"There you are, Evernt," the girl said.

Evernt—his name. That was it, Evernt Lanmarc, the eldest son of three
brothers of the House of Lanmarc. It had been eons since anyone had spoken it.

"Remember my name," the girl said.

Evernt searched her face for clues, her bright, shining eyes illuminating his, flooding light into the deepest corners of his mind. The fog lifted from his mind, revealing a rush of memories, faces, and names.

"Ze..." he muttered, "Zenobia?" He gripped her arms. They were twigs squeezed in his palms. "You don't belong here." He then moved his head back a little and shook it, reexamining the girl's features. Realizing he was mistaken, he eased his hold on her. "You're not..."

"No, I'm not," she confirmed. "We are the ones you've entrapped as tokens. Erased our names and identities and made keepsakes of us in the image of your sins."

"Has my time finally come to account for what I've done to all of you?" Evernt asked.

The girl smiled sadly. "You've accounted for it every day since," she said. "But have never learned our names. But now the time has come for us to forgive you."

Evernt released his hold on her entirely, jolting back from her. "You cannot," he exclaimed in horror. "I do not deserve—"

"No," she interrupted, her face flashing with sharp contempt before softening again. "You inflicted great pain upon us. Stripped us of all our rights, our will, and our dignity as people. But you cannot take our freedom to forgive. This isn't about you. It's about us. The one grain of freedom you can never rob us of our power to choose to hate or to forgive our oppressors and tormentors. I forgive you, Evernt Lanmarc. We forgive you."

"But..." Evernt began, only to abandon his speech, his mouth still agape.

"That is the one thing you cannot take from us," she repeated. "Perhaps you don't deserve forgiveness. That is no longer our concern. Be not mistaken. This is not you purging yourself of your ghosts nor your reckoning, but your ghosts purging themselves of you."

Tears stung his eyes as his gaze fell. He nodded in recognition of her words. His heart constricted, emptying itself like a sponge being squeezed dry. They did not pity him. It was his vanity that pitied himself. His millennium of self-flagellation served no one but himself. With a deep inhale, he peered back up at the girl. Her face regarded him with an even demeanor. "What is your name?" he asked. "So I will remember you and all the others. And not just what I did to you."

"Sopheena," she said, then returned his tiger mask to him. She glided past the knight to join the others, her voice lingering softly, poignant as honeyed lemon drops in his ear.

"We must fix what is broken in the world, even if we didn't break it. But especially if we did. Atonement isn't found in self-pity nor self-hate, but in fixing what we can."

She disappeared into the collective arms of the villagers. They turned away, slipping into the smoke that swiftly obscured them, making them hazy specters, before erasing them completely, and they were gone. The billowing smoke quickly filled everything, surrounding Evernt, who remained kneeling in the mud, holding onto his mask. The smoke filled every possible space, and in an instant, it was the only thing Evernt could see or breathe.

"Sopheena," he whispered. As soon as he spoke her name, the world fell silent, leaving only the sound of his breathing. "Zenobia," he whispered next, and the smoke receded, revealing the twinkling granite of the cave.

Memories rushed back, sharp and painful, like an avalanche of jumbled fragments, everything the knight had forgotten. He strained to wrangle them into some sense of order, leaving him momentarily bewildered. But then, all fell into place, and his mind became clear. Whether what had just happened was real or a dream, he could not deny its impact. Though he felt shame in wanting forgiveness, in hoping it was real. He knew he did not deserve forgiveness, but could not shake Sopheena's words. He could not deny her resolve nor his new purpose to fix what he could.

He looked at the wooden mask, tracing the painted lines of its fierce expression. With deliberate tenderness, he placed it on the ground. He was no longer denying who he was, who he had been, who he was now, and who he could become. Evernt rose to his feet. His legs felt sturdy, his bulk lighter. Leaving the mask next to his discarded armor, he swiftly carried himself towards a new cave passageway, heading towards Bobby Porter and Zenobia Mulhick. He was ready to help rid the world of his brother—the Ashen Knight.

THIRTY-SEVEN

FEAR IS a powerful motivator. Zenobia understood this, at least peripherally. Fear worked much like a wall—its imposing presence didn't just keep people out but convinced them to give up before they even tried to enter the safe space it protected. It stunted one into debilitating inaction. Zenobia had often seen others become terrifyingly torpid with fear while she soared, sailing high, in mighty leaps and bounds over or through numerous walls. But lately, she couldn't shake the feeling that fear somehow wormed its way inside her, performing a dark alchemy, turning her blood to stone, just like all the other cowards she pitied. Now, in the utter darkness of the tunnel, as she crawled forward, a single word formed in the void before her psyche:

PHOBOPHOBIA.

What was this word? Why was it clawing at her mind? Maybe she had seen it among the many pages of the librarian's word collection, sheaves upon sheaves listing dreads and disorders. But the longer it lingered at the fore of her thoughts, the more it felt like it was being stitched onto her heart. It brought an unwelcome revelation: she wasn't fearless. She held deep in her a fear after all: the fear of having fears.

She slowed, her body heavy in the dark, becoming almost too heavy for even her strength to carry. The anxiety turned her limbs to lead. Her heart dredged through the thickening oil of her building Bitter. Her mind anchored itself to the single horrific dream that now seized her. The same one she'd had on Captain Knapp's boat, her recollection of it just as vivid and hopeless as when she first had it:

She thought at first that she had awakened at the base of the Very Very Big Hinterland Maple Tree. Her head rested on the softest pillow she'd ever smothered her sleepy face into. A warm hand played gently with her hair, her mother's sing-song voice in her ear: "Wake up, Zenbee, wake up." Zenobia lifted her head and opened her eyes to a bright sky, the sun, a large yellow orb radiating warmth across her. Her mother smiled at her. "I love you so very, very much."

Zenobia rubbed an itch from her nose, glancing around with dopey eyes. Golly grazed nearby happily. It almost seemed like the perfect day. She yawned, asking, "Where's Daddy?"

"He should be appearing shortly," her mother replied.

As if on cue, her father came bobbing up the hill in his gangly gait and grinning wide, his tin cup in hand. "Function over taste, my sweet Zenbee. Function over taste," he howled and chuckled, slurping his black brewhaha. He knelt by her, kissing her forehead, and in that moment, it was perfect. Until he sighed. It was a sound full of exhaustion, carrying the weight of a man resigning himself to the unyielding clutches of fate. She smelled burnt earth on his breath.

"No matter what happens," her father began, his voice rich with affection, "we love you and always will. We're so proud of you. You're clever and brave. Your heart's strength can pump the blood of a legion of warriors into victory and overflow the cups of a host of Angels with the purest passion. I've always boasted there is nothing you cannot do, powered by that incredible strength you possess, matched only by your astonishing love." He paused, his eyes glistening with admiration. "Remember this, my sweet Zenbee. If something ever should appear impossible, don't tackle it all at once. Approach it step by step, bit by bit. Do this, and you'll find a way."

Zenobia's heart swelled, tears forming in her eyes. But her father's face shifted, his features growing suddenly gaunt and troubled. "Sometimes," he then said, his voice now tinged with sadness, "there are things you can't change. And what's done is done, and you must accept it."

Her father's wilting demeanor disturbed her greatly. She turned to her mother for comfort, but she was gone. A black mark on the ground where she had been. Golly, too, had vanished. Everything slipped away. The air grew hotter. The white-hot sun drew closer, its heat unbearable as it fell from the sky like a flaming comet hurtling toward them. The air spun with cinders and ash, an infernal wind swirling around them.

"Daddy!" Zenobia cried, her voice barely audible over the roar of the apocalyptic storm.

"There's nothing you can do," Hulmick said gently, his eyes filled with such warmth and love that it was almost painful. His lips continued to move, but his voice became lost in the rush of wind. But she could read the shapes of the words his mouth formed, repeating: We... love... you—

FLASH.

If there was a boom, Zenobia was deaf to it. After the searing light swallowed everything, all sound cut abruptly into a deafening silence, and her vision blackened. She seemed to drift, weightless in a numbing void, until sensations returned like a shock of tiny stabbing needles puncturing every fiber of her muscle and tissue, starkly reminding her of the tender flesh she was heir to.

A stench filled her nostrils, sharp and acrid. The scent of charred, ossified dung. It was what she imagined Death's rotting corpse might smell like. Then came the susurration of air, like the staccato gasps of a dying man whispering in her ear. A bleary glint of light emerged from the darkness, sharpening into the sight of a wasteland that bled into the shadowy umbra of a dark sky.

She stood, shins buried in ashen sand, surrounded by countless dunes of desolation. Their hazy crescents curled with wispy, vaporous tips in the wind. The world was painted in one shade, the monochrome of black grief. Where the towering Very Very Big Hinterland Maple Tree once stood was now a brittle, splintered trunk, its former majesty reduced to dark ruin.

Zenobia bent, her fingers digging into ash and earth, searching for remnants of her mother or father but finding only gritty soot. The final sensation to return was the biting salt of her tears on her lips and tongue as she tasted her great sorrow.

Then she had awakened, cradled on the boat, her face pressed into the damp fabric layered over Bobby Porter's belly. She had wept, unable to care how she managed to find herself in Bobby's embrace, simply letting herself cry.

And now, in the tenebrous belly of the snaked Ingress, Zenobia sat idle, knees drawn to chest. She rocked back and forth, gently wiping tears from her cheeks. Boy, was she utterly exhausted from crying. Would her eyes ever dry? Would her heart stop churning the relentless Bitter through her veins, fueled by unremitting dread and hopelessness?

"Bit by bit," her father's voice whispered in her head. "You'll be able to achieve the impossible."

Was it true? Could she overcome the impossible task of accepting loss? Her heart and guts plagued her with the feeling that her daddy might already be gone, though she didn't know for sure. She clung desperately to that uncertainty like it were the last ember on a cold winter night. But if he was truly gone, could his wisdom still hold true? Could she carry her anguish, learning to live with it step by step, day by day, until the vise of grief loosened, unseizing her heart to let it patter unmoored and un-bittered once more?

No! Absolute poppycock.

"Poppycock," she muttered aloud with a shaky voice. She loved her father, but he had a bad habit of talking in silly dad-talk. "Function over taste?" Taste was a function, a function of the tongue. That silly galoof. She adored a million such silly expressions and goofy phrases from her father and found comfort in his nonsense sense of humor. "Poppycock" was a far better word than "phobophobia." And love—love was a powerful motivator too.

It was just a nightmare, she told herself. That was all it was. She wouldn't let a stupid nightmare stop her from saving her father. She wouldn't fear such poppycock.

Zenobia scuttled forward, pushing onward. Soon, a dim light glimmered at the far end of the stone tunnel. It was faint, but against the absolute blackness, it seemed bright. Only when she reached the mouth of the exit did she realize that she'd been crawling, or more like climbing straight upwards. For how long, she couldn't say.

Hauling herself up, she emerged topside into a bleak and desolate forest. A thick fog hung heavy in the air, tingling against her skin like a million tiny mouths biting at her. She crawled out of the stone snake head's mouth, its gaping jaw pointing straight to the sky, the structure protruding ten feet from the ground like an ancient pylon.

Her feet landed with a wet squelch on shadowy mulch. The stench of sulfur was thick and suffocating as the heavy mist obscured the twisted, crooked trees around her. There were no signs of life, no sounds to comfort her, only the low, hollow wails of wind whirling through rotted-out tree corpses.

"Reckon thisyer might be the Ashen Forest," Zenobia said out loud to ease the eerie quietness with her own lively voice.

"Bobby?" she shouted. "Tiger Knight?"

Her calls were pointless, perhaps, but the silence was unbearable. "Bobby?" she called again, louder this time.

Only the ghoul-like gales answered her, and somewhere ahead, a low rumble shook the earth beneath her feet. It was almost imperceptible, but she could feel it more than hear it. If this was the Ashen Forest, she thought, then Fire Mountain lay just beyond. And the rumbling, she was sure, was the mountain's volcano venting its wrath.

She started walking in what she hoped was the right direction toward Fire Mountain. As she trudged along what vaguely resembled a trail, she occasionally called out for her companions; her voice didn't resonate very far before being eaten up by the fog. Then came the unsettling sounds of branches snapping, their brittle echoes cracking just beyond the veil of mist and skeletal trees to her left. Zenobia couldn't shake the unnerving notion that the sounds were following her. At first, she reasoned they might be expected for this dead forest, the remnants of limbs toppling under their own decay. But the persistent, deliberate rhythm of the noises made her doubt this. They seemed too intentional, too specific, as if something—or someone—wanted her to hear them. It wasn't hard to imagine the sound as the violent snap of bones crushed in the jaws of a monstrous predator. She pressed onward with heightened vigilance, her hand reflexively reaching for a sword no longer at her side.

The thin path morphed into something unmistakably man-made; its surface was worn smooth by the relentless footfalls of countless travelers across epochs. Though still half-buried beneath layers of decaying duff, the serpentine trail widened, its edges more defined with each step. This must be the path to Fire Mountain. A shiver ran down Zenobia's spine as the hairs on the back of her neck prickled, her mind consumed by thoughts of reaching her journey's end.

Then, the trail came to an abrupt end. Zenobia halted, her gaze stretching across a large, oval clearing that had appeared suddenly in the heart of the dead woods. The field hissed and steamed, pocked with fumaroles that jetted columns of vapor into the air. The stench of sulfur hit her hard, wrenching a gag from her throat. It took several moments to noticed the clearing's centerpiece: a ring of seven towering obsidian stones.

Each monolith stood at least twenty feet high and five feet thick, spaced evenly in a ring formation. Their sheer black surfaces seemed to drink in the dim light. During her homeschooling, Zenobia was fascinated by Fire Mountain and its surroundings, including the Ashen Forest. She had devoured every book she could find on the subject, their value exceeding that of her family's dirt farm. Yet, strangely, not a single text had ever mentioned this eerie, magnificent sight.

The focal point of the massive ring of megalithic stones was a crude altar hewn from the same black, glassy rock. Resting atop the dark, polished platform lay a glimmering sword—THE SWORD OF AEGIS slashed the words across Zenobia's inner thoughts like a blazing brand. Without wasting another breath on gawking, she sprinted toward the weapon.

At first, the distance to the altar seemed no more than a hundred yards, but as she ran, the entire concentric structure appeared to stretch away from her. The closer she pushed, the farther it receded. She skidded to a halt, her chest heaving as she scanned her progress. The sword now appeared at least two hundred yards away, and the field expanded tenfold. Spinning around to get her bearings, she only managed to disorient herself further, the dizzying sensation overwhelming her. Determined, she turned back toward the shrine and started running again.

Time and distance warped into a maddening paradox. It took her three times longer than it should have to reach the site, yet she still had not reached the altar. She stopped again, bending over with her hands braced against wobbly knees, her breath coming in labored gasps. The altar seemed impossibly distant now—four hundred yards, give or take.

"Dang!" she muttered under her breath, frustration boiling over. Was the field expanding, or was the sword shrinking? She steadied her breathing and dashed forward again, only to meet the same infuriating result: the distance grew with every desperate step.

Reaching the sword felt utterly impossible to Zenobia. She slumped to her knees against the moldering ground, her breath heaving in shuddering gasps. Saving her father seemed cruelly out of reach. Exhaustion struck her more frequently and vigorously now than when she first left home, a lifetime ago, or so it felt.

A pestering sense of hopelessness clung to her relentlessly, sending crippling waves that eroded her resolve. It was as if she battled an emotional succubus, a dark twin birthed from her nightmare on the boat. This twin now stalked her, hiding in the shadows of her heart, launching endless assaults of despair. Each attack felt like a barrage of arrows piercing her soul, leaving it perforated and deflated. Zenobia couldn't draw a breath without tears cascading from her eyes. She sank onto her back, the forest floor's damp decay seeping into her skin as she closed her eyes. Against the darkness of her eyelids, she saw a negative image of her face, her twin whispering insidious truths: *she was not special, it wasn't her fault, it was simply the cruel nature of the world she was born into. The odds were stacked against her, and surrendering to fate was inevitable. She should accept it.*

Step by step, and you'll find you can achieve the impossible. The words swept through her like a cavalry charge, summoned from the depths of the same dream that had borne her dark twin. It was a silly tactic, just more of her father's peculiar brand of dad-talk, but it felt no more absurd than running toward something only to have it grow farther out of reach with every stride.

The thing about reaching bottom, Zenobia thought, is there's only one way to go. Up. Step by step. That wasn't so bad. She could do that. With her father's words glowing like embers in her mind, her tears slowed, then stopped altogether with each steady breath.

She stood, the prehistoric circle of standing stones now barely visible in the distance off to her left. Instead of aligning her path with the stones, she focused on her feet. She took a step, releasing any concern about reaching a specific destination. She took another step, choosing to move forward without thought of where she was heading.

One step at a time, her breaths grew steadier, each exhale unraveling the swirling storm of emotions inside her. Step by step, she focused on the motion of her body, letting her thoughts drift unimpeded as if she were a passive observer within herself. Watching her boots rise and fall—left, then right, then left again—the rhythm became her anchor. Time melted away as she marched onward, her nose pointed to the ground, her chin resting against her chest, rising and falling gently with each breath. Her world narrowed to the simple act of pacing, without hurry or care, beyond observing the earth pass beneath her boots.

Step by step by step by—

Whack—the top of her head collided with something hard.

"For Port-sake," she cursed, rubbing her head as waves of pain struck her, each sharper and more biting than the last. "Dang it!" She stomped her foot against the ground in frustration. "For the love of dirt, darn, dolly whopping, crotcheting, craggily, fisstermonkey..." she spat with venom, her voice rising louder with each nonsensical word. Finally, the pain faded from a smart sting to a dull throb across her crown, and her stream of curses dwindled into a muttered grumble. She looked up and found herself staring at her reflection on the smooth, dark surface of an obsidian monolith. Oh boy, she thought, if I ain't a sorrowful lookin' thang.

She had made it, somehow. Absentmindedly yet mindfully, she reached the ancient site and the outer ring of stones encircling the altar. Zenobia sidestepped the tall pillar she had collided with, revealing the prize at the center: the Sword of Aegis.

The altar comprised four squat, boxy pillars that jutted out from the earth and supported an oblong tabletop made of the same dark, glassy stone as the pillars. The sword's design was stark and unyielding, its razor-sharp edges and angular hilt embodying a severe elegance. The entire blade gleamed with an untarnished silver sheen, catching the light in an almost otherworldly way. No matter where Zenobia stood, the angled presentation of the weapon seemed to follow her, giving an eerie impression that it was pointed directly at her, waiting.

She trampled across the ring barrier, pacing toward the weapon. Two or three strides into the inner circle, something ensnared her ankle. She glanced down. Her foot sank rapidly into the earth as if she had stepped into a pool of tar. The dark, syrupy bog pulled her deeper. She yanked at her leg, but the harder she pulled, the more it sucked her in.

Quicksand?

Zenobia knew from her readings not to panic if caught in quicksand; struggling only made it worse. But now, her other foot became locked beneath the dark sand, and she was buried up to her knees. Thinking fast, she bent at the hips and splayed her arms wide to distribute her weight. It worked. By the time she was waist-deep, her descent halted. She held still, daring not to move until she figured out what to do next.

"Ahhh," purred a honeyed voice. "This site has existed since before time was possible." A pair of black paws padded into her line of sight, claws flexing like curved daggers. It was the manticore, Kilrok.

Zenobia groaned, rolling her eyes. Of course, she had to deal with this beast on top of everything else. Nothing ever came easy—except pain and burdens.

"I was hoping for our little god-prince," Kilrok mused. "But I'm not disappointed. I'm pleased that it's you who's entrapped here." His grin revealed too many yellowed, razor-sharp teeth.

Beneath the earth, Zenobia worked her buried legs, trying to kick free. But the more she fought, the more the earth solidified around her lower half, compacting from sand to stone.

"It's an odd thing, really," Kilrok continued, pacing playfully around her like a cat taunting its prey. "I've known this sanctimonious ruin for as long as I've known the Ashen Forest, yet it was not created by the Old God. The dead god. No, it was the New God who dumped it here. And yet, it is as ancient and integral to our history as the world itself."

He paused for effect. Zenobia imagined he was savoring the drama before delivering his next revelation.

"You see, the boy, your little traveling companion, your friend and savior." The beast let the words linger, his grin widening. "He is the one wholly responsible for your predicament." A deep gurgling chuckle rolled up from Kilrok's rank gut. "Yes," he sneered, "I now understand the truth of your portly boyfriend."

Zenobia squirmed while Kilrok laughed harder.

"I have witnessed many valiant but unfortunate souls seek this place over the eons," he went on. "Only to find its glory cut short from their grasp."

Sick of his voice, Zenobia paid little mind to the words that seeped from the beast's slicked throat. But his incessant chattering was giving her time to think, to plan, to figure a way out.

"They all struggled, just as you do now," he continued. "And when they saw my approach, their struggles only grew more desperate."

He stopped pacing, lowering his grotesque face until they were nose to nose. "There is a beautiful sparkle in a man's eye when terror takes hold. When he sees his imminent death." Kilrok's tawny eyes seemed to frantically search for something within Zenobia's glassy orbs. And when he appeared not to find it, he disappointedly turned away, hissing, "But, your eyes, girl... they are dull."

Zenobia smirked. "Reckon that's on account of yer borin' jibber-jabber. You ever eat with that stinker of a-mouth or jus' yap on 'til your victims die of old age'n boredom?"

Kilrok's growl vibrated the air, his hot, rancid breath washing over her face as he turned back to her. Zenobia clapped her hand over her mouth to keep from gagging. She squeezed her eyes shut and held her breath until she sensed him withdrawing.

Peeking through her lashes, she saw the beast's back, his gaze settling on the shimmering sword cradled on the altar.

"They all sought the Sword of Aegis," he mused, "the fools all died trying to wield its power, by my tooth and claw, every single one of them." He spun back to her. "Live by the sword, die by the sword, as they say. Or, in this case, be eaten near the sword." He chuckled at his own wit.

"The lore of this sword is absurd, really," he continued. "The only way to wield the power of the Sword of Aegis is by refusing to. How's that for logic? The only way to use a weapon is to never desire it." He snorted. "Logic born from a child's mind, no doubt. Killing is necessary. Killing is natural. It is the edict of the natural world: to suffer and die at the hands of those who are stronger, more cunning, and more ruthless. Eat or be eaten." Kilrok paused again for dramatic flair, letting his slick tongue slip out to lick his lips before continuing, "Well, as useless as the Sword of Aegis may be, it makes for an alluring bait, drawing in my next meal. Or at least half of 'em."

Zenobia snorted back. "I bet ya yammer and yak like this to all yer poor ole corpses, don't ya? Chewin' off their ears long after you've eaten them faces like a jabberin', gossipin' lonely little ole bitty."

Kilrok roared and lunged at Zenobia's head, his fangs snapping mere inches from her cheek. "And I bet your father is dead!" he snarled.

Zenobia went still.

Kilrok drew in a slow, deliberate breath, savoring the moment. "No..." he purred, "I know for a fact your miserable father is dead. Sacrificed to the Enlightened Fire. All because of your little plump boyfriend."

Zenobia barely flinched as his tongue slithered from between three rows of glistening teeth and licked a slow, viscous trail down her cheek. The sensation barely registered. Because she was already gone.

Kilrok's words—"father" and "dead"—shattered something already fragile within her. Allowing her dark twin to unfurl and lay siege against her heart, paralyzing her muscles useless against the abyss that tore open beneath her, ripping out her soul and dragging her into unimaginable depths of despair. She wasn't just sinking into the quicksand—she was collapsing inward, folding into herself, spiraling into the churning acid of her stomach. The outside world faded. Her identity obliterated. She was no longer Zenobia, no longer human, just a barely animated sack of bone and meat, relinquishing itself to oblivion.

Then—

A flicker.

A glint of blue light caught her eye.

She gazed down at her endless descent into the void. Amid the nothingness, amorphous blobs of glowing blue pulsed and wobbled, delicate as soap bubbles. One drifted close enough for her to peer inside, revealing a disembodied bird's eye view of her trapped body, waist-deep in the dark sands, encircled by the obsidian stones. A ghostly projection of her death scene.

The Sword of Aegis shimmered against the darkness. Kilrok loomed over her limp form, jaws stretching wide to gobble up her exposed top half.

Then, in an instant, she was gone.

The quicksand swallowed her completely, leaving Kilrok snapping at empty air. He recoiled, momentarily stunned, before realizing his zesty meal had eluded him again. A furious roar raged from his throat as he glared up at the sky and seemingly into the void. Though their eyes met for a fleeting moment, she knew he couldn't see her. He stomped in circles around the empty space where she had been, waiting, hoping she might reappear, even pawing at the ground, now solid.

"Always with the chitchat," he grumbled, his voice thin and distant. "If only you didn't prattle on, old man, you'd be napping with a full belly right now," he hissed.

He lamented to the empty space, "Is it my fault the company I crave to gossip with is the same as the company I crave to eat?"

A growl thundered deep in his chest as he howled to the phantom winds, "How the truest truth in all the universe is none more true than how unfair and cruel life is to me."

The scene faded, and the blue light dimmed except for the Sword of Aegis, which lingered within the bubble. Then, with a soft pop, it was no longer contained but floating freely in the void, distant yet unmistakably real. It drifted toward her. Or perhaps she drifted toward it. In the void, it was impossible to tell.

As the sword neared, its form twisted and shifted. Its gleaming edges softened, reshaping into the luminous outline of a woman, silver and radiant. Zenobia squinted against the brilliance, searching for familiarity within the woman's soft features but finding none.

"Am I dead?" she asked.

"Do you feel as the dead do?"

Zenobia frowned. "Reckon not. Less'n the dead feel like a sorry sack of pain."

The woman smiled. Though her face was unfamiliar, her voice certainly was not. The Oracle Akasha.

"Is m-my d-daddy...really gone?"

She already knew the answer, but still grasped onto an ever-fraying thread of hope.

"Yes. He is gone."

She could sink no further than she already had. Numbed beyond consciousness. Untethered from emotion, from anything or anyone. She was the void personified.

Only the vague sensation of flesh pressing against something cold and hard. A slab? A coffin? Perhaps she did feel as the dead do.

"Lost child," the Oracle called to her, "there is a way to bring back that which the child has lost."

The Oracle's voice was a dull whir in her ear.

"There is a way for the father, the mother, and the bovine to be resurrected." The words drifted through Zenobia's mind, sluggish and distant, until their meaning ignited a spark in the darkness. Zenobia sharpened her gaze on the Oracle. "You sayin' I can git my family back?"

"Indeed, yes indeed."

"Well, how?" Zenobia's limbs twitched, her attentiveness alight with renewed excitement.

"There will be a great cost of course. But should you do this one thing, it will rid Helcyon of the Ashen Knight once and for all. And return to you all you have lost."

"What mus' I do?"

"Only Bobby Porter can perform these miracles. Therefore, the boy's fate is your fate. You must persuade him to remain in Helcyon. Then what you desire will be yours."

Zenobia's mind fevered with delirious visions of life as it once was. Her father, leaving the door open, letting the morning winds stir her mother into a squawking arousal, slamming the door shut with a bang that would rattle her from this current nightmare. The world had never been perfect, but it had been far better before the Ashen Knight came to their door. And, to some extent, before Bobby Porter.

Bobby liked her. That much was clear. Not surprising, really—boys who weren't scared of her always seemed to. They got an eager look, tried to prove themselves, and insisted on doing things for her, which only made her laugh. But if she could get him to stay—if he could make the world right again—she'd make it up to him. Might even give him that darn silly peck he'd been so giddy over. Well, that didn't matter. He'd made a vow to her. He was supposed to use all the power he had to get her father back. She just needed to remind him of that.

The Oracle's soft contours wavered, unraveling at the edges before reshaping, returning to the hard-edged form of the Sword of Aegis.

"This sword," the Oracle's voice resounded, disembodied now, fading like a ghostly melody, "is the key to the boy's return from whence he came. But for Helcyon to be free of the Ashen Knight and to shine once more as a peaceful and prosperous realm, the boy must not use it. The boy must stay."

The Oracle's words faded into silence, and Zenobia was left alone, adrift in the void, the Sword of Aegis floating beside her.

The manticore's words sailed through her mind: *To wield the sword, you must not want to.* But the more she tried to unravel its cryptic meaning, the more the logic tangled into a jumbled mess. But she began to make some sense of it. To destroy the Ashen Knight, Bobby must not use the sword to return home.

Persuade Bobby to stay. This was the only chance she had now to save her father. Her entire family.

Ignoring the deep, twisting pull in her gut—the one whispering something was wrong—she reached out and captured the sword's silver hilt. The cold bit into her flesh—then the void ripped away.

Pain crashed into her. She jolted upright, jarred from the darkness into a burning bright light. It quickly dimmed into an orange flicker. She sat on the ground, her soul tethered again to every fiber of her flesh. Every pang of her heart, ache of her bones, the chill of her skin, the burn of her eyes—all signals her mind was reconnecting with her body.

Just before her vision fully returned, she swore she heard the hurried patter of fleeing feet. When her sight cleared, she found herself alone in an underground chamber. Lit torches lined the stone walls, illuminating the vaulted space she had dropped into. Skeletons—hundreds of them—littered the floor. Or rather, half-skeletons. The lower halves of bodies, remnants of those swallowed by the altar's hungry sands. Half to the beast. Half to the ruins. Equal shares in their spoils.

She was swallowed but remained whole and intact. Yet something felt... missing.

Her right hand?

She exhaled in relief. It was still there, fingers locked tight around the Sword of Aegis. But it was numb, deadened up to the wrist. She concentrated, willing her fingers to move. A twitch. No more. It was like trying to move an object with her mind. With some effort, she pried her grip free using her other hand.

As soon as her hand no longer touched the sword, pain stabbed through her nerves as feeling returned. She flexed her fingers. The pain subsided quickly. Now she felt whole again. Except for her heart, which still felt missing. Even the Bitter was gone. She knew now, without a doubt—her father was gone. As were her mother and Golly. But she also knew now that what was lost could be found. She just had to find Bobby.

Zenobia rose unsteadily. Her knees buckled, but she caught herself, bracing against her thighs. She had straightened too fast—dizziness swept over her. She took a breath. With her head bowed toward the floor, she spotted fresh footprints in the thick dust. Someone had been here. And had run.

When the room stopped spinning, she forced herself to stand upright, wobbling slightly. Her body screamed for sustenance, muscles weak and trembling. She hadn't eaten in days. She was running on willpower alone.

No time to dwell, she got to work. She ambled over to one of the many severed skeletons. A pair of legs still precariously attached to a hip by a casing of pants. A bit of spine jutted out at the top, cut clean where the beast had chomped down on the poor fool. By the fine fabrics and elaborate stitchings and embroideries, the fashion of these fancy pants, along with these bones inside, belonged to noble men. Only the rich could afford the time to obsess over such occult exploits. Only they had the luxury to chase mystic treasures, not for more wealth, but for abject power.

She stripped velvet pants from a long-dead noble, using the material to wrap the sword, careful not to touch it directly, lest it deaden her hand again. A belt from another set of legs fashioned into a sling draped the weapon across her torso. Then she scavenged with more care, taking her time to rummage through piles of bones until she found a pair of tiny feet small enough to match her own. She tore off the soft leather boots, and small bones and dust spilled onto the floor as she shook them clean. Then, she stuffed more velvet cloth inside before sliding them on. Still too large, but far better than her old worn-out ones.

Now, she was ready. Armed with revived hope, despite a sickness gnawing at her core—she chalked up to hunger—Zenobia followed the fresh footprints through the only opening in the chamber. Toward, what surly had to be, Fire Mountain. Toward Dragoon Keep. Toward the Ashen Knight and Bobby.

THIRTY-EIGHT

BOBBY HAD grown accustomed to Helcyon's myriad oddities. Its peculiarities coiled and twisted, woven through every molecule of its creation, like the double helix of DNA. The world's logic followed dream logic yet remained as solid and real as the forest trail he trundled down. Hitting the soles of his weary boots as he trudged for what felt like forever. The cracked, hardpan clay of the desert-like woodland floor wore his flimsy boots thin. His knees ached, bruised, and scraped raw from crawling through the Ingress.

He had long since given up calling for his friends. His throat was too parched, lined with smoke and dust that it croaked whenever he hollered their names. With no clear direction, he pressed on, following the winding red-powdered trail. As he ambled on, kicking up red dust, his gaze lifted to the endless sprawl of smooth Ghost Trees surrounding him. Their chalky, bleached-bone bark loomed like skeletal sentinels, their brittle limbs clawing skyward. Where leaves should have been, the branch's tips were set aflame, burning with never-dying embers, setting the sky ablaze in an unnerving canopy of hellfire. A pervading din of white noise filled the air, the crackling clinkers creating a sense that Bobby was walking through an apocalyptic forest doomed to burn forever. Amazingly, despite the flames, the Ghost Tree bore no signs of charring—a testament to Helcyon's strange and unyielding dream logic.

Bobby froze. A faint weeping teased his ear.

Zenobia? Had he finally found her?

Heart pounding, he crept forward a few steps, then paused again, tilting his head and turning his ear toward the sound. He listened intently. It was not a trick of his senses—a low lamenting drone persisted. Unmistakable human misery.

Forgetting about his exhaustion, he lunged toward the sound, his breath wheezing as he pushed himself ahead. His hacking cough nearly drowned it out, but he held onto the sharp wailing, letting it guide him. Please let it be her.

At last, he stumbled to a tittering halt at the edge of a small clearing. At its center, a campfire gnawed on bone-white twigs and ossified wood. Seated upon a ghostly log was a brooding man, his long silk-white hair veiling his face as he sobbed into gloved hands. His shoulders, arms, and chest shimmered with silver-plated armor, beneath which he wore a regal purple velvet doublet. A matching damask cape draped over his back, and his suede breeches tapered tidily, tucked into his tall leather boots.

Sensing Bobby's presence, the man's shuddering stopped. He grew unnervingly still before slowly lowering his hands, revealing a young, grief-stricken face. The firelight cast a soft orange glow across his features, except for his icy-blue eyes, which remained untouched by its warmth—a hard hue of the coldest blue. His gaze locked onto Bobby, his expression shifting as if struggling to determine whether the boy before him was real.

Finally, he spoke in a soft and sorrowful tone. "Won't you please join me by the fire?"

Bobby hesitated. His legs ached to rest, and an empty log beckoned across from the man, but something about the stranger unsettled him.

"Please," the man implored, "I have been alone for ages. Your company would be a great comfort."

Bobby remained reserved. The man's face was kind, but his voice carried a ghostly undercurrent that sent a shiver down Bobby's spine. Still, he was relieved to finally find someone in this desolate, burning forest.

"Can you speak?" the man asked, rising from his log.

Bobby flinched. The stranger moved to the far side of the clearing, gathering an armful of petrified wood before returning to his seat. He gestured toward the empty log. "Please," he repeated.

Reluctantly, Bobby crossed over and sat, resting his satchel on his lap, his hands folded over it. He caught the man's gaze flicking to the bag before returning to him with a melancholic expression.

The man dropped a piece of wood into the fire, watching the flames crackle and pop as it rose between them. "I wish I could say I'm happy for your company, but I'm afraid I don't know what happiness is. So, I'll say your company is an amusing surprise."

"Why were you crying?" Bobby asked.

The man let out a deep sigh. "I don't know. Maybe it's not one thing, but many. Perhaps everything. I have known only misery. The world itself is grief manifested." He gestured around them. "I mean, look about you, boy. The world is on fire."

Indeed, the treetops burned in an eternal blaze.

"Where are we?" Bobby asked.

"The Red Forest."

Bobby recognized the name from his map. The Red Forest stretched along the northern side of Fire Mountain, forming an angry rash across the landscape. To the south was the Ashen Forest and the Sword of Aegis. He was close—practically at Dragoon Keep's back doorstep. It explained the burning leaves, their flames fueled by lava rivers coursing beneath the earth, flowing through the trees' roots and igniting the branch tips.

"I need to get to the Dragoon Keep," Bobby said. "Do you know how to get there?"

"Dragoon Keep?" the man repeated, with uneasiness. He leaned in, the firelight sculpting shadows across his face, deepening the lines until he appeared much older. "What is your name, boy?"

"Bobby Porter."

The man studied him before withdrawing from the fire, returning his face to a youthful orange glow. "I was afraid it was you."

Bobby tensed. "What do you mean, afraid?"

"We've met before. But neither of us looked the same then."

Bobby's stomach tightened. "When did we meet before?"

"First in your world. Then thrice in this one, each time in a different guise." The man extended his hands, studying them as if seeing them anew. "And now we meet again, and I have changed once more. This is all your doing."

"How am I responsible?" Bobby replied with a huff.

"If I were to hazard a guess," the man mused, "it is because you need me to be more familiar."

Bobby's fingers tightened around his satchel. "Who are you? What are you?"

The man exhaled solemnly. "I have been given many names. To some, I'm hope and respite; to others, tragedy and cowardness. For you... you may call me Infandous."

A strange, bone-claw-like grip tightened around Bobby's heart. As he looked at Infandous, he felt an inexplicable urge to cry. There was something so deeply sorrowful about the man that it was contagious. His eyes burned, but no tears came. It was almost torturous, the need to cry but not being able to..

"When did we meet in my world?" Bobby asked, his voice tight. "How am I different? Why are you afraid of me?"

"You have many questions I'm not sure you are ready to know the answers to. Some answers are like a fire—they can illuminate but also burn and disfigure. Some people can't resist reaching deeper into the flames, blind to their true intensity until it's too late."

Bobby stared into the fire, searching its core. The hypnotic flickering depths of the dancing flames lulled him into a trance.

Infandous's voice dipped into a whisper. "Ahh, you see, I'm afraid I might give you the wrong ideas."

"What sorta ideas?" Bobby asked without looking away from the flames.

"When we first met, you saw me as a stranger. Later, you saw me as an invader. Then, a monster. But now, near your journey's end, I fear you may see me as a friend."

Bobby drew his satchel to his chest, guarding the book.

Infandous let out a heavy sigh. "I suppose," he continued, "the reason I weep so profusely and so profoundly is that, although I relieve the suffering of those I befriend, I create suffering a millionfold in those around them. I am drawn—no, compelled, addicted to a certain kind of tender sadness that festers in broken hearts. I seek to help those as lost as I am, yet my embrace numbs them, and I am left to suffer an eternal cycle of loneliness."

Bobby could feel Infandous's icy-blue eyes piercing through the firelight and into his heart. Yet, he could not tear his gaze from the ensnaring flicker of the flames, already lost in their hypnotic glow. Infandous's squeeze around his arm hardened. His voice was low but insistent. "I ask you, Bobby Porter, what gives you your pain?" Then Infandous's voice grew distant, becoming lost in its own echo. "When I first laid eyes on you, all I saw was a guilty little boy full of shame—"

A door materialized in the fire's core. It did not burn.

At first, it was just a miniature door, white and familiar. Then it grew—or perhaps Bobby shrank—until it filled his entire vision, framed by the fire's quivering light. The flames faded as his peripheral vision darkened until only the door remained. It was the door to the attic back home.

Bobby watched as his hand reached out, turned the knob, and pushed the door open. He felt himself moving, yet it was as if he were a detached observer, viewing his own actions from within his head, peering out through two eye-shaped holes as though he wore a mask of his own face. He watched his feet move forward, stepping carefully onto the narrow staircase behind the attic door.

A low, haunting moan droned from the top of the stairs. Bobby pressed on, clinging to the railing, dragging his feet upward step by step. His heart seemed to catch with each creaky step he took until, at last, he reached the top—and the moaning stopped.

Most of the attic lay in shadow, the low ceiling disappearing into the darkness, giving an impression of endless height beyond the void. At the center of the room sat an old steel desk. Its surface was illuminated by a harsh, narrow circle of light cast from a desk lamp, a spotlight that revealed a heavy-framed, punch-key typewriter.

Bobby found himself drawn to the desk like a moth to a flame. He approached, bellying up to the typewriter. A yellowed sheet of paper, crinkled and stained, sat poised in the typewriter's roller like a limp, flat tongue. Black, eroded letters stamped upon it formed a short poem. Staring at the words, Bobby understood: these were his father's true final words.

DEEP INTO THE FRAY

THE ONLY THING THE SOLDIERS COULD BRAY

I'M DEEP IN THE FRAY

ALONE, TRAPPED, AND AFRAID

DEEP IN THE RED

MY HANDS SHAKE

MY MIND IS LEAD

SILENT SCREAMS AND PAIN FILL MY BRAIN

I'M DEEP IN THE RED

I'M DEEP IN THE FRAY

ALONE, TRAPPED, AND AFRAID

MY WEAPON: THE ONLY WAY OUT OF THE FRAY

Beside the typewriter rested his father's pistol.

Bobby watched through his own eye holes as his fingers stretched out, reaching to give the gun a gentle stroke.

"Don't touch that!" a voice boomed from behind him.

Bobby jolted, spinning around instantly.

Everett Porter—his father—sat hunched in his old armchair, his face twisted in a sour expression, the flickering, ill-blue static from the old square TV set across from him illuminated his features in a cold wash.

"What did I just tell you? I told you to never touch that!" His scarred hand shot out, pointing directly at Bobby's belly.

Bobby looked down. Somehow, he was already holding the gun, the cold, heavy metal resting firmly in his sweaty palms. He could feel its weight as if it had always been there.

His father shot up, stalking toward him, his face darkening from a sickly blue to a deep crimson. Shadows slithered with sinister intent within the crevices of his expression. The veins in his neck pulled taut like cords strung tight, bursting to their breaking point.

"Why are you up here?" he scolded. "Why are you bothering me? Why aren't you asleep?" He towered over Bobby, wrenching the weapon from his hands before grabbing him by the collar of his pajamas. Shaking him violently, he waved the gun in Bobby's face. "These are dangerous," he growled, his jaw working in an exaggerated grind, his stubbled beard bristling. "Don't be a stupid kid. It's not a toy!" Everett shoved him, forcefully letting go. Bobby stumbled backward, cracking his spine against the corner of the steel desk, before dropping to the floor.

Pain shot through every nerve in his body; thankfully, his senses were dulled by his being behind the mask of his own face. Everything felt second-hand, like a memory of a dream. His bleary vision fixated on his shaky hands. They were empty, yet the phantom weight of the pistol lingered in his palms.

A sharp, high-pitched moaning stabbed his ear. Was he crying? No. The wetness that clung to his face was his father's spit as he wept so close to his ear. Bobby turned his glare to Everett.

There he was, crumpled on his haunches, patting Bobby's head and back with trembling hands. "Are you all right?" he asked, tears streaming from his sunken, dark eyes. "I'm sorry. I'm sorry. Did I hurt you?"

Everett's eyes, swollen and bloodshot, stared deep down the eyeholes of Bobby's face mask. It was as if he could see past Bobby's mask, peering into the real Bobby within. His lips quivered. His rough hands clawed at his son, pulling him into his bony chest for a desperate embrace. "I didn't mean to—I love you. I didn't mean to... I love you so much. You know that, don't you?"

The press of his father's wet jowls against his cheek made Bobby's stomach churn. The cloying smell of sweat and alcohol enveloped him. A sickness roiled in his gut, the acidic gurgle of resentment and dread clawing his insides. He swallowed the bile creeping up his throat.

Everett pulled away but still held onto him, vigorously patting his head and caressing his wet cheeks, almost pleading. His father's face was ravaged and beaten down by grief and the weight of the world. Bobby was part of that world.

"You..." Everett whispered, his voice cracking into a low and guttural moan. "You love me, don't you? I know I've changed... But you still love me, don't you?" He knelt, his posture wilting, his entire being a portrait of dejection, desperation, and pitifulness.

Bobby's stomach clenched. A great, searing, caustic burn erupted in his chest and climbed into his throat. His vision wavered from behind the mask as his head shook from side to side. And then—he spoke.

A single, simple syllable. So small. So ordinary. So often used against him, it shouldn't have held any power. But this time, it devastated. It destroyed.

"No."

Then, from somewhere deep and dark and unguarded, the truth surfaced.

"I wish you would die."

Everett's face slackened. The shock melted away, dissolved into a quiet, numb acceptance. The knife had been driven into his back—and twisted. And he welcomed it. His shoulders fell. His whole body seemed to deflate as his son's words settled in.

Everett then twisted away, retreating into the darkness of the attic, his pistol glinting in his hand.

Bobby lurched to his feet and bolted down the stairs. As soon as his foot hit the bottom landing—

BANG—

He jumped at the single pop, every muscle in him tightening, nerves firing like electric shocks. For the briefest moment, the pain was so intense he imagined walking on the sun would pale in comparison.

He stood frozen, staring at the backside of the door at the bottom of the attic stairs. He didn't want to turn around. But trying not to look was like trying not to think of a pink rabbit after being told not to. His breath shuddered as he faced the staircase again.

No! No, no, no!

This wasn't how it happened—not quite like this. Time here was compressed into its sharpest edges. Yes, the key elements were familiar, except the details felt... warped. There was no gun. Not one he had ever seen or touched. Not until after the *pop* woke him. Later on, he knew exactly what type of firearm it was, thanks to extensive research. An obsession that earned him a ban from Googling. Yes, said those words. But he didn't really mean them. He loved his father. He didn't want him dead. Not really. What he'd just witnessed—it all felt wrong. It didn't happen like that. Not exactly. Not so quickly. Not all at once.

He peered through the eyeholes of his mask, up toward where he had just come from at the top of the stairs. His heart caught in the rapid fire of thunderous claps in his chest. His breath came in quick, shallow gasps, muffled by the mask's suffocating hold. He knew what he'd find at the top. He knew because he did find it. The picture flashed across his mind with horrifying precision, but the reality of it remained cloaked, just beyond his sight.

He stared up in dread, and then—a pale octopus tentacle slithered into view. Then another. And another. Red eyes, where suckers should be, winked at him, beckoning him forward. Bobby took a step toward it, back up the stairs.

"If only you could rewrite the past," Infandous said, his voice hissing like ice crystallizing in the air. "If only you could erase the guilt..."

Bobby took another step, his feet inching toward the undulating mass of eyes and tentacles awaiting him at the top.

"The guilt of killing your father—"

No!

Bobby forced himself to a standstill midway up the stairs.

With a frantic motion, he tore the mask off his face. Plunging first into darkness before his vision burned back with light and to a full field of view. He was in the Red Forest again. Infandous, still gripping his arm. But the silver-haired weeping man was gone. In his place was the monstrosity Bobby knew far too well. A thick, white tentacle coiled around his left forearm, its slick skin lined with a throng of winking red eyes of various sizes. The appendage tightened.

"Good," Infandous susurrated. Not with a mouth, but with a trespassing voice that burrowed into Bobby's psyche. "I do prefer you to see me this way... as a monster."

Another tentacle wrapped around Bobby's right arm, lifting him off the ground. He dangled above the fire; limbs splayed helplessly before the creature. His satchel tumbled from his side, landing in the flames with his book inside. Sparks erupted, flames blazing skyward, licking at the twisted mass of Infandous's appendages.

The creature shrieked, flinging Bobby backward. Crashing into the dirt, Bobby rolled to a stop just hairbreadths shy of the now-raging bonfire. The heat singed the front of his hair. Within the fire, his satchel shriveled, peeling back. His father's book lay exposed, its edges curling, turning black. Bobby didn't think—he sprang into action, thrusting his hand into fire. His fingers closed around the book and yanked it free.

The pain came after. The blistering agony. He gasped, clutching his wounded hand and book to his chest as he scampered backward.

Across the fire, Infandous writhed, his scorched limbs recoiling. He slithered back into alignment with Bobby, his many eyes blistered and blackened along his burnt tentacles, narrowing their focus on him. "You belong to me, boy," he hissed.

"No!" Bobby screamed, "I'll never belong to you."

"I follow where the hollow hearts lead me." Infandous's syllables stretched, slow, and sinuous. "I go wherever the lost and broken call. And oh, how this place is in shambles. You need me, Bobby Porter. You've claimed me just as your father did."

"No!" Bobby screamed the word again, this time with purpose and conviction, no longer as a weapon of rejection or hate but out of love and desire for life—his life, Zenobia's life. He pictured Zenobia's unbreakable resolve, her stick-thin frame strong with defiance, hands squeezed into fists, jaw clenched, teeth ready to chomp, gapped tooth and all, and her scarlet mane a raging, silky fire fluttering in the wind. Bobby rose to his feet, imagining her by his side.

Infandous's cluster of bloodshot eyes regarded him with unsettling curiosity.

With his uninjured hand, Bobby opened the book to a blank page.

"With this incantation," Bobby declared, watching the blank page fill up with perfect text:

TRICKS AND SPELLS TO AID YOU IN COMBAT:

SPELL 1. TELEPORT FRIENDS TO HELP YOU IN YOUR BATTLE.

INSTRUCTIONS: PICTURE A FRIEND AND
REPEAT FORWARD THEN BACKWARD:

"ERUJNOC LATROP OT NOMMUS SDNEIRF MORF EREHT OT EREH!"

Why Bobby made his spell so difficult for him to intone was a complete mystery; perhaps he just needed more time to master the delicate art of weaving words into the book's pages. Nonetheless, he persisted, chanting the reversed incantation forward and backward, over and over. His tongue tripped on the tangled elocutions, but his focus remained sharp, imbuing each syllable with intent and meaning.

Then, the atmosphere shuddered.

A wild wind blasted through the clearing, whipping the campfire into a roaring frenzy. A sudden, piercing-sucking sound followed—then the fire collapsed inward, vanishing with a blinding flash of blue light. In an instant, the entire forest of burning leaves extinguished, plunging the world into sudden darkness.

For a heartbeat, only silence reigned. The dim glow of the ominous red clouds hung overhead in the sky. It reminded Bobby of that blackout back home, in that moment of eerie stillness when the world seemed suspended in time—until the earth trembled with the distant rumble of Fire Mountain's core, and time moved again with a surge of sound. The treetops sparked, one crackle, then another, rising to a crescendo of flames roaring back to life. And in the renewed light, beside Bobby, stood Zenobia; her jaw fell open in shock.

"Zenobia," Bobby shrieked, rushing to sling his arms around her—only to stop short as he caught sight of her incensed expression. The energy of his excitement stalled in his chest and rerouted to a twitching eye instead. Gulping hard, he steadied his voice. "You're really here."

Zenobia wobbled where she stood, eyes darting about the unfamiliar space. Confusion and sickness were written on her face. She finally landed her gaze on Bobby.

"Wha..." she stuttered, "what in Hel—how'd I git here?"

"I teleported you," Bobby said excitedly.

"Is my innards showin'?" she asked, eyes slightly spinning.

Bobby shook his head. "No."

"Sho feels like it." Zenobia took a deep breath of air and steadied herself. "So... ya can tella-port folks now?"

Bobby held up his father's book and nodded. "With this book, I can."

Zenobia cocked a skeptical eyebrow. "Well... I'm glad I found ya."

Despite the dire circumstances, Bobby couldn't rid his lips of a garish smirk that crept across his face.

"Now that you're here, together we can fight—"

But as Bobby turned back toward Infandous, the monstrous form had shifted again, melting from the grotesque octopian abomination into a milky-white puddle that seeped down between the cracks of the hardpan ground.

"It is best you view me as nothing at all," Infandous gargled, his voice a liquid burbling through the air. "I am nothing until I become something reasonable. And then I'll be everything to you." His final words slurped into silence as the last drop of its viscous form vanished.

Zenobia crossed her arms tightly. "I see yer makin' friendly with all sorts of wrong folks."

"You heard that?" Bobby asked, astonished.

"I ain't deaf. Just feelin' mighty stupid. I was ready to storm the Dragoon Keep when all a-sudden, Imma staring at yer..." she cut herself off, Bobby sensing she was censoring herself before continuing, "...face."

"Do you... do you know what that thing was?"

"Ain't got a clue," she said, her voice hard and her glare sharp and cutting. "But thisyer tel-a-portin' trick might've come handy sooner, ya know."

"I... I just learned how to do it," Bobby muttered, avoiding her gaze.

"Don't matter none now," she said, her slender shoulders shaking slightly. "Ain't no need to hurry to Fire Mountain. It's too late. The Ashen Knight already done killed my daddy." She turned away from him, struggling to hold back a burst of tears.

"Bu... but that can't be," Bobby stammered to her back. "My dad told me that you save him. That's how the story is supposed to end. You save him. He didn't give me any details. He didn't want to spoil it—but he can't be dead."

"Well, he is. Dead as a coffin nail," she said without turning. Then, softer, almost inaudible: "And yer daddy is dead too, ain't he?"

"Yeah," Bobby whispered, "dead as a coffin nail." He picked at the singed edges of his father's book. "Your dad's gone 'cause mine never finished the story. He died before he could write the happy ending."

The silence that followed settled over them like a heavy, wet blanket, broken only by the crackling of burning cinders above. Bobby's chest constricted with the sharp pang of abandonment. Despite the tightness crushing him from within, he yearned for more, a suffocating embrace, the overwhelming comfort of his mother's arms. He didn't care if her cheeks were dripping with tears. He just wanted to bury himself in the warmth of her lavender scent. Nothing in Helcyon smelled of flowers—only the acrid stench of burnt earth and scorched remnants, and Bobby was sick of it. He ached to weep in her arms, partake in the sorrow ritual, and drown together in mutual misery. But she wasn't there. He was alone.

"You reckon you can bring 'em back?" Zenobia asked, turning back to face him. "With that book of yers, you think you can bring 'em back to life?"

Bobby stopped chewing his lip, suddenly aware of the metallic zing of blood on his tongue. He ran his hand through his messy hair in frantic thought. "I... well... maybe? You mean your dad?"

"I mean all of 'em—my pop, my ma, even sweet ole Golly. The Oracle said that yer the only one who can."

His eyes fell to the book. If he could conjure the teleportation spell from his imagination, along with the Sword of Aegis, as he believed, maybe he could do more. Perhaps there was something to his being some kind of deity after all. Back home, he couldn't muster a tear—but here? Well, he still couldn't produce a tear—but perhaps he could bring back the dead. "I can try," he said, his voice firm.

Zenobia's face softened.

Carefully nursing his injured hand, Bobby cracked open the book and began flipping through the pages. He thumbed past the histories of places, ancient sites, mystical objects, and figures of importance. Skimmed over numerous bungleroot recipes and practical tricks on capturing, skinning, and mending goblin-rat fur garments. He hurriedly scanned chapter after chapter until finally reaching the section on arcane spells and incantations. His eyes caught briefly on a charm for turning oneself into a lion, but he pressed on until he found his newly minted teleportation spell glistening on the page in perfect text.

And then... more blank pages. One after another.

"Hmm," Bobby groaned, chewing his lip again while flipping the pages back and forth. He stared at one of the blank pages, straining to will into existence a resurrection spell. He focused forcefully until his vision blurred, and it felt like his skull might crack under the pressure. But nothing came. The page remained stubbornly, frustratingly empty. A headache began to pulse behind his eyes. He exhaled, defeated. "Nothing here on bringing people back from the dead."

Zenobia's face fell, her features sinking back into her familiar sullen expression. The optimism in her eyes receding once more.

The vice of disappointment and failure tightened around Bobby's heart and throat—

No. Not now. Giving up is not an option.

"Wait," he said, straightening his spine. His fingers motored back through the sections, the pages flying until his finger landed on the passage he sought. His eyes lit up. "*Black Star*. It's a magical sword."

Zenobia cocked her left eyebrow. "That s'pose to mean sump'n'?"

"The Ashen Knight is immortal because of that sword. *Black Star* traps all the souls of everyone it slains. Maybe if we get it, we can reverse the process and bring them back."

Zenobia looked like she was on the brink of screaming. His eye threatened to twitch with abandoned madness as he braced for her anger, for her to lash out, to call him an idiot for such a stupid idea. It wasn't the first time he had chased this kind of foolish hope. He had once believed that if he could just understand the weapon that took lives, just maybe he could bring the person it killed back. Hours upon hours were consumed scouring every detail and fact about every type of gun there was. But that fragile hope had been crushed the moment his mother discovered his search history. It was what ultimately got him grounded from the Internet.

But Helcyon wasn't his world. Here, weapons had powers beyond just killing, especially magical ones. Here, the impossible wasn't bound by reality or logic. Here, anything could happen.

He just had to believe it.

"Alrite," Zenobia finally said, snapping Bobby's attention back to her. She seemed hopeful, and not disappointed or angry, as he had expected. "It's as best a plan as any, I reckon. We're bound to kill the Ashen Knight after all."

"Okay," Bobby said, invigorated. "Let's get moving." He took a confident step forward but stopped when he realized Zenobia hadn't followed.

"Dontcha reckon tell-a-portin' is quicker than walkin'?" she asked.

"Oh, right." Bobby chuckled nervously. "I reckon it would be." The words slipped out, loaded with unintentional mimicry of her accent. His body tensed immediately. He hadn't meant to mock her. Her way of speaking was just... catchy. But when Zenobia's expression remained unchanged, giving no sign of offense, he let out a quiet breath and relaxed, figuring she paid no mind—or just didn't plumb care.

Bobby split the book open once more and found the spell to conjure a new Ingress. One that would launch them tearing through an interdimensional portal at light speed straight to Dragoon Keep, where they would finally face the Ashen Knight once and for all.

He cleared his throat. Breathed deeply. And spoke the words of the spell with a strong and determined voice.

THIRTY-NINE

SLIMSY SQUATTED in a cool corner, sinking deeper into the shadowy alcove within the great hall of Dragoon Keep. His buggy stare locked on the specter, Nex, with its perfect skull and the hollows that bore into its bone face, never graced with eyes—only endless pits of pure nothingness. The specter was draped in crimson robes that flickered at the fringes like fire plasma, melting into hazy edges as it hovered beside the Ashen Knight. Nex seemed unaware of his covert presence.

Slimsy's desire was simple: to sit in silence and meditate over the significance, or insignificance, of his own existence. Was there meaning to his life beyond servitude and cunning tricks? If there was any at all to begin with. Without fulfilling his master's wishes, would his life hold any purpose? He often felt sick with the tasks he was charged with, yet he completed them without hesitation or question. Today was no different. Or was it? He couldn't recall a time when he had never felt sick. Perhaps it was just the fate of a devoted Dazzelf always to endure the sensation of acid eating away at his stomach, climbing through his intestines, and burning up his throat, except today. Today, there was a soothing coolness in his guts. For the first time, he executed a plan of his own design, and it stirred a strange, unnameable feeling within him.

His talent for illusions had always been meant for those unfortunates who crossed his wide, sparkling gaze. Nothing could fool him. His enchantments merely nudged or fortified the delusions already festering in his victims' minds, solidifying them into verisimilitude. He liked to believe his dazzling was merciful—offering fleeting relief from the cruelty of reality. But he couldn't even lie to himself. He knew the truth. He was an accomplice to life's traps and tragedies, enabling the endless cycle of torment and protracted suffering.

Now, under the eclipse of the blood moons, his talents became amplified. He could conjure flesh and apparition alike with disturbingly convincing realism. His illusions were substantial. Tangible enough to be touched,
held, and carried away. Didn't that make him worth something? Did he
now have enough power to end the suffering with one final, colossal lie? Or
was it possible for a lie to be so immersive that it became truth? In Helcyon,
Slimsy believed so.

He envisioned Helcyon without the Ashen Knight. Would there still be
use for his lies then? There was always use for lies, wasn't there? As long as
minds could think and dream and tongues could twist sound into speech,
lies would never lose their value. And humans would pay that price with
their folly.

Slimsy watched the Ashen Knight stalked back and forth before the great
orrery, the red glow of the blood moons saturating the entire castle and world
beyond. There was an electrical charge in the air. The mechanism's seven
spheres, representing the blood moons, hovered just shy of perfect alignment.
Once the final sphere clicked into place, the orrery froze with a resounding
gong, and Slimsy could taste the oncoming freedom of a new life.

"He should have returned by now," boomed the Ashen Knight.

"He has," Nex replied. A long red finger, the color of muscle beneath
flayed skin, stretched from the wraith's crimson sleeve and pointed directly
at Slimsy's hiding place.

"Come out of hiding, you foul thing," commanded the burnt knight.

Slimsy crawled out of the shadows, standing as tall as his crooked spine
allowed, and trudged toward the pair.

"As slimy as a snake and nasty as goblin-rat puke," sneered the knight,
his burning eyes locked onto the Dazzelf's trembling form. "I would have
scorched you from existence long ago if your deviousness weren't so useful."

Nex's empty stare bore into Slimsy, who came to a shuddering halt at
the knight's feet, head bowed low.

"I trust the worms from your rotting mouth have wiggled into the girl's ears?"

"She's believed what I told her, yes," Slimsy replied. He couldn't help but
notice how close "worms" sounded to "words." Perhaps there was a worm
for every word he uttered to feast on the rot of his lies, turning the world
to mush?

Suddenly, Slimsy felt Nex probing deeper into his thoughts. He braced himself, closing off his mind to all but obedience, yet the specter's dark voids pierced deeper inside his lumpy head. Slimsy prepared to flee—but then Nex shifted its skull upward as if catching the scent of something in the air.

"They are here," the wraith's vaporous voice hissed.

———

THE GRANITE TUNNELS of beneath Fire Mountain were endless, winding, and oppressively hot, lit by the radiant glow of molten lava rushing through the underground channels.

Evernt wished he had brought his tiger mask so he could perform the ritual of Immolation, properly sacrificing his animal form to the flames that danced atop the fiery rivers of lava he had traversed and scaled during his ascent before returning to the surface as a man.

It was a custom he carried from the forgotten provenance of the Order of Fire, a rite of passage for those born into the House of Lanmarc. In Fanggul, the village he called home, he preserved the tradition, though the meaning had been altered. In the Order of Fire, the ritual symbolized burning away a child's weakness and baby fat to emerge as an adult.

He forgave himself for the oversight. His mind was lost to the delirium of his vision, reckoning, revelation—or whatever had stripped him bare, reforged his purpose, and left him with a deeper, fuller understanding of responsibility.

The heat boiled him like an egg, sweat soaking every fiber of his garments and pruning the skin of his swollen hands as he scaled the jagged subterranean cliffs, climbing out from the belly of Fire Mountain. Sweat stung his eyes, blurring his vision, but in his mind's eye, he saw with perfect clarity every name on every gravestone he had helped erect, every horrified face that had gone silent and still beneath the slice or stab of his deadly blade. He carried with him the customs of every culture he had erased from Helcyon, their histories lingering in the breath that filled his lungs. With each inhale and exhale, he was to breathe life back into their stories, resurrect them from the buried past and into the open air for posterity.

The weight of it all was not a burden; it was his duty. His honor. To tell the true horrors and atrocities of war, not as an outsider, but as someone who had been entrenched in the mud and blood, perpetrating them. He was to bear witness to the truth of his cautionary tale. So long as he was cautious not to make it all about him. Again.

At last, he clambered onto a plateau, stumbling into a chamber where the oppressive heat gave way to a cooling wind. Here, the connecting tunnels leveled out into a gentle incline, filling Evernt with hope that he was nearing the surface. The craggy walls gradually smoothed into chiseled stone slabs, and the rough caverns transitioned into the network of vaulted catacombs.

"I must be within the Dragoon Keep," Evernt mumbled, assuring himself.

A wave of exhaustion seized his limbs, slowing his movements to a heavy, unsteady slog. He willed his body to stay upright, to keep moving, but flesh obeyed the mind only to a point. He had reached that point and surpassed it hours ago. His body, pushed beyond its limits, finally revolted, refusing to carry him an inch farther. Without ceremony, he collapsed where he stood, careless of his surroundings.

Helpless on his back, Evernt stared up at the arched ceiling of the wide but low stone chamber. An enormous storage vault, he pondered, though he could do little but ponder. Rolling his eyes back, he viewed the crypt-like space upside down. Not far from where he lay, rows upon rows of statues loomed. Though illuminated by the flickering torches along the walls, their dark features were indistinct, their purpose unclear.

Evernt recalled the many myths surrounding Dragoon Keep, particularly the legend of its Dark Army. Soldiers carved from the very dark stone of Fire Mountain, eternal talismans sworn to guard the dead kings in the afterlife. These stories had been drilled into him and his brothers, preparing them for the day they would storm the stronghold to end the war once and for all. They had been trained for every possibility.

Now, as he stared at the throng of dark statues in the chamber's silence, he wondered if at least one of those legends was true all along.

Evernt gasped. Had one of the figures moved? Or was it just a trick of the torchlight's dancing shadows?

Forcing himself over onto his belly, he righted his perspective. The ache in his muscles subsided enough to once more bend to his will, though with sluggish protest and giving only a fraction of their strength. Rising to his full height, he saw the chamber stretched far back. The rows of statues multiplied into a vast army of stone. One figure stood apart from the rest. A short, portly figure with a crown atop his head.

A child.

Wearing a royal military uniform, its crowned head barely reached Evernt's waist. He pushed himself to his knees to study the boy's features at eye level. A cold understanding took hold—the statues were not made of Fire

Mountain's dark stone, as legend claimed. They were formed from compacted charcoal. The emblem on the boy's armor was unmistakable: the coat-of-arms of Prince Horee, the last king of Dragoon Keep.

This was not the Dark Army of his childhood stories. It was something more terrifying—the Dark Army of the Ashen Knight.

A sudden fissure erupted across the boy's face. Evernt shot upright, stumbling backward. Cracks split across every figure in the chamber like invisible lashes. A sharp, dry, splintering chorus vibrated in the air as faces, limbs, and torsos fractured. Noses crumbled, ears shattered, and coal dust spilled to the floor in ashen piles.

Evernt's hand flew to his sword as white bone clawed free from its charcoal shell.

An army of skeletons stood where their petrified figures once had, their bony forms swaying, their jawbones grinding and clicking, their teeth gnashing empty air. Their eye sockets were hollow and sightless, their heads swaying in a state of blind stupidity. But Evernt knew they could still sense him through the sound vibrations that traveled through their bones. They were waiting, listening for him to make a move.

The scrape of his boot against the stone floor sent them into a frenzy.

They jerked toward him, limbs twitching. Evernt parted his stance, gripping his sword in both hands. The nearest skeleton snapped its jaw, teeth clattering with anticipation.

"Let's dance, you brainless bag of bones!" he roared, waiting as the rattling bone-army lurched straight for him.

The first to reach him was the child-king himself. With a powerful stroke, Evernt cleaved the boy's skull from his shoulder, shattering it into dust. But ten more skeletons lunged for him before he could take another breath. Then twenty. Then fifty.

They swarmed, a relentless tide of bone and rage.

Evernt slashed, bashed, and tore through the horde. His sword cleaved through spines, splintered femurs, and sent skulls bouncing across the chamber floor. Yet for every one he cut down, more clambered over the fallen, their razor-sharp, bony fingers reaching, their jaws snapping.

His blade lodged in a rib cage. He yanked, but it refused to budge. A sudden force wrenched it from his hand. More skeletons piled onto him, clawing at his chest, his face, his arms, raking deep, bloody grooves into his flesh. A jagged jaw clamped onto his shoulder. He roared in pain, kicking and thrashing wildly, but the tide of bodies smothered him, swallowing the last flickers of torchlight.

He was drowning in them.

The skeletal flood forced him to the floor. The back of his head struck stone with a crack, sending his brain to buzz. Then, his limbs faltered. The clawing continued, shredding his skin, gouging his arms and legs. He couldn't move. He couldn't breathe. The weight pressing down grew heavier and heavier.

The grinding of bone against bone flooded his throbbing head, drowning out the sound of his own weakening heartbeat.

From out of the darkness, a cold, bony hand clamped around his throat. Somehow, without flesh, without muscle, it squeezed with pure force. His windpipe collapsed. He gurgled and choked on his own blood, squirming helplessly like an insect crushed beneath the thumb of a tormenting giant until the pressure became unbearable.

Then—darkness. Silence.

Then, from somewhere deep in the void, an insignificant voice spoke.

"Evernt Lanmarc, you have tried and failed to give meaning to your life. All the years you accumulated, many by cheating Death, have amounted to a big fat nothing. You are now to become nothing more than another mindless minion in the dark army that has captured you."

The judgment came from a familiar voice, one that was too familiar. It sounded as much like his own. As it did Sopheena's. And his wife's. And his brother Likho's. And Amduat's.

Then the voice faded, and Evernt sank into perfect, silent blankness.

FORTY

ZENOBIA'S GUTS felt twisted and wrung out as if she'd been turned inside out and trampled by a stampede. A piercing cold knifed through her skull, splitting her mind into two warring halves—loving, innocent Zenobia and hateful, vengeful Zenobia. Then, a hellish wall of heat slammed into her, stealing her breath. Fire Mountain had arrived.

Deafening explosions of fire and ash vomited thunderously from Fire Mountain's summit, the violent roar hammering her ears at this close range. Clamping her hands over them, she let her stomach settle and her mind stitch itself back together. Just fifty yards ahead, the volcano spewed cinders that stung her eyes like frenzied fireflies. Thick churning plumes of smoke blotted the sky, their dark purple coils twisting like monstrous tendrils. Below, molten lava cascaded in fiery torrents, carving the land into a chaotic, hellish landscape of scorched rock and burning rivers. They had indeed arrived at the furious doorstep of hell.

Bobby shouted, but the storm of sound swallowed his voice. Zenobia caught sight of his frantic gestures, pointing toward a rocky terrace. It was the crumbling gatehouse that marked the volcano's rough-hewn entrance.

Zenobia nodded, and they rushed toward it.

The ground was treacherous, fractured into broken strips by bubbling rivulets of magma. The gaps widened as they neared the volcano, each jump growing more perilous. Bobby barely landed one, his arms pinwheeling as he teetered at the brink of a molten river. Zenobia lunged, seized his collar, and yanked him back to safety.

"That's another notch," she smirked.

"What?" Bobby screamed over the wailing hell-storm winds.

"Oh, nothin', don't you worry none."

The final gap was too wide for Bobby.

Zenobia crouched, motioning for him to climb onto her back.

Bobby hesitated, staring at her, his face tight with worry. She remembered the last time she had carried him, and it hadn't exactly been pleasant.

Zenobia rolled her eyes. "Do I hafta pick you up like a baby?"

"No," Bobby said, finally clambering onto her back. He wrapped his arms around her neck so tight she nearly choked. They wobbled for a moment, an awkward, top-heavy, drunken creature before she found her balance and took off. Bobby screamed in her ear as she launched over the chasm, flames licking at her heels. They landed hard. Zenobia's feet hit solid ground. Bobby slid off her back, stumbling, his legs rubbery, knees knocking.

Then, they were on the move again. Slipping past the crumbled gatehouse, they entered the volcano's gaping mouth.

Inside the hollowed-out volcano, the world hushed. The raging hell storms died down to a distant murmur. Before them stretched a massive roiling lake of magma. A narrow stone bridge spanned over the exploding yet quiet jets of flames, leading to an island where the hulking silhouette of Dragoon Keep loomed, black against the infernal glow.

Zenobia and Bobby exchanged a grave look, then stepped onto the bridge, single file, Zenobia leading the way. They moved in silence, like soldiers marching to their doom. Below them, the heat pulsed as the fire writhed just ten feet beneath them. Zenobia's eyes flicked down to the boiling lava. What would it feel like to drown in fire?

She turned her gaze upward. Above the Keep, a silent vortex churned, a swirling eye of darkness at the volcano's heart. She glanced over her shoulder at Bobby, giving him a nod, but his gaze remained fixed on Dragoon Keep ahead. The fortress seemed to have risen straight from the volcanic rock, its blackened stone shimmering with the dark sparkle of the earth. It seemed less built and more like it had grown from the rock itself.

As they neared the bridge's end, yet another threshold in a grueling, relentless series of thresholds, Zenobia stole another glance at Bobby. This time, his gaze was locked onto the sword strapped to her back—the Sword of Aegis.

A wave of nausea hit her. Her mind fluttered, and for a moment, she felt as if she were teetering on the edge of something monstrous and crumbling, barely holding herself together—just like the world around her. Maybe it was the heat. Maybe the lingering effects of teleportation. Or maybe it was from nerves. She was close now, so close to confronting the Ashen Knight.

But no—that wasn't it. She suspected it was Bobby.

She'd started to like the doughy little deity. She felt for his plight, his longing to return to his world, where she was sure he belonged. Where he'd be happier.

But she wanted her family back. And that meant keeping him here. If she told him what the Oracle had said about the sword—how it could send him home—he'd leave. That, she was sure of. She could absolve him of his vow. Tell him they could turn back. Hand him the Sword of Ageis and let him go home.

But she didn't. She swallowed the words like bitter pills, each one churning up a wreak in her guts.

And if he stayed... was she gonna have to put up with his annoying habits forever? Would it matter as long as she had her father, mother, and Golly back?

Her stomach twisted, the knot working its way up to her chest.

As they stepped off the bridge and approached the imposing gate of the Keep, Zenobia halted. Bobby did the same.

"Bobby Porter," she said, her voice clearer than she expected within this vortex of sucking sound.

Bobby looked at her. His mouth twitched.

It used to be his right eye that often winked at her—a habit she found oddly amusing. Lately, it was his mouth that wiggled, like he was either trying to suppress a smile or summon one for her benefit. Her stomach twisted tighter.

"Yeah?" he finally said, his lips skewing into a lopsided, puckered line.

"Afore we go on in there, I oughta tell you... the Oracle gone and tol' me yer my fate."

"How?"

"Dunno how. All I know is..." She paused, carefully sorting through her thoughts. "Whatever happens, you gotta do everythin' in yer power to save us. Like you done promised. If you stay here in Helcyon, yer liable to save my family. Bring 'em back, just as they were—fussin' over how many bungleroots to plop in the dirty water for supper."

"If I do stay, does that mean I'm stuck here forever?" Bobby asked.

The question tightened around her throat like invisible hands. Zenobia shifted slightly, angling to conceal the sword on her back. She forced a shrug.

"Dunno," she answered meekly.

Trying to soothe the gnawing in her gut, she blurted, "But if ya do stay, I promise to make it up to ya. Swear I will. Cross my heart and hope to die, I do. I ain't given to beggin', but I ain't too proud neither, not if it means gettin' my family back.

Shoot, we can even be kin if ya like."

Zenobia watched Bobby's face shift through a series of expressions as the weight of the choice settled in. Would he make the sacrifice for her?

He had the power to bring her family back, and part of her hated him for it. That hatred made it easier to keep the truth from him. Well, not lie exactly... but withholding still left a tight coil in her guts, like a snake wrapping around its prey, squeezing a silent confession from her—selfishness was, indeed, part of her character.

And she hated that part of herself.

A groaning screech shattered the moment—an interruption Zenobia was grateful for. The portcullis of the Keep shuddered open, revealing a dark throat beyond. Without saying anything more, they stepped inside.

———————

THE GRAND HALL was cavernous and barren, with the only illumination coming from the eerie, red glow of the Blood Moon Eclipse, which seeped through unseen cracks in the stone. The walls were naked—no torches, banners, or furnishings—just a cold, empty space of glittering black stone, as if the castle had been long ago abandoned.

"There's something not right about this place," Bobby muttered, stopping in his tracks.

Zenobia cocked her head, her voice mocking. "Ya reckon?"

"No. I mean. It seems like a trick."

A deep, resonating purr rippled through the hall like velvet ribbons of sound.

"The blood eclipse has come to a head," came a smooth and unsettling voice. "And my taste buds are at their peak. The flesh of children, marinated in fear, has never been more exquisite."

Zenobia and Bobby spun toward the sound as a shadow detached itself from the far wall. It moved with a sinuous grace, effortless and predatory. Kilrok emerged into the light, his saturnine fur glistening, his golden eyes sharp with amusement. His lips curled back, revealing fangs in what could be a smile—or promise of violence.

"Always chasin'," Zenobia said, unsheathing the Sword of Aegis. She tore strips from the cloth she carried it in, wrapping it around her palms before taking the hilt. Even through the fabric, the cold bit into her fingers. "Yer like a pathetic cat tryin' to catch a mouse jus' to please yer owner. 'Cept we ain't scared, and we sure ain't runnin' no more."

"Tis a maddening game for us both," Kilrok mused, circling them with lazy precision, his barbed tail flicking. "But all games must end."

Zenobia smirked. "Good. Means we won't haveta hear yer yappin' much longer."

"You going to fight him?" Bobby asked, voice edged with worry.

"Well, I ain't gonna tickle his underbelly none." Zenobia brandished the sword.

Bobby's jaw dropped, his eyes locking on the blade. "Hey, is that—?"

"Sumpm for the kitty to chew on. You bet yer bottom." Zenobia hoped the battle would distract Bobby from asking too many questions about the sword. She swung it, slicing the air with surprising ease.

It seemed to work. Bobby pulled out his book and cracked it open. "Well, I'm gonna help," he declared, flipping through the pages, likely searching for another spell.

Zenobia scoffed. "Good idea. Tire him out readin' the whole dang social-economic history o' Pangia. Reckon boredom'll do half the job for me." Her wryness peaked with the alignment of the blood moons—or maybe it always sharpened when she was nervous. Or anxious. No more talkin'. She paced, preparing to meet the beast in an epic standoff.

Bobby mumbled as he hastily searched the pages, "History is very important and can be interesting too, you know."

Zenobia knew he wasn't about to start narratin' economic policy—he was about to do something astonishing with that book. How? She did not know, but she left that kind of knowledge to the gods for now. Maybe one day she'll understand. Maybe one day, she'd wield that kind of power, too.

But not today.

Today was for skinnin' a cat. One wearin' the ugliest human mug in all of Helcyon.

BOBBY WAS DOING two things at once—well, three. First, he tried to rub the spasm from his eye. Second, he flipped through his book in frustration, searching for the page he'd seen before—the one that would enable him to fight. And third—despite himself—he was watching Zenobia, admiring how she stalked straight for the manticore, the Sword of Aegis flashing in a blur of silver arcs. Even with the sword, he knew how deadly the manticore was. His heart pounded in anxious beats. His fingers, damp with sweat, fumbled across the pages until he finally found the one he needed. He licked his dry lips and uttered the incantation, his gaze darting between the book and Zenobia, who now stood head-to-head, toe-to-toe with the beast.

The moment Bobby spoke the words, the ink on the page melted away, sinking into the parchment before bleeding back in as lines intersected and weaved together into the likeness of a lion-head pendant. As swiftly as it appeared, the illustration grew out from the page, solidifying into something tangible—something real—resting atop it. He tore the amulet free from the book.

Zenobia screamed.

Bobby looked up, just as she vaulted over Kilrok, her blade slicing clean through the manticore's lashing scorpion tail, severing its barbed tip. She landed in a controlled roll, skidding into a poised, battle-ready stance. She was amazing.

Moving quickly, Bobby looped the golden lion amulet around his neck. The moment the ornament graced his chest, a brilliant blaze of light erupted, and something surged through him—a pride of lions roaring to life inside his bones. A dazzling brightness engulfed him, and when it faded, he was no longer a boy.

He was a majestic lion.

Not the small, cute, and cuddly cub from the Feral Forest, but as a true full-grown King of the Jungle (though, for the record, lions don't live in jungles, and tigers are the bigger cat—but you get the point). His tawny mane swayed in grandeur, his claws scraped against the stone floor, and he felt raw, untamed strength coursing through him for the first time. His lungs expanded, his bone-crushing jaw stretched wide, and from deep in his chest, a resounding rumble rose—swelling—before exploding into a thunderous roar, shaking the chamber and halting everything in its tracks.

"The boy has sure grown," Kilrok sneered before striking at the momentarily distracted Zenobia, his claws slashing across her weapon-wielding arm.

She recoiled, pressing her free hand to her wound, blood spilling down her sleeve. The gash was deep, her grip on the sword unsteady.

Bobby charged.

Within three driving strides, he slammed into Kilrok, claws and fangs tearing into fur and flesh, unleashing a flurry of vicious strikes. Kilrok countered with brutal efficiency, whipping his now-truncated tail and driving his teeth into Bobby's neck. Pain cut through him with agonizing precision.

Zenobia tore a strip from her tunic, tightening it around her wound. The numbing effects of the sword dulled the pain as she lunged back into the fray, weaving through the chaos of claw and tooth, her blade flashing in an upward arc. She struck true—slicing Kilrok's neck, severing an artery. A dark surge of blood sprayed across the floor as the manticore staggered back, shrieking, retreating toward the shadows, head bowed low, painting a bloody trail in his wake.

Bobby, still in his lion form, and Zenobia, brandishing the Sword of Aegis, stalked after him. The beast slinked deeper into the dark, its black fur dissolving into the chamber's inky depths. His sickly yellow eyes flickered in the darkness one last time—then vanished.

Bobby slowed his pursuit, a strange scent prickling his senses. The taste of burnt steel clung to the air.

The shadows weren't broadening because they were nearing them—they were moving, creeping closer, reaching for them.

The golden hairs across his lionized form stood on end. Something was wrong.

He growled, trying to warn Zenobia, but as a lion, words failed him. His voice was no longer his own.

Zenobia rushed ahead, chasing Kilrok into the shrouding blackness. The moment she crossed the sharp divide between light and darkness, a blade shot from the void—piercing, impaling—driving straight through her—

Bobby's roar cracked through the air, shaking the very foundation of the Keep. But as his cry of anguish stretched on, it lost its power, shifting from a mighty lion's bellow into a pitiful wail of a boy. The enchantment unraveled in an instant. His body shrank, his mane disappeared, and he collapsed onto the cold stone floor—nothing more than his weak, human self once more. The golden-lion amulet crumbled to ash, streaking his shirt with dark smudges.

Then, a brutish figure stepped out of the darkness and into the dim red light, his iron boots echoing each heavy footstep. Bobby had never seen the Ashen Knight before, but the moment he emerged, he knew.

With a swift, savage motion, the knight wrenched his blade from Zenobia, the sound of tearing flesh sickening.

Her sword clanged against the floor, abandoned. Zenobia clutched at the gaping wound in her abdomen as she stumbled, then crumpled with a sharp, gasping breath. She barely seemed to register what had happened. Her trembling fingers pressed against her blackened, smoldering wound. For a moment, she only stared stupidly at it. Then, slowly, her head lifted toward Bobby. Her delicate face contorted, twisting from shock to something far worse—fear. A deep, visceral terror flared in her verdant eyes, the kind that came not from the pain but from the realization of what lay beyond one's arrival at their personal terminus. They had reached the end of everything.

Bobby was seized within the time-freezing gap between a hummingbird's heartbeat. His pained visage was reflected in the trembling disks of Zenobia's wide, terrified eyes, which swelled with unshed tears. Next to his reflection, within the waxing gawp of her pupils, lurked a dark, hooded figure eagerly waiting to claim her.

The ghastly skull belonged to Nex. Its deathly face slipped casually from under its hood, its permanently bared grin gleaming. Bobby realized the specter's reflection didn't loom outside her—it was inside her, behind her eyes. Stretching deeper into her soul, wrenching it from her body with unseen hands.

She never had the time to close her eyes.

Her wound flared—a burst of sizzling embers and burning cinders, smoking out her soul in one exhaled plume. In that suspended hummingbird moment, it became a single rippling flame, sweeping outward from her wound, rolling over her entire body in a scorching wave. Flesh turned to char—green eyes to coal stones.

At some point, Bobby's screaming stopped.

He found himself kneeling across from Zenobia's ossified form, the ringing of his cry still resonating in his ears.

The chamber around him wobbled. Fractured lines appeared in the air, thin as spider silk, shimmering into view at just the right angle of light. The very contours of the hall wavered—the silk threads vibrating—before the illusion peeled away, refashioning the space around him. No longer bare and lifeless, the hall bloomed into existence, now adorned with gaudy torches, heavy tables, and gilded chairs. And at its center stood the towering orrery, its blood-red lunar models pulsing with an intense glow.

Nex and a strange-looking, tiny man stood near the giant mechanism, the man's odd, google-eyed gaze fixed in horror.

Staring at these inhuman characters, Bobby felt an enormous heat ignite within him—a fever of rage rushing through his core. They needed to pay.

They needed to be erased, incinerated, burned from the very pages of Helcyon, purged like a disease in a baptism of fire—a cleansing inferno.

With a final surge of wrath, Bobby snatched up his book, flung it open, and thrust it forward—pages fixed on the monsters who took everything from him, arms locked as if aiming a weapon. From its splayed pages, a blinding light erupted, a concentrated beam like sunlight through glass.

"I'll kill all of you!" Bobby screamed, sweeping the blazing light before him.

The intense ray pulsed through Nex in burning waves, making the wraith wither and shrivel until it was nothing more than red wisps of smoke scattering into the air. The small bug-eyed man yelped and dove behind the orrery, narrowly escaping with only a scorch mark on his arm, but where the light had touched his skin, great red welts bubbled and blistered.

Bobby turned the beam upon the Ashen Knight, who stood unmoving against the storming pulse of light. Its force clawed at his armor, the iron plating cracking and fracturing at its weakest points.

"Die, you monster, die!" Bobby commanded, pushing closer, each stride more certain, his resolve hardening with every vengeful utterance of the word "Die". His hands held the book like a conduit of divine fury, raw energy surging through him, focusing into a concentrated death ray.

The Ashen Knight strained, his burnt form resisting the overwhelming force. Slowly, he stretched his arm outward, his charred gauntlet peeling away under white-hot assault, flaking away into dust. Beneath it, his fingers—exposed to the blaze—eroded to the bone, curling against the intensity, clawing at the very fire consuming him.

"Die, die, die!" Bobby cursed, his voice rising over the deafening drone of the blasting beam of light.

The Ashen Knight twitched, his skeletal hand contorting into a series of grotesque, mangled postures—his fingers flexing into twisted symbols, forming a malignant semaphore incantation. The moment he shaped the fifth crooked gesture, Bobby's hands burned molten-hot, the book blistering against his palms. A sudden flare of star-fire heat ignited the cover into flames.

Bobby bellowed and dropped the burning book. The instant he let go, the light ray snuffed out. He watched, stunned and crushed, as the book withered under the harsh blaze, its pages curling into blackened shavings. In seconds, it was gone—reduced to a charred stain upon the stone tile.

"If you are to get anywhere in life, boy," said the Ashen Knight, "you must learn to withstand the fire."

Bobby slung his dark gaze up from the blackened stain to the bright burn of the burnt knight's watch, feeling equally angry and helpless. Now that his father's book was gone, all his power was demolished into soot. How could he have ever thought he could win? Not with his unlucky blood.

His fleeting rage hushed into a dull, sinking emptiness. He turned back to Zenobia's charred form and reached out, his fingers grazing her shoulder. He knew even the slightest touch would cause her to crumble completely at his feet, rendered as nothing more than a heap of black powder. But he still wanted to touch her one last time.

"We have much in common," spoke the Ashen Knight.

"No!" Bobby screamed. "We have nothing in common."

"Our father abandoned us. That is one thing we have in common."

Bobby couldn't bear to look at him. His gaze remained on the coarse powder partially covering the Sword of Aegis at his feet. He could feel the oppressive heat of the Ashen Knight boring into his back, his presence suffocating, his words rasping against Bobby's ears.

"Do you know what you are capable of," the burnt knight continued, "once you master and endure the fire?" He let the question linger like a smoldering ember before punctuating, "Anything and everything. There is a way for us to mutually benefit from each other."

Bobby clenched his jaw and ripped the Sword of Aegis from Zenobia's ashes, inciting a whirl of dark dust into a stinging cloud. He spun on the burnt knight, blade raised, and screamed, "All I want is for you to die!"

"I'm sorry, son, but you cannot kill me."

The burnt knight swung *Black Star*, the blade sparking as it clashed against the Sword of Aegis, swatting the weapon from Bobby's tenuous grip. The sword clanged across the stone, spinning out of reach.

The Ashen Knight stepped forward. "You cannot fight fire with fire, boy."

But Bobby didn't flinch. He jabbed his face up, forcing himself as close as he could to the burnt knight's blazing eyes, and in a menacing, even tone, said, "I've killed with only my words before. And I'll do it again. To you!"

The Ashen Knight let out a guttural chuckle. "I see you've learned what all killers come to know—that after your first, the rest come all too easy. But if you believe your words can kill, boy, you've vastly overvalued your importance.

"Still, it is true that you were responsible for your father's death. In his final hour, the only thing he clung to was you—the cherished love of his son. And you had nothing to offer him except contempt and rejection. You wished him dead, and now you must accept it."

Bobby felt his eyes sting. His heart dropped like a lead ball into his stomach. He stumbled back, lightheaded. The Ashen Knight's words stabbed him like blades driven into a living voodoo doll. He crumpled, shrinking away from the sharp words. Tears ached to spill—but wouldn't come. Couldn't.

"Be honest, boy. You care only for yourself. You cannot cry because you have no heart. You and I are not so different. We hate the world and want to watch it burn.

"In your world, your father left you. Your mother sees you as nothing but a burden. A living, festering scar. No one cares about you there. You are powerless. Unwanted. Weak. Useless. Repugnant. A walking target for derision and ridicule. A fat loser."

He sneered.

"And that girl you grieve over? She didn't want you. She used you."

The knight gave a sinister chuckle, gesturing to the ash on the floor. "And see how that worked out for her."

He withdrew his towering bulk from the quivering Bobby.

"Best to forget that world, boy. Best to leave it behind forever." He then motioned to the black stones of Dragoon Keep. "Here, however, you do have an opportunity to be something great. Revered as a god, even. You could do more than kill with your words. You can create worlds with them."

Bobby's cold gaze roved over the dim surroundings, taking in its bleakness.

"But for those fruits to ripen," the burnt knight continued, "you must remain here while I take your place there." The knight moved close to Bobby again. With a slow, deliberate pressure, he pressed his dark, bony finger into Bobby's chest. "In your cruel world."

Stay here, and you shall never be alone again. They will adore you, praise you, love you. You will be the savior of Helcyon, worshiped for all eternity."

The Ashen Knight's voice lowered to a near whisper. "You can bring back everything and everyone you lost here. Even your precious Zenobia."

"I can't bring back my dad!" Bobby yelled scornfully.

"No," the Ashen Knight answered, almost sympathetically. "You cannot bring him back any more than I can return to my Lianna. Fate is cruel and absolute in that regard.

The biggest lie ever told was that life is supposed to be fair. It isn't. It can't be. If you want fairness, you have to force it into existence with an iron grasp. But before you can achieve that, you must break free from the shackles of the past and take control of your future—a future that can be whatever you want. But only here."

The knight waved his skeletal hand in the air behind him as if performing more mystic hand signals, which concluded as soon as a sallow man lumbered out from around the orrery, his posture hunched.

Bobby let out a gasp.

The man's pale features, sharp cheekbones jutting out from his hollow face, pin-point eyes sunken, vacant, and permanently latched open as he stumbled forward in a slow, absent-minded gait.

Was this a living corpse? A puppet? Or something worse?

The more Bobby stared, the clearer the grotesque likeness became. That nose—protruding and crooked, the same break as Everett Porter.

His fingers dug into his palms.

This emaciated man could be his father's twin.

Or was.

A chill rippled through him, his blood draining away, his body feeling plundered of his spirit.

"Born in the image of our father," the burnt knight said. "Brothers born at different times during the war, but with the same face. The eldest and most idyllic of us was Evernt. Such a tender heart. So easily broken."

"Tiger Knight?" Bobby whispered, mesmerized by the decayed reflection of his father.

"Now a mindless soldier in my Dark Army. But you can bring him back. You can bring them all back."

Bobby's guts coiled, twisting tightly, strangling his insides.

"But, how?" he screamed, hearing his own desperation, pining, pleading. The hunger to end this nightmare ravaged his voice.

"I will show you, my boy. But you must be willing to let me lead you."

Bobby's hands twitched. His cuticles were already frayed and tender, but he clawed at them anyway, tearing at the raw skin until grime and old blood mixed beneath his nails. His palms blackened with the remnants of Zenobia.

He had inhaled her dark particles, a terrible smell of burnt hair and barbecue that turned his stomach and made his mouth water.

He hated it.

"Our father left us this broken world," the burnt knight continued, "but I can imbue you with the power to fix it."

"Tell me how!" Bobby demanded.

But he didn't want to fix anything. He was tired of trying to fix things. He just wanted his struggles to end. To annihilate the world that had given him nothing but pain, to shatter it with the destructive sonic power of his shrill tone. To destroy everything with his speech. To obliterate the Ashen Knight to dust.

Except there was nothing left to destroy.

And the burnt knight was right. Bobby was too unimportant. Too useless. Meek. Powerless.

He also knew somewhere deep in his unlucky blood—he could not kill the Ashen Knight. Because the Ashen Knight was all that remained of him. The only force left propelling him forward. His hate. His rage. His grief.

The Ashen Knight lifted *Black Star* before Bobby.

"With this sword, you will rule Helcyon."

Bobby glared at the inky steel blade, its looping lines of refracted light swirling in hypnotic evolutions, shifting like something alive.

Power.

Abject Power.

Every negative emotion Bobby had ever borne swirled at its fringes, drawn into the dark blade's depths, spiraling in endless torment. He fought against the bone-deep cold creeping through him, but exhaustion was winning.

He could feel himself separating, fracturing into splintered fragments. His psyche detaching from his body, his soul retreating from his pulsating heart. Chaos and upheaval unraveled his very foundation. There was no unity with himself. No sense of identity. Just his warring, broken parts racing toward complete self-destruction.

He was ready to give up. Give in. Give the sword everything inside him that made him human. Because being human meant nothing but loss, disappointment, and pain. The cursed trilogy of his past, present, and future.

What was the point?

He stopped resisting and let the numbness envelop him, like the cold mud of the creek back in his schoolyard—how he had let it consume him as he sank deeper into it.

His rage, his pain, dulled, dissolving into a nebulous haze as his agency resigned. He drifted into a listless observer, his body moving only as an instrument yielding to a vague belief that the Ashen Knight knew what was best for him.

And so, without a word, Bobby hunched in silent obedience.

"Follow me, boy," the Ashen Knight said, sheathing *Black Star* before clomping off through an adjoining passageway.

FORTY-ONE

BOBBY OFTEN felt at odds with his own body, as if his lumpy flesh were a separate entity stitched onto him in mismatched patches. But now, he felt entirely hewn from it. Much like his vision in the Red Forest, when he had stared deep into the campfire flames and seen his life distorted through the flickering lens of a warped memory. A pair of floating eyes, and nothing more. Now was much the same; he could do little but be a spectator, detached and passive, as his feet and legs moved of their own accord, following the Ashen Knight deeper into the labyrinthine stone passages.

Dim corridors twisted and collided, merging and breaking apart, slipping ever downward into the irregular obsidian depths of the mountain, its walls shimmering with a starry sparkle like an endless night sky swallowing him whole.

Behind him trailed a tiny, slim figure—man or creature, Bobby could not say—standing nearly Bobby's height. His bulging, buggy eyes glimmered even in the tunnel's deepest shadows. Awkwardly, he held the Sword of Aegis, the blade scraping against the ground as he dragged it along. The weapon was clearly too heavy for his frail figure to wield.

Bobby wanted to ask who he was—and why he had brought the sword—but his lips, like the rest of him, couldn't be bothered.

Farther back, the Tiger Knight trudged along, vacant-eyed and gaunt without his tiger mask. Whether he had always looked so broken behind it or if the Ashen Knight had beaten him down into this sorry, pathetic state, Bobby couldn't say. But it no longer mattered. Bobby found himself caring less and less about anything and everything, especially about the who or why of this nightmare or even what was to come next. The Bitter within him had succeeded in breaking him down, shaping him into nothing more than a doughy, malleable automaton.

What came next was the Cave of Enlightened Fire.

The Ashen Knight stood before a black oblong stone slab. "The Enlightened Fire demands a sacrifice," he said, his voice raw and eager as he extended his sword toward Bobby. "Place *Black Star* into the Ingress Dies Redux."

Bobby's body complied. He took the sword and ambled up to the glossy obsidian table. The blade slid in all too readily, embedding to its hilt. Almost instantly, the solid, glassy surface dissolved into a bubbling tar bath, *Black Star* firmly locked in place.

"Now you must offer your immolation," the Ashen Knight commanded, gesturing toward Evernt, who swayed in place, expressionless. "You must give to gain."

Bobby's hand shuddered in protest, but his meager defiance crumbled. He guided Evernt to the edge of the seething tar. His former friend did not resist, only slumping forward like an obedient dog awaiting its fate.

And then, in a cold, creeping realization, Bobby understood. Until now, he had been a passenger—a passive outsider in his father's unfinished story. But now, under the Ashen Knight's influence, he had become an active participant in his father's doomed fantasy.

Without reservations or even an iota of compunction, Bobby shoved Evernt in.

The tar seized him instantly. There was no scream, no struggle, only the briefest, feeble flailing before he was consumed whole.

The tiny man stepped up beside Bobby, his globular eyes fixed on him with what looked like a permanent expression of distress. He propped the Sword of Aegis next to Bobby and waited, blinking not once.

After a moment, he spoke. "Take comfort in knowing that once he enters the tree... he'll no longer exist. Erased into oblivion."

"What tree?" Bobby asked. "Who?"

But the slim man offered no further explanation. He simply motioned to the sword.

Wary of the tiny man, Bobby grasped the hilt and watched him retreat into a shadowy recess.

The ground rumbled. Then shook. Then, it cracked apart. Molten lines splintered beneath them, venting bursts of scalding steam. The tremors worsened—until the entire floor collapsed, crumbling into a blazing chasm that nearly stretched the length and breadth of the chamber.

The Ashen Knight yanked *Black Star* from the tar, raising it high.

"You must follow me into the Enlightened Fire." With that, he stepped off the ledge, dropping into the inferno.

The tiny man nodded urgently at Bobby.

Bobby tightened his grip on the Sword of Aegis. The blade gleamed—bright and clean—and for a moment, he swore he saw his mother flitter pass in its reflective steel. His throat squirmed, squeezing out a shallow gasp. But when he looked again, the steel held only his unfortunate, sallow face.

He inched forward, stepping to the edge of the abyss, the flames licking at his toes; he embraced the sword in both hands and leaped into the fire.

AFTER DROPPING INTO the chasm, Bobby became gradually aware that he was already pacing along the trench floor of endless flames, not remembering the fall or the landing itself. The firestorm raged and howled at all sides and high above, yet the flames did not touch him. Instead, they arched around the Sword of Aegis, drawn to its north and south poles, forming a protective bubble of light.

In the distance, a dark void formed amidst the fire. As Bobby advanced toward it, the void took shape. A small, secluded island hovering just above the endless field of flames. At its center, rising from plush blue turf, stood the Very Very Big Hinterland Maple Tree, crystalline and frosted, an enormous beating heart encased within its translucent trunk.

With some effort, Bobby clambered onto the soft ground of the island and found the Ashen Knight waiting at the base of the giant glass tree.

"Your world lies through there," he said, motioning to the tree's pulsing core. He offered *Black Star* once more for Bobby to take. "Only you can cut into the tree so I may traverse into your world."

"And what will you do there?" Bobby asked.

"I will do what you cannot. Stand up for yourself against injustice."

Bobby tightened his squeeze on the Sword of Aegis' hilt, white-knuckled. He didn't like the idea of unleashing the Ashen Knight into his world, but would it really be all that bad? The knight wouldn't hold the same power there as he did in Helcyon. Especially not without *Black Star*. If he even made it there at all. Maybe he would vanish for good, just like the strange little man had said. Then he'd be really gone at last, and Bobby could set things right.

He stepped toward the tree, preparing to strike.

"No," the Ashen Knight bellowed, "You must pierce the heart with my sword. Cast the Sword of Aegis into the flames. Take ownership of *Black Star*."

Bobby moved to the escarpment, ready to discard the sword into the sea of flames—when he caught his reflection again in the blade. His father's same thousand-yard stare met him in the steel. Under all his excess fat, the resemblance was uncanny. The same nose (unbroken, of course), the same ears, the same chin. And now, the same hopelessness. He was doing his finest imitation of the same dull, glazed-over dead gaze his father had worn in his final days—a look that spoke volumes about giving up.

Bobby lifted the sword, bracing to cast it into the waiting roar of flames below. But the blade shuddered in his grasp. The silver surface rippled like water, and suddenly, its reflection presented something else—a peek into his bedroom back home. He angled the blade slightly, revealing a figure sitting on his bed. His mother. She sat hunched over, weeping into his pillow. The sound wasn't audible, but he felt it. Was the sword showing him the present? Was this happening now, in his world? His mother lifted her head, her eyes red and swollen. And then she looked directly at him. It was impossible. She couldn't see him through the sword's reflection. Could she? Her lips moved, speaking without sound, yet he still understood every word.

"Where are you, baby? Please come home," she pleaded. "Please. I love you."

His breath caught in his throat. Why was the sword showing him this? A tug, deep and insistent, pulled at his heart. He was so close. He could taste the salt of his mother's endless tears.

He could go back.

The thought struck him suddenly, like a punch to the chest.

He could go back.

Back to the attic.

Back to the oppressive world of judgment and cruelty. Labels and diagnosis.

Back to the urban insanity and kids who hated him just because.

Back to his suffocating mother, alone in the house that felt vacant and unbearable without his father.

He hesitated.

And then—

He let go.

The moment the Sword of Aegis slipped from his fingers, the pull on his heart unraveled—like a string untethered.

The blade plunged into the inferno, swallowed instantly by the fire.

Bobby exhaled. A deep chill settled in his chest, his stomach squeezing into something heavy and dense—like a collapsing star.

The Sword of Aegis wasn't just a weapon. It was his way home.

"Good," the burnt knight said, nodding approvingly. He placed *Black Star* into Bobby's hands. "Now, you must cut your flesh. Let your blood flow into the blade, and the Blood Moon's anneal it. Only then will you have the power to pierce the heart."

Bobby drew the razor edge of *Black Star* across his palm. Blood streamed down his hand, seeping into the dark swirls of the weapon's thirsty steel. He lifted the sword high beneath the hidden Blood Moons. The weapon vibrated in his clenched hands. A surge of raw electricity seared through him, burning away the numbing Bitter that had clung to his insides like thick tar. His senses sharpened. For the first time in his torpid life, he was hyper-present. No longer just a passive passenger, held down by the sludge of his unlucky blood. He fastened both hands firmly around the sword's sinewy crimson hilt, and hurled himself forward, plunging *Black Star* deep into the tree's pulsing heart.

The sky cracked open, thunder rupturing the heavens. A bolt of lightning and fire struck the crystalline maple tree, igniting intense flashes of heat and sparks where *Black Star* had penetrated. The tree fractured, splintering deep into its ancient trunk, its core nearly shattering. The wound had widened where *Black Star* had punctured, pieces breaking away in great, splintering chunks—exposing something raw beneath. A soft, fleshy interior.

The Ashen Knight seized Bobby's hands, his ironclad grip crushing over Bobby's fingers. Together, they drove the blade deeper. The gash tore wider, the tree's wound spreading open, revealing a muscular tunnel at its center.

The Ashen Knight lunged forward, his hulking frame clawing and tearing violently as he forced his way inside. The living tunnel shuddered around him.

And then he was gone.

Bobby was left standing before the pulsing wound, feeling light-headed and drained. He thought to step back. Maybe even lie down. But his feet were no longer touching the ground. He was drifting upward, weightless. Higher and higher, he floated, rising toward the crown of the maple tree. Below, black, viscous liquid gushed from the tree's wound in surging waves, spilling over the island's edge. The flood drowned the fires, sending up a curling haze of smoke and burnt oil. The world beneath him began to collapse, engulfed by the rising sea of dark waters.

Then he fell.

———————

W~HEN~ B~OBBY~ ~AWOKE~, tall blue grass swayed around him in a gentle breeze. The sky above was heavy and gray, sailing high and soundless. He eased himself upright, still clutching *Black Star*. A dry, heaving belch lurched from his throat. His hand twitched involuntarily, and he flung the sword as far as he could. *Black Star* flopped a few feet down the hill, its dark shimmer dulling.

A sudden bout of hiccups invaded his throat, jolting him as he gawked down at the little dirt farm and abandoned hut at the bottom of the shallow ravine.

He was back, back on Zenobia's farm.

Bobby spun around, gasping, motionless at the sight of what was left of the Very Very Big Hinterland Maple Tree. Nothing remained but a jagged, blackened stump, no taller than Bobby himself. The rest of the tree—

Gone.

A silence hung over the tree's charred remains. And in that silence, something inside Bobby broke. Out of everything he had endured—his father's death, his isolation, being thrown into this living nightmare, even witnessing Zenobia's traumatic death—it was this. This, of all things, this lifeless, ruined corpse of what had once been a soaring, beautiful tree—was what undid him. And then—

Bobby finally cried.

His mouth opened and howled and moaned and wailed. He shuddered feverishly as he curled into himself, rocking back and forth. Heavy, wet sobs wracked through him. The grief poured from him in a deluge, and now that it had begun, he feared it would never stop. This—this was what he feared would happen all along. That if he ever let himself cry, he would never be able to stop. He would be nothing more than a sodden heap of useless, bawling flesh. A broken record of spiraling sadness stuck playing on repeat for the rest of his days.

"You did a good thing," came a voice, cutting through his sobs.

Bobby sniffled, stifling the oily Bitter trickling down his cheeks. Lifting his head, he wiped away the blur of tears with the back of his hand, then saw the tiny man standing near the burnt maple stump, his large, unescapable eyes set on him.

"It might not seem so right now," the tiny man continued, "but you'll see. Great, wonderful, amazing things are to come."

Bobby scraped his sleeve across his face, noticing the dark tears staining his shirt. His voice came out hoarse. "Who are you?"

"I'm Slimsy. A Dazzelf, and once a servant to the Ashen Knight." He chuckled to himself. "But no more. Now that burnt brute is gone. Yes sir. I'm free from his fiery rule. No longer will I do his lying. If I am to lie or deceive, it'll be for myself from now on."

"Why do you tell lies?"

Slimsy shrugged. "Technically, I only assist with the lies people already tell themselves. I help affirm their fatuous imaginations and fantasy-driven desires as something that seems real, genuine, and true. It's a gift of our kind."

Slimsy moved closer, giving Bobby a ginger pat on the shoulder. "But you—you can make real things really happen. You can manifest whatever you like. Only you could rid Helcyon of the Ashen Knight. And that's something to be happy about. Proud of, even."

"But I can only do those things here," Bobby said sourly. "And what good is that?"

"Well, then," Slimsy gestured around them, his arms sweeping across the dismal landscape of Helcyon, "where better to be stuck than in a place where you can be a god?"

Bobby glanced down. The Bitter surrounded him, thick and viscous, polluting the blue grass beneath him. His pants were soaked in the slick, oil-like substance, the residue of his sorrow pooling around him.

"I cried," Bobby murmured in amazement.

"Yes," Slimsy said. "I saw."

Bobby rubbed at his puffy eyes. "I thought—I thought I wouldn't ever be able to cry again."

Slimsy cocked his head. "Is crying a good thing? It often seems like a bad thing."

Bobby let out a cleansing sigh. "No," he said. "It's a good thing."

Slimsy nodded. "Well, then. How about doing something about all this?" He motioned once more at their bleak surroundings.

Bobby looked around, catching onto Slimsy's meaning.

"Oh," he said. "But—I don't have the book anymore."

"You can write a new one."

Slimsy stepped up to the splintered, charred tree trunk, twisted off a blackened twig, and handed it to Bobby.

Bobby took the charcoal stick, meant to be a stylist, then looked down at the pools of Bitter surrounding him. Somehow, he knew what he needed to do. Perhaps he had known all along. Maybe it was because he had watched Zenobia turn Bitter into something useful, as her ancestors had done before her.

He focused his mind, sharpening his thoughts into a clear picture of something new. The black liquid quivered—then rippled. Then, it began to gather itself, pulling together like liquid metal drawn to a magnet, amassing and solidifying into the shape of a hardcover book. The final drops of Bitter absorbed into the now-defined tome, its surface hardening, taking on the feel and look of a clothbound cover, rich and unblemished, as if freshly mended. Golden text shimmered into existence across the front:

> THE TRAVELER'S GUIDE TO HELCYON: SIGHTS, HISTORY,
> TIPS ON HOW TO STOMACH ANY BUNGLEROOT DISH.

Bobby opened it. The first page was crisp, white-blank. He crumbled the charcoal stick over the page. The dark powder coated the surface, then moved—vibrating, melting into ink that transmuted itself into a script. The ink spreading outward, filling the page, then bleeding into many others, inscribing itself in divine, perfect text:

> WITHOUT REMEMBRANCE, THERE IS NO MEANING.
>
> WITHOUT MEANING, THERE IS NO PURPOSE.
>
> WITHOUT PURPOSE, THERE IS NO SPIRIT.
>
> HISTORY IS THE CONTEXT BY WHICH WE
> PREDICATE OUR IDENTITIES.
>
> WITHOUT RECOGNIZING OUR HISTORIES, WE WILL NEVER
> RECOGNIZE OURSELVES—OR WHERE WE'RE HEADED.

A shaft of golden light poured onto the pages. Bobby and Slimsy looked up as the dark sky began to burst, beams of light puncturing through, breaking apart the clouds until the murky pall dissipated, revealing a breathtaking, brilliant blue sky.

Slimsy shielded his eyes with his hands. Without eyelids, squinting was not an option. The brightness became overwhelming, forcing him to turn away, setting his gaze to the ground. The world had transformed. The large, bright orb of the sun radiated freely, while the seven smaller pale moons that had once been in tight orbit broke away from their alignment.

A blanketing warmth enveloped Bobby. He felt at peace. More than that, he felt wholly comfortable in his own skin for what seemed like forever.

The pages beneath his fingers continued to flip rapidly, blank sheets filling themselves with words:

> THE FIRST FAMILY WAS NOT THE LAST, AND CERTAINLY DID NOT FIND THE END OF THE FAMILY TREE TO BE THE END OF THE FAMILY. THE ONLY CHILD OF HULMICK AND HYLN MULHICK, ZENOBIA MULHICK, HAD SUCH HEART AND STRENGTH THAT THE GODS WERE CHARMED AND BEWITCHED BY HER. HOWEVER, BE SURE NOT TO MISTAKE HER FOR A WITCH. NO, SHE IS AN ALCHEMIST AND MIGHTY WARRIOR WHO WON THE HEART OF BOBBY PORTER. SHE TAUGHT THE YOUNG DEITY WHAT DIFFERENTIATED LOVE FROM SELFISHNESS. HERO FROM COWARD. HOPE FROM HOPELESSNESS..

Bobby wasn't sure if these words were his or if the book had a mind of its own. But at the moment, he didn't care. The words sounded right, and they made him smile. They made him think of Zenobia; alive, passionate, caring, and brave.

Laughter and cheers drifted over the hill. Bobby twisted his head toward the sound, then glanced back at Slimsy. The tiny man, still cowering from the brightness, smiled at him in an awkward, contorted way as if attempting an expression he wasn't accustomed to.

"A new story has begun," Slimsy said, wincing against the light. "And this one is solely yours."

Bobby pressed the book to his chest and pushed himself to his feet. He rushed to the very top of the hill and stood in awe.

Below, Zenobia was smothered deep in the arms of Hulmick and Hyln. She held her parents tight and close, refusing to let them go. Each of them laughed, rejoicing at their reunion, faces soaked with clear tears of joy.

And there was Golly, too, chewing mindlessly on a mushy pulp of blue grass.

"Well, I'll be a dancing tiger," came a bright, familiar voice to Bobby's right.

Evernt sauntered up beside him, his face aglow, his features healthy and luminous, untouched by suffering. The face of his father's youth, before the tour, before the hushness took hold of him.

"You did it." His voice was full of warmth. "You defeated the Ashen Knight and saved Helcyon."

Bobby suddenly felt the corner of his lips turn downward, slumping into a frown. The memory of pushing Evernt into the tar resurfaced like a sickness in his gut.

Evernt caught the look on Bobby's face and smiled knowingly. "Don't look so glum, cub. You did what you needed to. I was already gone."

Bobby let out a slight croaking sound but said nothing.

"It's okay, cub," Evernt added, "I'm back now. Better than ever."

"Bobby!"

Zenobia's voice rang out. She broke free from her parents and bounded up the hill, her strides effortless.

Before Bobby could react, she slung her arms around him, swooping him up, lifting him clear off the ground in a fierce hug that squeezed the breath from his lungs. Her bony frame dug into his flesh, but he loved it—the warmth, the strength, the certainty of her. Then, she planted a kiss on his cheek. Wet. Unapologetic. Bobby's entire face ballooned with a giddy bliss. It was the sweetest gesture she had ever bestowed upon him. And though she lifted him high with her strength, he felt he was floating on cloud nine.

Then—

She dropped him.

Bobby collided with the firm ground, the impact jolting him into a rude awakening—the gravity of his choices crashing down around him.

"Oh my gosh!" Zenobia's voice cracked with alarm as she stumbled forward, her joy draining away, steps slowing as she neared the remains of the Very Very Big Hinterland Maple Tree. She stood still, a statue of shock, staring at its demolished state. The mightiest, most magical living thing in all of Helcyon—now reduced to a charred stump.

For what felt like forever, she didn't speak. Then, when she turned to Bobby, her face darkened, her voice trembling.

"What have you gone'n done?"

Bobby's mouth opened to answer, but no words came. Just a cold prickle creeping up his spine. A phrase surfacing in his mind instead.

"History may not repeat itself, but it sure does rhyme with itself."

Mrs. Palmer's words.

Why he thought of them now, as always, he didn't know. But they struck him like a hammer, nailing terror into his heart.

History does have a habit of doing the same thing over and over, because people forget. Because they're short-minded and prone to habits—many bad ones.

Evernt's voice came up beside him. "The thing about purging ignorance from your past," he said, placing a consoling hand on Bobby's shoulder, "is that you cannot purge the past itself. Only see it more clearly."

Above, a cloud crept back across the pure blue sky, casting a long, creeping shadow over them only.

FORTY-TWO

I **WILL NEVER** cry.

It doesn't matter how many stupid shrinks my mom sends me to. I get it—she's scared. Though I'm not sure if she's more afraid for me or of me.

Two whole days. That's all I was gone for. But it was enough to break her mind. Now, she hangs over me every single minute like a prison guard. I'm fine. I can take care of myself.

The shrink keeps asking what happened in those two days. I keep telling her, nothing special, but she's not buying it.

Mrs. Palmer won't let it go either. She keeps clacking on about some stupid enormous tree that disappeared from our backyard as quickly as it appeared while I was gone—like it was magic. I keep telling her I don't know anything about it. But she seems to be doing magical thinking of her own, 'cause she keeps saying I do. She's as batty as an old loon in a zoo for head cases. Probably watches too many crazy fantasy shows. I told her I knew a shrink she could see. She scoffs, shocked at my changed behavior, clicking her tongue and her false teeth. I'm no different than before, I keep telling her. I'm just fed up with everyone always acting like the world is falling apart.

But I keep seeing the shrink. I put up with her condescending tone. I know the meaning of condescending because that's a word my mom loves to use about me now. Anyways, I put up with the shrink. I fake smiles. I'm pretty good at it now. I tell her what she wants to hear, except for those two days, but besides that, I play along just so I can get my internet privileges back.

After asking a million times, Mom finally relents. The first thing I do is go on social media. It's easy to find out exactly where Brock lives in my neighborhood. A kid from school is invited to his birthday party. The address is right there on the invitation. Google fills in the rest.

Brock is the worst.

He never lets up. Even after I come back, he still gives me a lot of trouble at school. Telling the whole class how happy he was when I went missing. Hoped I was kidnapped and murdered by some pervert. He even made up a song for the entire class to join in on. *Joy to the world, Portly Porker is dead. Joy to the world, Portly Porker is dead*, and on and on.

The teachers don't do anything. They just send him to the principal's office for detention. As if that did any good, he keeps doing it.

So I get his address. Sneak out in the middle of the night. Take my dad's old metal lighter. For kindling, I use the pages of his story—the one he wrote for me. I soak them in barbecue lighter fluid. The grill hasn't been used in years.

The fire starts small but burns pretty fast. It spreads.

I crouch in the park across the street and watch Brock's house go up in flames. The heat warms my face.

Brock, his parents, his little sister—they all flee, their screams mixing with the roar of the fire and wail of the distant sirens. After a while, they watch in horror as their home turns to ash. Plumes of oily, black smoke rise, swallowing the moon and darkening the night.

And for the first time in a long time—

I smile. A *real* smile.

ACKNOWLEDGMENTS

I probably bit off more than I could chew by making *Helcyon* my first novel and my first real venture into prose. But hey, that only makes finishing it all the more satisfying. I could not have completed this book without the support of so many wonderful people throughout the many years it took to finish. So I want to thank my family: Bill, Liz, and David, and my wife, Marion. To my friends: Ryan, Heidi, Gerry, Ursula, Josh, Danielle, Sam, Elaine, Celeste, Jose, Jared and Janel. And a special thanks to my Sherman Oaks writing group, who were there from the very beginning: Scott, Kit, Rebekah "K", Megan, Arthur, Stevie, Kevin & Doug, Alex, Chelsea, and Hilary. Your insight, honesty, and fellowship helped shape *Helcyon*. Without all of your kindness, encouragement, and guidance, *Helcyon: The Ashen Knight* would have remained more a fantasy than a fantasy novel.